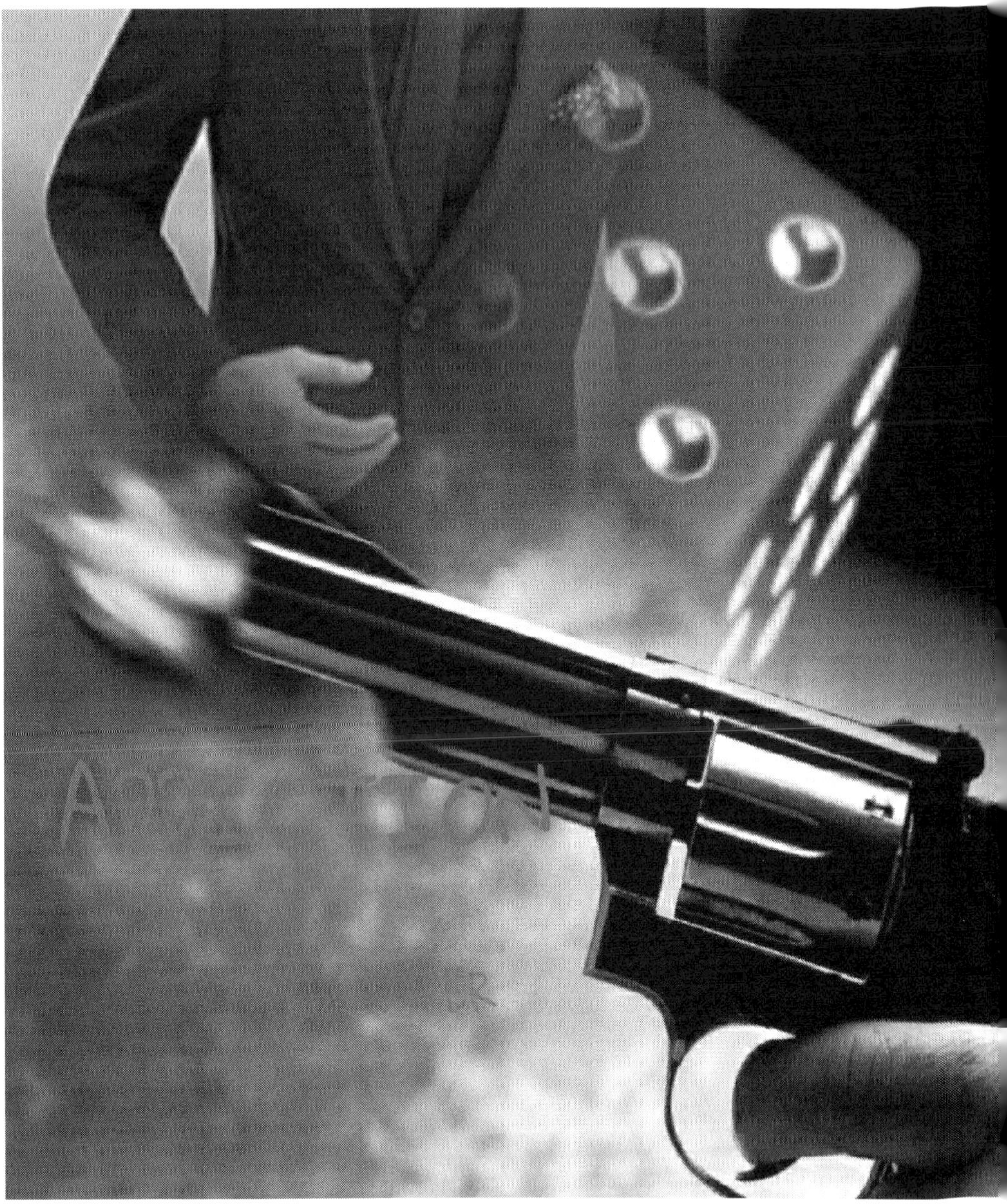

Addiction

By Vyper

To you,

Hello my dear reader!

Thank you for choosing my book

I hope this book will bring a flicker of hope, a splosh of knowledge and a of positive vibe.

I wish you to enjoy the story!!!

With love Vyper!!!

Table of Contents

Copyright
Connect with Vyper
Acknowledgement
Prologue
Chapter one
Chapter two
Chapter three
Chapter four
Chapter five
Chapter six
Chapter seven
Chapter eight
Chapter nine
Chapter ten
Chapter eleven
Chapter twelve
Chapter thirteen
Chapter fourteen
Chapter fifteen
Chapter sixteen
Chapter seventeen
Chapter eighteen
Chapter nineteen
Chapter twenty
Chapter twenty-one
Chapter twenty-two
Chapter twenty-three
Chapter twenty-four

Chapter twenty-five
Chapter twenty-six
Epilogue

Copyright © 2021 Vyper
All rights Reserved

No part of this book may be used or reproduced in any manner or whatsoever without written permission from the author.

This book is a work of fiction. References to real people, events, establishments, or organisations, or locations are intended only to provide a sense of authenticity, and are used fictitiously. All other characters, dead or alive are figments of the author's imagination and all incidents and dialogues are drawn from the author's mind's eye and are not to be interpreted as real.

Connect with Vyper

Facebook group
https://www.facebook.com/groups/vypersreaders

Instagram
https://www.instagram.com/vypersreaders/

Twitter
https://twitter.com/viper6566

Acknowledgements

To all of you!

Thank you for your time and interest in reading this book.

Thank you for allowing me to share with you a piece of my imagination, and take you in a memorable adventure.

Enjoy reading!

With love Vyper!

To my husband: Thank you for all your love and support. Thank you for all the understanding and care. I wouldn't have done it without you! I love you!

To my parents: Thank you for all those years of sacrifice and effort. Thank you for the education and support. For the example you showed us to never give up, no matter how hard life can be.

I love you both equally!

To my brother: You are one annoying person sometimes, but you are my support and determination. You push me beyond my limits (in a good way) ... that's why I eat your chocolate when we were younger :)). I love you tremendously!

To Slav: My dear friend I would like to thank you beyond words, this book is here only because of you! You were the one who believed in me when I didn't. You saw something in me that I didn't (still don't see it). I know you will never take the credit you deserve for this book, so here it is...Thank you for all the support, encouragement and trust you had and still have in me. You are one special person in my life.

To all readers: Thank you for taking this journey. Buckle up and enjoy.

With Love Vyper!

PROLOGUE

I lived and died in 25 years more than others in a lifetime… or so it feels.

What is life anyway?

A constant reminder that we are mortal in more ways than one. A constant reminder that we are fragile, addictive and we can be torn in pieces.

People say that being physically beaten within an inch of your life is the worst that can happen.

I say the worst fight is the fight with your soul. Once you lose that fight you are turned into … nothing. Coming back from nothing is so hard, you need will, power, strength and a reason. Such a strong reason to feel almost like a... addiction.

Because everyone has their own addiction in different forms and levels, but he… is my addiction.

I was numb until him, I believed that life for me has no meaning, that I had no reason on this green God planet, that my purpose is to be just another shadow on the surface of earth, but I was so mistaken, I was here for him and he was here for me and only me alone. Together we will serve a purpose greater than both of us.

His blue eyes are my escape and my demise all at the same time, I was dead until him, and I will be nothing without him.

But even then I still need to let him go, because like anything in life even love has an expiration day. And mine reached its point once he set foot in that hotel room, but then again how do you stop loving a man who is the whole meaning of your universe?

The answer is simple… by carrying his child without him even knowing.

CHAPTER ONE

SVETLANA

A child is supposed to be their parents pride and joy, the product of their infinite and true love.

Instead, I was their worst nightmare.

The curse they could not get rid of.

A constant reminder of how their hopes and dreams turn into ashes.

It was a warm April morning, around 4 AM to be exact, when I decided to make my appearance in this world. Little did I know, that instead of happiness, I brought pain and sorrow.

My mother was informed, she should stay with me in the hospital longer than intended. As I underwent more detailed medical investigations, due to my hard breathing and constant tiredness.

Soon days became weeks, weeks became months, and months became a year. A year passed, before my mother was able to leave the hospital with me. On the verge of madness and mental instability, she returned to an old wood house in an almost empty mountain village. In Altai.

Our house is on the edge of the village, at the other end of a street not too crowded. In the corner of the street with hidden houses covered with tiles, an old house, with plank shutters on the two old dried wooden windows. With glass far too thin to protect us from outside temperatures, either too high or too low.

As dusk falls, the light bulb, hanging from the smoky ceiling, flickers under the weather-yellowed lampshade, scattering glints of ruby.

From the street you can see everything in the yard and in the flower garden. The dry wood fence is too short to provide the privacy we need.

The garden in front of the house, holds two old acacias proudly wearing their white flowers, like bunches of snowdrops. On the ground, a few tulip bulbs bloom in the spring and turn into a joy of colours. Next to them, like a guard, a large bush of red peonies is making its mark. In May, his blood flowers spread a strong scent, which can be felt throughout the yard.

You could feel everything going to sleep in the evening except, the stream not far from our house.

I liked to listen to the water flowing on summer nights, looking at the starry sky. I could find peace in the dark, under the stars that looked down on me from afar.

In the morning everything came back to life, the rooster sang fiercely at sunrise. God, how I hated that rooster.

Birds chirped through the trees, children's voices could be heard nearby. None of this matters to my mother.

Ivanka Petrov, my mother is a medium high brunette woman, lean and curvy, she had an oval face with a mouth too big for her face, both physically and figuratively. Brown eyes, that were too sad all the time, and an angry temper most of the time. Her dark hair was shoulders length, but always kept in a nice bun at the back of her head. She was always dressed like a lady, it did not matter what she did around the house.

"These clothes are out of fashion for so long, I really need new ones."

She always complained to my father about her clothes. My mother was always beautiful to me, no matter the clothes she wore.

"I know darling, and I will buy you the moon soon. I promise!"

My father said to her. Ivan Petrov was a tall guy, about a head taller than my mother, thin but good-looking, with broad shoulders, darker blond hair. Square face, thin lips, and clear blue sky-like eyes on summer days.

And he did keep his promise to her, but not before he ruined me for everyone until…him.

My only joy was my brother Maykl Alexei Petrov or Misha, as I call him. At that time a blond boy with wavy hair and blue eyes. A screwy put only on blunders.

He was the person who distracted me from my father's betrayal, even though he didn't even know he was doing it.

"You are the biggest mistake of my life. I shouldn't have had you!"

My mother's bitter and full of venom confession came, after she found out that dad played and lost all our food money at the casino in town not far from the village.

He had this problem. Once in a while he would go to town and spend the night in the only casino there, as he played… and played… and played. Until, either came home with no money or with more debts.

After my mother's confession, no matter how much me and her tried, to this day, we have nothing but a very dysfunctional relationship and crave for love and affection for one another.

One night, when I was fifteen, my father came home and what happened next changed my life completely.

I had a family, but I haven't.

I had parents, but I was an orphan.

I was alive, but dead in so many ways,

I tried and tried, until exhaustion, to be perfect for them, for her. Nothing would be enough, no matter how much I tried.

At the age of twenty-one I underwent a heart surgery.

"I want to leave this house and never come back. Would you help me?"

I asked Vitaly, my father's best friend, two years later.

"Of course I would. Pack your bags, tonight you are out of Russia."

"They will murder me before I step foot out of the house. How would I go?"

"Don't worry about them. Just be ready, I will pick you up as soon as I finish everything. Don't forget, I am always here for you and I have your back no matter what they say. You are important for me!"

I knew I was. Apart from Vitaly I had my brother. He never disappointed me, always was there for me in everything, never agreeing with my mother's behaviour toward me.

Maybe that's why I always made a priority to never let her or anyone come in between two of us. I will be there for him the same way he was for me and we will never fight for serious matters, like who will take the family inheritance or who will run the company…he could take it all.

I did not want a dime. Not after everything. Promised myself, I will be someone in life on my own, not because my parents helped or anyone else for that matter.

I have a big ego. It wasn't always like that, but after moving to London and providing for myself, I swear, I will let nobody bring me down again…well more than I already am.

In this past year I managed to put myself together as much as possible. I have a decent job, most people do not know about.

Made some friends, two actually, but it is more than I need. Given the fact that I am not a communicative girl, some would even go that far and say I'm a cold, selfish and ruthless bitch. Which is fine with me, as long as they let me be. This makes things easier and helps me keep guys as further away as possible.

I do not need or want a relationship, let alone someone to spend my day in day out time with, I do not need someone's touch or kiss. Not after… hell no! I am better off alone and I made peace with that!

"So, do you want to go out with me? Come on? It's been more than an hour since I'm asking you the same question."

The guy says as he tries to grab my hand. I wanted to react but Arthur was faster.

"She told you three times no, now get lost."

Apparently, he wasn't happy because he started a fight with Arthur, which led to a full panic attack for me.

"It's done, he's gone. Don't worry. Let's focus on the show. I have to walk in twenty minutes so I need my make-up spotless."

Arthur was telling me. He's a tall, muscular boy with broad shoulders, brunette with yellow-green eyes, you've said he's a cat sometimes. Oval face and half-full lips. He always has a smile on his face and warm eyes when he talks to me.

I was trying a career in makeup and this fashion show was important to me.

Arthur has his debut for a famous fashion house.

We became such good friends, he is the only one who knows me head to toe with everything I am and have lived so far. Probably because we have never been physically attracted to each other. He once told me that I am the sister he wishes to have had. I promised him, he would always be my second brother.

And the only girl I managed to keep a friendship with, is Renesmee.

She's taller than me, thin but curvy, blonde with brown eyes, round face and thin lips. When you see her, you say she's spitfire, but she is gentle and sensitive. She likes shopping, and loves gifts.

We fit in many ways, but when we argue an entire neighbourhood knows about it. Renesmee often tells me, she doesn't understand, how I can be so quiet with such a volcanic character and that hideous French of mine.

They are my only friends and my family except my brother. These three people are my life and soul or what is left of both. Any time when family words come around in conversation, they are the one that come to my mind.

Family is not always blood related. In my case this is so true.

Family is people that make you comfortable, people that are there for you no matter the mistakes or the hard times, people that support you and make you see the light at the end of the tunnel.

Happiness in the hardest time.

People that will take a leap of faith because you are important for them! This is what these three are for me and me for them.

Even if we never had spoken these through words, they are spoken by actions every day.

They are my GRACE from heaven if something like that exists!

CHAPTER TWO

RUSLAN

I'm the first born of my family.

My father's pride and my mother's love.

The biggest from the three, two boys and one annoying sister. No matter the level of her annoyance, I still love her very much and over protect her with everything I have, despite the fact that my protection drives her crazy.

I had everything I could ask for and even more in this life. I lived in the most beautiful village in the Altai Mountains of Russia.

Our big house was on the edge of the village, a small mountain village with small wooden houses and fences.

Our house is the largest in the village. It has five rooms, one for each of my brothers, including me. A huge room that belonged to my parents and a guest room. The house was made of attic that meant we had the bedrooms upstairs, the kitchen, living room and the bathroom, were downstairs.

Living room was my favourite room in the whole house.

It was a big room with a huge fireplace, in the middle of the kitchen's wall.

On the right side of the fireplace were the windows and they were quite big, the wall facing the fireplace had a large sofa. On the left side of the fireplace we had a big table, where we had dinner together.

Dinner was always the most important meal, we would dress nicely and all of us would be present no exception.

Everything was very rustic, typical to the mountain area. The ceiling had some thick, but visible beams from which hung some iron chandeliers with three bulbs each.

The winter evenings were wonderful. Outside, snow would be so thick, sometimes it reached the middle of the entry door, and fire was burning inside. We listened to the wood burning in the fireplace, while my father read the newspaper and my mother told us stories about dragons and bears.

My mother was a tall, thin woman with very beautiful curves. An oval face, blue eyes and full fleshy lips. Her light blond hair was long and wavy, reaching to the middle of her back. She was an elegant woman, always had a new dress, or a new shirt.

Her perfume had a scent of pine and every time she took me in her arms I felt like I was embracing the pine forest at the top of the mountain.

My mother is the most important person to me to this day. She liked to spend a lot of time in the kitchen. The tastiest dishes were made by her, even to this day, I have not eaten food as good as hers.

Our kitchen was not very wide, but it was longer.

It had a window on the same wall as the living room window, under it were the kitchen cabinets, aligned nicely in the most perfect line I had seen as a child.

We had some suspended cabinets, my mother said they were fashionable, my father said my mother put them up there with a purpose, although I didn't understand at the time what the purpose was.

At the kitchen window we had a coloured curtain depending on the season. I liked the autumn curtain. It was yellow and brown and gave a pleasant warm light at sunset, I really like the sunset.

We had a table glued to the wall opposite the cabinets with a coloured table cloth depending on the season as well, I liked the summer one, it was coloured with all kinds of fruits, and I hated the winter one. Same table cloth with Santa Claus. I haven't believed in Santa since I caught dad with the presents under the tree.

"Wow, you see Santa left the present right in my arms, can you believe it?"

Dad lied to me.

"Amazing dad. You saw Santa? Can I open my present now?"

I tried my luck, even if I knew he wouldn't let me open. But, it was the escape I most definitely needed.

"Tomorrow, boy. Everybody needs to be present, so we can have a family picture before."

Das said to me. This was our tradition, we took a picture every year before opening the presents. Displaying a sad face I ran up the stairs, happy that he believed I believed him.

My father had the same stature as my mother, he always joked that mother wears heels only to be taller, so that people would think she was the boss in the house. My mother was the boss, but I never told my father that.

He had wide shoulders and very well defined muscles, dark blond hair, with blue eyes like the sky, in the same shade as my mother's. He had thin lips and thick eyebrows. To me, he looks funny when he smiles, but he always had a warm smile and eyes full of love. Especially when he looked at his wife.

Dad is very serious and frowning when he is angry, which doesn't happen often. He made a rule, in our house everyone had to be happy and smile, he said that when my mother smiles everything stays still.

Although, nothing was standing still, but I understood what he meant by that on my wedding day, when she really smiled at me, for the first time.

My father was the best politician in our area, everyone loved him and he was highly respected.

"Ruslan, come and see what Nikolai brought you."

Dad said to me one day and I ran outside.

"A horse? That's so amazing and so big. Can I ride it? Does he have a name?"

"Yes, of course you can ride it, it's yours. But, it doesn't have a name yet, you need to name it."

Nikolai said to me laughing.

"Caesar!"

I said as I tried to hop on the back of my horse, a big black mountain horse with a white spot on his forehead.

Nikolai, also taught me how to ride it, and I did that at least twice a week. To my mother's horror and my father's amusement

Nikolai is my father's younger brother, he is the biggest man in our area. Tall with very wide shoulders, meaning he's so big that when he stands in the doorway, the door looks so small. Uncle has a square face with brown yellow eyes, lips thinner than my father's, oriented inwardly to mouth and eyebrows as thick as dad.

Sometimes, when he doesn't shave for a few days in a row, he looks like Santa Claus from the pictures, only that he has black hair, like ebony.

"Believe me, you don't want to see your uncle angry. He looks like a mountain executioner or like a Viking."

Dad warned me one day, only to agree with him years later, when I did see my uncle angry.

When I was about fifteen years old, Nikolai took me for the first time to the only casino in town. He was so proud of that casino, "the fruit of his work" uncle calls it. There I learned to play poker and roulette, I was very good at poker, but roulette always fooled me.

"Happy birthday kid. She will make your day special. Make sure you treat her nice."

Nikolai said to me as he introduced me to the read head that looked like Victoria secrets models. Damn, she was hot and I was horny.

The following day I went to Nikolai and requested the same present.

"It would be nice if you would let me 'borrow' that brunette, last night I saw the sky full of stars."

He laughed so hard, I was afraid the casino would fall on me,

"Boy you are a romantic!"

Romantic or not, that was the night my life became better and worse. I was in that casino more nights that my parents liked, fucking almost all the girls my uncle head in his staff. At one point I caused so much of a drama that he forbade me to step inside the casino for the following year.

Our village was small but beautiful, my only problem was the stream was on the other side of the village. I would have liked to be closer to the water.

But, I went there every time I took Caesar for a ride.

I liked to listen to the water, sometimes I stayed up late in the evening to see the stars. It was a place on the mountain from where I was able to see the sky full of stars, and I could see the girl with black hair and green eyes lying down in her garden, looking at the sky, I would pretend she knows we watch the stars together. Until, one day when I never saw her again. I thought of her many years after she was gone.

Like I said I was a lucky child and man… until, the day I found out about my mother.

She is dying, a little faster with each day passing, and I am not referring to a normal death, like every one of us. I mean… cancer.

She fought with these ugly and ruthless diseases for the last five years, but now I can see it take a toll on her. Sometimes, it is hard to look at her and see this fragile woman standing in front of me. I would just like to scream "What did you do with my mother!" but, it's in vain.

I was there when doctors said she has less than nine months…

How fucked up is this?

We need nine months to come into this world, and she has nine months until she will leave this world…

Until she will be nothing more than a lifeless body, to look at.

Often I wonder if this is some sort of punishment for my past mistakes, if this is God's way to bring me back from my gambling addiction?

Immediately, after we found out that mother has cancer, dad moved us to England, so she could receive the highest quality medical care. To have access to the best tests, of course it was a plus for his political career as well.

When we arrived in England, my parents bought a house in a small town next to the sea, not far from London. Saying the breeze would make her feel better and the small town giving her the peace and quiet she needs.

It is not a very big house. It has three bedrooms, two bathrooms, living room, kitchen and a garden in the back of the house.

It doesn't compare with our house in Altai, but it's more suitable for them and my brothers.

I decided to live in London, alone. Being too hard for me to see my mother tormented every day by this merciless disease.

This house is welcoming, but not warm as the one in Altai, maybe because my mother opted for an interior designer, instead of taking care of everything herself.

The walls of the house have neutral colours, the wall of the staircase is devoid of pictures. The living room that was once my favourite room, is now so formal, I feel like throwing up.

With almond-coloured walls and a huge TV instead of a fireplace, that's used too few times. In front of it a black sofa matched with some cream sofa-chairs and a coffee table I'm not even sure what dark colour it has, a red carpet on a black floor. In the right side of the living room is the dining area, with a massive wooden table and matching chairs.

Everything is so elegant, but lifeless.

"Mother, we talked about marriage so many times. I told you I will try my best to find a suitable woman to marry and have children. I promised you."

"I know, but I have so less time and I would really like to see you married, until…"

"Don't you even dare to finish that sentence!"

I came to visit my mother after not seeing her for a full week.

Because the weather is still beautiful for September, we decided to sit outside in the garden.

As we took our place in the chairs at the table, I stared at her and saw tiredness and concerned in her gaze. I don't know if it's because of me or because of this disease that it's eating her alive.

"I promise, I will get married until… And you will have your chance to see me married and expecting a baby. Not me of course, my wife will expect a baby, oh for the love of God, you got it."

That was a huge promise coming from a man who doesn't believe in love.

She smiles bright and all her face lights up, a flicker of hope in her blue eye. Contented with my promises she asks me with so much joy.

"Are you serious?"

"Yes, I'm serious, mother!"

What the hell got into me to promise this? I have no clue, but I'm deathly serious, as I spoke the words with conviction.

What she will never find out, is that I will get divorced after she passes away. And of course I will pay a doctor to say my wife, whoever it will be, is carrying my child. I am not that worse of a man to abandon my child and I will never be! But, for sure I cannot even phantom the thought of bringing a child of mine in this world.

All I am thinking is, how many points are in my gambling machine? How long until I hit the next jackpot? How drunk will I get? How long will I spend buried in between some girl's legs, to fuck away my loss frustration?

Because I totally know by now, most of the time you lose and just a few times you win. But, for some reason, I always manage to find my way to the next casino, to the next roulette, or a choice of gambling device from so many displayed next to a very long wall, in almost every casino I walk into…

"Are you sure?"

Mother interrupts the thoughts about my addiction.

"Yes, I am sure!"

I assure her.

"And how will you do this, when you do not even date? When was the last time I saw you with a girl by your side?"

"When I was twenty-two!" I answer truthfully. "It was Felicia. But, who told you I don't date? I have dated this girl, in the last two or three weeks!"

I lie, thinking of the little "ant" who's always dancing when passing the Thames River, walk-away. It's the most beautiful thing I saw in a very long time. I find it amusing, so amusing that I called her "my ant"…To be totally honest, I didn't even know I enjoyed the show so much until she did not come the next day. It was like I missed my private dance and something was missing. I found myself pissed off for the whole day because of her…whoever she is.

Where the fuck this thoughts are coming from?

"Date? In the last two or three weeks? Are you serious?"

I believe she's getting on my lie, but not really sure about that.

"Yes mother! I date! I have dated this girl for nearly three weeks now, and spend time talking to her on the phone constantly!"

Talking on the phone? Constantly? Me? Well, even I realise how stupid that sounds. Hopefully my mother will just let this one go. Otherwise, this will lead to more lies and I am not at all comfortable lying to her. Never was and never will, not that I lied to her in the past. Not until… now. It's for her own good, I say to myself.

"Good then! I would like to meet her!"

She states so matter of fact that I am left without a breath, for a few seconds. Recovering quickly, I display my most charming smile.

"Of course you do!"

Later that afternoon, I say my goodbye and walk out the door doing the only thing that crosses my mind. I call my best friend Arthur.

A British model and a loyal friend, to me and to everyone he knows. Of course he picks up at the first ring.

"Are you sleeping with your phone or something dude?"

"Fuck off! I had my phone in my hands, I wanted to call her… never mind, what do you want?"

I realised he said… her. And my curiosity gets the best of me. He doesn't date just like me. We both were toasted by a girl and never dated again.

"Who's her?"

"What do you want?"

He asked, deflecting my question.

"I need a favour, a huge one! It's for mom!"

I clarify and he doesn't question further, knowing what a hard fucking blow was for me to learn that mom has cancer, and the fucker it's not going away.

"OK! Again, what do you want?"

He asks, slightly annoyed he needs to push it so far!

"I need a girl to marry!"

I say cold and without feelings, it's like I was asking him to buy me a bear.

"You need what? Have I heard you right? YOU?

Married? Is this a sick joke?"

He asks every question a little more shocked than the one before.

"Yes you dick! I promise mom I will marry and expect a child, before she passes away!"

Even I can't believe how ridiculous it sounds when I say the words out loud.

"A child?"

He shouts in my ear, forcing me to pull my phone away. Fucker, he knows this is not me.

"Look man, I need to see you and explain. I have a plan, she will not know what the hell is going on, but I need her to find peace!"

It kills me that I will go to this extent, to make my mother happy in her last months of life. Especially, because I never lied to her, ever. No matter the worst, I was always truthful with her and she was always there….until now.

She always said to me "Lan, no matter if you are deep in the valley or on the highest mountain, I will be next to you as long as you don't lie to me!" And I never lied to her… until now.

But she will not find out!

She can't!

It will destroy her worse than cancer does.

Realising I'm still on the phone with Arthur, I say.

"Will you help me then?"

He sights, contemplating at my problem and the risk involved, but decides to help me in this crazy plan.

"This is insane, but I will help you. Just to make it clear is for your mother. Meet me at the coffee shop. I will send you the address."

Checking the address I say.

"That's next to my apartment. I will see you there in an hour. What the fuck are you doing in a coffee shop, anyway?"

He hangs up without an answer.

It's fairly easy to get to the café, especially because it's on my way home. It's a nightmare to actually find a place to park around this dam café. Once I manage that, I go inside and find Arthur talking to the waitress.

It's surprising how big the café is. Especially for London's café, where they are small and crowded. This one is large. Two rooms, both open view, with floor to ceiling windows. There must be over twenty tables on this side of the café, all of them hard wood with metal chairs. Strange combination, but not bad looking.

Green walls with black doors.

The bar and the grill are in the other room of the café, which is a bit smaller, but has the same green walls with black doors and same tables with chairs.

For sure the owner has a strange taste in decoration or another definition of beauty when it comes to painting the walls.

This thought makes me smile, earning me, a stare from the waitress that Arthur was talking to.

A medium high girl, brunette with a way too big French for her oval face, it's like she wants to hide behind her hair or something. Her eyes are a mix of green and light brown. They look familiar, but I can't place them in my head. I wonder if they change according to her mood. Why do I wonder that?

Looking down, hello boobies.

I mean she has a big enough chest, her boobs can fit perfectly in my large hand. She is curvy and from what I can see, her ass is just as fine as her boobs. With a pair of a little too thick thighs, but long enough legs. Standing close enough to her, I realise her high fits perfectly under my chin.

I could hold this girl and have my way with her, if she would like to lose that two number larger widow outfit she has. I suppose it's kind of a uniform since everyone looks like they are at a funeral …get a grip Lan. What the fuck is wrong with you? I scold myself internally.

"Anything you like, babe?"

I ask her, as I spread my perfect smile across my face.

Her reaction shocks me, she looks like I just slap her across the face. What the actual fuck just happen? I didn't say a thing to her. Most importantly, why do I care?

Turning my face, I see Arthur staring between me and her.

"Hey man. Thanks for meeting me!"

I greet him as the waitress is gone and I take a seat.

"Hi! What the fuck was that?"

Pointing in the direction the waitress just disappeared and continues "…and no problem, anything for your mom!"

What? I am confused now.

"What was what?"

I ask, to make sure I follow what he's point is.

"Anything you like?"

He repeats, in a worst attempt to be me.

"That? I was just trying to be nice, and who knows maybe score something. She has a fine ass!"

I say smirking and turn my gaze, maybe I can catch another glimpse of that ass. Only to be welcomed with a very pissed Arthur when I turn back my head.

"She is nothing of what you are used to! So step back! Besides, you are looking for a "wife" don't you?"

He says the last part more like a joke.

What the hell is his problem? Who is this girl to him? And why does he care? Is she "her" who he referred when we spoke on the phone? That's why he is here in this café, instead of our usual 5 star in Canary Wharf?

"Yes, that's exactly what I am looking for!"

I say, to distract myself from the hundred question list that decided to pop in my brain.

"Will you help me?"

"What do you need help with? Aren't you perfectly capable to charm your way in marriage?" He's mocking me "What's your plan here? You said you will explain if we meet. Speak!"

I begin to speak, but I am reduced to silence the moment I hear her.

"What would you like to drink?"

"I would have a strong cappuccino."

I answer her question. Now that she's closer, I admire her face, her half parted lips, like she is struggling to breath. I am getting lost in her, but she nods and breaks the connection.

Turning to Arthur she speaks.

"It's a virus on your computer that gave whoever the access they needed to break into your social media account. I will do my best to find that trace. Closed and make sure they cannot get back inside your computer again."

Her voice is soft, similar to my mother when she explains something. I'm so lost, she envelops me. When suddenly, my brain decided to work and make sense of what she said. Virus, computer, trace access…

"Are you a hacker?"

I ask, apparently aloud, since she looks at me like I had grown another head. What's the deal with this girl?

"No, I'm not! I just returned a small favour to a friend."

And with that she disappeared.

For the next half an hour I am going through my plan with Arthur, making sure he understands what I want to do, and what type of girl I need. In order to make my mother believe that I fall for her and I truly want to marry her.

I was both relieved and disappointed, that my coffee was broth to me by a dude, instead of her.

What is with this girl?

Arthur tells me he might know someone who can help me with my problem. A girl he knew for a long time, she did something similar and she would most probably do it again.

He pays for the bill and we walk out the café, going to meet that girl. As I walk to my car, I can see her there. Staring at her, I have the strange feeling that I want to get to know her. She seems so familiar, but a total stranger at the same time.

CHAPTER THREE

SVETLANA

"Have you heard about Renesmee? She told me, they had another fight… again."

I was talking to Arthur, when the hair on neck started to raise. Turning to see who was next to me, I was reduced to silence, well more that I normally am.

He is tall, well defined muscles that I can see through his tight T-shirt. Light blond hair and his eyes. Oh my God, his eyes, the most perfect sky blue I had the privilege to see. Oval face, a little elongated. His chin is slightly wide, but he has well defined full fleshy lips, that I could kiss forever.

What? Since when I want to kiss someone?

I am staring. I know I am, but cannot stop, even if my life depends on it. He's like some kind of ruthless Russian fighter model, straight from the magazine cover. In this God forgotten café.

As he comes closer to where I am glued to the floor, I see that I fit perfectly under his chin. It's like if he stands right in front of me, he can place his chin on top of my head.

I want to ask him how he even knows this café, but then, I realise that he said something to Arthur and now he is looking at me.

Is he checking me out, no that's impossible, I make sure every morning to be as unattractive as I can get. Still, decent for work.

"Anything you like?"

He asks so cocky, I turn my face and walk away, not before seeing that smile on his face.

A smile that makes his face light and his eyes look smaller than they are. Jesus that smile, if displayed more, I could do anything he asked me to!

What is wrong with me and since when I have this kind of thought?

When I get to the bar I realize, I forget two things. One, to ask this Greek God, if he wants something to drink. Second, to let Arthur know what I found on his laptop.

I smile, which looks more like a grimace and walk to their table, again.

As I approach, I hear Arthur speaking with "Mr Muscle".

"What do you need help with? Aren't you perfectly capable to charm your way in marriage? What's your plan here? You said you will explain if we meet. Speak!"

What the heck? He plans to marry and needs Arthur help? What is going on?

Making a mental note to ask Arthur what is going on. Then I ask myself when and why I became so nosy? I made sure to not date and most important not to care about people around me, unless is any of the three people I care the most.

"What would you like to drink?"

I ask him, after he answers, I turn to Arthur. Telling him about my discovery, I am prompted with a question.

"Are you a hacker?"

Mr Muscle asks, I deny and nearly run away. Placing my order, I ask one other colleague to deliver it. I don't intend to interact with this guy anymore.

The rest of the day as usual, without interruption, and I am glad for it.

Nobody, except Arthur knows I'm a hacker. I worked my brain hard to become the best black hat in London at least. Hoping, one day this knowledge will help me do good for people in need.

I want to be able to save as many people as I can, I know first-hand how to be without salvation, when you need it the most. Until then, I would like to keep this for me and Arthur, which I know for sure will not say a word to a soul, if I don't want to.

"You son of a motherfucker! You bastard!... arh!"

After three days, I caught the bastard who broke into Arthur's computer, and accessed his social media. I even made sure he will not be able to come back again, but made a huge mistake. I connected to a server I shouldn't.

Problem is, I don't know how to undo my mistake. I mean, I'm above average hackers, even if I still have more to learn. However, I know for sure, what I did is as stupid mistake as a "skiddie" can make. And I'm not someone who does not know how to write their own code, I made sure to learn and get as much experience as possible. And here I am praying someone on the other side will not see my mistake.

Amazing, just so fucking amazing, no matter what I try to think nothing comes to my mind, so I do one thing that I know will calm my nerves.

I decided to take a walk by the Thames River, that will settle my nerves and I will have time to think.

I love this part of the river. It's nice and it's always quiet.

I positioned myself at the highest point of the walk away. From here, I can perfectly see in both ways of the river. I am fascinated by the ferry's.

How they make circles around each other, carrying people and cars from one side to another of the river.

They are big white and blue boat platforms going in a perfect circle, looking like some force pushes them above the water, as they slide.

Behind them you can see Canary Wharf buildings, creating the illusion of a smaller version of New York, Beautiful buildings. I like to watch them at sundown, when all the lights are displayed, you can see all the red lights on top of the building. How they trace a red line in the sky, signalling planes their position, it's so peaceful.

I love the mornings when there is nobody on the street and I can dance while listening to the songs that play in my headphones at a maximum level. Sometimes wondering if I want to get myself deaf. Good thing, nobody pays attention to my dancing skills, which are non-existing.

Except, the last two days I missed this view, my bus decided to be late in the morning, and I had to hurry for my shift at the café.

I'm watching the water current that creates small waves on the surface of the water. Watching the ferry taking rounds on the river as well.

Half an hour later, I decided to call Arthur and ask him to meet me in the morning, to return his laptop, because I finished my job. Heading home, to rest for tomorrow, because it's a long and busy day. As always in Saturday's at coffee shops. Everyone decides to eat out, especially families with kids. It's like family day or something. I wouldn't know, because we never had that home.

On my way home, I call Renesmee asking about her day and what is going on with that relation of hers. I laugh when she says to me, that her boyfriend doesn't get the hint to fuck off.

The night goes quickly. I wake up an hour and half earlier than my shift is. Take a quick shower, brush my teeth and walk out the door to meet Arthur by the river. Getting there I see Arthur's already waiting for me with a coffee and sleeping eyes.

"Morning! How are you?"

I greet him as he kisses my forehead and smiles. He always does that, it's like a father's gesture, or the way my father supposed to be. But, I decided to become a monster.

"Morning! Good! How are you? Have you brought my "charming keys"?"

He asks, referring to his laptop.

"Charming keys?"

I laugh

"Yes, charming keys! You know, all the baby girls that are writing to me and we meet, and do stuff. Stuff you never want to know about!"

He laughs and I join him.

"Why the hell would I want to know about your sex life?"

"Just saying, maybe you want to know something funny other than your usual criminals and hex, mex codes."

"Mex? It's hex and decimal codes, not mex codes. But, if you are that good who knows? Maybe, you can invent a new way of communication and name it MEX code."

I say and laugh so hard, that I need a minute to realise suddenly we are not alone anymore, and by the time I do that I'm greeted with the most amazing smile….fuck.

"Morning!"

He says to us and for the first time I get the hint of a Russian accent, a cold chill runs down my spine. Scratch that, a very cold chill runs my spine.

I stare at Arthur and he is unaffected, of course he is. It's his friend not mine, but for some reason he gazes at me, as if asking for permission to introduce us.

I slightly nod in agreement. I do not want to embarrass Arthur in front of his friend, it was me who insisted so many times to keep me away from his glamorous life as a model.

"Morning!"

Arthur says to his friend, then turns to me.

"This is Lan!"

Gazing at him and before I can stop myself I ask.

"As in Local Area Network (LAN)?"

We all burst in laughter. When we get a grip of ourselves, Lan answers.

"Local area yes, but not network, just a guy!"

Gazing at me, he smiles again. God that smile will be the end of me, and this is a strange sensation, I am supposed to be dead inside from a long time.

"And this is Lana!"

Arthur announced, before I can go deeper into my thoughts.

"Local area network antenna?"

Lan speaks first, and we start to laugh again.

"OK you geeks! This is funny and all, but I need to go because I did not sleep last night. Baby girl and all that."

I crook my nose and Lan frowns looking between the two of us.

"Oh no, no, not with me! God no!"

I say a little too quickly and loud, for this time in the morning. Before anyone can say something I head for work, leaving the two looking in my direction, like I grew another head or something.

CHAPTER FOUR

RUSLAN

"This is my offer! Leave it or take it, it's up to you. I will not change my conditions."

The girl in front of me said. She's a good looking model, slim, fit, long leg, blond hair. All that, but something doesn't please me. I'm uncomfortable around her, and she irritates me.

"Thank you, but I will pass it this time."

"Suits yourself!"

Turning my face to Arthur, I see he has a shocked expression. Before getting in my car he asks.

"Can you explain to me why you refuse that offer? She said she wants no complications, no kids and she will play along the pregnant part. It was the simplest deal you could ever find. Don't say it's about money, because it is not. So, care to share?"

He has a point here, but I had no answer. I had no clue of what just happened or why.

"Honestly, I don't know. Something didn't feel right."

He nods, turning his back to me heading to his car. On my way home all I could think about were her green-brown eyes and that hideous uniform that makes her look like a widow.

I wanted to know why she reacted the way she did when I asked her if she liked what she saw. Who would be offended by such a simple question? And yet she was.

After getting home that night with a frown on my face and a bruised ego, I decided to settle for my laptop. Trying to catch some work that I neglected in the last couple of days.

The place I call home is a two bedroom flat, with one bathroom, a service toilet, living, kitchen and a small hallway on the side of the Thames River.

The entrance to the apartment is through a hall in shape of "T", bathroom wall being one of the hall walls, if you turn left and pass the bathroom, you head to the kitchen. If you turn right first and pass the service toilet, straight ahead it should be in one of the bedrooms, but I changed that in a home office. I liked that it faces the water just like the bedroom does.

My office has white walls and mahogany furniture. A huge bookshelves that covers the whole wall and has a built-in desk, in the middle, holding my big computer screen. A second desk table in front of the built-in desk. I keep my laptop on and used as a work table. In between the two desks I have a white leather office wheelchair, making it easy to move between the two.

On the other side of the middle table, another two chairs. On the opposite wall is a sofa bed which I never used, but I wanted there for no specific reason, a light grey laminate with no carpet. I use this office only for private business or personal use.

Next to the office is the bedroom, which has mahogany walls with the dressing room on the left, as you enter, and the windows on the right. The bed, an upholstered low profile platform bed, is placed next to the wall facing the door, right in the middle.

A square arch frames the bed with a wooden decoration giving the feeling that the bed would be actually positioned in front of a wooden door lit with LEDs of different colours.

On each side of the bed is a bedside table with lamps in the shape of snail eyes, directed towards the bed.

I didn't care what colour the bedroom was, I don't spend much time in it and when I do it, it's just to sleep.

On the loft, next to the bedroom, is the living room. This was always my favourite room and it's a huge room for that matter. Unlike the one we had at home in Altai, it does not have a fireplace. I wanted to create one, but I gave up the idea.

No matter how many fake chimneys you will have, it will never be like a real one.

I put my dining table on the same wall with the kitchen, which is the wall facing the apartment entrance. Opposite the dining table I have a floor to ceiling window. On the right I have a massive flat screen, I have no idea why it is there since I do not watch TV. Probably just for décor. Opposite the TV is a sofa with a coffee table.

All the living is to be black, white and blue. Walls are white, and the furniture is black with blue decoration.

I love this apartment, it's my first accomplishment. My first serious investment. Followed by many others of course, but this was my first.

I head to the office and take a seat at the desk, opening my laptop and all the applications I need. Just to be greeted with a notification, someone connected to a server they shouldn't have access to…

Great, just fucking great…this will be a long night.

Three days later, I wake up to a beautiful morning in London, despite the fact that it's the end of September. The weather is still hot, and mornings are not so freezing.

I still have my laptop open, running a searching program, but at least I have an ID for the fucker who broke into the server.

@рыба12. Who the fuck puts their nick as fish these day? Probably a stupid kid who wanted to show off and got lucky to break into our server, anyway in a matter of minutes, I will have their phone number and the most probably a name for that number too.

After having my shower, I made my coffee and went on the balcony from my office, to enjoy probably one of the last wonderful mornings this September has. The view of my apartment is amazing, facing the river, from the seventeenth floor, I have a clear image of Canary Wharf buildings. I love to watch them at night. The ferry, that looks just like little child bath toys from up here. You can see all sorts of buildings by each side of the river, and it is a magnificent view every time.

I don't mind the sunrise, but my favourite is the sunset, when the sun mixes with the clouds and spreads a magical fire colour that slightly fades into darkness.

It makes me think of my mother and her time on this planet, in this life... As soon as I look down, to see if I am lucky today and get my "private dance", I see my "ant" with none other than Arthur. He bends and kisses her on the forehead.

Before I realise what I was doing, I am standing in front of them outside my building.

What is wrong with me? What am I supposed to say now?

Way to go Lan, way to go! I do the only thing that I know for sure it will never go wrong…smile.

Couple of minutes later, after a small interaction and apparently my wrong assumption that Arthur is sleeping with this Lana chick, she starts running. Like literally running, claiming she is late for her shift. Fuck, this is the chick from the café, "my ant" works 5 minute from my house. This must be a joke from the sky…again!

I stare at an irritated Arthur, as I study him I question.

"What's with her and you? Are you sleeping together?"

He's eyes are so wide, I am afraid they will go out of their socket.

"No man!"

He shouts and I put my hands up, in a defensive mode.

"OK! Just asking!"

"I know, but it's nothing like that. I am just a little over protective of her. She had a lot of hard times in the past and she's like a sister to me."

"A sister?" Now I am officially confused. "Man you don't have a sister, or you do?"

"Are you fucking deaf? Like a sister, not my sister! Of course she is not my sister by blood, we have been friends for a long time!"

Friends for a long time, like since when? How do they meet? Why did he never say anything to me? I know all his friends we kind of grew up together, why I know nothing about her? And what the hell is with so many questions in my head??

Instead, I focus my attention back at him asking him if he wants to come up and sleep at my place. I can see he is tired and it would be nothing out of the ordinary. By the time we go back inside, I should have the scan result of my online searching. I will be gone to catch the fish fucker who broke in my server anyways.

Once he agrees we go back in the building, to the elevator and up to the apartment. Arthur tells me all about that "baby girl" he supposed to fuck last night, but stood him up.

I really try not to laugh in his face, I still cannot imagine how some chick can fool him like that. He is known for not being in situations like this, maybe other way around. He claims this chick is different. Whatever!

Back in the apartment, I go straight to my office as Arthur goes straight for the bedroom.

"Did you change the bed shits from your last fuck?"

"Fuck off!"

I respond to his question and he chuckles.

Looking down at my laptop... BINGO

I have a hit and most important I have coordinates for the number I found, now this was easier than I expected.

Taking notes of my finding I realise that the address is not far from here, actually walking distance. I decide to type coordinates in my phone GPS and head there, to see if I can find this fish fucker. Making a mental note to stop at café and try their food on my way back. Not because I really want to eat, but because I want to see Lana.

Ten minutes later, I am standing in front of the café, equal parts terrified and trilled … this cannot be happening.

If I am right, which I am positive I am, she is the fish fucker and I can try to blackmail her into getting married with me…

Jackass move, I know. Still a move, and this will give me the time to actually know this girl. If I am wrong, doubtful. Who the fuck is my fish? Am I comfortable knowing that he is here and she is here as well? Are they working together??

With all these questions in mind I decide to go in and take a seat at a table.

I didn't see her yet, but I know she is in because of our encounter in the morning. Some guy took my coffee order and I contemplated if I should call the number I found.

If it's hers, she will pick up or at least call back. If not I will not embarrass myself in front of her. As I debate what to do, I see Lana talking to a guy, they look friendly enough for her to be relaxed in conversation, but I still don't like it. What can I say? Jealousy it's a powerful sentiment and I hit the call button. As the phone rings, and rings, and rings.

She goes from stiff to more stiff, until she excuses herself and goes to the bathrooms. Ten second after she enters the bathroom my phone rings in my hand, staring at it… her number. At that moment, I feel like I won the biggest jackpot gamble ever.

"Welcome to Paulscorp Security! My name is Dimitri, how can I help?"

I greet her, glancing around to make sure nobody sees me, as I make my way to the ladies bathroom. I found her inside with the back at the door, disconnecting the call at the same time she said.

"I had a missed call from this number!"

Bending down and whispering in her ear "ryba" which is the meaning for fish in Russian.

In the mirror next to me, I see all the colours draining from her cheeks. Closing her eyes, taking a deep breath. Turning to face me, she opens her eyes. Shock is displayed on her face, clear as the day, and something else…maybe fear?

CHAPTER FIVE

SVETLANA

I was in the small part of the café, serving Danny, an usual customer. He is very shy and barely speaks to anyone, except today he opened up a bit more to me and surprised me with a small talk. My phone started to buzz in my pocket, at first I believed it was a text or something, but the thing would not stop buzzing. I realise it must be a call. Trying my best to get away from Danny, without scaring him, but in time to answer to whoever decided this very moment to call I said,

"Nice to see you today, Danny!"

By the time I managed to get inside the bathroom, my phone call stopped. I tried to ring back, it rings twice before I heard a man speaking.

"Welcome to Paulscorp Security! My name is Dimitri, how can I help?"

I start my reply when someone whispers in my ear… "ryba".

This cannot be happening, not now, not ever. How did he find me? Who is behind me? Most importantly what the consequences will be?

I knew I made a stupid mistake, but I never thought they would put so much effort in finding me, in person.

I didn't open any folder or access any information. They know this, don't they? But, I think it does not matter anymore because in a matter of seconds I will find out who it is, and what will happen.

Closing my eyes, I force myself to inhale a sharp breath, too sharp in this very moment. I feel my blood draining from my cheeks as I turn slowly to face whoever this is. Forcing myself to open my eyes, praying this is just my imagination playing tricks on me and no one will be here, no such luck. Instead, I am greeted with those blue eyes and his smile. This cannot be true! He said ryba, how does he even know that? And in that very moment a wave of fear runs down my spine.

I am positive, by now shock is displayed on my face. Trying to recover the best I can, I say.

"What are you doing in the ladies toilet?"

"Deceiving, I see! I found you ryba!"

He says so sure of himself.

"I don't know what you are talking about. And my name is not ryba, you short memory person!"

I say trying to sound unaffected.

"Nice try! But it's not working."

He says, smiling even brighter and taking a step closer.

This might be a problem in this tiny bathroom, I wasn't touched by a man since…him. And, I do not plan to let anyone start now.

"Don't touch me!"

I said through gritted teeth, I saw him put his hands in the air and take a step back, at the same time with the walls coming in. I am on the verge of a panic attack. I can feel it, trying my best to calm myself down. I take small regular breaths.

"I am not going to hurt you! However, I want to talk to you about my findings on the company server!"

"I don't know what you are talking about!"

I try again, with no good result apparently, because he tells me.

"Stop pretending, I know for sure It was you! I will wait for you to finish your shift, so we can talk without interruption!"

He got out of the toilet and I let out a breath I wasn't aware I was holding. He did not touch me, thank God for that, and backed away without a fight, strange. I take a moment to compose myself. Staring at my image in the mirror, I understand why Lan back away without a fight, I am white as a ghost.

My shift goes on without any other "surprise". By the time I need to go home, I can see Lan standing outside the café, waiting for me to finish…that's just great!

Needless to say I tried to come up with thousands of different scenarios of how to flee before he got here, none of them worked. Once outside, I lead the way to the river side alley. At least to be somewhere where I can think. We take a seat on one of the concrete benches and I'm waiting for him to speak.

"I have a proposition for you."

"Okay, I am listening!"

I have no other choice, because even if "physically" I did not open any folders to access the information, the method I used to be there braked at least three different criminal laws and four acts.

"I am not going to take any actions against you for accessing that server if... you marry me!"

He says so matter of fact, I need a minute to realise he is serious. I am positive my face is somewhere on the concrete, at my feet.

"Marry you? Is this some kind of joke? Because is a very stupid one!"

I bite back, before he can say something I say what Arthur said to him at the café.

"Aren't you perfectly capable of charming your way in marriage?"

He frowns and looks like I slap him. Great… feel that jackass.

"Don't talk about what you don't know!"

He bites back, closing his eyes, takes a deep breath and continues in a calmer tone.

"It's not like that! I don't really want to marry, but I promise my mother I will marry before it's too late….for her!"

Confusing me more than ever before, I frown.

"Why would it be too late for her?"

Trying to get some clarification.

"Look we can make an agreement, some kind of contract if you like. Put down some rule that only the two of us would know."

"Why would you do that? Why me?"

"I would do anything for my mother's happiness and because you just broke a few serious laws! Look, I am not a total ass in here. I know this is a lot to ask from you. Especially, because we don't know each other.

Take it this way, I need your help and you need mine. Simple as that!"

"You still didn't answer my question. Why is it too late for your mother?"

I ask pushing my luck, and never in a million years actually hoped for him to answer so honestly.

"Because she is dying of cancer!"

At that moment, I wished to never ask the question, in the first place.

"Sorry!"

Was all I managed, looking down at the concrete floor.

"So, let me understand, you want me to go meet your dying mother, lie to her, with a smile on my face, that I'm happily in love with you and we are going to marry? What kind of person do you think I am?"

Shock, angriness and something else is displayed in the way he stares at me as realisation hits me. I was thinking out loud. Shit!

"I know it sounds terrible, but it isn't. Or at least not for me! I am not some cold heartless ass, but I want my mom to find peace in her last months of her life, and if marriage is what she needs, that's what I will do! I just need your help and you need mine. Like I said, I will not go further with my findings on the server. Even more, I will make it look like it was not there in the first place!"

He says a little too fast, but I can see his sincereness when he speaks, and to my surprise he's calmer than I expected.

Weighing my options, which are only two in real. Like going through real trouble with authorities, and everything that includes breaking in that server. Or agreeing to this insane plan of his, which is still a jail sentence, but at least I have the opportunity to actually make it on my own terms as well.

"Ground rules and contract you said?"

"Yes, I said that!"

"Okay, I will do this!"

He's staring at me, not believing I just agree to this. But, again he didn't give me much of a choice, either.

"So, how is this going to go? We meet to put together a contract? What kind of rules are allowed?"

I question him at such speed, that he starts to laugh.

"Well we need to agree on a day, seat down and discuss the contract terms and conditions!"

He explains, like discussing a business deal not his life, or my life for that matter.

This is insane.

I am insane.

Except, it's a bit too late to go back now.

An uncomfortable silence sets between us, gazing his way, I notice for the first time his big hands. A lion head tattoo with the word King, is skilfully drawn on the back of his right hand. It suits his hand and is so well drawn, that looks so real.

"It's a beautiful tattoo! Does it have any meaning or you just like it?"

Curiosity gets the best of me as I further admire the peace of work on his hand.

"It's my zodiac sign and of course, I'm the king in my own life."

He explained and I burst in laughter, of course he is. It's so hard to actually picture him anything else than muscle and rudeness, commanding any room he is in.

"What?"

"Nothing, you were so funny in all your seriousness I'm the king of my own life!"

I try to make a male sound that comes like a bear roar, which gains me a smile from him, and we laugh further.

It's a nice experience and gives me the hope that maybe this is not such a bad idea after all. Few minutes later, we agreed that he would let me know the day of our "meeting". Saying our goodbyes, we part ways.

I pull my phone and call Vitaly.

He is a broad-shouldered, muscular man with long hands and legs. A diamond-shaped face, curly black hair, blue eyes and fleshy lips.

He has a hand as big as my head. When I was younger, and even now sometimes, when he puts his hand on my head, he covers it.

Despite being the best MMA fighter, and having his own training room, he is the gentlest person I have ever met. Even gentler than Arthur and he is very kind and gentle to me.

Vitaly was with me on the darkest night of my life and has remained motionless with me, to this day. He is the father I did not have and any problem I have, his door and arms are always open for me, no matter the time.

My father and he were good friends until that evening, after that all changed and Vitaly supported me more than it did them. He brought me to London and sustained me, until I got to where I am today.

Always telling me that I can do whatever I want.

He picks up on the second ring and answers the call with his usual.

"Hello princess! How are you? And what can I do for you tonight?"

The way he speaks makes him sound like some kind of gigolo or something, but I know he doesn't mean any harm. In fact it was him that helped me the most without even questioning my reasons, I will always be thankful for that.

When I first came here, I was crushing at the flat on top of he's gym, no one ever knew I was there. I had access to the gym anytime, I mostly used it after everyone left. I like to be alone.

Vitally was there for me without intruding, always telling me people will open at their own peace. I guess he knows what happened, but he has no idea who did it, no one does except Arthur. I would have never mentioned that to anyone, I wouldn't have said a word to him either if it wasn't for that idiot colleague of his, who didn't get no for an answer.

"Hello! You there?"

Vitally's voice brings me back to the moment.

"Yes, yes I'm here! Sorry, I disconnected from my body for a second, I want a race tonight!"

"Hmm, that bad? Okay! Ten o'clock, in the usual spot!"

He ends the conversation. That's what I like the most. Vitally, doesn't need words to understand me, and he always protects me like I am his own daughter, only if that were true…

By nine o'clock I am at the garage that I keep my beauty in. I made a point to keep my car away from everyone, except Vitaly and Arthur. The less people know about me, the better.

Well if I think better people know me in bits and pieces. Except of course Arthur, who knows everything and I mean everything about me. When the garage door opens, I take a look at this beauty. Peace and happiness fills me.

It's a red, orange and black Chevrolet Camaro ZL1 from 2016 modified, not only on the inside which is all red and black leather with sport seats. But, on the outside as well. With a 6.2L supercharged V-8 engine, developing 650 horsepower and a prodigious 881Nm of torque. Enabling a benchmark run of 0-100Km/H in just over 3.5 seconds.

The outside is mainly black with red and orange starting from the trunk to the middle of the car, representing fire. It looks like half of the car comes out from flames every second you look at it. Ironically it's exactly how I feel all the time.

Bumper is so low, I am grateful that London does not have too many holes in the road. I love this car. "Freedom" is my escape, my peace and quiet, and yes I named him freedom. Because he is my freedom and he will be the only one to actually hold me. I am officially nuts, I am talking about the car like it would be a man.

Ten sharp and I am in our usual spot in Trafalgar Square, at the north entrance of St James park. Same picture as every other time, a lot of tuned cars, a sea of people minding their own business.

Some betting who will be the first to cross the finish line tonight, probably me. I didn't lose a race in the past year, but nothing is for sure, especially because we never know what to expect after the "Go" signal. Some are here just for entertainment, and some are here to race, like in my case.

Of course we are all racing illegal, which makes the race even more interesting. You not only need to stay focused in crossing first the finish line, but you need to make sure you don't fall in any police traps. Judging from this point of view, you could say I am an adrenaline junkie. We meet here, agree on the race route and fire the engines.

I love the roar of my car.

The feel of all that horsepower at my feet.

The way my car sends me in my driver seat, every time I speed up to the finish line, it's amazing.

Routine is the same every time, except this time I am competing against… him.

"Not you again!"

I tell myself with a roll of my eyes. Tonight, it's supposed to be about me and only me. I'm supposed to be free, not thinking how to stay focused on kicking his ass. There is no way in hell, I will let him win this. I never lost a race this year and I am not planning to start with him.

 Praised myself for the choice of my outfit tonight. Black jeans, black hoodie and a face mask that came straight under my eyes. Similar to a small ninja, the only visible part of my face is the eyes. And because the hood of my top is coming down so low on my face, the only person who knows who I really am, is Vitaly.

He is the person who would pay the fee and collect the winning price for the race, we would meet the next day to give me my share, which most of the time was more than I would hope for.

It was quick and easy money, and the race will give me the freedom I need to clear my head. Except tonight, Lan is here, sitting right next to me, our cars are so close that I am really grateful for the hood on my face and the tinted windows. I'm trying my best not to look in his direction, because I need my head clear for the race and what is next after.

Same drill at every race, an almost naked girl points herself between the front of our cars, making signs with her hands as she says her part. At "GO!" I release the clutch and adrenaline takes over.

This is the most alive, I get to feel in life. Carefree without problems, without my father, without thoughts, without…. just me and the car, pure adrenaline.

I follow the race route, as changing gears gaining more speed and becoming more alive, by the time I realise any of this, I won the race!

OW MY GOD I WAN THE RACE, I beat him! I am laughing out loud as I see him, in the rear mirror.

All angry and frustrated, talking to Vitaly, he's asking for a rematch. I wait for a few seconds to see if Vitaly would signal me to retake the race, as the signal doesn't come, I start my beauty and go away from there, from… him.

Once on the hill at Alexandra Palace, I take in the beauty of London at night.

It's so peaceful and so refreshing.

I love the quiet times, the dark, the silence and the stars.

Surprisingly for September in London, tonight I can admire a clear sky full of stars. Lying down on the hood of my car it's a memorable moment. The hood is still warm from the engine, the breeze is not as cold as you would expect to be around this time of the month. I don't know how much I stayed there, maybe I have even fallen asleep, not sure. Opening my eyes, I can hear an engine roaring behind me. I would always know a tuning car engine, and this is one. Jumping to my feet I go straight to the driver door hoping to have enough time to get inside the car, before anyone notices me.

I am thankful I had enough time to even turn my car around, and go down the hill. When, on the other side of the parking lot, I am prompted with an image I will not be able to easily forget.

A blonde is giving what appears to be a blowjob, to none other than… Lan.

"What the fuck? What is he doing here and who the hell is that blonde?"

No this is not true, my mind is playing tricks on me. I need to take a break and think of something else, maybe someone else. I am sure I have seen right when the blonde says to him.

"Lan, tell whoever to kill the light we are not making a porn movie here!"

That's my queue to speed by them, like a bat out of hell. By the time I got home it was five o'clock in the morning. I couldn't sleep anymore, either because of the nap I took on the hood of my car.

Or because their image is still engraved in my head.

I am not sure. But, I do the only thing I can think of… I work on the bloody marriage contract.

CHAPTER SIX

RUSLAN

After parting ways with Lana yesterday, I called Vitaly for a race.

I need it time to think of what I am getting myself into. It's for mom, I tell myself every time, but is it? I mean yeah she does not look bad, but she is not exactly my type of girl either. On the other hand marriage?

I never saw a woman so disgusted by the idea of marriage until her. What? She did not dream to have a special day, in white dress and all this shit women mumble about?

But then again, she will have none with me, so maybe that's why. I took away from her the dream of being a bride and stuff. She can get it back. It is not like we are getting married for real, we will get divorce as soon as my mom passes away…wow.

Only, the thought makes me cringe at what a dick I am towards a girl I know nothing about. Maybe, she is well intentioned.

What about the hacking stuff? I mean, things she pulled to even connect on that server, she must be good. I know I have a good firewall, but apparently not so good if she breached.

Now, there are two options, one my firewall sucks, which is impossible. I am one of the best out there. Option two, she is good, better than I gave her credit for. I mean when I look at her it is like watching death in person, all pale face and black outfit she's just missing the scythe in her hand…man, I am a dick. Talking like that about my future wife.

My Audi Spyder V10 tuning, brand new, is still waiting for me to test it in tonight's race. It has 1,035-horsepower, while torque substantially increased from 477 lb-ft to a 737 lb-ft of torque, and will rocket from 0-62 mph in 2.7 seconds. I am sure whoever I compete against, will cry big tears and pay me loads of money at the end of the race. Thinking of that I smile and head to the shower, cool myself down and get ready for the ten o'clock tonight.

Once I get in Trafalgar Square, at the park entrance I scan the place for Vitaly's car, so I can get to him and pay the fee for the race. I spot the most amazing car around here, a Chevrolet Camaro black, red and orange. The way it is painted looks like the first half of the car gets out of the flames that are displayed on the back of the car.

I envy the dude who owns this car, but when I pay a closer attention dude is weird, who the fuck wears ninja style close this days, especially to a race. I laugh all to myself and look for Vitaly.

We take our positions at the start line and at "GO!" my car speeds. Sending me further back in the driver's seat.

I love this sensation, the adrenaline that comes with the race, it clears my head most of the time. Except today, this fucker with the nicest car seems to be on my nerves and if I don't pay much attention I will lose the ra…fuck!

"Fuck! I lost the race!"

This is unbelievable, ninja fucker beat my ass 2 seconds away… 2 fucking seconds.

I am so pissed right now I want to blow his head off, I go to Vitally and make a scene, informing him that I want a rematch, no such luck.

"Go and cool off! You are too hot headed for another race, I am not sending you to certain death!"

Vitally orders me, of course I am not happy, but have no other choice. So, I do what I know will give me a choice.

I take the first blonde I can find in the parking lot…at least this car served for something, if not for race…

Heading to the only place I know for sure it will be empty and quiet, not happy at all that I bring the blonde along, but now I need a blowjob to release some tension.

It was just a horrible day, forcing Lana into marriage because of some jealousy impulse. Jealousy…where this came from?

Losing the race, and now being forced to actually listen to the blonde saying something about a fashion show or something.

Once I reach Alexandra Palace parking I stop as close to the entrance as possible, this is my usual place, and I really don't want anyone to see me with this blonde chick, whose name I can even remember.

Turning to face her I say.

"Get off the car, I don't want the car to smell like sex and have stains on the car upholstery, it's a brand new car!"

I am being a dick, but at this moment I don't care. As soon as she starts to suck my dick, I imagine someone else's lips wrapped around my cock…oh *that* lips of hers…I imagine *her* moans, as *she* sucks my cock… When suddenly, the blinding light of the headlights strikes me like I am on a theatre scene, what the hell…?

"Lan, tell whoever to kill the light we are not making a porn movie here!"

The blonde chick brings me back to the parking lot, that's it for privacy. When the car speeds by us I realise it's the fucker from the race. Pointless to say all I was thinking at this point was to follow the dude and ask for a rematch, dam my ego was bruised. Except, Blondie had other plans and went back doing her job, and I just let go.

By the time I get home, I am exhausted. I hit the bed and fell asleep, dreaming of a certain brunette with too big of a French for her face.

Next day, I wake up late in the afternoon, head to shower and think that maybe I will have time to get a coffee at the café. Meet Lana, so we can decide for a day to get together and talk about contract and fuck… the rules.

What rules should I put? I never did this before and I have no idea how this will go. In all honesty, I don't even know why I said to have a contract and rules, but I said and I will not back down now. I don't want to freak her.

With my hair still damp I am heading to café, find a table and expect her to come and serve me.

When a guy shows up to take my order, I ask about her and he tells me that she had family problems and left the café at 2.30 pm today.

Two hours ago. Family problems? What family problems? Is her family here? Then I realise, I have no idea about anything, because I don't know anything about her.

That's my first rule, tell each other everything about families. If she will be my wife I need to know how many crazy aunts I need to deal with, or intrusive mother, grandmothers and all shit.

All this thoughts remind me of Alan Walker song "Lily"

Lily was a little girl

Afraid of the big, wide world

She grew up within her castle walls

Now and then she tried to run

And then on the night with the setting sun

She went in the woods away

So afraid, all alone

Which made me wonder, was she alone? Was she scared?

Give you everything you've been dreaming of

Just let me in, ooh

Everything you wantin' gonna be the

Magic story you've been told

And you'll be safe under my control

Just let me in, ooh

Would she let me in? Would she be safe under my control?

Get a grip Lan, where are all these thoughts coming from?

This is something that I do for my mother. After, I divorce and we parted ways. She will find happiness that she deserves, not a gambling additive that doesn't know when to stop before, is too late.

Even if I don't gamble anymore the addiction is still there and I'm afraid that one day I will snap again, in that person from before. She will be another victim, another broken soul, another pair of empty eyes.

Walking back to my apartment I go straight for the office, I will try to catch up work. Fix the mistake Lana made in the server, as I promised. Head back to sleep after. If she doesn't turn for her shift tomorrow, I will give her a call to set up the day for this meeting.

CHAPTER SEVEN

SVETLANA

By the time I finished with the contract, it was time for my shift at the café. It was an easy day, until Misha called me that my parents arrived today in London.

Needless to say that's exactly the last thing I need in my life. My only saving grace was the house Misha rented, it was big enough for everyone. I

A gothic style house with sharp, peaked rooflines, towers reminiscent of castles, arched windows and entryways characteristic of Gothic architecture.

The style gave facades an imposing stance, and most of the building showcased vertical lines. I know it has a garden in the back, but in all honesty, I did not pay attention to this house. I will not be here long. So I am not interested in making memories here, or with this family for that matter. I know that this house looks massive compared with my studio-flat from Woolwich, but I was more than grateful for this place, imagine me and my parents in that small apartment. Will kill each other, especially that I still have to meet with Lan and discuss the contract. Hope, it will be sooner rather than later. By the time I got to the house my parents were here and my mom was complaining to Misha.

"I don't understand your sister, she knows we are coming a long way. How could she not be off today and cook for us? When you were little children I didn't let you starve."

I rolled my eyes, because I can repeat word by word what she is saying. I heard it so many times over the years that by now I am unaffected by her drama.

"Hello mother! Nice to see you too!"

I say as she turns to face me, only to see her cringe at my black outfit and say a little too loud.

"Svetlana, darling what are you wearing?!"

Of course, only she would care what I wear, how I behave, if I have make up or not. And the worst, she would use "darling" like I am some treasured person she really cares about.

When we both know all she cares about is her and how many sacrifices she made in this life for "us". Guess what? Her comfort is still a "sacrifice"... for us. So we would have a proper education.

Seriously now! Who does she think she fools?

It's a mystery for me, why am I her daughter?

I guess someone up there wanted to make a joke, not sure to who, me or her.

"My uniform mom!"

I say as I pass my father, we have an agreement to never touch each other, if not extremely necessary. Instead, I nod and go to the kitchen.

I need space from her, from them. Jesus they are here like 5 minutes and I feel the walls crumbling on me. Of course mother being mother, follows me in the kitchen, irritation visible in her voice as she speaks.

"Svetlana, first you don't walk away from me like that. Second, how much is left until you finish that school of yours and get a proper position, like a manager or something in a decent place in this city.   I educate you to be better than a waitress in a Godforsaken place?"

Her words make me cringe, but I don't bother replying. She will never understand that I have enough money to live a good life in London, actually scratch that she doesn't know what I do, and that I have enough money to live a decent life in London, or anywhere in this world for that matter. She will never know the truth again, crossed that bridge once, not going back there. Later on Misha orders pizza for him and dad, I get grilled spicy chicken wings and mom a chicken shish that she complains about, but eating it anyways. I really don't understand her, if she doesn't like something. Why does she carry on doing it? Well in this case eating it.

Dinner goes with mom talking for everyone, telling us how my aunt thinks she is smarter than mom, how I don't know what cousin didn't do God knows what. I stopped listening like an hour ago, it's the same old stories. After dinner I go upstairs and lay down on the bed, trying to catch some sleep before Vitally calls me for another race. Or maybe Lan will text me to let me know when we meet. Thinking of that I remember my phone is in my bag down the stairs, heading down for the bag I met my dad in the living room.

"You are not going to talk to me again? Are you going to avoid me for the rest of our stay in London?"

Now that's a new one. He has some nerve coming at me like that!

"I think we said what we need it to be said nine years ago!"

I said through gritted teeth, looking him in the eyes I continued.

"What else do you want me to say to you? Be happy I am in the same room with you after what you did, and didn't say a word to a soul. Be happy that I stand her…"

I stop myself when I see Misha coming from outside. Grabbing my bag I head to my room…well the room was designed for me, and wish that I had my car with me so I could bolt out sooner. Worst case scenario, I call Vitally and ask him for a ride. He would come to the end of the world if asked, I know that.

Checking my phone, I have three missed calls and an email from @Astra* What the fuck? Astra?

Opening the email it simply says "I undo your mistake!"

What the heck is happening?

The only mistake I had was the server and except Lan nobody knew about it. Is Lan @Astra* no it cannot be, but then again I know nothing about this guy. Not even his first name, and I am supposed to marry him. Have I lost my mind? Yes I did, apparently.

Making a mental note to call Arthur and ask a few things about Lan, that will help me to go online and have a deeper search on the "subject. I pressed the call button for the number that called me three times until now. It answers the second ring.

"Look who decided to return my calls!"

Lan says into my ear.

"Hello to you too! Why did you call me three times? What was so urgent that you could not text me?"

I ask, as I hear some girl calling his name and memories of him and the blonde surface in my brain, making my blood boil…whoa chill girl…he's not your husband, yet. And even then, it will not be a real marriage. Ignoring the woman he says "I emailed you!"

"What are you, Astra? As in The Astra?"

My voice is so loud I'm surprised my mom did not knock on my door, I hear him laugh on the other side of the line.

"Did you have any doubt?"

"Wow very subtle, you pompous ass!"

I start to laugh and he joins me.

"On a serious note, why did you call me?"

"Because, I wanted to know if tomorrow it's a good day for you to meet and discuss the contract?"

That will give me a reason to escape from here. I reply until I won't change my mind.

"Yes of course!"

We chatted nonsense for another ten minutes and hung up. I fell asleep. Waking up in a pool sweating to a nightmare, the same as every time my father is close by. No matter how many locks a door has, it will not keep the demons away.

I can see that the sun it's rising in the sky, and decide to take a shower, thanking Misha. He switched the rooms with me, because this room had an en-suit bathroom. I owe him big time for that! After shower, I go downstairs to the kitchen and find my dad at the kitchen table. I would love to turn around and go back where I came from, but I'm cut short by my mother.

"Good morning Svetlana! Have a sit and drink your coffee, we need to talk!"

I wonder what drama she has to face at six o'clock in the morning. I stand next to the kitchen cabinet with a can of Pepsi in my hands, just to prove that she is not giving me orders, or at least not anymore.

"Tell me!"

I demand, curious to see what she has to say.

"Do you remember the Ivanovich family?"

If I remember? I never forgot them, I can't! Every time someone tries to get close to me, I remember them. My mother's question made chills run down my spine, and barely manage to ask.

"What about them?"

"Well they made your father play again, after so many years, and now he owes them money. Money we don't have, but I know you do! So because we are family, I made so many sacri…"

As soon as she says the words "made" and "play" my mood goes from angel to devil in 2 seconds flat.

Needing time to process where she is going with all this, but realisation sets in sooner than she can finish. I hold my hand to stop her. Not again! Not after so long! Why is this coming back now? Wanting to find the answers to all the questions, I don't even bother to control my voice. In full scream I bite back.

"He played? And you want me to pay his debt? How much?"

By now, I look like a bull who saw red in front of his eyes.

"Fifty thousand!"

Dad says, speaking for the first time this morning. Turning my head towards where he stands at the table, I can see he is ashamed of what he did. He does not even dares to look me in the eyes, as he says the amount.

"Fifty thousand?!"

Shock is all over me and I feel my blood boiling with anger.

"Are you out of your damn mind?"

I shout not caring if the neighbours will hear me.

"Young lady language, he is your father and he made a mistake. We just need a deposit to pay the first instalment, until we sell the house. He will be here soon to collect the payment."

Mom tries to calm me down, she knows they need me. But, it gets just the opposite, I feel my head spinning, words like father… mistake… deposit… sell the house… payment… are playing in my head like a broken record.

I am going back in time to the only memory I have since I was happy, truly happy… the old house with the blue veranda, the small room with old traditional carpets. A rocking chair with my grandfather in it, an old pick-up with the same old disc playing. Me dancing happy and carefree, my father being my king and I his princess. Never understanding why my granddad's green eyes would hold so much disappointment in them every time they gaze my father's way. And just like that I am plucked from there to reality, tears coming down my eyes. I cannot stop screaming.

"Are you out of your minds…mistake? What mistake? He made the same "mistake" nine years ago and I was the one who paid that price, my life was ruined not yours apparently…"

Wanting to continue, I take a breath and something catches my eye, turning to see what it is, I feel like being slapped across the face.

Lan... is in the doorway, his face mirroring the same horrified expression as mine or maybe worse, I am not sure anymore. We both say "You" at the same time.

I never had the pleasure to meet Ivanovich's son in the past, even if he was there that night. Dad had kept me busy by beating the hell out of me, when finished with what he did to me before. All of that being part of the grand education "how to be a proper Russian wife for a Vory member man."

Vory V Zakone, the code for organised crime or "the underworld power and money" how my father explained to me, a week before that night. Once in there we would miss nothing, he said. But, I was in need of training, because Vory man needs a strong capable wife. And the biggest leader around our area was Nikolay Ivanovich. Who will soon be my husband, my father informed me. I should be proud that he made such a deal for me. Because, Nikolay is a powerful man and will provide everything for me and... them. I never met Nikolay, but I already hate it. I was only fifteen at that time and in no need of a husband. I wanted to finish my school and be a lawyer, not get married and be at a man service. My mother's voice brought me back to the room.

"Dimitri! Welcome! Do you know each other? Please have a sit and let's talk. Svetlana was making coffee!"

Clear fear in her tone, not for me that's for sure.

Until I'm able to process what is going on, he replies.

"I'm good, standing…thank you!"

The last words are for me more than for them. For what he is thanking me I'm not sure, but I have no intention in playing nice and prepare coffees for any of them. Never leaving his spot in the doorway, it makes me feel trapped inside.

"Dimitri, how much will be the first payment, Svetlana will write you a check!"

Mom says so sweet like she was trying to make him fall in love, except I bite back.

"I will not write anything to anyone…, *looking my father's way I continue*,… you did this to yourself *again*, but don't you think for a second that you will drag me down with you. Not again, not after everything!"

My voice is hoarse, more tears run down my face, I am so angry at my father, at Lan, at all of them. When I hear the word "Marriage" from Lan's mouth I think my hearing is not good. The way my parents stare at him, I have the confirmation. I did hear the right word. We all look at him like he grew three heads and six eyes in the last second.

"No one needs to write any check if... I marry her!"

In another dimension of time and different circumstances, I would be very grateful for what he said. Giving me the exit I need from this family, but, we are not in another dimension and the circumstances are not different. What he offers is the death of me, before I can formulate a word, both my parents answer for me in unison,

"YES!"

My long, long time ago best friend words played in my head

"For your parents, you're just a bag of money, they will cash at the right time!"

Well, apparently now is the right time and my price tag is fifty thousand. Both me and Lan, flinched at their response. He tried to mask it. I saw it. It was quick ,but it was there. Staring at my parents, dad has regret in his eyes, unlike mom that has a smile on her face.

"Yes what?"

Lan brings our attention to him

"Yes she will marry you!"

Mom clarifies.

"OK! Sealed!"

And with that they struck the last nail in my coffin, sealing it and sending it directly to the pit, without so much of a look in my way.

My chest started to feel heavy, my breath slowed dramatically. Seeking my escape around the room, I see Misha for the first time and attempt to call his name, but darkness is quicker. This time I welcome her, as a pair of strong hands wrap around me. Normally, I would kick and scream, now I don't care anymore, I am dead anyway.

When I come back to my senses, a heavy breathing next to my ear, and a large strong hand around my waist. It's like, it's not his hand, but my father is next to me in bed, and his hand heads to my breasts.

"NO, NO, not again, not this."

I am thinking as I jump out of the bed taking the cover with me, hitting the hard floor or maybe a wall, I am not sure. I am left without a breath, the light comes on and I see his blue eyes. I go back hitting the wall so fast and so hard, I have the feeling that either I will mould into the wall or I will break it and fall on the other side of the building. His eyes never left mine, he is here! Again!

"You promised, you will never touch me again!"

"Again? I never promise to not touch you!"

He says and he starts to laugh so hard, coming closer... and closer... and closer, until we are face to face and the blue shade of his eyes begin to change to a deeper blue. Concern is displayed in them, these aren't his eyes anymore, this are Lan's eyes. I know my father is here and I do the only thing I can think of. I start to scream so hard that my lungs hurt, not being able to stop myself anymore. I scream until I hear Arthur's name… Arthur is coming! He will save me from my father, darkness comes again.

This time everything is numb.

I don't feel.

Nothing hurts anymore.

Everything is good, everything is smooth, like floating on a cloud made just for me. I hear Lan's voice, but it's so far, far away and it's fading by the second.

I like it here, I don't want to go back, and I don't want to feel anything. Here is like falling from the highest mountain, straight into nothingness. This is what freedom Is?

Maybe yes. Anyway I have made up my mind. I am not going back from here.

CHAPTER EIGHT

RUSLAN

After ending the call with Lana last night, I got a call from my uncle, Letting me know that I need to go and collect a debt of fifty thousand euro from an old "friend" of his, Petrov.

The same guy that gave us a hard time nine years ago. He's some Vory wannabe, a total douche. I'm given an address that I memorise in my Spyder's GPS.

I need to be there by eight o'clock, but the faster I am there the faster I can come back and call Lana to set the meeting. So, we have that wedding sort out, and another perk to that meeting, I can see her again. Man, I start to like this weird girl.

By seven thirty I'm in front of a Gothic style house, looks massive on the exterior, I bet it's not so big on the inside.

Paying attention to my surroundings, I hear someone screaming. It's never good to walk in any woman's screaming competition with her husband. I bet this douche wife had enough of him. I ring the bell and the door opens to reveal a tall blond lean guy, too skinny for his high with a pair of grey-blue eyes.

"Morning"

"Morning. In the kitchen they are waiting for you!"

I smile and walk inside, from the screaming match I can realise they are "very happy" to see me. Getting in the kitchen doorway, I'm stunned to see the last person I was expecting to find in this house, let alone to be the one in the screaming match with Petrov.

What the hell is Lana doing here?

Why is she screaming like that to this douche?

Before I can say something she turns to me and says "YOU" at the same time with me.

Once the woman, who I know for sure is Petrov's wife, informs me that Lana will write a check for me, I put two and two together.

Lana is Petrov's daughter. The same brat daughter, who was trying to run away from home with a drug dealer that stole my uncle's merchandise, nine years ago.

Only Petrov's grace was that he caught the guy and his daughter, before they actually took off.

Nikolai recovered his merchandise and Petrov got a place in "the family". Never actually found out what happened with his daughter at that time. I remember the story clearly from nine years ago.

Well that was something, this is something else.

Never seen her so fiercely, and it's a nice show to watch, until I catch what she's saying to Petrov.

"… you did this to yourself, *again*, but don't you think for a second that you will drag me down with you. Not again, not after everything!"

What the hell? Again? After everything? What is she talking about? And before I can think, I shout out the word "Marriage", a deafening silence spreads across the room, with three pair of eyes staring at me like I lost my damn mind.

I clarify my intentions and they agree way too soon for my liking. Well this worked better than I was expecting, two birds one stone.

Pleased with myself, I gaze at Lana, who is about to pass out as she says "Misha".

I hurry to wrap my hand around her and catch her before she hits the table corner, in the middle of the room. Taking her in my arms, I got her in my car and said my goodbyes, to Petrov and his wife, who looks way too happy to marry her daughter with me.

Happier than any normal mother would be in her position. I was expecting hell on earth for this, not applause.

Something here is not matching, making a mental note to clarify this with Lana when she wakes up, I drive back to my apartment.

Once there, I try to wake her gently, but no such luck. Great! Taking her in my arms, I am grateful the lift is fully functional, not that she is heavy, but ten flights of stairs with her in my arm would put me to sleep.

Inside of my apartment I am heading for the bedroom, gently positioning her on the bed and I start to undress her. Who knows when she will wake up, but at least she should be comfortable.

I take a second to admire her naked body on my bed. Jesus, this woman is so beautiful, full breasts, perfect for my big hands, she is chubby but not fat. The way she is positioned looks like she has a flat stomach, but I saw her standing and I know that's not the case. She is curvy…fuck me. Chubby, chubby, but she is the most beautiful woman I could see to this day. Just like that, I feel my cock stir to life and my blood navigate south.

"Get a fuckin grip, she is passed out man."

I tell myself and pull one of my T-shirts on her body.

Once the job is done and Lana is safe between the sheets of my bed, I head straight to the bathroom for a cold shower and maybe a blowjob to release some tension.

After shower, I dry my hair in a towel, so I will not wet the pillow, and lie in bed next to her. I must have fallen asleep, because I feel my hand wrap around her waist and suddenly she bolts out of bed like a scared cat, hitting the floor with a hard thud.

I open the light next to the bed glancing at the digital clock that says 2.45 a.m.. Yes, I definitely fell asleep. Lifting myself off the bed, I reach out to take her in my arm, but as soon as I try to touch her she starts to scream like I was planning to murder her.

If she doesn't stop I will have to explain to the police why I have a next to naked screaming woman in my bedroom.

But, because she doesn't stop screaming, I call the only person I know for sure will pick up the phone three o'clock in the morning no questions asked.

At the second ring Arthur's sleepy raspy voice says "Hello!" As soon as he hears Lana screaming goes into fighting mode.

"Is that Lana screaming? What the fuck did you do? Did you touch her?" Whoa man chill…

"Touch her? I can't make her stop screaming. Arthur, please come to my apartment!"

I say, pleading this time, but I don't care. As soon as I mention he's name she stops screaming, but faints again. Now, I'm not sure if it's he's name that makes her stop, or the fact that she faint. It doesn't matter anymore.

She stopped screaming, one less explanation to do. I'm unplugged from my thoughts when Arthur speaks again.

"What happened? Why did she stop screaming?"

"She faint!" I say "How long until you are here?"

"Five minutes tops, I am on my way!"

Five minutes later, on the spot, he is in my apartment, placing Lana back on the bed. It's not that I liked to see her there, but I was scared to actually touch her.

Yes for the second time in my entire life I was shit scared to touch a woman. First time was when my mother told me she got cancer. Even though I knew it's not contagious, I was afraid to touch her. Not to make her disappear.

After making sure she is still asleep, we head to the kitchen. I began telling him what is going on. If I am to do this, I need him in my corner. Especially, because he has some connection with her that I will never understand or maybe never have.

Better the first option, I can work without understanding. I want my connection with her to be stronger than theirs. Shit! Now I am jealous of their friendship.

I explain to him what happened from the beginning, like from the server thing. He listens without interruption and when I get to the last part, the bed part, he frowns and scratches the back of his head. He does that when he is nervous, I know I will not like what comes next out of his mouth.

"Look man, this is not my story to tell. But, I can tell you this. Avoid touching her, like at all. Especially, before she is ready to talk to you. Give her time to come back from wherever she is now. Lana went through some crazy shit in the past, because of her father. And she was all alone. Her mom does not know a damn thing from what happened with her. Believe me, no matter how bad you want to beat her dad in telling you, think of this. Once she is better, she will not forgive you for that! Trust me, I understand you. I wanted to murder the guy when I found out what he did, but that will not change the past. Try to be here for her, if you really care. If not let me take her out of here. She doesn't deserve to go through that again. This is all I can say!"

"You know you cannot just say shit like that to me and aspect me to behave like nothing happened. Give her time, not touch her and all the above shits! I need answers, and I need them now! And what the fuck is with "don't touch her" thing? What the fuck is going on?""

I bite back at him like a caged man. I fell like a stupid nursery kid in between college guys. I can't see the bigger picture…

"What she went through with her dad it was because of a drug fucking dealer that wanted her to go with him. Of course if I would be in her pops shoes, I would have murder them both. No matter how much I dislike the guy, I'm on his side with this one!"

I state, angry as shit. Arthur's reaction tells me that something isn't the way I know.

"Or you know a different version of the story?"

I ask, terrified of what he might say, but still needing to know the truth.

"Look man! I can tell you that I know for sure there was no fucking drug dealer to begin with!"

I feel like he just knocked the last breath from my chest. I knew Petrov was a lying fucker, but I never knew he was that big of a fucker. If there is no drug dealer in the story where all that drugs came from? It's not like Petrov could afford to buy them back then? Could it be worse? Could he have sold her like he did earlier today with me? To who? Who touched her?

For everyone's sake I hope this is not the case. Otherwise, I have to speak with Nikolai to hide his body once I finish with him. Trying to calm myself down I close my eyes, take a few deep breaths and ask

Arthur if he wants a coffee or if he wants to sleep? We decided to go to sleep and I let him sleep in the bedroom with Lana. No matter how much it pains me that I cannot be there for her, I head to the office. I have an extendable sofa bed there.

"Not yet, but soon…"

I'm cut short from my monolog, when the doorbell rings. Wondering who might be, I'm heading to open the door.

"I think it is Renesme. I told her about Lana. It will be best, all of us to be here when she wakes up."

Now this is awesome.

Opening the door, I'm coming face to fate with a blonde fury.

"Where is Lana? And what the hell did you do to her?"

She barks at me so angry that I'm sure she would chop my head off, if not in need for direction.

"She's in the bedroom and I did nothing to her. Nice to meet you too!"

I say the last part full of sarcasm, trying to close the door, she replied.

"I wouldn't close that door just yet. Misha is coming. He was parking the car. Turning around to see where he was. I come face to face with a too tall and very pissed version of the Casper phantom. Great another one.

"Anymore coming?"

I ask as I gesture for him to come in, but what happens next surprises the hell out of me. Making me realise that I am left without air in my lungs.

Angry Casper wraps his hand around my neck screaming.

"It was you all along? I've been waiting for you since I was twelve years old! I promised myself everyday, once I put my hands on you, I will make sure you will never breathe again!"

Man he is true to his words, I barely breathe. The lack of oxygen in my brain makes my eyes water and my thoughts hard to gather.

What is wrong with this family?

"Misha it's not him, he saved her this time! It's not him!"

Arthur says and Casper lets go of my neck, as very welcome and necessary breath comes to fill me. Taking in my surroundings, Arthur holds an even more pissed Casper as far away from me as he can. Renesme closes the door demanding he should keep his mouth shut. We all head in the kitchen, before we wake up Lana.

Since when did this apartment become the podium of a circus? What is going on? And, why is everyone in my apartment?

I would like to get them the hell out of here, but again I need answers.

I hold my hands in the air, in a defensive gesture, and speak to Casper with conviction.

"I have no idea what you are talking about. But, I sure want to know, because I don't know your sister man!"

Looking around the room he nods and sits down. I can see he's relaxing at my statement, but still keeps his guard up. I need to give him credit, he has a strong hand despite the fact that he is lean.

Staring me dead in the eyes he starts.

"You were there that night! I know you were, I saw you!"

"I was where? Which night?"

This game is confusing. What is he talking about? Clarification follows as he speaks.

"Nine years ago you were at our house back in Russia, my father did this to her, for you!"

My eyes are wide and everyone is looking at me like I am some kind of monster.

"For me? I don't know what you're talking about. I was there because he needed it to pay a debt, just like early today, well yesterday!"

I try to explain.

"That's what he said to everyone. That he needed it to pay a debt because Lana wanted to run with a drug dealer, and he caught them at the last minute…"

Terrified, I glanced at Arthur. What he said to me minutes before, I heard it all over again, this time from a different guy. Have I been lied, that night? Did Petrov lie to Vory? Casper continues his story and I force myself to pay attention. Despite the fact that by now my blood boils with anger.

"…all that was a big fat lie. Actually, that was the night of my sister initiation in the big education of "how to be a perfect Vory wife" for the guy who was in our house, to testify first hand at my father's promised "education". As a proof to Vory his word is law when it comes to them. He beat her, until she couldn't stand anymore. She needed to be brave and handle a beating from her husband, without bitching to everyone in the family about that.

To be fair, I always thought it was more than the beating he did to her. But I have no other proof to that.

Except the fact that after that night she was not the same again. She could not stand to be touched. If it was not for Vitally, she would be dead from the beating itself. One way or another she is dead. As soon as I heard her scream I called Vitally. He took her out from there and straight to hospital. Everyone knew she tried to run away but she was caught in fact, and that was so far from the truth… I promised myself that night, once I find the fucker she was beaten for, he will lie six feet underground. To this day she doesn't smile the way she used to, she is always guarded and afraid. Let's not talk about the fact that she never had a proper relationship with a guy. She tried, but she couldn't. They think I don't remember, but I do. It's all here, in my mind!"

He points to his temples and tears run down from his eyes.

Despite the fact that he is a mature person now, all I can see in front of me is a small boy who couldn't protect his sister from his father's rage. He looks so defeated and broken, and I respect him more than he will ever understand.

"What Petrov did to her was not initiation to any Vory shit! He said she tried to run away with that guy and the guy owed Vory a lot of money and merchandise. We dealt with him, and let Petrov deal with his daughter. We would never interfere in the family, unless a cruel act of violence happened there."

I said angry as shit at the douche of a father they have, but before anyone can say something I continue.

"Vory never asked anyone to maltreat their family or kids, Vory protects their own! I don't know what he tried to prove, but it was not for Vory, and sure as hell was NOT for me! I knew about her and you from your father's stories. I never met any of you in person before. Until, last week when she broke into our company server, I didn't even know she was in London. I was there that night, but it was not for what you think. He had to pay big money to Nikolai, my uncle, and by the time I got to your house Vitaly's car was storming out of your street. I never knew a single thing about all of this and I can assure you, Vory did't know any of this! But, I can promise you they will know and take measures, I will get married to your sister and keep her safe from all of this!"

By the time I finish my statement I am breathless and everyone including me is silent. What did he do to her? To his own flesh and blood? This is beyond understanding.

"Well If that is true and your Intentions are pure, you need to know this! Whatever you think you know, think again. They plan to use this marriage and secure their place in this Vory family thing. I heard them speak after you left. Probably they believed I stormed out after you and Lana. They said once you marry her the payment is done, and the right in the family is bought and sealed with marriage. Especially, because you are Nikolai's nephew."

He says, full of honesty and concern, at the same time.

"Fuck! I am stupid! I play straight into their hands, haven't I?"

And here I was pleased with myself that I killed two birds with one stone, when in fact, I was the one hit by the fucking rock.

"Thank you for letting me know their intentions, I can assure you this will never happen. Nikolai will be aware of your parents' game!"

I promise myself to stay true to my words, speak with Nikolai and inform him about this. I will make sure she is safe from her father. Exhausted from all the things that happened in the last 24 hours and the emotions from the conversations, I do my best to guide everyone in finding a place for them to sleep. For the first time since I acquired this apartment, it feels so small.

CHAPTER NINE

SVETLANA

I wake up to a dark room, but a lot of voices. At the beginning it's like voices are talking all together, maybe screaming. I am not sure, but after a few seconds, I start to distinguish everyone's voice…Lan for sure, Arthur, and …Misha? What is Misha doing here, and why is here?

I try to stand but my head feels so heavy, it takes me a minute to be able to lift myself in a standing position on the bed.

Listening carefully, I hear Misha talking about the darkest night of my life. I didn't know he was there to begin with, and for sure I had no idea that he called Vitally and everything that happened after.

I always knew Vitally and I have a different connection. He acts like a father figure to me. He never mentioned a word about this, not even a single one. That's the reason he helped me escape as soon as I brought it to him. He witnessed what my father did. Does he know everything? He took me to hospital, but then again nobody knew about it. I need to talk to him about this.

Hearing Misha cry I stood up slowly and went in the direction of his voice, careful not to make a sound, I don't want the attention on me. Once the conversation is over, with both Misha and Lan making their confession, I hurry the best I manage back to bed and pretend to sleep. As soon as everyone falls asleep, I try my best to get out of the apartment.

Ten minutes later I am in the building hallway, heading to the lift fully dressed and grateful no one heard me on my way out. I still have no idea where I am, maybe once I am outside I will figure it out.

Stepping out of the building I realise that I know this view, in fact it's where I used to feel free and enjoy the morning on the way to work. It's where Lan lives, then I realise I just came out of his apartment. I put my garage address in my phone GPS so I can get Freedom. Safely inside my car, I decide I have two stops.

One is at Vitaly's gym, he practically lives there since I left his flat.

Next stop is Alexandra Palace hill.

I really want to see the sunrise, dash clock says five minutes past five in the morning. If Vitaly answers the door I will not have time to see the sunrise, but still he is my first stop.

I park the car in front of the building. I'm heading straight to the gym, noticing lights are on, probably he's training before everyone comes in.

Inside the gym, which is actually a huge room with a caged ring in the middle, a lot of punching bags, weights and a rope jumping space. It's always smelling like man's sweat in here, probably because the windows are small and so high that it's impossible to open. I hear Vitally growling at someone. Turning my gaze towards the sound of his voice, to see who he screams at, I see Vitaly on the other side of the caged ring. It's impossible to see the other person, because of Vitaly's broad back. But,I can understand very clearly what he is saying when he opens his mouth next.

"If you dare so much to look at her, I will personally tell Nikolai what a piece of shit best friend I had. I covered for you and your bloody mistakes for so long. Now leave her alone! For fucksake"

His voice is booming inside the room.

Soon I realized he's talking to… my father!

My blood runs cold. Out of all places in London he needs to be here? At this time? Why?

They both look in my direction, probably because I said something or done something, not sure. In a split of a second a "Fuck!" comes out of Vitaly's mouth, joined by a big frown on his face. Showing clear frustration, because of the conversation I just walk into. Making his way in my direction, he gives me a clear view of my father, who is equal parts ashamed and angry.

Ashamed of what he did and angry because Vitaly threatened him? Not sure of either one, but I sure as hell wanted to run out from here as fast as I could.

The only problem was, my feet would not move. My father is still on the other side of the room, not even looking at me. He tried his best to look like he came to visit and I intruded. He has the nerves to ignore me completely…

"How much did you hear?"

Vitaly asks with kindness in his voice, breaking my stare.

"Ahem… probably the last part."

Turning to my father, he says in a no joke tone,

"You can go, but remember, I was serious!"

Facing me, he says.

"Let's sit down."

I nod, not able to form words. I see my father disappearing, on the same door I came in just a few minutes before.

"I was afraid of this moment, but somehow I knew it would come. I will tell you everything you want to know, without lying to you. I must say it will not be pretty and you may not like what you hear. However I will not lie to you!"

He's telling me. So nonchalant, like we are talking about candies. We make our way to the caged ring stairs and sit down on them. Looking at him I can see the pain in his eyes, more than it ever was before.

"You know everything he did to me?"

Emphasising on the word everything.

"Yes! I know, everything!"

I close my eyes, tears coming down my face as he continues.

"I am sorry I wasn't there before, he was supposed to be at the casino, not home alone with you. Misha got there first because Sergei wanted to see if your father would keep his promise. As soon as you screamed, Misha called me, I couldn't get to you fast enough. Unfortunately!"

More tears run down my face and I don't bother to hide them, it's no use. He saw me at my worst and he is here, always has been here for me, like the father I never had.

"I didn't know at the beginning…"

He answered my silent question.

"…but once in the hospital, the doctor said to me you had internal bleeding and they needed to stop it. I told them you are my daughter and I will sign any paper they need, paid him enough to keep his mouth shut and tell nobody. Two weeks later you went back home. It was the most painful thing that I have had to do. Letting you go back to that house, was hard. I made sure your father never touched you again. I always watched from the shadows. You needed to gain your confidence in yourself first, and then in everyone else. I was there if you ever needed me. When you came to me and told me you want to leave that shithole of a house, I couldn't be more happy and proud of you. So, I did the only thing I could to make sure you got away from them. I threatened them that I would reveal to Nikolai what I knew. Your mother agreed to let you go as soon as I finished that sentence. The rest you know!"

Whoa this was more than I could understand. I knew some things but not the extent of them.

"Why did you help me? I mean he was your best friend?"

I ask, needing to know.

"We were never best friends, I mean for the world yes, but your father hated me. He could not stand the idea that I was better than him in any fight I got myself in. When I got my first professional match, he tried to pay a few guys to break my bones, so I couldn't fight. It turned out people were more afraid of me than him. They told me what he was up to. I respected him, even if he deserves nothing of that, because of your grandfather. He was the one to lead me on the right path ,when I was younger, and made sure I have a decent life. I owed that old man everything I have, including you! Even if you are not blood related to me, he was more of a father to me than my own was. I promised your granddad I will always look after you and Misha, and I will always do that, until my last breath."

He says, gazing in the distance. Like he is talking to himself more than with me.

"Anything you need, anything, I will give it to you! I will help you in any way I possibly can, just ask."

Without thinking I spit it out.

"I am marrying Lan and I want you to be there!"

"You what now?"

He shouts, making me jump. He brings his hands up in the air, like a defensive gesture.

"Sorry!"

He managed so low that it was barely audible.

I go on and explain what happened in the last twenty-four hours. It feels good to be able to talk to someone about this and know they will be there for me.

I can see he goes from peaceful, to pissed back to peaceful, angry, concerned and so on with every word of my story, but never stopping me. We both need this to be out, we both kept inside for so long.

I admit to him that I don't dislike Lan, but I am afraid of what will happen when time to fulfil my duties as wife will come. Because after what happened with my parents, I doubt there will be any rules.

What he says shocks me to my core.

"If all this is going to happen, you will need to be honest with him. It will make it easier for him, but mostly for you. This is a big and important matter to be kept away from him. I have two reasons for that. One and most important, this is none of your fault. What happened with you, was not your fault. Second, if he doesn't know he might hurt you without intention.

It's not pleasant to know your wife doesn't want to sleep with you in the same bed. Let alone have sex with you, but she refuses to provide you with any logical explanation as to why that is happening. I would go mad in his shoes. So, I cannot blame him for that. And, if you're not honest with him, I cannot murder him if he does hurts you!"

He says as the weirdness of the conversation becomes easier.

Never had this type of conversations with anyone until now, and being here with Vitally makes it easier.

"Okay, I will think about it. One more thing, please keep the secret of Freedom and racing! It was nice to kick his ass in the race!"

We burst in laughing. A nice and strange feeling of peace and relaxation gets to me. It's good that I came and talked to him. I say my goodbye and head for the Alexandra Palace hill.

It's pouring rain outside by the time I'm there, but I don't mind. I find it beautiful. It's like this little girl of God is all angry and crying. When the flash of light strikes the sky followed by the thunder, I am positive that she is in full mode screaming at God.

I laugh all to myself, thinking back at how happy I was with my granddad. How I used to make sad faces, so he will put me on his lap and tell me stories. How I pretended to be sad and he pretended to believe me.

"That's not the pick-up disc song!" the little girl says "No it's your phone silly!" granddad replied, and I opened my eyes. Staring down at my phone. Misha's name is on display…

"Hello!"

"Oh God! Where the hell are you, we were looking for you EVERYWHERE, I nearly paid a team of divers to look for you at the bottom of Thames River. You lunatic woman!"

He managed to calm himself down by the end of the sentence.

"Is she OK?"

Three different concerned voices scream in the background, and I can distinguish each and every one of it…Lan, Arthur, and Renesmee.

"Yes she is fine!"

Misha says sarcastically.

"You are fine, yes?"

He asks in a more concerned voice this time.

"Yes, I am fine! And I'm not on the bottom of Thames River, so hold your money. I will be home in an hour."

"Home? Where home? You are coming to my apartment so we can talk, I will not leave you alone in that matchbox you call apartment."

Lan voice boom through the phone.

"Shit sorry! It was not an order, it was a request"

He corrects and I laugh to myself, Renesme must elbow him in the ribs, after the sound he made. And the image of the two of them fighting, it's one of entertainment.

"I will call you as soon as I am outside the building, I didn't pay enough attention where you live this morning when I stormed out of the apartment, sorry!"

I confess and I hear four "hmmm" at the same time. Renesme speaks first after.

"No worry sis, just call me and I will come down to get you!"

Man she is demanding. I nod like they could see me, hung up the phone and head back to park my beauty. An hour later I'm at the apartment with a plate full of food. Some chicken with rice, and four pairs of eyes looking my way.

"You know you are staring right? I can't eat like that. I mean unless you guys want to count how many spoons of food I introduce in my mouth…"

I hear Lan mumbling something that sounds more like "I would like something else introduced in your mouth", but I am not sure because the next thing I see is two different hands heating the back of his head at the same time and I start laughing at the synchronisation, even if the thought of what he said terrifies me.

This makes me think of Vitaly's words from earlier today. I take in how these people are staring at me like I am some kind of rare alien or something, which makes me laugh even harder.

"That's something I didn't see in a very long time!"

Misha says followed by a hard "hhmm" when Arthur's elbow connects with his ribs.

God, I love them. In moments like this I'm grateful for each and every one of them. I look up and I see the most beautiful eyes staring back at me and a smile is spread across his face. That smile will be the end of me, I am telling you. And in that moment I make the decision to be honest with him, no matter what the outcome.

Before I can change my mind, I gaze into his eyes and speak.

"We need to talk, now!"

Not giving myself a chance to overthink this decision. Without saying a word he stands and holds his hand expecting me to take it, but when my eyes go wide he says "This way!" and we are heading for his office. Once in there a soft song of Alan Walker plays through his laptop speakers. "The end of times" How ironic is this? I think as I listen the lyrics

"When things are right

Then you just know

There is something in your eyes that brings me home

'Cause when there's love

You don't let go

So as long as you're with me

You're not alone, you'll never be

How wonderful. It feels like the songs speak for him at this very moment. Except, he doesn't know how I crave for these words to be true. To be spoken by him to me.

I wanna tell you what I feel and really mean it

I wanna shout it from the rooftops to the sky

'Cause if you ever need a friend

You know I'll be it

From tonight until we see the end of time

This is my reply to him, or at least it is in my head. I really want to tell him *everything* and hope at the end he will still be here.

I'll cross my heart and hope to die

We're always and forever I'll be by your side

When days are dark and stars don't align

We're always and forever 'til the end

The end of time

Are we? Could we be? till the end of time?

When we look back and when we're old

We'll see your footprints next to mine along the road

And I don't know what the future holds

But as long as you're with me

You're not alone, you'll never be

Will it be, until the end of time? Do I have another chance at happiness? Maybe a family of my own? I can't stop thinking about it, even if I know it's not the right time for this.

The song is nice and brings a light of hope, but I need to speak before I change my mind. I'm afraid of what will happen…no I can't go there, not now. Instead, I start to speak.

"I don't know how you want to do this marriage thing, but I was wondering if the terms and conditions are still on the table?"

He looks at me a bit puzzled.

"Despite your parents, I am not an ass. Told you that already, and yes the offer is still on the table!"

"Do you have any rules?"

"I want to see yours first!"

He replied, not answering my question. I nod and take out a paper from my backpack, unfolding it, I handed to him.

Rules

1 The most important no physical contact at ALL

2 A Prenuptial agreement/ financially independent

3 One night a week at my apartment ALONE

4 A dog named ALPHA

5 A LOT of chocolate

After he reads the paper, he stares at me.

"A dog and chocolate?"

Making a funny face. I know that's not what caught his eye, but he tries to make me feel better.

"Well I need to keep fit!"

I say, as I walk my hand up and down my body, laughing. I see a glimpse of lust in his eyes but it's so fast, I wonder if it was there in the first place.

"What dog would you like?"

"A Caucasian Shepherd dog!"

I say proud of myself.

"Woman, you don't want a dog, you want a big ass bear!"

He says surprised. But I changed the subject.

"Now you know my rules. Tell me yours!"

I demand

"I have only one!" he says "Tell me everything about you, and don't let anything out!" gesturing at the paper.

And just like that, I had my opening to start talking about the darkest night of my life, hoping that at the end of the story he will not look at me with disgust or mercy. I wouldn't stand the look in his eyes for any of the two.

Taking a seat on the sofa, I motion for him to do the same as I take a deep breath to calm my nerves and start talking.

"I have to tell you something, but I want you to listen carefully and don't interrupt me, please. I am not sure I have it in me to start all over again, if you stop me once."

Nodding, he agreed, and I started my story.

"Like a week before that night, I could tell that my father started to pay more attention to me than normal. It felt good to be his centre of attention. Never, in a million years thinking what his true intentions really were. That, his intentions are totally different from those of a father. I could tell that he was trying to get my attention and make me feel more comfortable around him than I normally should. Again, I did not think anything of that. He came home that night and came straight to my room. I could see he was drunk and smelled the liquor on his breath as he came closer to me. Telling me I was beautiful all grown up looking like a woman, and I should expect men to look at me differently… I asked him what he was talking about. He never said these things to me before. What he said rendered me silent and broked to this day.

"Look at you! How beautiful you are, your body changed in the most amazing way a man could dream of. If thinking properly you are more gorgeous than your mother is, and I will show you what a proper cock means and how it feels to have it in you. I will make you a great and happy woman!"

With that he pushed me on the bed and started to undress me. I tried to scream and fight him off but it was no use, he was stronger. No matter how much I pleaded with him… How much I told him that this is wrong… what he is doing to me is wrong and I don't want that… it did not matter. He just cupped my breast with his hands and proceeded to give me "pleasure" as he stated. But with each and every touch… with every kiss… he was killing me more and more… Once he opened his pants and parted my legs I became quiet, realising I have no escape from him… from what was about to happen… When he finished, he expected me to be happy and pleased with what he just did to me. Instead, tears were running down my face and I refused to look at him. I did not want to believe that my father became the monster I heard about only in the news… I think that just made him even angrier. He started to shout that I am a worthless woman and I don't know how to be grateful to a man for the pleasure he gave me… with that his fist started to fly, until I could not feel anything anymore..."

By now tears run down my face as I went down the memory lane of that horrifying night.

"It was like I could feel my soul departing my body… like the peace wanted me, but I was fighting against it… I really wanted to be able to surrender. Except, no matter how much I wanted it… that would not happen… peace decided to go further and further away from me. When I opened my eyes, I was in a hospital room lying on the bed, pissed at the world that kept me instead of letting me go…"

By the end of my story more tears were running from my eyes, I felt both exhausted and relieved. It was the first time when I told this crucial horror experience to someone who could turn into something more than a friend, and he didn't run away. He never stopped me from talking or reliving it. He was patient and gave me time to speak, at my own peace. Except for the soft music from the laptop neither one of us was talking. I was afraid to look his way, because of what I would find in his gaze… Was it mercy? Was it disgust? Would he still want to carry on with this crazy plan of his? Hell, could he even look me in the eyes…

I could not finish the thought because two soft fingers cupped my chin, making my head turn to face him. His eyes are soft and kind, something I did not expect to find.

"You or any other girl for that matter should not experience something so horrible like what your father did to you. You have nothing to be ashamed of, it was not your fault. I have only one question… the scar on your chest is it from… that time? I saw it when I brought you here, after you passed out at the house."

He asks, sounding so shy. It's kind of funny to look at him now. Never could have had a picture of a man like him being shy, ruthless maybe, but definitely not shy.

"No, the scar is from my heart surgery, it happened when I was twenty-one!"

He looks at me like I just transformed myself in some horrible creature.

"You have heart problems?"

The shock displayed not only on his face, but in his tone as well.

"Yes, it's not something that gives me hard times! Everything was fixed in surgery. I got used to it by now, and made peace with that long time ago! I am sorry!"

I blurt out before he can ask anything else, even though I don't know why I apologised.

"Why are you sorry? It's nothing to be sorry for. Again, not your fault."

"Well after your reaction it kind of makes it!"

"Shit sorry. I didn't mean it like that, I'm just amazed how many things you went through in such a short time."

He clarifies, leaving me speechless to that. I have no idea how I should feel or say now, I am grateful when he continues on a calm tone this time.

"Coming back to our rules… I have time. I will never force you into anything you don't want. Not after everything you went to. However, I would like to spend time with you and maybe sleep in the same bed with you. And I mean it, just sleep with you in the same bed. I think it will help us to be more comfortable around each other in public. It will be weird to explain why I can't hold hands with my wife… but of course baby steps."

He spoke so fast I believed for a second he would suffocate. He was nervous about this as well. I could tell that.

It was so funny to watch him struggle with what to do and what to say. It feels like he was confused for the first time and doesn't know how he should react to that. But, he recovers quickly and changes the subject

"Another thing… prenuptial contract. If you really want I am OK to sign it. So, you will be sure I do not want to force you financially to stay with me. However, I am to pay everything that comes to expenses for this family, that includes your outfit as well. Because no offence, that black cloth you are wearing all the time, makes you look like a widow… and will be left at your place… And the work at the café should stop."

"Whoa, widow, hmm? And why would I stop working somewhere I enjoy being? Who the hell you think you are? Just because I pour my heart to you, it doesn't give you the right to insult me!"

I am fully screaming, not caring if in any minute the rest of the guys will be here.

Closing his eyes, taking a deep breath, he calmly said

"I didn't mean to insult you. I was just trying to explain that you are beautiful and it's no need for you to hide behind that black outfit of yours. I am next to you and nothing like what you've been through will happen to you anymore. Not as long as you are my wife, at least! That I can promise you. And how would I explain that the daughter-in-law of the most powerful diplomat is a waitress?"

I can see confusion in his eyes, but before I change my mind I state "Well we will have an intimate ceremony and no one will ever know who I am, because I'm not a piece of meat you can display for anyone to look at!"

I am a volcano in full eruption…

CHAPTER TEN

RUSLAN

"She is gone! I am not telling him, you are!"

Two voices are whispering, it's like a muffled fight and it would be comic to listen if they would not talk about someone being gone. Chill ran down my spine and jumped to my feet from the sofa I was sleeping in, after the last twenty or so hours we had.

Who is gone? My mother?

No that's not possible I am thinking while I open the office door a little too harsh, only to find a very angry Renesmee and a frustrated Arthur. As the door opens both their heads turn my way and shock is what takes place on their faces instead. What is with these two anyway?

They look like they want to murder each other, but in the same time to fuck each other till the end of time.

"It's not my fault!"

Renesmee's statement brings me back from my thoughts.

"What's not your fault?"

I ask as Arthur states.

"It's never your fault!"

"OK you two, get a grip! What happened? Is something with mom?"

I ask Arthur more than the blond fury.

"No, no, not your mom. It's amm... Lana!"

He says after a moment, sending me straight in alert mode.

"What's with her?"

I ask a little too fast.

"Well she was sleeping with Renesmee..."

He starts only to be cut short by the blond fury.

"Come on! Now it's my fault? You were there too remember?"

Putting my hands between the two of them, more like a referee, cutting through their bullshit play.

 "You can fuck your stress after. What happened? What's with her?".

"She is gone!"

Arthur says.

"Gone? Gone where??"

I ask, as panic settles in.

"That's the thing, we don't know? Misha called everyone he knew including Vitally. Who said she was there very early in the morning, but she left like an hour ago, nothing since then. The way he looks, I wouldn't be surprised if he starts to call all the hospitals around London."

"Fuck! This woman will be the end of me!"

I realised what truth I just spoke, and the fact that I was thinking out loud, by the frowning look Blondie gave me. In a matter of weeks and minimal conversation, I care for this woman more than I care for anyone, except my mother, in this world.

Hearing Misha saying "Hello" in his phone we all head his way, while he continues "Oh God! Where the hell are you, we were looking for you EVERYWHERE, I nearly paid a team of divers to look for you at the bottom of Thames River you lunatic woman!"

What a sense of humour he has.

Once everything is cleared and we know that she is ok, fury with blond hair decides to cook some chicken and rice. We have a decent meal in a comfortable silence.

Or at least for me it was comfortable, before fury's phone rings and she heads downstairs to bring my future wife back to the apartment.

As she sits down we all make sure she has a plate of food on the table and a glass with water. It feels like she is some kind of celebrity and we go out of our way so she will enjoy her staying.

Once the things settle, and we all calmed down, she looks at the plate and back at us.

After a brief comment about us staring at her, she starts to laugh like really laughing. A few seconds after staring at how she could not stop laughing, realisation hit me hard. This was the moment that I fell for her… hard and fast.

She was the most beautiful person, so happy and carefree. I couldn't stop watching her. I was staring at her, I knew I was. She raised her eyes and gazed me in the eyes.

"We need to talk now!"

Cold runs down my spine. Not saying a word as I stand and hold my hand for her, seeing her eyes getting bigger in their sockets, I just lead the way to the office.

When we get in, music plays softly from the laptop sited on my desk. She takes in every word of the song playing, like contemplating what the song is saying.

At some point in the song she turns around and asks me what I want to do in regards to my plan, if the rules are still on table? Of course they are. I am not going to hurt her more than her parents already did. For some strange reason, I find myself wanting to protect this strange woman in front of me from all the world's ugliness. I let her know about the fact that rules are still on, and ask her about hers when she hands me a paper to read.

Looking at the paper I see five rules. The first two catch my eye, but I decided to tease her about the last two.

When she fires her response about her needing to stay fit and gesture to her body, I feel my blood get warm. I try my best to focus on what she says, instead of letting my mind go in another direction. I ask what kind of dog she wants, when she informs me that she doesn't want a dog, she wants a bear. Changing the subject we talk about the rules. I let her know I have only one rule and give her the opportunity to tell me about hers, curious if she will bring up that night Misha was talking about. Maybe enlighten me why the hell she despises to be touched so bad. I know her brother said it's about the beating, but I doubt it's only that.

As soon as she motioned for me to sit down I did just that and listened to her carefully. I see the struggle in her, but as soon as she starts to speak and go on about that night, my blood starts to boil with furry towards her father.

She is flesh of his flesh, blood of his blood. How could he do that to her? How could he ruin her like that?

After all that he is the one to be angry she didn't enjoy it?

This is beyond fucked up insane. By the time she finishes I am happy for the silence, because I need a moment to calm myself down before I storm out the office and go for a kill.

I will make sure he will not touch her ever again. Turning my head towards her to let her know that, I see her crying and ashamed.

Why is she ashamed? Of me? Of what he did to her?

Without thinking, I catch her chin between my long fingers, turn her head so she will face me and staring into her green eyes I let her know none of this is her fault.

Asking about the scar I saw, and she explains that she had a heart surgery.

This woman is something else I swear. I mean if I wouldn't have had to change her close the other night I wouldn't even know she has heart problems. Then and there I decide to be honest with her and tell her that if she wants a prenuptial contract I will sign one for her.

I will make sure she doesn't need to pay a dime for anything, she's been through so much that this should not be a problem for her from now on. I would never ask her for anything, even if we divorce after my mom passes away. Like the plan was at the beginning, and still is. Or not? Before I can clarify everything I was thinking she screamed.

"Who the hell you think you are?" Confused by her question and surprised that no one broke the door, I now close my eyes, take a deep breath and explain to her that my intention wasn't to insult her. She is the most beautiful woman I saw and she doesn't need to hide behind her outfit anymore.

What I left out from that, is the fact that I will murder everyone who will as much as look her way in the wrong way. Of course she needed to pick up on the fact that I was telling her to quit her job at the café. I said that of jealousy, more than the fact that I would actually give a fuck what people or press would say for that matter. I need to use everything at hand, just to be taken aback by her statement.

"Well we will have an intimate ceremony and no one will ever know who I am, because I'm not a piece of meat you can display for anyone to look at!"

She explodes like a volcano in full eruption. Of course, I would not think of her like that. I would like to present her as my wife for various reasons. One, she will be protected by Vory members, and her father or some other men for that matter would not lay a hand on her again. Second, I will show off how lucky of a son of a bitch I actually am.

"I never thought you are a piece of meat. As for the wedding ceremony we still have a discussion pending. Why do you need to take everything I say the wrong way? I am not here to hurt you!"

I say as calm as I can, not wanting to fuel her burst more. She looks at me surprised by what I said. Opening her mouth to say something, but nothing comes out and she closes it back. After a moment of silence I speak.

"OK! How are we going to start this? Because, I promised my mother she will get to know you."

"When?"

And like always with her, I am confused by the question.

"When what? When I promise or when she gets to know you?"

"Well I was thinking about the second part, but you can answer the first part of the question as well."

She says more calm this time as she tries to smile. And just like that I find myself relaxing. What is she doing to me?

"I was planning at the end of this week, but giving everything. I am not sure if you are ready for this."

I answer honestly.

"Well giving the fact that time is not on our side, how about Sunday sounds? And what do we tell her? She will want to know how we met and how long we have been together. When will the wedding be? How did you propose to me? If we want her to believe a word we say, we need to be synchronised in this lie, don't you think?"

She fires the questions my way making it hard to follow her.

"First, I did not propose to you, yet. I mean she knows I want to marry, but I did not say I asked you. Second, let's stick with the truth, well as close to the truth as possible. Of course avoiding your family contribution to this wedding. She doesn't need to know that, and you don't need to go through that embarrassment again. We met through Arthur at your café, sorted. Sunday sounds good. I will let her know we are taking them to lunch."

"Them?"

Confusion on her face.

"Yes them, my parents and my brothers."

"Oh!"

She does a perfect "o" with her mouth and my mind goes wild.

"I want to ask something, but please don't get me wrong. This is all a lie anyway. Can we please skip the wedding party? I don't know, maybe have something intimate? With just your parents and brothers, my brother and friends, and unfortunately my parents as well? You know because of your mother's sake."

She asked, but as soon as she said "intimate" her cheeks were filled with the most beautiful shade of red I saw on someone's face, she was so sweet all red and shy.

"Well I believe a bit earlier you demanded just that, but we will talk about this. Now let's get through Sunday first. How about that?"

She nods not saying a word.

"Well then with all that settled let's start again!"

I say, taking my best posture in front of her I start.

"My name is Ruslan Dimitri Ivanovish!"

"My name is Svetlana Rebekah Petrov, nice to meet you!"

She says with a smile on her face, trying to mimic my posture.

"Svetlana Rebekah, will you do me the honour to take lunch with me and my family Sunday at 2 pm?"

I ask, displaying my most charming smile in return.

"It will be my honour to accompany you to lunch, with your family!"

And just like that we stepped in this wedding game together, without knowing what to expect further or what the future holds for us, for that matter.

Days have gone in a blink of an eye and now is Sunday. I am a nervous wreck and I shouldn't be.

Me and Lana spent more time together and we became more comfortable with one another. Well she became more comfortable with me touching her.

First I got to hold her hand for five minutes straight, until she pulled back. Later that evening I tried to touch her arm, at first she flinched back so fast, I was worried she would lose her balance. It took a few times until I managed to wrap my fingers around her arm.

Next day, I tried to wrap my hand around her shoulders and her reaction was like a punch to my stomach. She tried to hide it but with no luck.

Yesterday I managed to hug her without pulling back. She's got so far in these last few days, I could see she is trying hard to accept the fact that someone is touching her. That I touch her. I will do my best to be the only one who touches her in this way. Man, my jealousy and something more… could be real love? … is getting stronger the more I spend my time with her.

Her progress makes me so proud of her. However, we agreed to hold hands in front of everyone, but limit ourselves from touching each other as much as possible.

As I wait in my apartment office, I can help but wonder. How will she look? What dress will she choose to wear? I am plucked out of my thoughts when her furious blond friend announces that Lana is waiting for me in the living room.

As soon as I step foot in living I am left without breath.

She is wearing a dark red off shoulders dress, long until above her knee. A pair of black stilettos. Her hair is braided on one side and on the other is loose coming to her shoulder.

Natural makeup with eyeliner that highlights her green eyes.

I noticed that her eyes are changing colour depending on her mood, for example when she is angry her eyes get such a dark shade of brown, that I am surprised they open so much when she is shy or cries.

Judging by the green in her eyes, I am thinking that she is struggling to keep her tears at bay. Her lips are coloured by a shade of dark red that matches her dress. She is so beautiful that it pains me to look at.

And for the first time since I met her, her French is out of her eyes. Man I am lucky!

"You…"

I try to say something, but my mouth is dry. Clearing my throat, I try again.

"You are so beautiful!"

"You like it?"

She asks surprise in her voice, as her fury friend and Arthur laugh at my expense… traitors. I nod in response for her. I cannot trust my own voice and I don't want to give these two another reason to laugh.

The ride at the restaurant is fairly short, in equal parts a blessing and a curse.

Blessing, because I am not sure how much restrain I have left in me to not touch her body. And the last thing I need is to scare her off. Especially, after evolving so much in this beautifully strange relationship of ours.

Curse, because I would really like to spend more time with her by my side and not to share her with the world.

Once we were at a restaurant, I gave the hostess our names and she guides us at our table where my family is expecting us.

Only to feel my head spin and my blood run cold, when I see *her* next to my sister at the table. This is just fucking great.

After introductions are made *she* speaks.

"Ruslan I am so happy to see you. It's been a long time!"

Heading my way and wrapping her hands around my neck before I can react. Taking her arm down from around my neck, I ask her through gritted teeth.

"Felicia what do you want and why are you here?"

CHAPTER ELEVEN

SVETLANA

After the office discussion we agree to take it all over again.

He pretended we introduced ourselves to each other, which was nice and funny. But since we were never introduced to each other properly, I think that kind of made sense.

Once the Sunday lunch was agreed, we established to spend more time together. To be able to accustom to each other, which in real was the code for me to get used to him touching me.

One day, I managed to let him hold my hand for 5 min, I really had to fight the urge to pull my hand out of his. A couple of times I was so sure I would vomit from the stomach pain. It got easier as the day passed, but I had to force myself to look at him, actually look at him and realise that it's him who holds my hand. I even asked him to hold my hand with his right hand, so I would know in my mind that it's not my father who holds my hand. Sounds crazy, but it works for my mind to understand the difference between the two men.

The worst part was when he tried to cup my shoulders with his arm. I felt like he's caging me and instinctively I pulled out of arm reach. It pained him to see that and I tried my best to appear unaffected, putting a smile on my face but it didn't do the trick, he saw right through it.

I tried to breath and asked him to try again, looking into his eyes the whole time I managed to not pull away the second time.

For some reason that blue eyes of his, bring peace to me.

Yesterday, I wanted him to hug me, so I made sure if someone tried to hug me, I would not jump back and be awkward. It was a welcome accomplishment, because it was the first time when I did not feel the need to pull back. Meaning that I started to trust him or at least my body did.

In between touching sessions with Lan, I managed to go shopping with my crazy friend. Man she loves shopping, unlike me that I hate being dragged to the mall and all that. I will never understand why this woman loves to waste her time like that. But, it was better than I expected. She knew this fashion shop and after trying what felt like all the clothes from that shop, I agreed on a dark red dress with no shoulders. Rest of the day went pretty well with more hugging practise. By the time I got to bed I was exhausted.

It's Sunday and I am a nervous wreck as Renesmee applies my makeup. I try my best to keep my nerves at bay, but it's so difficult.

At one o'clock sharp, I am in the living room waiting for Lan to come out from his office. As he steps in the living room, I am breathless, he is wearing a black formal pointed toe dress shoes, black slack trouser with a white shirt and a black suit jacket.

The last three buttons of his white shirt are open revealing his skin, a shiny gold necklace at his neck, freshly shaven and his hair is styled toward the right part of his face in a messy style.

At the sight of him, I feel a strange sensation going through my body. It's like a warm feeling, so foreign I don't even know how or what to call. He tries to speak but the only word that comes out is "You..." After another attempt he managed to compliment me.

I ask him a little too excitedly "You like it?" and my two best friends start to laugh at our interaction, Lan nods not able to form words and we leave for the restaurant.

The car ride to the restaurant is nice and quiet, honestly I preferred this way because at how nervous I am right now, I am not sure if I can manage a conversation.

When we arrive at the hotel a valet takes the car keys from Lan and we enter the hotel that our restaurant is in.

A big hallway with the small welcome desk where the bellboy normally stays, is on the right side of the door we just entered.

In the left side of the hallway, is the concierge area and in front is the main reception desk. The concierge area is some kind of a blue with a world map displayed on the back wall. Despite the fact that the reception area has no windows, it's well lit by some bulbs that look like tears with a hint of yellowish light. We give our names at the reception, and Lan tells the lady that we have a reservation at the restaurant, whose name I don't remember, on the first floor.

She politely informs us that we can take the lift or choose the stairs. I suggest the stairs, so I have more time to breathe and admire the location. The staircase has the shape of a spiral with the same bulbs light and the walls are covered in mirrors. I wonder how much time they need to clean these mirrors, and how many swearings the owner gets, every time a child leaves his prints on them. At that thought I smile and Lan asks me what is so funny. As I tell him what I was thinking, we make our way to the reception area of our restaurant. A small hallway with black floor tile and a desk positioned on the right hand side, is a hostess area. A tall to slim girl dressed in a business suit, with a tag that says 'Linda', takes our name again and leads us at a table in the far left corner of the restaurant. A breathtaking view displayed from where we are seated at the table. Is the most beautiful view of the Thames River and The Shard building.

The way you enter the restaurant, you can notice that the big room is split in three by the four couches that are grouped in sets of two. Positioned back to back in a way that looks like a big booth.

In the right hand side it's what appears to be the grill side open space kitchen area, the same as you see in movies with chefs that are cooking in front of the guests. A grey carpet with blue and yellow lines lie on the floor. Wood tables and upholstered chairs with blue leather on the inside and yellow on the outside.

As we make our way to the table, I notice the restaurant has a floor to ceiling window that displays the beauty of Canary Wharf buildings and a perfect view of Thames River.

It's so beautiful in the broad daylight, which makes me think. How beautiful it can be in the night time, with all that buildings lights on?

I am so taken by the restaurant view, that I don't even notice Lan is all tense next to me and squeezing my hand a little too hard, until we make the presentations.

First, I am introduced to his father who looks like an older version of Lan, the only difference is that his Russian accent is stronger than Lan's. He is dressed in a black dress suit with shoes to match his outfit and a navy blue tie.

As he stands to shake my hand, I notice that he is as tall as Lan is, he is freshly shaved with a pronounced jaw line which makes him appear tougher than I believe he is. A pair of brown eyes meet my green eyes and a smile as charming as Lan's.

"I'm Dimitri, Ruslan's father!"

"I am Svetlana and it's nice to meet you!"

Next in line is his mother, that despite the fact she has cancer, she is still as beautiful as she was before. I assume! A dark blond hair woman, with the same blue eye as her son's, red lipstick on her thin lips that make them look a bit fuller than they really are. Round face and a happy look on her face. A little too thin for her stature, as I assume because she does not raise from her sit. Her cocktail black and white dress hugs her body perfectly. She looks stunning.

"I am Elena, Ruslan's mother! It's nice to finally meet you!"

"Pleasure is all mine!"

A muffled laugh coms from the girl sitting next to his sister.

His sister is the spitting image of her mother, but the younger version. She wears a dark green one shoulder cocktail dress and when she raises to shake my hand, I see that she is as tall as Lan is. Her dress just accentuated her fit body, unlike me she is tan.

More tanned than anyone could get in London in September, I guess she just returned from holiday. She manages to plaster what seems to be her best fake smile.

"I am Julia nice to meet you!"

"Nice to meet you too!"

I reply, not sure if she is fake just with me or she naturally is disgusted by the world.

"My name is Vladimir and it is nice to see that my brother has a girl finally, this will be interesting!"

A brunette young man, that cannot be more than twenty, says. He wears the same black dress suit and shiny shoes like his father, but unlike Lan his hair is charcoal black and his eyes are dark blue, cosmic blue. Square face and full lips that make his grin look so devilish on his face. Like screaming danger every time he displays that grin. Between so many blonds in his family, he looks so out of place, just like me in this moment. At that moment I decided that I like him and we could be good friends in time

"Nice to meet you Vladimir…"

I say but I am cut short by the girl who until three second ago was next to Julia, but now is in Lan's arms.

"Ruslan, I am so happy to see you. It's been a long time!"

What the hell is that? I mean she looks like a model, nearly as tall as Lan. Wearing a pink corset dress that makes her perfect shapes to stand out. Lean body with big boobs and curvy hips, only these dresses are so short, that I am afraid if she stretches her arm a little longer Dimitri will be prompted with a perfect image of her ass.

A pair of pink shoes that look hideous. I guess it is supposed to go with the dress, but someone please tell this girl she has such a bad taste in shoes or maybe she just chose wrong this time for all I know.

Her long light brown hair is a little longer than her shoulders and curly. She has an oval face with too full lips. I can see the Botox in them from where I am standing. It looks like duck lips which make me think of Mr Donald Duck, and I am fighting not to burst in laughter at that thought. Dark brown eyes and a smile even faker than Julia's.

Whoever she is I hope she will not be around much, because I can't stand her. Is this jealousy that I feel toward her? I am positive, I never felt that way toward anyone, my father included. Lan's surprise me by taking her hand down from around his neck and biting back.

"Felicia, what do you want and why are you here?"

OK! So who is she?

Now, I am confused.

It's supposed to be a family lunch not a family drama, but I am plucked out of my thoughts when Lan's arm cups my shoulders.

I try my best to not flinch, we worked hard for this moment. I don't want to ruin it, and he states so matter of fact.

"Felicia, this is my fiancée Svetlana, now stop embarrassing yourself further!"

Shock hits me at the same time as Julia and Vladimir nearly scream in unison "Fiancée?" Julia's voice is full of shock and disgust, while Vladimir's more like a comic chuckle. Dimitri nearly chokes on the glass of wine he drinks and Elena smiles brightly, as I try to fake a happy smile.

This announcement should not be out just yet. I could see Felicia's face fall but she recovered fast, turning to me with the same fake smile.

"Nice to meet you Svetlana, I didn't know you two are engaged. We never got that far!"

She says more to Lan than me. Oh perfect a crazy ex, that's what I have missed from my life at this moment.

"Felicia sit!"

Dimitri says, before any more interaction can take place, bringing everyone attention to him.

"Now let us sit down and eat, because I am starving and my treasure here is hungry as well."

He kisses his wife's cheek as we sit down and she smiles warmly to him. You can see from their gestures that they love each other so much, even after so many years together.

For the first time, I am thinking if me and Lan we will get that chance in all this game of ours. I can see everyone is hanging and waiting for explanations about the announcement, but like a great lady she is Elena asks Lan.

"Dear how are you? It's been a long time since I saw you last time."

I think sensing the tension that just builds around us, she wants to light the air before going full blown into an engagement discussion, which I am not prepared for.

"I am a good mother! We are happy to be here and I am pleased to see you are feeling better. That makes me feel better!"

He says as he relaxes his shoulder, a sign that he is beginning to feel comfortable again. We attempt to make small talk while the food is served and eaten. This could go better than I was anticipating, except in that very moment Felicia speaks.

"So how do you two meet? In a casino you are playing or a club? Or do you still race and meet her there?"

I understand she was suggesting that he might pick me up from the parking lot, and memories with him and that blonde come to my mind, forcing me to push it back. But, then I make sense of what she said, he is playing in a casino?

"None of that!"

I manage before he can say something to embarrass me further.

"We actually met in the café I am working at. He was meeting Arthur there, and that's how we met!"

I clarify, stating the truth but leaving out the motive of their meeting.

"A café?" she asks in full disgust "What happened with five star restaurants that you are accustomed to? And what in the God name Arthur was doing there? I need to tease him for that. When did he go so low?"

I cringe and roll my eyes at her statement, but keep my mouth shut. I really don't want to go in full discussion about that right now. It will only create tension and for sure it will be too stressful for Elena. Gazing in her direction I smile kindly and shove a potato in my mouth, I will be busy chewing instead of talking, as I hear Lan speaking.

"Since when you are such a pristine bitch, Felicia? When you came to London you used to eat in that kind of place as well. You are modelling, because of Arthur. So stop pretending!"

I choke on my potato as Elena and Julia say at the same time "Ruslan!" After a few more coughs later, I excuse myself and head for the restroom. Hoping to get some privacy and recover myself. As I head to the restroom I hear an angry Lan continuing to tell Felicia.

"Mind your fuckin business and stay out of this or I will make sure to hurt you as much as possible!"

What the hell was that? She just called me a cheap bitch just to be thrown under the bus by Lan. Whatever they have I don't want to be in the middle.

Once in the restroom, which is big with a half full mirror wall, that gives you the impression the room is twice as big as it really is. With a toilet cubicle on the opposite side of the wall and square sinks placed under the mirrors. I put my hands on the edge of one sink, closing my eyes trying to calm my breath, but soon I hear the bathroom door opening. When I open my eyes I see Felicia, great!

"Hey I did not intend to insult you in there… but I just want to warn you, he is not marriage material. Whatever he said to you is not intended to last. Probably he does what he does for his mother, and I can assure you as soon as she is gone, he will come back to me. He always does. That's how we are. We have known each other since we were fourteen. And it was always like this between us. Why else do you think I am here?"

She states and my mind is spinning. I know we agreed to have a fake marriage but we never agreed that I will have to stand his ex. And for sure I never agreed to listen to how she insults me and puts me down, like I am a worthless cloth. I speak the first thing that comes to my mind.

 "How do you feel about that? How do you feel to be someone's 'filler'? How do you feel when you know that when he sleeps with you, he is thinking of me? That even though he is fucking you, he wants me? His body is with you, but his mind and soul desire me as much as he desires his next breath?"

I ask and I step out of the restroom, not wanting to hear what she has to say anymore.

Back at the table everyone's eyes are on me, which makes me feel a bit uncomfortable. Elena speaks first.

"How do you feel dear?"

Not sure if she means about the potato situation or about what just happened with Felicia.

"I am good thank you! I didn't mean to scare anyone. I was just a bit clumsy with my food"

I smiled. Lucky for me this lunch doesn't carry on too much, before I know we are back in the car. Total silence, but for the first time since this lunch, I am grateful for the silence.

My head is still spinning from the discussion with Felicia. How would she even know about the agreement I have with Ruslan? Are they still talking or she just implemented that out of frustration?

"I can see the wheels spinning in your head. You can ask me anything, I will be honest with you. We are in this together."

Lan's statement brings me back to the car.

"Are we in this together?"

He frowns.

"Why would you say that? I made sure she apologised for what she said. That's why she followed you to the restroom."

I start to laugh, man he is naïve if he thinks she came there to apologise.

"Well, her definition of apology is way different than mine."

I say sarcastically, but serious at the same time

"What did she say to you? And more importantly, why didn't you tell me right away?"

"For the start, I did not want to put your mother under even more stress than she already was. Second, you would have made a scene there and again, that is not what your mother needs. Third, since you and her are so close, I can assume you already know what she told me. So, I will tell you this, no matter what my parents did. I will not let you or anybody else, for that matter, to insult me or use me like I am some worthless person. I know what happened to me in the past is hard to handle, but I didn't ask to be broth in this game of yours. For everyone's sake, keep your girlfriend away from me next time you decide she should join us for family meals!"

I scream my frustration out to him.

CHAPTER TWELVE

RUSLAN

"So how do you two meet? In a casino you are playing or a club? Or do you still race and meet her there?"

As soon as Felicia's words leave her mouth, I have only one desire, to wrap my finger around her throat and choke her to death.

How dare she bring this now, if in front of everyone? After what she did back then, she is not one to talk about anyone. Especially not about Lana, like that. She doesn't even know this girl. She doesn't know how hard she tried to make sure this lunch is as good as it can be. How hard she worked to pass her fear of being touched, so she will play along in this game of mine.

I know, I am nothing more to Felicia than a bruised ego and a desperate desire to forgive her for sleeping with my best friend. A friend she is in a relationship with.

Why the fuck is she even here?

I am trying to be on my best behaviour for my mother. I hear the exchange between Lana and Felicia, but when she starts to talk about teasing Arthur and the way she was speaking to Lana, I just can't keep my mouth shut anymore. Biting back at her.

"Since when you are such a pristine bitch, Felicia? When you came to London, you used to eat in that kind of place as well. You are modelling, because of Arthur. So stop pretending!"

I see Lana nearly dying over a potato, as my mother and sister shouts my name in unison, but I am too angry to think straight and pay attention to anything that happens around me. Lana excuses herself and heads to the restroom. Turning back to Felicia, I spit out.

"Mind you fuckin business and stay out of this. Or I will make sure to hurt you as much as possible!"

At my angry statement she replied.

"Look I am sorry, I didn't mean to insult anyone, but I know you never frequent those places and imagine my surprise."

She says softly and sweetly, just adding up to my disgust toward her.

"You see I had good intentions. I will go and apologize!"

She goes in the same direction Lana went, a few minutes ago. Turning to my mother I explain.

"I am sorry, she was just talking rubbish about people she doesn't know. Or in Arthur's case helped her to be where she is!"

"Don't worry about me, I am a big girl. This is not the first time I needed to deal with Felicia's bitter jealousy. But, you have a lovely girl here, make sure she goes untouched by Felicia's venom."

Mother says sweetly. She is the best mother I could have been given.

"Fiancée? Hmm?"

Dad says with a grin on his face.

"Yes fiancée, I wanted to introduce her to family before breaking the news, but Felicia's comment just made me blurted out."

My brother laughs and my sister is so shocked, she just doesn't say a word. I can see she doesn't like Lana at all. Well, there is no surprise here, I was sure this would happen. I need to find a way so the two of them can be in the same room, without setting it on fire.

Baby steps Lan, baby steps. As Lana returns, followed by a very shocked Felicia, I just wonder how their conversation went. I make a mental note to ask about it, in the car on the way back home. Lunch goes smoothly, not long after that incident, we say our goodbyes and head home.

I am trying my best to get Lana to speak, never expecting what she replies to me about Felicia. By the time she finishes her stamen, she is fully screaming.

I manage to park the car in my usual spot at the apartment.

Insult…use…girlfriend…agreed to join the family meals? What the hell is she talking about?

Turning to ask her about that, she is already out of the car. Heading toward the entrance of the building, with her shoes in her hands. Getting out of the car as soon as I manage, I try to catch up with her. Man, she is fast for such a smurf. I get to the lift just in time before the doors are closing. Not being able to keep it inside I start to scream.

"What the fuck happened in there? What she told you? I haven't agreed with any of this. I sure as fuck didn't know she will be there! So clarify before I will!"

t I turn to stare at her and raise my hand to scratch my forehead, a habit I have when I am nervous, just to see a very scared Lana backing in the wall lift and raising her hand in a protective gesture.

She is fighting her tears. Fuck! The way she looks so scared and frighten, is just a punch in my fucking stomach. I want to murder that father of hers, right the fuck now

"I didn't mean to scream like that. I will never hurt you, but you need to talk to me. What happened there?"

I try again, this time on a calm tone and my hands in my pockets. Before she can answer, the lift doors open and she storms out going straight into my bedroom apartment, locking the door behind her.

Great job man! Great fucking job. I head for the office, I need to calm down before I am able to have a conversation with her, like normal people. No way in hell I will let this go. I need to know what happened there and make sure Felicia will not give her hard times. Half an hour later, I am calm enough to master the capability of taking all hatred that comes from Lana's mouth, regarding this situation. I decide to head to the bedroom and try at least to have a conversation with her, before any of that happens, I hear the front door slamming. You must be kidding me! Heading in the sound direction I found a piece of paper stuck on the door with the message.

Rule nr 3

One night a week at my apartment ALONE, starts tonight!

Amazing! No matter how angry and hurt I'm now, I know I need to give her time, if I want her to trust me. So, I do the thing I know will make me forget all this. I call Vitaly to let him know I want to be in for a race tonight, asking if the fucker with the cool car will be there. At least, I will set one thing right!

At midnight on the dot I'm in Trafalgar Square at the usual meeting spot, I find Vitaly fairly easy.

He is always parked at the park entrance. He assured me the fucker will be here, I made sure to tell Vitaly that if I win the race I want to see the fucker face.

I brought my Bugatti Veyron today.

It's a 2011th car in amazing shape. The Veyron features an 8.0-litre, quad-turbocharged, W-16 cylinder engine, equivalent to two narrow-angle V8 engines bolted together. Each cylinder has four valves for a total of 64, but the configuration of each bank allows two overhead camshafts to drive two banks of cylinders so only four camshafts are needed. The engine is fed by four turbochargers and displaces 7,993 cc, with a square 86 by 86 mm bore and stroke.

The outside of the car is black and white, with black coming from the back of the car to the hood in a form of "V", both of the front wheel sides and the doors are white. A matching black and white interior. White doors and sport seats, black steering wheel, dashboard and derailleur. Dashboard lights are blue providing just enough light to see the command board at night. After parking my car, I head to Vitally's way. Tonight Square is a packet, same scene every time. A lot of tuned cars, even more women, wearing next to nothing outfits. Blasting electro music and a lot of colour displayed around the pavement from cars neon's lights.

It's a nice and welcoming chaos where you are surrounded by a lot of people, but nobody is paying attention to what you are doing. Like being alone in the middle of a sea of people, which with me is more than okay. Every time I come to race, I am here for the adrenaline and from time to time I try to score a woman. Depending on the night mood she's blonde, brunette, red head or sometimes a mix of them. Yeah, threesome it's not really my thing, but I tried as well. I am a man after all and have my need and fantasies, but for the most times, I enjoy fucking one woman at the time. Except now, I would enjoy to fuck one particular brunette in special. Baby steps Lan, baby steps.

"Hey man!"

I greet Vitaly

"Hey!"

"Is that fucker here? I can't see his car yet."

I ask as he starts to smile.

"What the fuck you're smiling for?"

My question sends him into full laughter and gets me confused. What can be so funny? After a minute of laughter he speaks.

"I meant to ask you so many times. What makes you think it's a… him? Maybe it's a…she, kicking your ass every time?"

"Nah man, a pussy cannot drive like that. I have skills, but that fucker is mad driving, which qualifies it as a "him"." But, I cannot stop thinking that maybe he is right. That kind of driving skills cannot be a woman, nah it's impossible.

Vitally shake his head as I pay for the race. Turning my head to watch the dudes that draw a line on the pavement, I see that Camaro. Oh he came. Good! I bring my car to the start line and look the "fucker" way. Except, I can't see a damn thing because of his tinted windows and ninja style clothes. Again that outfit? This makes me think of the first time I saw Lana and her big French. The thought alone makes me smile and brings my cock to life, not now. I don't need this distraction.

As I watch the girl between our cars go with the drill of ready, steady…"GO", I turn on my music which is a song of Juicy J and Kevin Gates "Payback", the soundtrack of "Fast and Furious" my favourite. Making me think that this song is so suitable for the situations at hand, this *is* my payback to this fucker.

The race route of tonight has the start line at the north entrance of St James Park, going in a straight line towards Buckingham palace, rounding the Queens Victoria Memorial, which is a big yellow angel statue with a huge round fountain at the base, and back to the north entrance. It's an easy route, so it should not be a problem to win. I bought my Veyron for a reason.

As my music blasts through speakers, the chick in between our cars says "GO". I release my foot from the clutch, speeding up.

This time, I am faster than him. It will be easy, I just need to be the first to take the turn at the statue, and the win is mine. We speed faster and faster towards the statues, my adrenaline raises, helped by the music as well. It's like my soul will detach my body any minute now, but it's a welcoming sensation. At this moment it's just about me and my car… we are one.

When I approach the statue I use the loss of lateral grip of the car to initiate the drift, so I will not use my hand brake and slide easier around the statue. Except, I am too fast and too wide, creating enough space for the fucker to overtake me on the interior and sprint in front of me the second we finish the turn. I try to push my car to go as fast as it will, but something unexpected happens, fucker uses NOS (Nitrous Oxide System) and sprints out of the park. Not even looking back at the finish line.

I lost again!

FUUUCCCKKK!

This day could not be worse.

I don't care of the money, but I care of my ego.

Who the hell is this guy? Where did he learn to drive like that? Man I really need to beat this guy.. No one beat me twice in a row until him, no one!

As I stop to breathe and calm down my adrenaline, I see Vitaly coming my way.

"How do you feel, baby boy? You had your ass kicked, by "the fucker" like you say, twice in a row."

"Fuck you Vitaly!"

I say back and we both laugh.

"The fucker said to split the premium in two fair shares, one for him and one for you! You know? Gas money, time waste and all that."

He is teasing me and laughing.

"Fuck him man, I don't need his money. I want to kick his fucking ass!"

"You should buy a Camaro then, maybe you will have more luck."

He says and I swear more. I was serious, I did not need the money. Well, not from that fucker anyway. Even though it's a lot of money in the middle. But money is something that I have, more than I need. Saying my goodbye I head home. At least I will sleep after all that shit that went down.

Getting home I'm happy that no one is around and I am left with my thoughts as I take a shower and head to bed. Thinking that I have a discussion pending with Lana tomorrow, she will not get away with this. Night goes by with a dream about certain green-brown eyes. I wake up as my phone is ringing, and ringing, and ringing…

Who the hell calls in the middle of the night, but when I open my eyes, my nightstand watch shows 6.45. I had 4 hours and 45 minutes to sleep, seriously? Whoever is calling it better be important. I answer my phone as I hear her voice boom through the phone.

"I am calling you for the last 10 minutes, why don't you pick up your phone?"

"Good morning to you too, princess! I am good as well, how are you? Oh I know you are bored and wake up early in the morning!"

I say teasing her, just to get an even angrier voice.

"You jackass! I am at the entrance of your building, but I don't have a key and it's pouring rain outside. My shift starts in half an hour, so you better move your ass and open that door!"

Man, when she became so demanding? From the shy scared girl I met like two weeks ago, she became a force of nature now. Is it me that brings that in her or she was like that before?

"Hello? Are you there?"

She brings me back from my trance about her.

"Yes, I am coming boss lady!"

I get up from bed wrapping the bed shit around my waist, not bothering to put cloth on. I am coming back to bed anyway. I need to give her a pair of keys from the apartment. Soon we'll move together and it will be easier for both of us.

I push the intercom button so she can come into the building. When I hear a knock on the door I open the door. She is all dripping wet. The way she is staring and moving her mouth to say something, she looks like a fish that was just taken out of the water and it's in need of air. She is so damn pretty. I want so bad to kiss her right now, but I'm afraid she will turn around and run away.

Suddenly she brings her hands to her face, I frown and look down in confusion. Only to be aware that my morning hardness is visible through the bed sheet wrapped around my waste. I turn around and head to the bedroom as I shout to her to come in.

After throwing some cloth on, I go to the kitchen where I turn on the kettle to boil some water for coffee. I'm waiting for her to come out of the bathroom and when she does, I notice something has changed.

She wears the same black outfit, only this time her jeans are hugging her body like a second skin. Putting on display that ass and curvy hips of hers.

The shirt is exactly her size, not like the previous one with two sizes larger, evidenting her chest more than it should. I mean she is decent but sexy as hell.

Scratching my forehead I have only one thought, this will be hell worse than I anticipate it will be. Look at her, and she is terrified to be touched. What am I supposed to do? I am a man after all.

"Are you okay? Is something wrong with my outfit?"

No, I am not OK, and hell yes! Your outfit is sexy as hell, makes me want to bend you on top of this fucking table and have my ways with you. I want to scream at her. Instead, I plaster my charming smile and say.

"Yes, I am OK! And no, your outfit is OK. Still looking like a widow but it's OK, I guess!"

Man, I am such an ass.

"Let not start with this again, please! Tonight after my shit we need to talk. Agree how everything will go on, now that you told everyone we are engaged!"

"Yes we need to talk about that and about the fact that you run away. Without actually telling me what that bitch said to you, to make you run for the hill like that. Now you need to go to work, so I will wait until tonight!

Did you eat something? Do you have time to have a sandwich if I make you one?"

She nods and I proceed to make turkey ham sandwiches for both of us and we eat in silence, until she goes to work.

This feels amazing, I could get used to this. Before she went out the door I said to her.

"I will go and make a spare key for you. You will wait at the door anymore, however I will wait for you in front of the café tonight. Have a great day at work!"

And with that, she is out of the apartment.

Of course, by now I cannot go back to bed because sleep ran away Instead, I go to take a shower, brush my teeth and carry on with my morning routine. Once I finish getting dressed I take a look at the digital clock next to bed, it says nine thirty a.m. I'm out the door to find a key cutting shop, making a point to pass the café just to see her there. She has to stop working in that place. She is way smarter. Why does she kill herself like that? It's beyond my understanding

The day went by with me getting the keys done, then returning straight home, because of a call I received from a client. Talking to him I proceeded doing some work. I would have liked to go and see her but this was an important matter and it couldn't wait. Before I realise what time is, my intercom is ringing and Lana asks "Can I come in?"

I curse myself for not paying attention at the clock. As I let her in, I saw she was crying, before I could ask what was wrong with her, I was slapped across my face. Without time to react, I take it full blown…

Why the hell is this one for?

CHAPTER THIRTEEN

SVETLANA

Getting to his apartment after lunch with his family, I had straight into the bedroom locking the door to cool myself down before talking to him. I seriously believe he will come at least knock on my door and ask me if I am ok. But no, he stayed hidden in his office. After waiting for half an hour, I took a piece of paper remembering him about the rule nr three and stormed out of the apartment slamming the door behind. Maybe that will make him chase me.

Nope.

Not happened.

Ten minutes I waited in front of his building. To see if he will at least come and look for me.

Another, no show!

I head to my flat.

A little after ten Vitaly called me and asked me if I wanted a rematch with Lan.

Of course I agreed. At least I will give him another reason to be mad after what he did to me.

At midnight, I was at the start line not missing a bit. Turning my music up. Selena Gomez "Wolves" was playing, which is appropriate for this situation. I have run through the jungle of my feelings for this man, in a matter of weeks since I know him. And that makes it scary for me. I start to fall for this guy and this is not even possible for me.

Why do I even have feelings for him, when all he does is command me left and right? Blackmailed me into a marriage that I do not want. Agreeing with my parents at a price of fifty thousand for the same bloody marriage, he doesn't even want to be in.

As if all that is not enough, he gets to laugh with his ex or actual ex, or who the fuck she is for him, at my expense.

Nope that will not happen.

After this race I am going straight to my flat.

Have a shower and sleep until tomorrow.

Then, I will be with my head straight.

I will have a chat with him about all of this and find a solution to everything. The worst case scenario, I will pay him fifty thousand and get lost from here. I know Vitaly will help me settle anywhere and I know, I am a good driver and a good hacker to make the money back. But, before all of that. I will make sure to kick his ass again tonight.

As the bimbo between our cars says "GO " he sprint like a bat out of hell. He actually thinks that he has a chance to win?

I am not praising myself here. If he would pay better attention to the road, than to my car, he could actually see his gone a little too far and his spin will be just wide enough for me to pass him on the interior. Which is exactly what I do and sprint in front of him. As he tries to catch up, I push my car even further releasing my NOS (Nitrous Oxide System) button. Bringing me further into the driver seat and pulsing my adrenaline even higher than it already is.

With a fast glance in my rear mirror, I see him behind me which qualifies me as a winner.

AGAIN!

I don't even bother to stop now. I already instructed Vitaly to offer him half the money from the race. On one hand to see if he will actually take it. On the other to piss him off more, if he refuses the money. I know he has a big bruised ego, and he will jump at the next offer of a race I hand to him.

After parking my freedom at the garage I head to my flat, have a shower and get some sleep.

I wake up when my alarm goes off. I pack a bag with clothes to get me for a couple of days, just in case he agrees to let me stay with him, so we can become more credible and get to know each other better. Or at least enough to not make him want to kill me every time he sees me.

Getting out of my building I am welcomed by a pouring rain. I speed up to the bus station just in time to catch the first bus and I don't wait in the rain.

Once in front of his building I try to call him for ten minutes straight. As soon as he picks up the phone, I start to shout, being already angry and wet. I start to freeze in here and if he doesn't let me in soon, I will be late for my shift. He lets me in the building finally, I take the lift and knock on his door as soon as I am there.

As he opens the door I see a sleepy, naked Lan. Trying to say something, nothing comes out of my mouth. I am positive by now I look like a fish to him. Embarrassed, I look down only to be greeted by his morning hardness. Oh my God this is even more embarrassing. I cover my eyes with my hands and in a few seconds he turns and heads to the bedroom shouting at me to get in.

I go to the bathroom and change my clothes into my uniform, this time I made sure to get something that actually fits my body. Maybe in this way he will pay attention to me. I don't even know where these thoughts are coming from, especially when it's so hard for me to be touched.

Ready for work, I step in the kitchen. We chat and eat for a bit, before I get out the door he informs me he will give me a spare key for his apartment and that he will wait for me in front of the café when I finish my shift. Well that went better than I expected.

The day is pretty good until around four in the afternoon when all of sudden Felicia with Arthur walks in.

Seriously?

Out of all the coffee shops, he needs to bring her here?

I don't care if they are friends, but I don't want her around me.

Simple as that.

I go and take their drink order. When I return with the drinks and ask them if they want to eat. She makes a face like I asked her to eat mouse poison. Which I wouldn't mind, but I would not offer.

"Dear they don't have the food we normally eat, am I right Arthur?"

With a roll of his eye and an apologetic look he says,

"Just ignore her! She said, she wanted to talk to you about something that happened at the restaurant."

He clarifies. Oh, that's why you are here to spit your venom further, well good to know because I will not let you.

Turning to her I ask.

"What's there more to talk about? I believe we said everything we needed to be said there?"

"Oh no dear, Arthur here did not understand properly…"

A grin on her face. Staring at Arthur, I can see he has a frown on his face, looking at her like she was lying.

Maybe, she did lie to him.

With her everything is possible.

Before he has a chance to say something, she takes a key out of her purse and places it in my hands.

"Lan said, he did not have time to come and give you this himself, but it will be home by nine o'clock for the dinner, you will cook as a celebration that you are moving in together."

Me and Arthur share the same shocked expression.

Me, because this was the last thing I expected Lan to do. This is so low for him to actually go and spend time with his ex, then send me the key to his apartment, through her? Where the hell is he anyway?

Arthur on the other hand, I assume is shocked, because one, he did not know that we are moving together, hell I did not know either. That's why I did not say a thing. Second, he probably thinks the same of Lan.

As I looked up at her, I saw a victory smile. Telling me that was exactly the reaction she was expecting from me, like a fool I played into her hand.

I handed her the key back so fast like the key was fire in my hands replying.

"I don't know what gave you the idea that I do not have a key from his apartment already, but you are mistaken. I don't need a key from you, and if you would have a bit of self-respect, you would hand that key back to Lan. Just to let you know he left the shop just a few minutes before, he was here with his laptop working."

I lie, after the way her smile disappeared, I know she wasn't with Lan today. But then again, how does she have the key to his apartment? Before I can say something else, Arthur grabs her arm so hard, I am positive tomorrow she will have the evidence of that, on her arm. Dragging her out of the shop, so quickly she loses her footage, but he doesn't stop. For a second, I feel sorry for her, but just for a second. I know Arthur is the calmest person I met. Except, when he has enough, he's the monster you don't want to wake from his sleep.

I witnessed that when his colleague did not understand that I am not interested in his flirting.

She deserved this, because she caused it. After screaming to one another Arthur's return in the café.

"I am sorry. I didn't know what she was up to. You need to believe me!   I would never do this to you. Not after everything you did for me and all the trust you have in me. I was a stupid fool to believe her, I should knew better, because I know what kind of person she is. You have…"

He speaks so fast that I need a moment to react, bringing my hand up in the air I stop him.

 "I know you for so long, you never did a single gesture to hurt me. She is good. Don't worry! I am not mad at you, I am at myself."

"I will have a serious talk with Lan…"

"Please let me talk to him first, we have so many things to sort out with everything that is going on. Let me talk to him, please. Anyways he will come by the time I finish my shift."

"OK you have until tomorrow, but tomorrow I will talk to him. I know your parents are idiots, but he cannot treat you like that."

He goes out of the shop, gets into his car and speeds up.

I could not wait for the end of the shift more than I did now. When I was done at the shop I headed to Lan's place, taking my time on the river walk away. I cried for more than one hour and he was nowhere to be found. He said he will come after me at the end of the shift, but then again Felicia said he is busy until nine o'clock, well is quarter to nine so I try my luck at the intercom. I still don't have a key since I didn't take the key from her. Lan answers and I ask him if I can come in. Praying she is not in the apartment, laughing at my reaction from earlier today. As he opens the door and looks at me, he starts to frown. Before I realise what I am doing my hand connects with his face. I caught him unprepared as he took the full blow. I can see my handprint on his face that sent me over the edge…

"You son of a bitch! What did you expect? That I will come home and cook dinner for you? In the meantime, you have your ways with her? Maybe my parents are as low as they can get, for selling their child to a jackass like you…"

I point to his chest with my finger so hard, I am afraid that I made a hole there

"…but I am not them, and I will never be. What made you believe, I am some naïve girl that you blackmail around in marriage? Force her to stay home and cook you dinners as you're at your mistress apartment spending quality time? Hmm? Tell me, that low do you think of me?"

By now I am screaming my lungs out, and for sure at least ten other apartments heard everything I said to him

"How could you send me the key of your fucking apartment through her? Out of all people you know, you've chosen your ex, or actual or who the fuck knows anymore, to send me the fucking key of you apartment and you have the nerves to stand here and look me like nothing happened?"

I continue my screaming session, because I am not even nearly finished, I need to take it all out. I need to tell him that this is not OK, and I will not accept this kind of behaviour.

No matter the consequence.

The hell with the consequences.

I will deal with them later.

"Here I was thinking, that maybe, you really don't know she was a bitch to me at the restaurant. Here I was actually wanting to heal for you. And maybe, who knows? Have a chance at a real marriage…"

I say before I can stop myself, why did I even say that now? Well, it doesn't matter, because it will not happen anyway

"…well because of that, you could say I am naïve. I will agree with you, but only on that"

He tries to hold a smile, which sets me on fire even worse. So, I carry on, because now I have enough courage to go to war with this Greek God, standing in front of me… no, not Greek God. Just an asshole. A big one for that matter.

"I will pay you the fifty thousand that my father owes you. I will buy my way out of this marriage. I will write you a check and once I am out of that door, I am out of your life. You can bring you precious Felicia and fuck her ten ways until Sunday for all I care! You can fuck off both of you, at the same time!"

I say so angry and serious. I move to go for my bag which is next to the now closed door. Before I can take the next step toward the door, I am yanked back by the arm and slammed into a wall of hard muscles as his mouth seals mine, in a kiss so soft at the begging, but deeper and needier by the second. Without even knowing what I do, I try to open my mouth to say something, and he takes that as an invitation to shove his tongue in my mouth.

It's my first kiss ever, it's the closest I ever went with a man, except my father, but that was not consensual.

Well this is not either, but it does feel good, too good to be able to pull back, and a sensation of burning heat travels my body and settles down between my legs. For a few seconds I surrender myself to the kiss… to him.

After a minute or ten for that matter, I manage to make my body cooperate with my brain and step back out of his reach.

"Are you out of your damn minds? What the hell is wrong with you?"

The only problem with my stepping back was the direction I chose to go. Instead of heading for the door I head for the wall and now he is in between me and the door. Realisation hit me, I was going for the door when he pulled me back, that means he spun us around and positioned himself between me and the door. Just like that, panic set within me. What will he do to me? Hopefully not the same thing as my father did. Don't get me wrong, I figured out by now that I am attracted to Lan. I would really like to be able to sleep with him, like any other normal woman. But, now is not the time, not that it will ever be. I am sure as hell not prepared for that big of a step with him.

As he sees my struggle and probably the panic in my eyes, he speaks softly.

"I will never hurt you! Not with intention, and not in that way, for sure!"

I look at him terrified, questioning if his words are true.

"I don't know what got into me to kiss you like that, but I wanted to do it for a while now. Please let me speak, because I have no idea what you were talking about earlier. I had not seen Felicia in five years, until yesterday at a restaurant. I knew she was in London, but I made sure we are not in each other's way. I even told Arthur I don't care if they are friends, as long as I am not involved in that. I knew something was wrong after lunch, but you stormed out of this place and I wanted to give you time to cool down. Before we could speak about everything. I did not send any key with her. Hell, I didn't even see her, after her appearance at the restaurant yesterday. I am beyond confused. Why would you even think I spoke with her? Let alone send you a key with her. Out of all the people we know, I chose her? I was working at the firewall you broke in, and I had an emergency call from a company I work with, until the intercom ring and you came like a hurricane in war mode."

He says staring at me, confusion clear as day on his face. Staring back at him, it's hard to decide if he is lying or telling the truth, but for sure he is confused. I will work with that.

"She came with Arthur at the café, she put a key in my hand and told me you sent her to give me the key, because you are busy until nine o'clock. And I am supposed to cook dinner as a celebration for our moving in together night."

I explained to him and I can see his face changin, going angry as the words were leaving my mouth.

"Arthur brought her to the café? Why the hell would he do that after everything he knows about you?"

"She said to him she needs to apologise for what she did at the restaurant. I think his intentions were good, because once he saw what she did and heard what she said he dragged her out of the café and came back to apologies."

"Look I know it is too much for you all of this. And it is hard to trust me, because of everything I did, but my intentions are not bad here. I will never hurt you or treat you the way you think.

I will never put you down especially when it comes to Felicia. We need to be able to communicate with each other and tell each other this kind of thing, otherwise this will not be the first or the last time when she will come in between us. Like I said, except Arthur nobody knows this agreement we have and even he doesn't know about our rules. I am sorry I broke rule number one. I couldn't think of a way to make you listen to what I had to say!"

He says as he scratches his forehead.

"Take a shower in the meantime I will prepare something for us to eat, I did not have a chance to eat today. We can talk after that."

He says trying to light up the atmosphere between us.

"Is too late for me…"

His face falls at my choice of word and pain is in his eyes, and I clarify.

 "…to eat at this time!"

"What time is it?"

Looking at the clock on the wall he says surprised.

"It's quarter past nine o'clock already? Where did the day go?"

I smile shyly and shake my head as I go to the door to pick up my bag, he puts himself between me and the door.

"You're not going to stay?"

"I am. just taking my bag to go to the shower. I will join you in the kitchen as soon as I finish showering."

And that gets me his most charming smile, as he steps aside and makes space for me to grab my bag. I go to the bathroom and welcome the hot water over my body.

CHAPTER FOURTEEN

RUSLAN

As soon as she speaks, scratch that. As soon as she screams, like I am some deaf person or maybe she believes that my neighbours are interested in our …my private life. I kept my mouth shut. One, I never saw her like that, well I did see her angry but not toward me… then it was easy, because I had a clear head… now totally different. Even screaming she is the most attractive woman I saw. Second, most probably in this way she will spit out what is eating her alive. Maybe if she is angry enough, she will not think what she needs to say. She will just say the things the way they come. As she is screaming I pay attention to what she says, as well as what she is doing.

The way her eyes become that light shade of green.

How her lips move or her cheeks became flushed by that red colour that she has every time she is angry or shy.

I see how the redness spreads down her neck. As far as her shirt will allow me to see, it spreads down her chest as well.

The way she is pacing around and her eyes widen with every fury word she has to say.

She looks like a hurricane in a war mode, but she is the most beautiful form of hurricane that I will take any time we are together, with all her fury. As soon as she screams that she wants to heal, for me. I feel like I won the biggest jackpot any casino will ever reward me.

The second she tells me she wanted a chance at a normal marriage, I know I will do everything in my power to give her that.

I will be patient with her.

I will show her that she is worth waiting for.

When she goes on telling me agrees with me, she was naïve to think we can have a normal marriage, I fight a smile back that only sets her on fire even more.

My hurricane.

The most wonderful woman in all her fury.

As I am looking at her realisation hits me. I am in love with this woman more than she will ever know. I don't even hear the last words she says, because her beauty stunned me.

As soon as I realise she is heading to the door, I do the first thing I can think of. Grab her arm and pull her towards me, only to slam her to my chest and seal her mouth with mine.

Soft at the beginning.

I know how hard this must be for her.

I am prepared to take another slap across the face.

I will deserve this one, but when she doesn't pull back I take it as an invitation to go further, only for her to open her mouth to say something.

I bet.

I don't give her that chance.

I shove my tongue in her mouth caressing her tongue with mine, the most amazing sensation I had until now.

I know this is her first real kiss and damn sure I want to make as memorable as I can.

I want her to want me more than her fear of being touched.

I want her to crave me the same way I crave her.

As I kiss her, I spin softly. In this way I put myself in between her and the door. By the time my spin is finished, she pulls back straight into the hallway wall. It takes her a few seconds to realise the way she went, once she does that panic sets in.

It pains me so much, I would like to kill her father, with my bare hands. Like Arthur once said, it will be useless, because it will not change the damage he did to her.

Trying to ease her panic I say as softly as I can manage

"I will never hurt you! Not with intention and not in that way for sure!"

I see her stance relaxing and I go further with my explanation, once we finish our small interaction, she heads to the bathroom and I for the kitchen. Grateful that she stayed and hopeful that I will start to make my way through that wall she built over the years. Because, she found her way under my skin without even trying. She made me fall for her like I never did for anyone, until her. Even if I didn't gamble in a while now, I will never go back to any casino again, as long as she is with me. I will make her my most wanted price. She will become my new…addiction.

As soon as she sets foot in the kitchen, I'm at a loss of word. She is wearing a white tank top with a pair of shorts, too short. That's her pyjamas? Well good luck to me, for a nice and restful sleep. Which will be anything but restful, with the pair of blue balls she gives me right this very moment

She takes a seat at the round table in front of me. By the way she positioned herself, I can see she sits with a leg underneath her. Fully facing me, only to be given the best view, of that gorgeous chest, from where I'm leaning against the kitchen cabinet.

"Ahem, are you hungry?"

I ask, even if she already told me it's too late for her to eat at this time, and try my best to sound as cool as possible, but my blood starts to warm up. Chill man you need to talk about the wedding.

"I lost my appetite a long time ago, but I want to talk to you about everything that happened and what is going to happen."

She is so calm. How can she be so unaffected, when I feel like I've just landed in hell here?

"Okay!"

"Okay?"

She asks, confused.

"Yes okay. We need to talk, but you can start first."

Because I have no idea what I wanted to say anymore. But not saying it out loud.

"Well do you have anything to say about what I said before you…kissed me?"

What did she say before that? Damn, I have no idea, by that time the only thing I was thinking was her lips. How they move, and how they should move somewhere else…

"Earth to Lan? I am here, where are you?"

She waves a hand in front of me, from where she is standing it looks like she is waving me "hello".

"I am here!"

"Yes of course you are! What did I say?"

Shit! What did she say? I really need to focus on her words not her body.

"Sorry you caught me! I was drifting out, can you please repeat? I am tired!"

Lame excuse, but I cannot really say that I envisioned her on her knees in front of me. She will run as fast as she can from here…focus Lan!

"Well before you kissed me. I was saying, I will pay you fifty thousand and I will save you from a marriage you don't want anyway. I know we agreed to do this for your mother, but now that Felicia girl is back you don't need me anymore."

She says anger in her eyes at the mention of Felicia's name. What do I say to that? How do I make her see I fall for her, without her turning around and bolt out this place and my life?

I say the first thing that crosses my mind at that moment.

"We had an agreement before the thing with your parents… which is half true… and Felicia has no place in this conversation or between us for that matter. If I wanted Felicia to be my wife, I would have said so. I don't want her!"

I stated my truth, but left out the reasons.

"In that case, you should make sure you don't share details of our agreement with her anymore. Because that is not okay with me. I left my father to make a fool out of me, but don't think for a second, I will let you or your "precious" do the same to me."

She says calmly but clearly.

"Are you jealous of Felicia?"

I ask more out of curiosity, and I want to see her reaction. As soon as she hears my question her face falls. Surprised by my question or the fact that I called her on it, not sure, but I got my response.

She is jealous of Felicia, You cannot be jealous, if you don't have feelings for the other person. Then it hits me hard…she does have feelings for me as well, and she meant what she said about the healing and marriage, a bit earlier.

Well this will be nice. I will make sure to make her admit that she has feelings for me.

"Where did you get that I'm jealous of that girl?"

She asks, bringing me back from my thought.

"OK then. You don't have a reason to back out from the deal. I do not want your money. I need you to keep your part of the deal as I keep mine. The quicker we got married the better. You said you don't want any party, is there a reason why?"

I try to change the subject by pushing the wedding further on and not give her a chance to give me more arguments as in why I need Felicia instead of her by my side.

"Isn't it obvious? I can't stand my father, I hate to be around a crowd that will always want to touch me in a way or another. And frankly the only people that matter to me, are in number of four and you know them all."

She says and my heart breaks for her at the mention of her father.

"OK it's settled then, we have a private ceremony without your parents!"

I say as surprise is clear on her face. I bet she expected a fight, but to be honest the less people know I got married the better. Places I used to visit are not for her, and her being my wife will make her a target so they can get to me.

"Just like that?"

"Just like that!"

"There is only one thing you are wrong about, and that's the fact that I cannot skip my parents from the wedding. They need to be there, if you don't want to present your mother with either the truth or another lie!"

She says and she makes perfect sense.

"What would you like to do then? You cannot stand your father, I would like to murder him for what he did to you. But, I need to be on my best behaviour for you and mom. If they come to the wedding, a disaster will follow I am sure!"

I state as I see her shock at the mention of me wanting to murder her father, but she is calm when she reply.

"I will talk to Vitaly to be there and guard them. For some reason he is the only one who can handle my father despite everything and after so many years."

"Good then! I will let you talk to Vitaly and settle that. One last question, when you think we could get married? I don't want to put pressure on you, but I would like it to be as soon as possible. So, by the end of this week we can start to move your stuff here. I will sleep in the office and you can take the bedroom. I don't want to force you to sleep in the same bed, if you don't want to."

I say without stopping until everything is out, so she could understand that I will never force her to do anything she doesn't want or feel comfortable with.

"Given the situation we are in, it's better to be sooner rather than later.   I still need time to work on my flaws. How about the 22nd of October sound? Because 11th is Renesme's birthday and she wants to go to a club or something like that."

She says and I am taken aback, because I believe she would want to steal more. I reply before she has a chance to change her mind.

"It works for me, as long as you agree with it! So we have a date set for the wedding then?"

I ask, smiling like a fool, it's not like it will be true. Not for her at least, because for me this starts to become more and more real, and for some reason I would be the happiest if she would feel the same.

"Yes we have a date!"

She answered smiling shyly. After we finish our conversation, she stands up and steps toward me slowly and shyly, because I never know how to act around her. I'm just frozen in place.

I expect her to go to one of the cabinets, but she keeps coming, until she is in front of me.

Staring me in the eyes, such a bold move for her.

I can tell she is up to something, I am not sure what.

When she whispers "Don't move, I want to try something. So stay very still!"

Anticipation hits me.

Is she going to kiss me?

No she wouldn't do that, but then I feel her soft hands on my chest.

I see her lift herself on the tip of her toes as she comes even closer to my face. Bending her head to her left, she's so close to my mouth, that I feel her breath on my lips.

She is going to kiss me!

On her own accord.

I will be damned if I stop her.

When she is not moving, I wonder what she plans.

Is she playing or what she has in mind?

All those questions are out the window as soon as she touches her lips with mine.

She kisses me slowly and I follow her lead, I don't want to scare her away.

I know I need to have patience.

The kiss turned from soft to passionate and I tried my best to not scoop her in my arms and take her to the bedroom. I am a man after all. When I hear her moan, I know for sure I need to stop. I raise my hand with the intention of hugging her, but I'm afraid she will panic.

Instead, I bring my hands to both sides of her shoulders, hesitating for a second there, but I need to stop this. Until I still have some control left in me.

Holding her by the shoulders, I softly stop the kiss and touch my forehead of hers. Squeezing my eyes close, I say.

"We need to take it slow, don't get me wrong. I want nothing more than to take you to bed right at this very moment and bury myself in you, so hard that we would mould into one, but you are not ready for that, yet."

It breaks my heart to turn her down, especially after such a bold move from her side. But I know now is not the time. If I am not careful and patient with her, she will run and hate me later. I want her to be able to enjoy and feel the special connection between a man and a woman.

To make her desire me the way, I desire her. Because, fuck, I want her so much. Especially after these two kisses we shared.

"Aham!"

Is all that comes from her so I ask her "Can I hug you now?"

She nods and I bring my arms around her bringing her closer to me in a hug, not too tight, so I will not freak her out. I am surprised when she wraps her arms around my waist hugging me back.

I will never be whole again, after this. Minutes later, she pulls back softly and I let go. Not because I want, but because I know I have to.

"I will go to bed, I am tired and today was hard for me, especially after Felicia."

She says and I remember I need to give her the key for the apartment.

"Don't move from the kitchen, I am coming back."

Without another word, I head to my office and grab the key. Coming back to the kitchen, I find her sitting at the table with her head on her hands, bent on top of the kitchen table. She looks so cute there, watching her like that, I hear her breathing is steady. She must have fallen asleep. I step closer, careful not to startle her. I touch her shoulder and whisper her name expecting to wake her up. Instead she moans.

"I want you!"

So low, at first I am not sure I understand her correctly. I call her again, only to get the same response, fuck me! Is she dreaming about me? I bend and scoop her in my arms, careful to not wake her as I make my way toward the bedroom. Once in there, I lay her down on the bed, covering her with duvet. I shut the lights and go out the bedroom, before I am too tempted to lay down next to her.

CHAPTER FIFTEEN

SVETLANA

As I get in the shower, I welcome the hot water over my body. I feel the tension leaving and it feels good to relax. It was a hard and long day today.

I positioned myself under the shower spray as I recall the events of the day, when I got to the kiss a warmth traveled my body again and this time, a different tension takes place within me.

A burning desire to do it again. Will he kiss me again? Probably no. He said, it was the only option he found at the time to make me keep my mouth shut. Can I do it? Can I kiss him? Yeah sure, like I would have that courage to get up and kiss him. And then what? It's not like I am ready to be taken to bed.

What if he wants more after I kiss him? So many questions in my head will make me crazy. I never knew desiring someone is so stressful.

After what felt like a long shower, I dressed in my new pyjamas a pair of shorts and a white top. Renesme told me to buy this one, especially if I move with Lan. That girl is mad when it comes to this. Once in my new PJs, I make my way to the kitchen to find a standing Lan staring at me, like I am naked. At this moment I feel so shy and ashamed. I should've stuck with my normal PJ.

He asks me if I want to eat, even if I already told him no. We go on talking about what happened and what we do further on, agreeing on a wedding day. Finally! I will have time to prepare and work on my flaws. To be, as ready as I can be for that horrifying day that it is supposed to be my dreams day. Well, I didn't think of my wedding day, or a wedding day for that matter, not after what my father did to me. I was absolutely sure I would end up alone for the rest of my life. I would be that alone auntie from the stories.

I told Lan that on 11th of October is Renesme's birthday and we… as in me Renesmee and Arthur… supposed to go to a club, but with Renesmee you never know what is going to happen in the next five minutes, let alone three weeks from now. As we finished the conversation I felt brave enough to actually stand up and go to him. Instructing him not to move as I am going in for the kiss, hesitating in the last second. What if he doesn't want this, but then again he kissed me first and now he is not moving. With that thought, I close the gap between our lips and enjoy the kiss, this time for real. I mean, the one before was not bad, but this…this is something else. This is passion, this is need, this is feelings. Before I even can go on, two hands on my shoulders push me softly as he breaks our connection.

Why? It felt so good. He explains what he feels about this and I am shocked at how much desire is in his voice, how good all those words make me feel.

He does want me… for me.

After everything he knows, Lan is not disgusted with me. Even more, he wants me.

Lan wants to be patient with me.

I think this is the second I'm officially falling for this guy, hard.

He even asks me if he can hug me and I nod, not able to form actual words. As soon as I am broth closer to his chest, I feel like I am home. This is my home. I never felt like this and I want him to know that. So, I wrap my hands around him. Until, I feel a burning desire for more, but before I can act on it, I tell him I will go to bed and he informs me not to move from the kitchen.

OK?

He disappears and I go to take a seat at the round table from the kitchen. I put my hands on the table, in a hugging gesture and rest my head on them, Lan returns to the kitchen and tells me that I'm the most beautiful woman.

He doesn't want to be far from me anymore, He demands that I should love him. For some strange reason I do love him, and I tell him that. I tell him that I have a burning desire to make me his. To love me and fuck me like no one ever did before. I want to be his and him to be mine. Enveloping me in his arms, he kisses me with passion and need. He is so hard. I can feel the bulge in his jeans next to my pussy, through the fabric of our clothes. Lifting me in the air, he carries me to bed. Laying me down he penetrates me as we both say each other's name. Pleasure takes over and we mould into each other, falling into a blissful sleep.

An annoying sound starts to ring. My alarm.

When I wake up Lan is nowhere to be found, did he leave? Was he here to begin with? Oh God, I dreamed about him. I was in the kitchen last time I remember.

Opening my eyes I realise I am in the bedroom, so he was here, we slept together? For some reason a joy feels to me. As I head to the bathroom to start my morning routine, I see his office door open and hear a soft snoring. Picking inside, I see a peaceful sleeping Lan. Sadness feels me in. We didn't sleep together.

Why am I sad? I should be relieved.

Do I want to share the bed with him? Yes, I would like to try, at least. I'm sure of that. With that in mind I go to the bathroom.

When I finish dressing and I'm fully prepared for my shit at café, I go in the kitchen hoping to have enough time to make the coffee for him and maybe, if I am lucky, a few sandwiches. I try my best to not make a sound.

I manage to have half the job done when I turn around to look for something and I see Lan standing in the doorway. With only a pair of jeans on his, so low on his waist that I could see the V lines of his pelvis bone. Good Lord, have mercy. I was staring and I had to react. I say the first thing that comes to my mind.

"I nearly had a heart attack!"

I bring one of my hands to my chest, all the blood is drained from his face.

"Are you ok?"

He asks, so concerned. I think he will be the one to actually have a heart attack.

"Yes I am ok, I was speaking figuratively!"

I can see him relax.

"I made some coffee and sandwiches, if you like we can have a quick breakfast before I go to work."

I inform him, praying he will say yes. He doesn't say anything, but takes a seat and starts to eat. I want to ask him if we slept in the same bed, but I am afraid he will take this the wrong way and I decide to keep my mouth shut.

"I wanted to give you the key to the apartment last night. You fall asleep by the time I return. Here is the key."

He says as taking out the key from his jeans pocket and hands it to me. I nod and thank him, but he continues.

"I couldn't let you sleep here. I put you in the bedroom so you can rest better, ahem… What did you dream about? You were whispering when I scoop you in my arms and lay you down the bed. I was afraid that you would wake up screaming again."

He tells me as I feel cheeks blushing, when I heard that I was talking in my dream. I don't talk in my dreams or maybe I do, hell I don't know.

"Did we sleep together? I mean in the same bed?"

I ask so I would not answer his question. What exactly I would say… Ah I dream of us on the bed, kissing like the world would end? No, I cannot say that. He starts to chuckle and I am brought back to the kitchen.

"What is so funny? It was a simple question."

"Your face was priceless when you asked if we slept together. No we did not. I just laid you down in bed and I slept on the office sofa. I told you I would not hurt you, and you are not ready for more, yet. I promise as soon as you are, I will be the one to make you feel a happy woman. To show you how being together with a man feels, and how worth the waiting you are."

He says, smiling at the beginning but very serious and cocky in his statement by the end. As he speaks, I feel the warmth sensation feeling my body. It's like the room suddenly starts to warm more than it should. Someone should turn the heating down. I notice that lately he has this effect on me, but I will never tell or complain about it. It feels so good.   I wonder what else feels good. What he can do to me, to make me feel even better than what I feel now? Unfortunately for me, I cannot carry on my day dream because he interrupted it.

"What time are you going to work?"

Changing the subject for my benefit or his, I'm not sure.

"In the next five minutes I need to leave. Why?"

"Because, I don't want you to be late and blame me after."

He says and we both laugh.

Days fly by and before I know it's Sunday. Today I will move in with Lan officially. I was spending time with him and sleeping at his apartment… Our apartment now, from the day I went to see him that morning.

It feels good to know he is there, to have breakfast and dinner together. To get to know this handsome man at a different level than other people. He is so handsome when awakes. Sleep makes his eyes look smaller than they are, his blond hair is in all directions when he wakes up, which makes me feel all sorts of things inside. In the last few days I have a burning desire to stick my fingers in his hair. To feel what kind of hair he has, is it as soft as it looks? The ways he looks at me makes me feel the most special woman in his life.

The kisses we share every morning and evening before the bed, make me feel things I never felt before for anyone. Yes we make it a habit to kiss each other, every morning before I go to work and every night before bed. The only difference is, at night I will have the pleasure to rest in his arms for a little while, before actually going to bed with an aching desire to take him to bed with me.

The other day I was dreaming we slept together, he was holding me, caressing my face and making love to me, needless to say I woke up covered in sweat. The more days passed, the closer we became, This desire only grows bigger. He keeps telling me that I am not ready. If he will carry on like that I think, I will never be ready.

"Are you ready?"

Lan asks and brings me to present. I am in the kitchen with a cup of coffee in my hands as I frown and ask him with confusion.

"Ready for what?"

"Ready to go and bring your things to the apartment. What else?"

He asks me, as disappointments set in. What did you expect from him, woman? That he will take you on top of the kitchen table?

"Ahem, yes I am ready."

He looks at me with curiosity all over him.

"What did you think you should be ready for?"

A hint of a smile covers his face. Oh, he wants it as much as I do. Only if he would not be so afraid to touch me, like that.

Maybe, I should be bolder and make the first move? One day probably I will, until then I need a lot of courage and strength.

"Nothing."

I say blushing, and he let it go.

We made our way to his car, an Audi Spyder, the same car I kicked his ass at our first race, of course he doesn't know that. And we head to my flat to start moving my things. Day goes by so quickly between moving lunch and more moving.

It's around nine in the evening when we finish everything. As we sat at the kitchen table, me with a can of Pepsi and him with a cup of warm milk… He was telling me milk helps him to sleep, whatever…I ask him curiously.

"You know, at the wedding reception, we will need to dance? Because I don't know how to dance."

He is looking at me like I lost my head in the parking lot.

"Have I said something wrong?"

"You've never been to a wedding? Of course we need to dance, that's what you do at weddings. And… if you don't know how to dance we could get a personal dance trainer or something to help you learn."

He says with shock and amusement in his voice. For him, it's like I just landed from the jungle. I did not feel the need to go anywhere crowded. When I was younger, it was hard enough to go to school, let alone to make friends that will disappear as soon as I told them I don't like being touched. After the first year of high school it became easier, because by then everyone would stop trying to talk to me and that was amazing. I had a comfortable peace. Go to school and come home. Sometimes I would not come out of my room, which was good for everyone.

"No, I have never been to a wedding before, no matter how crazy it sounds. After that night, I kind of isolated myself, like outside was a deadly virus or something. It was OK with everyone. Misha would come from time to time to ask me to play with him, but I never went further than our own yard."

A frown was on his face and pain in his eye, more like mercy. I hate that feeling on anyone's face. That's why I don't talk about these things.

"Then I can show you the recording of the weddings I have been to, and we need to put you in dance classes. What bride doesn't know how to dance?"

He is teasing I know, because we agree to do something private so I bet dance is not involved, or at least if I have my way, I will skip this part.

"Or you could show me how to dance."

I don't know what got into me to challenge him like that, but I did and now is too late to take it back. Gazing at him I can see his eyes full with desire and lust. Oh, he wanted me to say that, before I can say something or maybe change my mind he says.

"Done, if you are up to it I can start lessons now, we just need music."

Speaking so fast I'm afraid he will choke over the words.

"I am!"

I say a little too enthusiastic that he actually offered. He takes my hand, which by now I am comfortable holding it, and leads me to the living room, where we have enough space for anything he would decide to show me. Under his TV in the living Lan broth an audio home cinema with so many speakers. I have no idea what they are all for. Connecting his phone to it, he chose a song and before he hits play he stares into my eyes saying.

"This song reminds me of you when we went to lunch, and the way you looked then."

He presses play and Chris DeBurgh song "Lady In Red" starts to play. I am surprised he even knows the song, for an electro music fanatic like him. As the song fills the room, he comes closer to me, taking one of my hands in his and wrapping his other hand around my waist. He instructs me to put my free hand on his shoulder.

He starts to sway us easily as the song plays. It feels so nice, so intimate, and so perfect. I follow his moves, I have never danced before. We dance as the song is going, I rest my head on his chest closing my eyes and inhaling his scent.

His perfume is unique to me. It smells like power and masculinity. Lyrics of the song just make me go into another dimension. Where we love each other, where we share this moment as true lovers, where we are dressed as the song describes.

Me in a long bright red dress and him in that black slack suit with his blond hair in a beautiful styled mess, where his eyes are on me and only me. I'm the only woman he ever loves. As I let my imagination go with the song, I heard him whisper in my ear "I love you!" at the same time with Chris DeBurg in his song. I lift my head to look into his eyes and ask softly "What?"

Instead of answering me he closes the gap between our lips and starts to kiss me softly at the beginning, like he always does. Only this time our kiss becomes something else. Something more, passion, need for one another.

I brought my hand, that was on his shoulder, up to the back of his head and I lace my fingers with his soft hair.

A moan came out of both of us, normally by this time he always pulls back and gives me the "you are not ready" explanation.

This time, I'm faster and lock him in place with my hand. He surprised me by hugging me tighter. Both his hands wrapped around me. One goes up in between my shoulders and the other one to the lowest point of my back just above my ass, but not touching it.

In this way he pulls me toward him so tight that at some point I am sure we would mould one another, which makes me feel how hard he is for me.

This sends the warmth sensation in me to a higher level. That and his needy kiss, making me all a ball of fire. More moans escape us as we continue kissing.

This is the longest and needier kiss we shared until now, I don't want to stop. I want him to take it further, scratch that. I need him to take it further. I need him to help me make different memories about this experience. I want him to be my first and last man that I will ever desire. Even, if biologically I am not a virgin anymore, because my father ruined that. I am a virgin in so many other ways and I want him to be my first. To show me what a real connection between a man and a woman means. What sensation an orgasm can give and how it is to be on that cloud of rush and pleasure that Renesme was talking all the fucking time.

But, he stops before I can go on. I see lust in his eyes clear as day.

"Don't stop, please not now. We both need this!"

He kisses me again and scoops me in his arms. I straddle his waist with both my legs, and he holds me by each of my ass cheeks, even more pleasure traveling my body at this intimate position we share as he guides us to the bedroom, never breaking the kiss. Proving me how well he knows this apartment. Once in the bedroom, he lays me down on the bed and he puts one knee on the mattress as he slides down between my legs supporting himself on one arm, so he will not crush me under his weight. With his right hand he cups the side of my face, staring in my eyes he asks."

Are you sure about this? I can stop now."

"I don't want you to stop! I want to know how it feels when a man makes love to a woman!"

I am sincere, even if we don't make love. We are not in love, but I will not say that now. Apparently, that's what he needed to hear. He slammed his mouth to mine and started to kiss me again. This time more passion in the kiss. He lowered his hand easily down my neck and even lower, until he cups one of my breasts, never breaking the kiss. He squeezed gentle and I can tell my nipples are hardening for him. He starts to make circles with his thumb over the material of my top and bra. Few seconds later, he lowered his hand to my waist and slid it under my top, so careful like I'm a bomb about to go off.

Well I am, but not because I will be scared of him. He brings so much pleasure to my body, I am afraid I will burst in pieces, if he carries on like that. Slowly, lifting my top until he needs to stop the kiss. Making me feel the loss of our connection.

He lifted the top over my head and out of the way, followed by my bra. The second I am naked in front of him, I become shy, trying to cover myself with my hands. Only to be caught mid-way by his big and strong hands. Cupping my both hands in one of his guides them above my head, gazing at me.

"No need to be ashamed of me. I will never hurt you, not in that way at least!"

He bends down kissing me softly, this time cupping my breast with his hand and massaging my nipple, harding like a rock by his touch. This feels so good…so good.

He kisses me on my neck and behind my ear, bringing more pleasure to my body. Lowering his hand straight into the waist of my track suit trousers and in my panties right between my legs. As soon as he touched my clit a loud moan escaped my lips.

I can feel him smiling on my neck as he continues kissing me. Massaging my clit further, a burning pleasure like never before fills my body, making me part my legs even wider.

That's his invitation to fill me with one of his fingers. An "Oh" escapes my lips as he goes on This is the best I felt, even better than when I race at full speed.

He continues kissing his way to my breasts. When he cups a nipple with his teeth, slowly biting. At the same time as he is thrusting me with his finger, I arch my back and scream in pleasure.

This sensation is so good, pure pleasure created by this Greek God only for me. Only to me. He goes on, and I feel so full of this energy, I'm sure I will combust in flames.

"Laaann!"

I come so hard, everything is spinning. I need a moment to recover. He placed sweet kisses on my cheeks, giving me the time I need to come back from the ecstasy wave, I was driving a second ago.

I know if I let this moment go on too much, I will give him time to overthink things and he might go away.

Wrapping my hands, which by now are free from his hold, around his neck bringing him closer to me. He tries to pull back, but I don't let him. Suddenly feeling bold. Maybe it's the adrenaline, I don't know. I kiss him.

"I want you. And I want you to make me yours!"

For sure is the adrenaline, I never say things like this. But my statement ignites something in him.

He starts caressing me again. This time, sliding my trousers and my panties down my legs, starts to kiss his way up my tights.

Oh! This feels even better than before, if that's even possible. I am so happy I chose to shave today in the morning. Thank God for small miracles... before I can finish my thank you prayer to God, I am broth to the present moment by Lan lips and tongue as they touch my clit.

Holly mother of all saints! This is amazing!

Feeling the need to touch him, I lower both of my hands in his hair and push his head further in between my legs.

This is… is…I can't find a word to compare this. As he licks my pussy, my back arches from the mattress and more moans escape from me.

I need more.

I need… him.

I need to feel him, like fully feel him. Letting my mind speak for herself I say.

"I need to feel you!"

Desperation in my voice. If I can hear it, even in this state, I am positive he can as well. He chuckles.

"You are very demanding and impatient. No worries, we get to that part too. I just need you to relax a bit more!"

Relax…more? Man, I will explode in pleasure in a minute. You better hurry up! Before I can say anything else, his mouth is on mine swirling his tongue inside my mouth. Sliding down between my legs he says.

"If you want me to stop, just tell me."

Not able to speak, I just nod. He positions himself at my entry and fills me in one quick move. I feel a burning sensation at the beginning, but as he stays still and lets me get used to him being there, the pain fades away. As I relax he starts to move, slowly at the beginning increasing the peace as the sensation builds up. I am in full mode screaming in pleasure.

Hope no neighbours are indoors, but I don't really care about it, this is too good to stop.

Pleasure takes over my body, I move in sync with him now. We both moan and kiss and moan some more. He caresses my body and plays with my nipples. I am sure, this time I will really explode. I hear him say.

"Be a good girl and come for me!"

I am riding a wave of pure ecstasy that I never knew existed. Not long after, he follows me as he says my name.

Falling on top of me for a few seconds. Both struggling to catch our breath. As he lifts himself up he says.

"I am heading to take a shower and dispose of the condom. You can join me for showe,r if you like."

A condom, when did he put a condom? Looking at him, I take in this beauty that is in front of me. This time being able to admire his body, in full disclosure in my sight. Well defined muscle, like I already knew. Long defined legs and a huge cock.

"That was inside of me?"

This question got me a full laugh and a yes. Sending me in a full shy mode. God I was thinking out loud. I will die from this embarrassment. But, I noticed he doesn't have any more tattoos apart from the one on his hand.

"Do you want to join me in the shower?"

He repeated his question and I shook my head in "no" response. I am not talking after embarrassing me like that.

"OK. So what happens next? Do you want to sleep alone or I can come next to you tonight?"

He asked me with fear in his voice. Fear of what?

"You can come back and sleep with me, tonight."

I say, until I am still brave, well an embarrassed brave.

"Deal."

And he goes to shower, as soon as he comes out, I take his place in the shower.

Thinking about what happened just minutes ago.

Will this change something in our crazy game of marriage?

Will we be able to step away from one another when this is over?

Or we will fall in love and stay married, maybe more.

I know I'm in love with him. He is my first love, hopefully my last too.

But, is he in love with me? Will he ever be in love with me? So many questions that make my head spin, and a small headache come to surface. Before panic sets in, I step out the shower and go to bed where I find a sleeping Lan, in all his beauty.

Looking at him how he sleeps peacefully. I realise, believing my father ruined me, is nothing compared with what will happen when this man decides to end things. I will be turned into nothing. I will become like ashes after a strong burning fire. With that realisation, I lay in bed next to him, pull the cover and shut the light.

CHAPTER SIXTEEN

RUSLAN

Days passed by quickly with her. We kind of have a routine of ours, we take breakfast together, before she goes to work. Kiss her once she is nearly out the door for her shift.

Taking dinners when she comes back, kiss and hug her before bed. I would love to sleep next to her, but she is not ready for that. I can see, she thinks she is, but I know she is not.

Sometimes she jumps, if I speak too loud.

Or freeze, if I come close too quickly.

She believes I don't see it, but I do. And it kills me inside, she still doesn't fully trust me. I will never hurt her, not in this way at least. I still have a lot of flaws, but I would never do that to her or any woman for that matter.

I have been raised better than that.

My mother made a point in teaching me how to respect a woman. Bring her flowers and always, no matter what, talk nice to a woman. Treat her nice and with respect.

Probably that's why I never did anything to Felicia, even if she did sleep with my best friend. Hell they have a five years relationship and I still didn't break their neck, as I probably should. I chose to go on and let them be.

Today is Sunday. Today it's the day Lana is moving in with me officially. I was thinking of this day a lot before, and I was terrified. But today, I'm happy. I feel good to have her here, to know that she is here with me. I can watch her sleep every night. It brings me peace to look at her how she sleeps. Maybe for many is creepy, but for me it's relaxing and brings peace inside. She is the calm in my storm. She thinks that her hot temper will make me leave, she is wrong, I am not scared of her.

Lana's hot temper will not be a problem for me. I will be the cold water to her hotness, and she isn't getting rid of me.

As I walk in the kitchen I see her day dreaming, which makes me smile. She is so far gone in her head, she doesn't even hear me as I approach.

"Are you ready?"

Confusion is all over her face. What was she dreaming at?

"Ready for what?"

I explain to her that we need to go and bring her stuff. Ask her what she was dreaming of, but I get nothing from her. Seeing redness surface on her face, I just let it go. Not wanting to embarrass her further. It takes all day to move her things to my apartment, for someone who looks like a widow most of the time, she has so many things. But what surprised the hell out of me, was the amount of makeup she has.

I don't get her, if she never uses make up.

Why does she have so many?

I got a clarification of that fact when I asked her. She told me she was a makeup artist, but she didn't like the way she was treated at a few fashions shows, and just gave up the idea of that.

It's around nine when we sit at the kitchen table. Me with my cup of milk and her with her Pepsi. She drives me crazy with that Pepsi, but I can't make her give up on it. She asked me a crazy question, if we need to dance at our wedding. Sure as hell I would like to have her in my arms, so I give her a positive answer. Only to be told that she never was at a wedding and most of her youth she isolated herself.

I felt so sorry for her, for all the experiences she missed out there. She could have had a nice teen age period, if she wouldn't have a shit of a father. That thought alone brings angriness to me. When she challenges me to give her a dance lesson, I jump at the occasion.

This will help me calm down and give me the chance I was hoping for, to hold her in my arms, more than what I do every night she goes to sleep. Once she agrees so excitedly, I take her hand and lead the way to living, thinking of a song that will make it easier to keep her close to me.

An image of her wearing the red dress, that makes things to my body every time I see it in my head, comes to my mind and I know the perfect song.

Chris DeBurgh "Lady in Red" song.

This will be our first dance together, I want to make it memorable for her to. I tell her this song makes me think of her and I see how surprised she is that I know the song.

She thinks I am an electro guy just because that is all I listen to around her, so I will keep myself in check. Not wanting to scare her off acting on my feelings and emotions.

Once the song starts I get closer to her. Take one of her hands in mine, her hand looks so small in my large hand, it's like holding a toddler hand. I wrap the other hand around her waist and pull her closer to me. Telling her to put her free hand on my shoulder, and she listened. By the way, the song is playing, we sway in sync. This song made me think, how would it be to actually have a normal relationship? A normal marriage? She rested her head on my chest. That alone makes my heart beat faster and my cock stir to life.

Get a grip Lan, is not the time for this yet. God if she knew how much I like her, how I started to feel about her.

If I could tell her "I love you!" she would understand what she means to me. Before I could even go further, she lifts her head and asks "What?" The way she looks at me is pure love. She is so beautiful that it pains me. Without thinking I kiss her not replying to her question. I start soft like always. Because, I always expect her to pull back if it's too much for her. Instead, she carries on. This time different, more passion, more need, she brings her hand to the back of my head and plays with my hair. I wanted to pull away to stop for her sake, but she locked me in place with her hand.

I squeeze her tighter in my arms, one hand between her shoulder and one just above her fine ass. Even, if I have itchy fingers to touch her ass I can't. Not wanting to scare her, I pull away only for her to tell me.

"Don't stop, pleeee not now. We both need this!"

Fuck me. I knew I needed it for a long time, but I never in a million years believed she needed it, too. That's all I need to kiss her back, bend just enough so I can catch each of her legs and part them as I lift her in my arms. By now she has her legs wrapped around me and makes me want her more. Probably she looks like a monkey that is holding me tight for dear life. I make my way to the bedroom with her. Never breaking the kiss. I know this apartment with everything it's in it, from the back of my mind. Because, memorising helped me not to break things every time I came home wasted from the casino. As I hit the bed with my legs, I bend and lay her down. I bring a knee on the mattress and lower myself between her legs, asking her if she is sure about this, if not I will stop. It will pain me, but I will stop. For sure I will need an ice cold shower. She assures me that she's okay with it and wants to know how it feels when a man makes love to a woman.

Fuck me hard!

I will make sure to make it as memorable for her, as it will be for me. She can be sure, I will make love to her, even if we are as further away as possible from being lovers. Or, from her point of view. I know I fell for her a long time ago.

Kissing her ever more she moans and I am fucking gone. So, in love with this crazy strange woman. I will never recover after this. I start to kiss her neck and behind her ear which gives me more moans from her. Oh, this is heaven! Lowering my hand, I cup one of her breasts and squeeze gently. I feel her nipple hardening through her bra and her top that drives me crazy. Deciding I need to feel it in my hands without the barrier of her top. I lower my hand and easily bring her top up so gently. I want her to feel comfortable with me, but most I want her to enjoy this. Once her top is out of the way her bra follows, she starts to cover herself. Oh no baby! You will not do that.

Catching her hands mid-way I tell her.

"Is no need to be ashamed of me, I will never hurt you, not in that way at least!"

Cupping her breast with my hand fits so perfect. It's like she is made just for me. Kissing her further, I lower my hand straight in between her legs. I start to massage her clit, more moans come from her and it makes me feel good.

So proud of me, but most so proud of her.

She came a very long way until this moment and looked at her now… displayed for me to admire and touch her… only for me to caress.

Carrying on, massaging her clit as placing more kisses, she comes so hard that she shakes underneath me.

Allow her to catch her breath. Still feeling the need of contact and I place kisses on her checks. She surprised me by pulling me to her and kissing me. If she doesn't stops I will fuck her for sure. But, I need to be able to control myself and take everything slow.

I think for tonight, I accomplish a lot with what I just did. Except, Lana's plans are different from mine's as she says.

"I want you. And I want you to make me yours!"

What can I say? Nothing! I take her trousers and panties off her and bury my head between her legs, as she puts her hands on my head and pushes me further into her.

Man she is brave! More than I gave her credit for.

"I need to feel you!"

Desperation in her voice, which makes me think of Trevor Daniels song "Falling." It's so appropriate for us, for our situation. Especially in this moment. I will make her fall for me. I will spend the rest of my life to make sure she falls for me and never think of another man. I chuckle at her comment and reply.

"You are very demanding and impatient, but no worry we get to that part too. I just need you to relax a bit more!"

I move up to kiss her mouth. Parting her leg further and telling her,

"If you want me to stop just tell me."

Not sure how I will be able to stop now. But she shakes her head no and I enter her in one quick push. Never having to deal with this before, I am not sure how to act, but for sure I don't want to hurt her. I stay as still as possible, until she relaxes, I start to move slowly at the beginning, but increase my peace as I see pleasure takes place instead of pain. She is so tight and she feels so good. Like this is home. After so many years and so many women, she is my home and she will always be. I will be ruined if she decides to ever leave me after all of this.

She ruined me for any other woman. I can see she is so close and I tell her.

"Be a good girl and come for me!"

She comes so hard screaming my name. It's like fireworks take place under me on the mattress, with my name on them. Seeing her unfold under me I come as well, feeling the condom I placed when she was so demanding earlier.

It feels so good, she is mine now. I'm the one man in this world to make her feel so much pleasure, to make her feel what pure love means. She is my pure love and I will make sure I will be the last man who ever touches her in this way.

I want nobody to ever touch her or make her feel this way. Man, I have a big ego and an even bigger jealousy. I know I will kill anyone who touches her from now on, because she is mine. Mine alone.

Lifting myself from her I tell her I will go to shower and ask her if she would like to join me. When she says "That was inside of me?" so shocked. I burst in laughter, she is so sweet and she just praised my ego without her even knowing. I repeat my question and she shakes her head no. I want to go to shower. But then, I don't know if I should come back or head to my sofa. I decide to ask her and I am so fucking happy when she agrees to let me sleep with her in my bed.

After I return from shower she takes my place. I lay down in my bed after more than a week. I'm thinking how wonderful this was. How I would like to repeat this experience with her. How wonderful it would be if she would fall in love with me as I fell with her. If she will love me as I love her. Then we will have a real family. As I am thinking about all this I feel my eyes closing and fall asleep before she even returns from shower.

I wake up wrapped in one another's arms. I was on my back and she was nearly on top of me with her leg between mines, my arm wrapped around her body. She has her head resting on my chest like it was her pillow.

I could get used to waking up like this, it is an amazing sensation to have her in my arms so early in the morning.

I try to get off the bed without waking her, because I really need to use the bathroom. After succeeding this, I head to the kitchen to make some coffee and sandwiches in a few minutes her alarm will get off. She wakes up minutes later and comes straight in the kitchen attacking the sandwiches and the coffee, she is so cute. We go with our morning routine until she goes to work and I go and see mom. Let her know about the wedding, and try to pull some strings to make sure no press will be present. Lana doesn't want to be in any tabloids or paper. Driving to Southend-on-Sea to see my mother, which is an hour or so out of London. I already feel Lana is missing. I never believed I would love anyone after Felicia. If someone would have told me, I would fall in love with this girl when I saw her, I would have laughed in their faces. Now, I cannot wait for the day we will get married. Hell, I cannot wait until the next time I will be buried in her warmth again. She is it for me. No one else. I pray to God to let her stay and not take her away like he does with mom.

Arriving at my parents home from England, I park the car and go inside, up the stairs and up to my mother's room. Dad said a couple of days ago that she is weaker these days and rests a lot.

I know she will be in her room, which is the one at the right, as you stay on top of the stairs. I knock softly, I do not want to wake her in case she sleeps. But, she responded.

"Come In dear!"

I walk in and I can see my mother in the double bed she has in the middle of the room.

A night stand and a lamp on top of it, on each side of the bed. Her huge wardrobe, the same colour of walnut wood as the bed and nightstands are, fills the left wall of the room.

As you face the bed, on the right side of the bed is the window where she has a small coffee table with two armchairs, where probably sits with dad when she is too tired to go out.

The wall behind her bed is a white, curtain and drapes are a shade of cream matching with everything in the room and offering as much light as possible.

I take a seat on the side of the bed she is in, bending so I can kiss her too skinny cheeks, letting her pin scent to bring back so many happy memories.

"How do you feel today? Dad said you haven't been yourself these days. As in, you sleep too much and pain starts to surface."

I explain, remembering the doctor told us that by the time she gets closer to her leave, the pain will grow as well. That happens when you have stage IV of cancer. I wait for her tired eyes to open. I take her in. She lost a lot of wait, her face drawn and all white, not like the old times when she had full cheeks, and a shade of red in them, much like Lana when is shy.

Her blue eyes are so tired without the spark for life that once was there and her voice is hoarse and tired.

This is the first time when I realise, she doesn't have much time left. It feels like a fucking punch to my stomach that brings tears to my eyes. I wasn't supposed to cry.

I was supposed to be here and gave her good news, to make her happy. At the end of the day, I came so long in everything I did including Lana and my love for her, because of the woman in front of my eyes. Only she doesn't look like the woman I knew. She doesn't have the energy that once made her the greatest mother of all. She still is the greatest mother, but without energy. If I could, I would trade places with her in a split of a second.

As she opens her eyes the second time, she realise I am crying like a fucking baby. Bringing her hand to my cheeks and caressing them with her thumb, like she always did when I was a child.

"Hey, don't cry I am here. I will be here to see you on your wedding day. I am just a little tired, because I woke up early today."

She smiles so kindly at me as she rests her hand on the duvet again. She encourages me, when it is supposed to be the other way around. But the more I think, I'm taken aback of this shit happening with her. I don't know why.

I mean I know it's hard for all of us, but I was always here with her. Always next to her no matter the stupidest thing I went through, she was there and I was there.

She is my best friend and soon, I will be forced to speak about her in the past. And that makes me burst in cry so bad. I bend and hug her waist through the duvet, just to realise how much weight she lost. She doesn't say a word, she just lets me cry my eyes out. She knows once it's all out I will be calm and able to speak. After what felt like a lot of time, I lifted my head and she smiled again telling me.

"Ruslan, what did you do to those beautiful eyes of yours? You made them red now."

We both started to laugh, she always said that to me after I cried. I nod and laugh some more.

"That's my boy see, all happy!"

"I actually came here to give you great news. Instead, I made a fool of myself. I am supposed to be the one to support you, not the other way around."

I said as she waved me off.

"Nonsense, I am your mother and I will support you no matter what, cancer or not. Now give me the great news of yours!"

"On the 22nd of October I will marry Lana, that's in about three weeks. So you better be there or I will be very… very mad on you!"

I say as I smile and she smiles back, a light in her eyes now. I gave her a reason to be happy again.

"You can make sure I will be there, she is a wonderful girl. But what I really want to know is this…are your fillings real? Because you do not fool me, my sweet boy. I could see that you like her, but unlike at the restaurant something changed in your eyes when you talk about her now. And I know for sure she loves you more than she will probably ever admit. The way she handled Felicia and what she told her in the bathroom proves me, she is so much in love with you. So tell me boy, do you love her?"

As my mother talks I frown at her words. How does she know what Lana and Felicia talked in the bathroom? Since she was at the same table with me at that time. Then again we are talking about my mother. She knows everything she puts her head to know, being there or not. I will ask her what she knows about that conversation, but I decide to start with her last question

"I do love her mother. I fall for her worse than I ever did for anyone before, Felicia included…"

"That cannot be true, tell me that you just lied now!"

A screaming and very demanding Felicia comes to me, as fast as light. As she raises her hand to slap me, I catch her in the air before actually making contact to my face. What the hell is wrong with these womans? What the fuck is she doing here in this house, in these room?

"First never, ever raise your hand to me again. Second, what the hell are you doing here? This is supposed to be a conversation between me and my mother. For your own good, speak before I will do something I will regret."

I warn her trying to keep my voice at bay and my anger in check, because of my mother's presence. But, when she doesn't speak I growl at her "SPEAK" so loud that even my mother jumps.

"Ruslan! I did not raise you like that!"

She is right she did not raise me like that. So still holding Felicia's hand I face my mother.

"I am sorry for scaring you. That is true you did not raise me like that, that's why she is still alive…"

Turning to Felicia and continuing

"…but we have some unfinished business to discuss. I will come back to see you before I leave."

I storm out from my mother's room, dragging along the woman I once loved, out of the house in the backyard. Here, I can scream my lungs out, because all my patience with this woman is gone by now. Not even hate I have toward her. Just disgust and irritation that she doesn't leave me the fuck alone, after so many years. She was the one to fuck my best friend and decide they want a relation behind my back. I was the blind fool that they made fun of.

I stop once I am in the garden, turning to her and grab her by both her arms, I scream.

"What the fuck you are doing here?"

She never saw me so angry, is understandable she is scared out of her fucking mind. But I do not care anymore, I am tired playing nice to her and with that fucker of her boyfriend. I am tired of all of this stupid game of hers. What she wants? Why now after so many years? Until she didn't know about Lana she couldn't even talk to me. Why the sudden change? Is she jealous?

Well, too bad because I don't give a fuck anymore. Not about her, not about any of them. Except, the woman I shared my bed with last night. The woman that showed me how is to be broken, but to fight as fucking hard to put yourself together for love. Realising she didn't say a work I scream louder.

"SPEAK! Before I make you speak!"

She is crying shitless scared, trying to speak

"Julia…Julia told me you are here and… I wanted to talk to you… I wanted to tell you that…that, I am sorry and…and, I made a huge mistake than… and I want you back!"

I expected everything, but not this. What the fuck? And why was Julia talking to her about me? I made it clear, I don't care if they are friends as long as they don't talk about me. My sister knows that and if she doubted me before about this matter, I will make it clear this time. She needs to fucking understand that.

"What the hell are you talking about? You are with Ivan and you've made that choice. It wasn't me who fucked him and laughed in your face. It. Was. You!"

I scream, not able to calm myself down. Well, maybe it's for the better, at least I have to say my part after so many years in this shitty situation.

"We broke up, we are not together for like 5 months now."

She says, so fast like this is supposed to make me feel better. Well it didn't, I don't care anymore about any of them. I will still have a discussion with Julia about that big mouth of hers.

"Why did you fucked his best friend too?"

I bite back, and she flinches.

"Lan, you don't understand I just felt alone. Because you were playing so much and you were more drunk than sober. I wasn't enough anymore. You left me before I did! But you were so selfish, you didn't even care to admit it to yourself …and when I couldn't take it anymore, you went and played the victim card."

She is screaming now and I let go, like she suddenly burst into flames.

"What are you talking about? I saw you at the casino, the first time you slept with him. I was there! I heard everything! You were so into each other, you didn't even see me in the corner of my uncle's room "because Lan never comes here" and that was before I started to drink. Actually I started to drink because sober I could not stand you anymore."

As I use Ivan's words to her she brings her hand to her eyes and starts to cry louder, I am so cold toward this woman, it's like my heart suddenly became stone.

"It was your uncle that told Ivan to use his room, because you don't go there. And, I bet it was your uncle telling you to stay there too, am I right?"

I feel like she slapped me across the face.

"Yes, it was Nikolai who told me. But what has this to do with everything?"

"Well you should ask him, why didn't he marry your priceless Lana then?"

She screams from the bottom of her lungs, as a deep voice calls her name "Felicia!" in both warning and angriness.

When I look away from her face, Nikolai sits in the doorway. For the first time, I understand why they are calling him "mountain executioners". He is even bigger than it was a few months ago, when I last saw him. Normally I am happy to see him. Now, I have a burning desire to break his neck and make him swallow his own tongue. That doesn't make any sense, but anyway the feeling is the same.

"What is she talking about?"

I ask in both warning and angriness. From the corner of my eyes, I see Felicia wanting to go back in the house, but I am faster than she is and much stronger than she is that's for sure.

In one step I am next to her, wrapping my hand around her arm, I warn her in a calm but angry tone.

"If you don't finish what you started, you may see a part of me that only Nikolai knows. And believe me when I say, it's not pleasant at all!"

This is more… the silence before the storm, a storm that is about to become a full blown cat 5 hurricane.

She looks at Nikolai pleading. For what? I don't know. He shakes his head no, in warning.

Just to make a point, I squeeze her hand so hard. I am positive tomorrow will have the evidence there. I hate myself for that, never hurt a woman and I don't want to start with her, but I need them to talk and I know for sure she will talk out of fear. The only problem is that she is more afraid of Nikolai than me.

"He is going to kill me!"

She says to Nikolai. So afraid and like I could not hear them.

"I am here you know! I can fucking hear you!"

I say as she cries.

"Ruslan! Let her go, we can talk like men. Your mother raised you better than to threaten a poor scared woman."

Nikolai says, so calm. Dam, the man knows me and he knows that if he keeps his tone low, I will calm down. I would never hurt her, more than I did.

"Nikolai, I respect you more than you understand, but… this time we are talking about my future wife. So… is better if any of you two speaks before… I go for your heads!"

I state, anger obvious in my tone as I stare in his eyes.

"Fine!"

He agrees as calmly as before. But whatever plan he had in mind is blown by Julia. Like a castle of cards blown by wind, when she screams.

"Petrov killed Ana and sold Lana to Nikolai".

And in a split of a second, next things happen. I am so stunned by Julia's confession, I feel like my hands transformed in jelly as I let go of Felicia's hand.

Causing Felicia to stumble on her feet. Nikolai closes his eyes, but in a split of a second opens them with a predatory look in them and wraps his even bigger than mine hand around Julia's neck, making me want to kill him. Even more like before, only if I would not be so stunned by what the fuck I heard. All these things happen so fast but so slow at the same time, I feel dizzy by the speed in my head. I close my eyes and try to process everything. Taking a few seconds, I open my eyes as Nikolai says to Julia.

"When I tell you to use Ana's name then use it. Until, then if you dare one more time to speak her name, I will not remember you are my niece. Now go in the house and take Felicia with you. I need to speak with Ruslan. ALONE."

And with that both women disappear in the house. Taking a deep breath, Nikolai guides me to the table that mother has in her garden.

"Please take a seat, calm down and open your mind. I promised you a long time ago that I will never lie to you, as you are like my son. I taught you everything you know, especially how to run a business. Today I need you to be more open minded than you already are and don't let your feeling for anyone come in between this."

He says as we take a seat. Looking at him, I am afraid that the chair will break under my uncle's weight, but I nod to what he said. He treated me like an adult all my life and he was always honest with me, no matter how ugly the truth was.

"Nine years ago, we found out that someone stole and sold our merchandise as their own. We tried our best to be as quiet as possible, especially because your father was looking at a career overseas. And your mother's disease being at the beginning, we wanted to be as quiet as possible, in case your mother got worse, as she did. We wanted your family to be able to move here."

He starts, but I cut him short.

"Mom has cancer for like 5 years, so this is a lie from the beginning, try again!"

I say starting to get angry again.

"No, your mom has cancer for like nine years. She fought with it and at the beginning she was strong enough and beat it. But three years later, it returned and it was worse than before. Then they decided to let you and your brothers know, it was too obvious to hide it anymore. So, like I said Vory supported your father and wanted to give your mother a chance to cure this disease. She was not only your father's wife but our sister as well. Your mother helped us more times than we can count. So this was our time to help her, to return the favour. Problem was that Petrov wife was too jealous and stupid. She always competed with your mother and wanted Sergei as her husband. Only Sergei did not want her, so to get back on Sergei she slept with Petrov, only to find out she was pregnant a few months after. She caused a scene and wanted to frame Sergei on that, but with no luck. She ends up marrying Petrov. He wanted to be in Vory before all this, but never trusted him enough for that. When all the drama went down between them and Sergei, I used that to wash my hand of them. It did work, until nine years ago when Petrov came to me one night and tried to make a deal. He told me he would wed his daughter to me if I let him in Vory and that will be a guarantee for me he will never turn his back on me. Of course I didn't agree to that. That girl was about your age, way too young for being someone's wife, let alone a Vory wife. She needed to grow and had a life ahead of her. Petrov went further and found out about Ana, it is still a mystery to me how he did this, but he did. I believed I was careful enough and no one would know, but apparently I was just in love. He manage to find our thief, again a fucking mystery how he did it, but he did it.

He told me that the fucker wanted to run with his daughter and when she refused, he raped her. He insisted he heard the guy telling someone that he did the same with Ana, just before killing her. Pointless to say, I saw red and no matter how many times that guy denied, I beat the shit out of him until he passed away. Beaten my anger, my frustration and what he did to

Ana, my Ana. With this, we agree to let Petrov get in the Vory family, with a few important restrictions that you know about. I had no reason to be against this anymore. He did what we couldn't do. He, an outsider, found the thief within our family, he scored more points that I couldn't dismiss. Except, at one point we heard that he hired a few guys to beat the shit out of Vitally, and that made me despite him more than I already did. You do not pretend to love someone like a brother, but hire people to kill him. I had no proof to stand in front of Vory. As you know, even if I am the president I still needed a solid proof for what was happening, other than some guy's words. Later when I talked to Vitaly, he told me it was a misunderstanding between the two of them. I heard that Vitaly by then was protecting Lana from her father. It made me curious but never asked, I knew better than that. However, I appreciate the hell out of Vitaly for that and told him anytime he needs help with anything, no matter what it is. Even if it is an illegal matter, I will be the man to help him. He stood in front of Petrov the way it did, even if I have no idea what he did. When Vitally came to me a year or a year and half back to ask my help to bring that girl in London, I boarded her on the first plane and got her out of Russia. Because I knew if Vitaly was asking for it, some serious shits was about to go down. I couldn't wait to put my hands on Petrov and get rid of him once and for all. Unfortunately, nothing happened. I still wait to find things about Petrov. This is what happened then and what the girls were talking about."

Nikolai finishes his story and with the exception of correcting his mistake about mom I didn't stop him. Listening every word he said to me, with more attention than ever. I knew I didn't like this Petrov guy. Now I hate the guy and that makes me tell Nikolai

"What no one knows, is this. The guy you killed with your bare hands was not your thief…Nikolai turns his head to look at me so fast I was afraid he will break his neck, and even if his eyes are so wide looking like walnuts in his head, he doesn't say a word. And I continue… Lana wasn't running with anyone, her father raped her that night pretending he is preparing her for you. And when she didn't appreciate the lesson, he beat her inches within her life. Vitally took her to hospital, because Misha called him that her father beat the hell out of Lana. I guess Misha and Sergei came home the wrong time, or in Lana's case the exact right time to save her from the beast she calls father, to this day. For all of this to get better, a couple a weeks ago, when I went to collect the debt from Petrov. I found Lana screaming at him like a lunatic, at that moment it didn't make any sense why she would scream at a man she doesn't know. As soon as I realised she was his daughter, I wanted her out of his reach. Even if at the time I had no idea what he did to her, and told them the debt will be paid if she marries me. They agree way too quickly, like she was some rotten merchandise they did not know how to get rid of. I found out later that night what the reason was behind the fastest agreement I had in my negotiations history. Misha told me, the deal was that they expected me to marry her and secure his place in the family. Only for Lana to tell me what happened with her that night. I decide that I will go on with marriage. Because one, I fall for this broken girl and two, because I work hard to catch Petrov with something, so he will never touch her again. I will find a way to take him out of the family. So far, I found out that the guy he was handed to you as "the thief" had a sister Ana. Not sure if it is the same Ana or not, but that it's what I found out until now."

By the time I finished my story, my uncle was a ball of anger ready to explode with eyes so big, I was really concerned about him. He looked like anytime his eyes would jump out of their sockets, like in cartoons I used to watch as a child.

"When were you planning to tell me?"

He asked me so low, I barely heard him.

"As soon as I would have more proof. This is the way that it is in Vory, no?"

He just nods. After a few moments or maybe minutes of silence he turns to me, places his hand on my shoulder and says with conviction.

"If you really love this girl, then go on and marry her. Don't do it for only your mother, and before you came with a lame excuse, I thought you to think the way you do. I knew what your plan was as soon as I heard about marriage. But again if you love her go on. Make sure you protect her from him. I will be there on your wedding day, to make sure Petrov is kept in control. If you don't love her then let her go. I promise I will make her disappear and I bet Elena will understand once I explain her how things are."

"I do love her, as in real love. I never fall for anyone the way I did for this girl. I will make it top priority in my life to protect her, not only from her father but anyone who wants to touch her in that way. As for my mother I would like if she will be kept in the dark. She has a lot going on. Vitally will be at the wedding too, so between you and Vitally I think Petrov will behave."

We discussed it a little longer, before heading back in the house to see my mother. By now she is soundly asleep, I just watch her sleep, thanking God that I have another day with her. After what felt like an hour, I headed to Julia's room.

Her room is like a little girl's room. All pink and purple, pink bed frame, purple wardrobe that is bigger than my moms, with purple curtains, pink makeup table with a pink furry chair to match.

What the hell?

I find my sister sitting on top of her bed, with some magazine in her hands, rolling her eyes when she sees me.

"Look, I thought we made it clear by now, do not talk about me with your precious friend"

I say as soon as I close the door of her room behind me. I am known for being direct, especially with her. She tries to defend herself, but I cut her short.

"I don't care about an explanation, I want you to tell me two things. One, why do you hate Lana so much, when you don't even know her? And second, I know you told mom about the conversation between Lana and Felicia in the restaurant toilet, and before you deny mom told me. You know, she tells me everything!"

I hold my hand up and count on my fingers as I speak. Bluffing the last part, but after her reaction, my weak poker hand of cards, just became my best.

"I don't hate the girl, she looks nice and she's kind of OK. I just really hate her father, after everything Felicia told me, he is bad. I am afraid she will take after him. And you will become the same way you were after Felicia. The only reason we stayed friends was, maybe you will get back together with her. But now she ruined everything and she will make Lana's life miserable, if you don't pay attention. She did say to Lana that you spent time together and you gave her the key to your apartment. She said that every time you fight, you will find a way back to one another. That's what they were talking about in the bathroom. But I need to tell you. I started to appreciate her when Felicia told me what Lana replied. And mom is a traitor, like always when it comes to you."

And with that she closed her mouth.

"What did Lana say to Felicia?"

Curiosity getting the best of me.

"Apparently, mom did not tell you everything, isn't it dear?"

She says the last part trying to make a voice like mom. I know she will say nothing more.

"You should know by now, that mom never tells me what she talks with you or Vladimir, she never did. She always told me that, in the way I am able to trust her, all her children should be able to do that. But with you, it was always easy, I know you have a big mouth."

She makes a shocked face, and screams.

"You jackass! I hate you!"

"Shhh! You will wake up mom! I love you too don't worry!" I say, leaving her room.

Heading to my car and back to London. By the time I am back in my apartment it's around half nine.

As I go into the bedroom to change for shower, I see a sleeping Lana. She is so beautiful it takes my breath away. Showering as fast as I could. I go back to bed, wrapping my hands around her body. Pulling her close to me as I drift to a peaceful sleep.

CHAPTER SEVENTEEN

SVETLANA

Ruslan woke up first the next morning preparing some sandwiches and coffee. As soon as I smelled the fresh coffee, I followed him in the kitchen carrying on with our morning routine until I left for work. Ruslan told me he is going to see his mother outside London. The day at the café was good until we were close to finishing. Felicia came apparently to see me, this girl is something else, I swear.

"Hello Lana, how are you? I am so happy to see you!"

"Why did nobody answer your calls anymore and decided to force me into a friendship?"

I ask sarcastically. Why would she be happy to see me?

"No darling, don't go so far. I just wanted to let you know that I spent some quality time with Lan at his parents property and he informed us that you will get married on 22nd of October. I just wanted to come and congratulate you personally. So congratulations!"

I force my face not to fall in her trap. Plastering the most honest smile I could master in that moment. Refraining my mind to envision some horror ways I could kill her, like right now. Man this woman has some nerves, this time I would not play into her hand. I make a mental note to let Lan know about this.

"Well I hope you enjoyed your quality time with Lan, because that's pretty much what you will have left once we get married. By the way don't you get tired of this spectacle that you play? It's not getting boring to keep running after someone who doesn't want you? I mean, yes you maybe spend some "quality time" with my fiancée. But at the end of the day he is marrying me, not you. How does that make you feel? I would have more dignity than to chase my ex around like a puppy, only to be left out every time!"

As I talk her face displays pure shock. She gets so red that I am afraid steam will come out her ears, like in the cartoons. At that thought I forced myself not to laugh in her face, I had to finish what I had to say. As soon as I finish my part of this conversation, I turn around on my hills and leave her there in the middle of the café, looking exactly like a lost puppy.

Once my shift is done, I walk to the apartment admiring the water, it is so amazing how at the surface it seems so calm. With only a few lazy waves traveling from one side to another, but if you go deeper all her currents are pulling you deeper and deeper. It makes me compare the river with Lan, at the beginning he seemed so calm and peaceful. The more time I spend with him he is pulling me deeper and deeper. Making me fall for him more and more. This is all so scary but so wonderful at the same time just like the river is.

Feeling tiredness taking a toll on me I go upstairs in the apartment. Take a shower and go to bed. Lan didn't return yet. I sleep so peaceful until the next day, I wake up with Lan's arms wrapped around me.

Two weeks passed like a blink of an eye, and here we are getting ready for Renesmee's birthday. This makes me remember I have only 11 days until my wedding with Lan.

In the end we are going to a club like previously decided. But of course Renesme being Renesme, she needed to change her mind three times until now.

We had a shopping session yesterday, because she has nothing to wear for her birthday. I was prohibited to wear black tonight. She was so serious that it made me laugh.

I have a sequin champagne dress with long sleeves and a neckline deeper than I am comfortable. At the middle of my waist it seems that the dress envelops me. Leaving some subtle folds on the right side, creating an optical illusion of a flat waist, which benefits my small belly. This dress is so short, the material reaches only a palm below my bottom.

At the slit on my right leg, corners are round that make it seem they fit into each other.

I matched the dress with a pair of silver sandals that have a strap passing over my toes and another strap wraps around my ankle.

I waved my dark blue hair, leaving it loose. It's long enough to pass over my shoulders, highlighting my face. Opting for make-up that is as natural as possible with a nude lipstick and a "cat eyeliner" around the eyes, highlighting my green-brown eye colour.

Admiring me in the mirror, I am proud of my achievement. It's a radical change from the black uniform that I wear every day, the same that makes Lan call me a widow.

I step out of the bathroom and head to living, where I find a bad boy style Lan in there.

Damn that makes me wet my panties. He looks so hot I may come just from looking at him. Yes we repeated that experience a couple of times until now. It felt even better, every time.

One day a neighbour told me "Ha, I heard you last night. You cheeky woman, next time don't make so much noise!" he was laughing at my expense. Me on the other hand I was so red and embarrassed, I just wished the ground to part and swallow me whole.

"Wow, you look…you look HOT!"

Lan says with a predatory look in his eyes. Still not able to form words, he looks hotter than I do.

A pair of black men's boots, a pair of ripped jeans at both knees and just below the pockets. With a silver chain hanging from the front of his right side to the middle of the back of his jeans. Moulded white T-shirt, which highlights his muscular chest and flat abdomen. A black leather jacket with silver zipper, on top of his shirt. Corners of the jacket are fastened in some silver staples, also at the base of the jacket a semi strap starting from the sides towards the middle of the waist. The way he wears his jacket open, creates the appearance of a "bad boy".

A long sour chain reaching to the middle of his chest, with a key instead of a pendant, hangs at his neck. I'm not sure if it has any meaning or if he just likes that chain.

Sleeves of the jacket raised on the arms highlighting an Armani masculine watch, with a tone of elegance in it. He once told me that it's his favourite watch, received from his mother as a gift on his twenty-first birthday "being major all around the world" ,Elena said to him.

His hair arranged in the same beautiful but messy style, directed to the right side of his head.

"Ahem, you look hot too!"

I say smiling and I bet by now I am all flushed red, like a Turkish flag. He comes closer not taking his eyes from me.

"Tonight I will be very busy keeping the horny man's away from you, if they fill anything close with what I do, they would wish to fuck you until sunrise. Which not only makes me jealous as hell, but murderous as well. Because you are only mine and you will always be!"

He bends and kisses me with so much passion and need that my legs become jelly.

What can I say to that?

This was the first he said anything about his feelings toward me. Well except when we danced, I wasn't sure he told me he loves me or he was singing, and I didn't ask. Not knowing what to say if he did say it to me or how to feel if he didn't. Now, he was telling me I am his forever? What did that even mean? So many questions and this kiss made me dizzy.   I did not have time to react, once he pulled away from the kiss, he informed me we better be going otherwise he will have his way with me. I will not complain at all, things he can do and the pleasure...

Ride to the club was made in his Veyron that brought back memories of us racing in St James Park. I smile and look out the window admiring the beauty of London. In this short time since I am here, I have come to love this city.

It's so full of people, like the city never sleeps and you are always surrendered by people, but at the same time you are alone, which is fine with me.

I like to be alone, I know I'm not lonely. Same as London is full of people, but everyone minds their own business. I'm surrounded by people, but most of the time I don't speak with a soul. I like to pay attention to their behaviour, the way they talk, the shape of their faces, for me is something so fascinating.

I am brought back from my thought, by Lan announcing that we arrived at our destination. Paying attention to surroundings, I realise we are at the same hotel as we were for lunch. Looking confused in Lan direction he informs me that at eighteen floor of this hotel is an amazing bar. For sure I will like it. He doesn't give me more details. Getting out of the car, he gave the key to a valet, coming around and taking my hand in his. We walk through the same door and hallway area with the main reception desk at the end. Except, this time a dark blond tall receptionist greets Lan ignoring me completely.

"Look who decided to make an appearance tonight. Good to see you! Same room like always?"

She asks, smiling wide and knowingly. What the hell?

"Hello Cecily. No, tonight I'm not staying. I'm here for a birthday party in Sky Bar."

He replied never letting go of my hand, but not introducing me either. What is going on? The way he behaved made me feel one of his bimbo's. Only to be absolutely sure it's not only my imagination, Cecily girl here, winks at my fiancée. I am boiling by now, not wanting to make a scene. I smile and follow him to the lifts. Once inside, I am not saying a word, even if I plot murder in my head. He doesn't say a word either, but smiles at me and I look away. I want to be angry at him for his behaviour, not become all sugary here.

We reach eighteen floors and pass two double doors to get in the Sky Bar. The view is magnificent, I am so taken aback by it. I need to take a moment to process it.

Eighteen Sky Bar, with spectacular views of the London skyline. An iconic style bar, with unrivalled views over The O2, Canary Wharf and Docklands. Glamorous and sophisticated.

As you enter the bar on the right is a huge bar that occupies all the floor. Near the glass wall are the refrigerators with juices, above them being a black melamine chipboard with all the alcoholic and non-alcoholic drinks, needed to prepare the drinks on the menu. About a motor in front of the refrigerators there is an elegant bar counter, made I think from the same material as the countertop above the refrigerators. In front of the counter some high red bar stools seats with golden legs, at least that's what they look in this light. The wall being made of glass with a view of the O2 arena. That side of the bar is lit by some LEDs that emit a reddish yellow light, creating a warm romantic atmosphere, with a strong enough light for the four bartenders to do their job without eye pain. The floor in front of the bar is made of black tiles.

On the left side of the room, the floor is covered by a zebra-like carpet, a huge sofa in the middle of the room and a rectangular table about the same size as the sofa. I assume for very large groups.

Around this sofa there are several low tables with matching armchairs that look blue, probably due to the lights. The wall is also made of glass, displaying an absolutely gorgeous picture of the buildings in Canary Wharf.

Same buildings I saw in broad daylight when I was last here, a few floors below, taking lunch with Lan's family. I was wondering how they will look at night. I got my answer. They are… absolutely magnificent. On each floor you can see yellow lights in different intensities. The logo of each company in a different colour. The buildings of the four banks are so tall they look like four Vikings prepared for fighting. It is a memorable panorama.

The room is lit with blue spotlights, you can see four pillars and next to them a tall lamp displaying a yellowish colour, in a lower intensity than the blue one. From where I stand in front of the door, it looks as if the side of the bar and the rest of the room are two different worlds. Something like heaven and hell, only in this case hell would be blue. After what seems to be an eternity, Lan guides me to the window at a table placed exactly in the middle of it. So close to the window the view becomes even more splendid, because from here you can see the river at the base of the buildings. It's a kind of mini New York at my feet.

Once at the table I can see Arthur, he is dressed elegantly in a pair of black shoes, black fabric trousers, a white shirt and a black suit jacket. His yellow eyes stand out as if he were a cat, his hair looks as if someone has just played with hands in it. When he sees me, he gets up and gives me a hug, telling me how beautiful I am.

Then, I turn to Renesme who has a dark green emerald-like dress, at the base in the shape of a mermaid with a completely bare back. The front of the dress has the shape of a tear turned upside down, with the tail of the drop extended to the left, behind her neck and down on the right hand forming a sleeve.

She looks gorgeous, with her hair caught in a stylized bun. This dress highlights her body, leaving very little to the men's imagination. Looking like a Victoria Secrets model, taken directly from the first page of a magazine. Her blue eyes are so bright and she exudes immense happiness when she sees me, telling me that I look gorgeous.

Looking around, I realize that there are more chairs than people, which makes me wonder, who else is coming.

Misha made his way toward us holding hands with a Barbie bimbo. Too big boobs, too big ass, too pink and most important too less material for that dress she was wearing. Way too high heels for her own good.

What happened tonight? Every magazine in London decided to display their best? Well, in the no-name bimbo case, she was coming straight from Playboy's pages. What was wrong with Misha and since when he was dating this type of woman?

Coming to think about it, we never actually discussed this subject. Looking at Misha, I can see he's dressed casual and elegant. A pair of blue sport shoes like, a pair of blue jeans and a blue shirt. Approaching and kissing me on the check he says.

"Wow you look amazing, this is mouth-watering for all the guys in here, including Lan. Who by the way, will be very busy at breaking necks tonight!"

He laughs as I ask.

"What's with you all in blue? Have you decided to become a taller version of a smurf? Where is your white hat?"

We laugh at the mention of our favourite cartoons. After all hellos have been shared and all the hugs given, we take a seat at the table. I see a seat is still empty. Who is to come? And just like that I hear.

"Hello guys did you miss me?"

For a second I wished to be Felicia's voice, but no. It had to be Cecily. Great, just fucking great! Even better, Lan is first to raise and kiss her cheeks. Is he fucking kidding me? Seriously, if he wants to score points with …her, he should at least do it away from me. I don't need to know about this. Yes we sleep together, but I know he is not in love with me. And no matter how much it hurts, I don't expect him to be faithful or pretend he is, but at least have some decency. For sure, I will not agree with him eye fucking any woman in front of me. Let alone…Cecily. Arh! She carries on greeting everyone, when it's my turn, I try to smile, still not sure what to do. Part, because earlier Lan did not say a thing about me and part, because for some foreign reason, I am so jealous of this girl that I cannot stand her. Then I hear Lan speaking over the music.

"Cecily she is my fiancée, the girl I told you about!"

What? When did they meet and talk? This is confusing, before I have time to say something, she hugs me and screams in my ear.

"I am so happy to know you finally. When he told me he would marry, I started to laugh in his face. Then he showed me pictures of you. You are more beautiful in person than any picture will make you justice!"

Trying to master a hug back, I feel like I was hit by the most powerful version of Katrina the hurricane. So many questions in my head, I am not sure where to end and where to stop.

We take a seat with Cecily next to me on the right, Lan on my left, followed by Renesme, Arthur, no-name bimbo, and Misha. For a little while we tried to do a small talk. I noticed bimbo saying something in Misha's ear and now she was a few seconds away from sitting in Arthur's lap, only to see Renesme plotting murder. Since when is she jealous of Arthur? We have been best of friends for a long time and never seen her react like that toward him. Before I can ask she says to me.

"I know you don't drink like the rest of us, so I ordered a bottle of Martini Bianco and some olives."

Smiling knowingly at me.

"A bottle just for me, you lost your mind! But thank you!"

"You owe me a race for that!"

She screams, exactly in time with music stopping between songs. The whole club is looking at us. I can see a horror on Lan and Arthur's faces, while me, Misha and Cecily display full shock. Bimbo is not paying attention to the conversation being too distracted by an annoying Arthur now.

"What?"

Arthur and Lan speak at the same time. As soon as she realised what she did, basically she just told me that Arthur betrayed my trust, except Vitaly he was the only one knowing about the race. I will have a pending discussion with him, as soon as I can have a moment alone with him. I need to play cool now.

"You know I like to go and watch races in Trafalgar Square. I keep telling you to come with me. Now you owe me a race to watch at."

We all relax, each of us for different reasons. Me because even if Arthur told her, she kept my secret. I presume Arthur for the same reason, even if he looks at me apologetically. I still shoot him daggers, Lan because he believed her lie. I need to give her credit. She was good. Looking at Misha and Cecily, I can see they are in conversation, not caring about the explanation anymore. What is going on with my brother?

Lan asked her more out of curiosity than anything, I believe.

"When was the last time you saw a race in the Square?"

Big mistake for him.

"When that guy with the most gorgeous Camaro beat your ass in that amazing race around the Queen

Victoria memorial. Man he was good and you were so pissed!"

She says as I see Lan getting angry at the memory, Arthur closing his eyes. Not sure if he is angry because Renesme shared with me one of my great victories, without actually telling me that, or because by now bimbo has her hands nearly to his crotch. I see he takes her hand away as Lan says,

"I will beat that fucker don't you worry. Even better, I will take you there together with Lana, so you can watch me kicking that fucker ass and make sure I will see his face once and for all!"

I start to laugh thinking that at that moment in time I will need a strong reason not to be present for the race, or another clone. I hear Renesme saying "Aham! If you say so."

As a pissed off Arthur leaves his seat, so fast that you would say he's on fire. Misha hands grabs the bimbo's hand and heads to the door. Renesmee starts to laugh and I am lost. What did I miss? Cecily is the one explaining me between laughs.

"Your brother's girlfriend was nearly given Arthur a blowjob here! I think it was not comfortable with either Arthur or Misha."

Who's this girl? Knowing everyone by the name and looking so comfortable with everyone around, except me. Lan is taking me out of my thoughts.

"Cecily you should tell Lana about the wedding idea you have."

"What?"

I ask, anger in my tone. Seriously, what the hell is going on?

"Cecily is Arthur's cousin, she is a wedding planner, and has a great idea about a private wedding. I bet you will like it."

Relieve is filling me. She's our wedding planner, Arthur's cousin. Cecily starts to tell me what she thought about our wedding. That one of these days she would like to show me the location, even surprised me by saying.

"Me and Lan never went further than best friends. He helped me a while ago with my ex, pretending he was my boyfriond, but even then we didn't share anything. Not even a kiss. We have known each other a long time and we consider ourselves like brothers. You are safe with me. No need for jealousy here. I want your wedding to be perfect and you to be a happy bride. Not stressed out of her mind bride. I even have a few dresses ideas in mind."

She speaks so fast that I have no time to think or reply to a comment. Instead, I just smile. We decided to meet following Wednesday, in case we don't like the location, she should have time to recommend something else. I agree with her and carry on talking about the wedding. More like she talks and I listen, glancing at Lan from time to time. The night passes by nice and easy, with both Arthur and Misha coming back from wherever without the bimbo. Thank God for that.

By the time we go home my head is spinning. I know Martini is not a strong drink, but for me it is. I don't drink at all. I feel brave now, because of the alcohol. I start to talk and tell Lan what I feel.

"You were a jerk to me at the beginning of the night, you know? You did not introduce me to Cecily, which by the way is a nice girl. But nooo, instead you made me believe she is one of your one night stands…alcohol was taking control over my mind, I was talking without a filter, too fast and too loud. Raising a finger to him I continue…which by the way, I never want to encounter one, or she will leave without a head."

Both me and Lan laugh at our comment.

"Are you jealous?"

"Me… no? Why would I be jealous? Is not like you love me or something. Hell, not even the marriage we plan will not be a real one. At least not for you!"

How much did I drink, to bring this on?

"What makes you think it will not be real for me, but it will be real for you?"

He asks as we step in his…our apartment. Once I hear the door closing behind him, I turn around too fast and lose my balance on this traitor's hills that make me land in Lan's arms.

"Because, you don't love me like I do!"

I say staring into his eyes as he replies in a raspy voice

"Are you sure about that?"

I have no time to answer because he bends and kisses me. Softy at the beginning like always, and needy a few seconds later. Pushing me in the hallway wall. Right hand wrapped around my waist, the other on my leg, finding her way under my short dress, straight between my legs. He starts to massage my clit, as a wave of pleasure hits me and I moan.

"You are so wet for me already."

He says as he kisses my neck and I lift my leg around his waist creating more space for his hand to carry on massaging my clit that feels so good. The hand that was on my waist, lowers down and cups my ass cheek as he comes even closer to me and lifts me up, which makes me wrap my legs around his waist.

In the next moment, or maybe longer I don't know, I am so lost in the pleasure he gives me. I feel him deep inside me, at this point I'm sandwiched between him and the wall, with my legs wrapped around him. The way he is moving, thrusting inside me, it feels so blissful I would freeze the time for this moment.

He covers my mouth with his as he caress my nipple with his thumb, adding to the pleasure building inside me.

I am so close and I try to tell him "I…I…am…" but his words are faster "Look at me!" demanding he continues "Come with me baby girl!"

I do as I'm told, staring at him as we both come so hard. In a second Lan turns us around, now he's back leaning against the wall, while sliding down and taking a seat on the floor. With me straddling his lap. Like riding a horse. I rested my head on the crook of his neck, trying to catch my breath, allowing tiredness and alcohol to take me to sleep, not before I heard Lan saying "Marry me!"

It's not a question, it's a statement. I responded "Yes!" anyway. I know this is the closest, I will get from Lan, to a marriage proposal and I fall asleep.

Before I know its Wednesday. We need to meet Cecily and go wherever to show us the location. An hour later we arrived somewhere in the Kent area, the view was breathtaking.

It's a small forest at the edge of a lake with an amazing restaurant. It seems so small from the outside, but once inside, I see the walls are made of glass. I fell in love with this location instantly and I name it, my "glass house".

On the outside looks more like a church, with the roof too sharp. In the middle, the building has a tower much higher than the building itself. It looked like the building was added to the tower. With the same sharp roof, only at its base was the entrance to the restaurant, marked by a white veranda with two supporting pillars.

On each side of the tower that divided the roof in two, was a triangular glass window. Positioned in such a way that if you joined the two triangles of glass, the facade of the roof would have been given.

On the entrance wall on either side of the door were two narrow slit windows, but almost as high as the wall. It felt as if the entrance wall had lines in it.

On the inside, a fairly large room with the grey tile floor. So clean and shiny, it felt like you were stepping on the mirror. Looking down, I saw my reflection almost perfectly. The walls were completely made of glass with supporting pillars from place to place for the roof.

In any point of the restaurant you were sited, could be seen, on the right the lake with small boats on it. On the left, a small and beautiful forest, not too very thick. It was like in a fairy tale!

I got to know and like Cecily. We found out, we have so much in common. She started to tell me, she envisioned arranging the room in such a way that we would do all the wedding process in here, including the reception as well.

I was so grateful for her and for this location. It could not be more beautiful. I know this marriage comes with an expiry date, but at least I will make some great memories to hold on to, for the time that I will be left alone. I know for me it will never be another man, after Lan. So... I decided to be present and enjoy every moment I have with him, no matter what happens after.

Once we agreed with the location and listened to her talking for two hours straight, we came back to London, starting to do our part in the wedding. Like going to look for wedding clothes. Needless to say I took a holiday from the café. Of course, fighting Lan in need of an explanation, as why I need to go back at all.

To be honest I don't know. I just liked the way I could look at people without being creepy. Since part of my job was to make sure they have everything they need, I had to pay attention to them. But for me it was fascinating to just observe them.

Lan took me to an Armani shop in Oxford street, where the sales lady was adamant that he should, under no circumstances, see my dress or I should see his groom's suit. It seemed stupid and hilarious, but I could not fight with the woman. She was determined and I just gave up fighting listening to her. Once that was done, I just needed to book my hairstylist, which I delegate to Renesmee. With all that done, I was waiting for my wedding day. Strange, but I was nervous. I could not believe, I am getting married to a man I actually love, but soon I will divorce. What king of twisted luck was this??

CHAPTER EIGHTEEN

RUSLAN

We were getting ready for her fury blond friend's birthday. Okay I like the girl, she's a good and loyal friend to Lana. I just enjoy the nickname I gave her. To me, she always looks like a small furry furious Chihuahua, barking every time she sees me. Because, every damn time she has something to say to me.

Oh, you make Lana sad today. Oh, you were a dick to do that, to say that. Man, this girl complained more than Lana did. Okay, Lana doesn't complain, maybe at all. And here I am, getting ready for her birthday. But, I know after her shift Cecily will be there too. Cecily is Arthur's cousin and a wedding planner. I met with her the other day, told her I will get married, only to make fun of me and give me shit. I showed her a few pictures I sneaked of Lana while she was at the café or she did things in the house, to keep her mouth shut. We need to make official pictures together. Then she started to take me more seriously as I told her I want to give Lana the most amazing wedding party, even if it's a private one. She agreed to meet me at the SkyBar. At the hotel she is manager at.

I became impatient as I was waiting for Lana to come out of the bathroom. I mean I know women take forever, but come on! Turning around, I am face to a new version of Lana…fuck…me! She is beautiful…

and stunning… and the most gorgeous woman on the entire planet. How come she does not see that?

"Wow, you look…you look HOT!"

I managed, suddenly feeling my mouth dry. This dress makes all her body stand out and hides the little belly she has. And that legs of her, man I feel all my blood navigate to the south and my cock stir to life. If we don't leave the apartment soon we will never get to the party. I will make her scream, louder this time. Just to fuck with the neighbour that embarrassed her the other day. I need to talk to him about complaining.

"Ahem, you look hot too!"

It is a simple casual bad boy outfit, nothing special. Admiring her I speak before I can stop myself.

"Tonight I will be very busy keeping the horny man's away from you, because if they fill anything close with what I do, they would wish to fuck you until sunrise. Which not only makes me jealous as hell, but murdorous as well. You are only mine and you will always be!"

As I speak I can see she is surprised to hear me speak like that. I never told her how I felt. Of course, I showed her every time we made love, every time we fucked, but I know she needed to hear the words.

The only problem with that is, I'm shitless scared to tell her what I feel. She will turn around and run away.

That is something I do not wish, or at least not anymore. Before she has time to recover and start a million question list, I bend and kiss her. Taking her hand in mine and guiding her to my Bugatti Veyron. I wanted to take the Audi, but she is too elegant and I feel the need to show off next to her.

Once at Intercontinental, we step in the hotel hallway and I see Cecily at the main desk. As soon as I see her, I glance at Lana and see she is not paying me any attention. Gazing back at Cecily I wink, this is our code she needs to be sugary toward me.

I used this one, a long time ago, when I needed to get rid of a girl. I'm not sure if she remembers. But she did and played along, adding more fuel to the fire. Asking me if I want to stay in my usual room. I don't have a usual room here, but Lana doesn't know that. I would love to introduce Lana to her, except rules of the hotel don't allow becoming too friendly with a customer. And she was already too friendly. I played my part as well.

"Hello Cecily, no tonight I am not staying. I am here for a birthday party in Sky Bar."

Next to me a boiling Lana, she doesn't say anything except smiles. I was a dick, I know.

It makes me feel good to see she is as affected by the attention I get from other women. As I am, when a man looks too much in her way. And tonight I need all the self-control I can master, not to start and break necks. Once we step foot in the bar she is so mesmerised by this view that for me is so familiar, by now.

I knew she would love it and I made sure we had the closest table from the window as possible, managing to get the middle one. The best view from this place. Lucky me, I scored points with my woman. I will need a lot of them, once Cecily comes up. That if Lana doesn't walk away before I manage to proceed with introductions. I guide her at our table and I see her looking at the building on the other side of the river. They are something else at night time, I will admit.

Even after so long that view at night still amazes me.

We greet and hug everyone as Misha comes with a bimbo, this kid is something else. Where did he find this bimbo Barbie?

Turning my gaze at Lana, she is so disgusted by the woman in pink. Misha doesn't even bother to introduce her to us. We take a seat as Cecily makes an appearance.

"Hello guys did you miss me?"

I am first to raise and hug her, thanking her for earlier in the lobby, gestures that nearly take my head off the shoulders by Lana. But again, she doesn't say anything. I decided it is time to put this wonderful woman out of her misery and I introduce the two of them to each other. Thanking God Lana did not run, until now.

"Cecily she is my fiancée, the girl I told you about!"

I see Lana's surprised expression looking at me and then to Cecily as she explain to Lana how excited she is to meet her, and just like that, I see Cecily hugging Lana, fuck! I did not warn Cecily not to touch her. I'm getting relaxed when I see Lana try to hug her back.

Weird hug, but she tried and I am so proud of her. As we take a seat again, Lana is in between me and Cecily, then Renesmee, Arthur, no-name bimbo, and Misha.

We talk nonsense for a while. Except, a moment when Renesme was talking about my race and the fucker, the night went on peacefully. Lana and Cecily started to share ideas about the wedding, agreeing to meet Wednesday to see a location for our wedding. I appreciate Cecily trying to put Lana at ease. I will thank her later for that.I saw Lana getting tipsy and became very talkative on the way back home.

"You were a jerk to me at the beginning of the night, you know? You did not introduce me to Cecily which by the way is a nice girl. But nooo instead you made me believe she is one of your one night stands…alcohol was taking control over her mind, and I cringe at the fact she believed that I will ever introduce her to one of my night stand. She raises a finger to my chest as she continues…which by the way I never want to encounter one, or she will leave without head."

Both I and Lana laugh at her comment."

Are you jealous?"

"Me… no? Why would I be jealous? Is not like you love me or something, hell not even the marriage we plan will not be a real one.

At least not for you!"

Fuck! I never thought she could actually have feelings for me. Her stamen is like a fucking punch to my stomach. Was I so selfish in this?

"What makes you think it will not be real for me, but it will be real for you?"

We stepped inside the apartment. I close the door behind me. I see how she tries to spin, but loses her footage, landing in my arms. Never expecting what comes out of her mouth next.

"Because you don't love me, like I do!"

She says, looking me deep in the eyes as I ask back in a raspy voice

"Are you sure about that?"

I gave her no time to answer, I bent and kissed her. Softy at the beginning as always, and needy a few seconds later. Pushing her in the hallway wall. Wrapping my right hand around her waist, finding my way between her legs with my left hand. I start massaging her clit and I can tell a wave of pleasure hit her, as she moans.

"You are so wet for me already."

Kissing her neck as she lifts her leg wrapping it around my waist, creating more space for my hand. I massaged her clit, sliding my right hand down her ass. I grab her and lift her to my level, locking her between me and the wall. This feels so good, but I need to be inside her. I managed to open my jeans and slide them down my legs, just enough to free my cock so I can hit home inside her. I cover her mouth with mine so she cannot scream. Man she is loud. I caress her nipple with my thumb as I am in and out of her, bringing pleasure to both of us. I can feel the pressure building down my spine and I know she is close as well. She tries to let me know she's close, but I'm faster staring at her, I demand.

"Look at me!"

She opens her eyes and stares at me.

"Come with me baby girl!"

We both come so hard.

"Marry me!" it's not a question. It's a stamen. I did not give her a choice. Like the first time, now as well, I'm so terrified she will actually say no. I am surprised when she says "Yes!" anyway and at that moment.

I make a mental note to actually buy a ring and propose to her, even if the wedding is already nearly planned and went through.

I will give her this memory, because I don't plan on letting go of her. As I am thinking about that, I decide that now is the best time to let her know how I feel, even if she said it first in a different form.

"I love you so much that it hurts!"

This time no response comes from her. Confused and scared of what I could see, I look at her anyway and realise that she is asleep.

She sleeps so peacefully, I am afraid I will wake her once I move. I need to get her to bed.

Before we know it's Wednesday. We need to meet Cecily and go with her in Kont, to show Lana the location. I wanted to be there, I saw a wedding there once. It was so beautiful. We travel an hour from where we live, but I would travel the world with this woman next to me. It's a beautiful location on the edge of a lake with a mini forest next to it. After two hours of Cecily and Lana talking about wedding, cakes, flowers and all that I could not give a damn about, we headed straight to Armani shop in Oxford Street. Here, I paid the sales lady fifty pounds to take Lana in a separate room, so she could choose her wedding dress. That will be a surprise, when I see her at the altar. I want this wedding to be real for her. I want her to look back and be happy about it, I know I will be.

This will be the day I will marry the love of my life, even if all this started as a game. I think mom's right universe does have a reason for everything.

After all the shopping was done we had home and I made love with her, for the first time in a long time.

Taking my time to admire her body, to memorise the shape of her breast, the way her lips would swallow after kissing her so much. The colour of her eyes, when orgasm hit her body. The pleasure I could give her as she would allow me to do that… only me.

I was lucky to have her and I will treasure her as many days I have left. We showered together and she sucked my cock, I in return made her come with my tongue. Every day, I would show her new ways to come and let her practise them on me. Because, finally she was off from that café, we could stay buried in one another more time and I couldn't believe time went so fast.

Today is our wedding day. I am a nervous wreck and have no idea what is around me, other than a nice decorated table, with some flowers on top of some vases that looks like a cannon that exploded flowers.

I am standing next to a glass table with one thick wooden leg, which serves as an altar. In front of me on the other side of the table, is an officer that will officiate the wedding. After that, a priest will take his place and proceed with the religious part of the wedding. Once this is done the reception will start. All in this same room, we did not want to change location and carry everyone along, deciding everything will be here.

I realise that the tables are arranged in a way that once she steps through the doors, she will walk down the alley in between the tables.

For everyone's sake, instead of her father walking her at the altar, Vitaly will. Her father lost that privilege the night he touched her. As soon as the doors are opening, I look at her and become more nervous. For some damn reason, I can't keep my tears. I'm not a fucking pussy, but she is so gorgeous.

All in white she looks stunning.

Her dress is white mermaid type with a layer of lace above all the other material. The top side seems to be a corset that is supported by the same lace that continues to the baseline of her neck. Making her boobs look even bigger than they are, probably offering the comfort they need. In between her neckline and the corset you can see through the lace. Her face is hidden behind a veil.

From where I am standing, she has her hair done in a nice stylized bun. As she comes closer, I can see she has natural makeup, like always the same eyeliner that makes her eyes stand out. So simple, but so beautiful.

She literally took my breath away. A tear comes down her cheeks and I am worried. Why is she crying? Then I see Vitaly patting her hand, in a father gesture like, realising she is as nervous as I am.

As soon as she is in front of the stairs, Vitaly lifts her veil, kisses her on the check and whispers something in her ear. I cannot make out what it is but I see her nod and gaze at me smiling. I am gone. I will die for this woman no question asked. Vitally takes her hand and places it in mine.

"Take good care of her, otherwise I will chase you till the end of earth, without a time limit. And once I found you, you will wish I never did!"

I smile as Lana whispers "Vitally!" and he winks at both of us.

Helping her claim the two stairs in front of the table. We face the wedding official and he starts the ceremony. I have no idea what he says, until we need to say our vows. Unlike the American wedding, we don't write them ourselves, they are already written. Which is amazing for me. I don't need to tell a story about my feelings and everyone to clap for Lana to know my feelings. My feelings are just for her and her alone. Dude, start to say.

"Today you are making an important step in your lives, you are getting married, and you take on new duties in relation to each other. Further time is not easy, however happy or sad enjoy life.

Ruslan Dimitri Ivanovich do you agree to take Svetnala Rebekah Petrov as wife, to love, respect and take care of her until death do you apart?

"Yes!" I say a little too loud and everyone giggles like babies.

Svetnala Rebekah Petrov do you agree to take Ruslan Dimitri Ivanovich as husband to love, respect and care about him until death do you apart?

"Yes!" she says as loud as me, not sure if she meant it or she just didn't want to embarrass me in front of others because I was so loud and excited.

"Now I ask the groom to repeat after me..." dude says as me and Lana face each other and hold hands "I, Ruslan swear to be worthy of your love, be loyal and respectful, I know this love is one forever. I will always be a loyal husband, reliable friend and mate."

I repeat every word after this guy, but meaning every word that leaves my mouth.

"Now the bride…" dude says and she starts to repeat every word looking deep in my eyes as she speaks "I Svetlana swear to be your support in everything, love you gently and take care about our love patiently. I swear I understand, respect and support you no matter what future present for us. I will always and forever give you my loyalty and love."

What she says after knocks the breath out of me "I love you!"

Lana whispers just for me to hear, if it's possible I love her more than I did before. She looks at me like I grew another head. Realising my reply to her was only in my mind, lifting her veil I kissed my wife. Whispering "I love you more!" and seal my mouth with her's.

Now she is mine and I am so freaking happy. I'm brought back by the dude who says "You need to sign before you kiss!" and everyone bursts into laughter including us.

As everyone applauded us we signed the marriage certificate and proceeded with pictures and religious part and all that until the wedding party.

At some point my mother came and told me she is so proud of me. I told her, I am happy that she is happy, I would like to speak with her as soon as possible, but now I need to go and dance our first dance as husband and wife.

Instructing the DJ Misha found, to choose the Jacob Lee song "I belong to you" as our first dance song. In my mind that was the most suitable song for us.

As the song begins, I take my wife's hand and start to dance with her holding her tight in my arms. Pretending is just me and her tonight. I spin her so I can admire her entirely. She is the most beautiful bride I ever saw, and I saw plenty until now. None of them stand a chance in front of her. The song comes to an end.

"You are the most beautiful bride I ever saw and I am the luckiest bastard with parents ever born, to be your husband!"

Kissing her lips, just to make my point.

Applause erupts again and I have to let her go, only to be broth face to face with her father.

She hugs me gently, her way of telling me to control myself as he says.

"Can I have the next dance?"

She froze and I am a ball of anger. She smiles and a strong hand lands on my shoulder. Turning to see who the hand belongs to, Nikolai is next to me and Vitaly next to her father. Lana smiles and says full of confidence.

"Of course, a bride should dance with her father. I promise to save a dance for each of you gentlemen."

She holds a hand to her father, who takes her hand in his and they wait for a song to start. My anger and anxiety only raise when I hear it's a slow dance as well.

I will murder that DJ, but I'm plug out from my murderous thought by Vitaly.

"I spoke to him before the wedding, he knows if he touches her again I will kill him."

He speaks low in my ear, so I can hear only. Nikolai squeezes my shoulder but says nothing. He doesn't have to, I know what he thinks. Before I can respond something unexpected happens…

Petrov leaves mid song, never looking back to Lana, ever again.   As we will find later on, this will be the last time either one of them would see each other.

CHAPTER NINETEEN

SVETLANA

My wedding day!

I am getting married today with a man that I am so deeply in love, but he has no idea what I feel. I mean yes, I gave him hints. I doubt he understood what I wanted to say with all of that.

When we arrived at the wedding location today, I was so happy and proud of what Cecily managed to do. She completely changed the place. I have no idea what Ruslan paid her, but she was worth every penny.

The porch pillars were dressed in white lilies and among them non-flammable red LEDs. The entrance had an arch of white lilies, in the restaurant tables were arranged in a ziz-zag shape on one side and the other near the glass walls, forming an alley with an altar at the end.

At the same time, keeping the middle of the room spacious enough to be used as a dance floor later.

Tables dressed with white table cloth, in the middle of each table a square mirror on which were placed vases in the shape of a trumpet with the foot filled with false crystals and LEDs of different colours, on the top of each vase were placed flower ornaments composed of white lilies and red roses. Each corner of the mirror holds a candle, as big and thick as a D battery.

Close to the edge of the table matching each chair in front of them, were nicely arranged cutlery plates and glasses, in each glass you could find a red napkin arranged in the shape of rose.

The number of each table was visibly placed in the middle of the table, being incorporated in a medium-sized photo frame. The chairs are also covered in a white cover, with a bow made of red veil material placed at the back of it.

It's a magnificent change. Especially, because of the glass walls that allow the late October sun to illuminate the room, creating a romantic feeling with the lake and the forest next to it.

I felt like Cinderella that found her prince at the end of the story.

On the opposite side of the entrance were placed some glass tables on a wooden foot, tall about the size of my waist and thick enough to support the glass that rests above them.

They were placed in such a way they formed an altar, that was first used by the registrar, then by the priest and then by the DJ. Thus escaping the turmoil of moving from one building to another.

Standing in the middle of this beautiful room I could not hold my tears, I would love Cecily forever. She gave me the most beautiful room to hold my wedding in. This was the moment I decided to fight for Lan as much as I can and maybe make him fall in love with me…

As I was crying Cecily came next to me in full panic.

"Oh. My. God! You don't like it, do you? I knew. I should have talked to you more, asked you about flowers and the colour and the table's arrangement and…"

I literally put my hand over her mouth and said with tears in my eyes.

"I will always be grateful to you for all of this. It's more than I could imagine. I have no words to describe how thankful I am. I just hope whatever Lan pays you it's enough for your effort."

By now she has her eyes in tears and hugs me. She is the person that hugged me the most. Now, I'm comfortable with her hugging me.

"If you like it why are you crying like someone died? You crazy woman, you scared me to death. Stop crying they will not be able to do your makeup and what is a bride without makeup? Don't worry about payment. I made sure to charge you soon-to-be husband triple, for short notice."

She has a crazy sense of humour, she is comic and sarcastic all the time. We kind of match in this way. Laughing we make our way in the room designed to be the bride's room. Renesmee made sure to bring a makeup artist and a hair stylist that now are changing my appearance in "the most beautiful bride" as Renesmee says for the hundredth time.

I am ready to get in my dress and nervousness finds her way in.

Is an open back dress in the shape of a mermaid at the bottom, with a built-in bra. Giving the feeling that it would be a corset under the lace that comes up to the base of the neck, it closes with a button on the back of the neck.

From the neckline to the bra it's a see through the lace making this dress both sexy and elegant.

I wanted my hair done in a curly styled bun that will help with my veil, which is long enough. I decided to have a veil, for some reason it looked good when I tried the dress.

My makeup is natural, except for my eyeliner that makes my eyes stand out. You wouldn't say I wear any makeup at all.

I can't wait to see what Lan will look like when he sees me. I am so nervous, I feel like I will burst in tears. A soft knock is at the door and I'm wondering who could be. I know for sure all the girls went to change in the other room.

"Who is it?"

"Vitally!"

I released a breath I wasn't aware I was holding. As I open my door Vitaly is so surprised, I see tears in his eyes. Please don't cry, I will not be able to hold my tears. This is the first time I see him with tears in his eyes.

"Come in, but don't cry! I will ruin my makeup and the makeup artist left the premises. I will be an ugly bride because of you!"

We start to laugh. He holds his hands up in a defensive gesture.

"Hey I will not cry, not because you will be ugly, but, because that is impossible. I'm an old guy and a fighter. Fighters don't cry!"

He's serious, which makes me reply involuntarily "AHAM" and roll my eyes and we start to laugh again.

"You look stunning! And I am serious, and so proud of you! I was hoping to get to see this day, to see you as a bride. After what happened and the way you isolate yourself from the world… Let's say I was afraid it wouldn't happen. I am the happiest person to see you here, because I know you came a long way to even be able to talk about this. I have only one question. I know it's not my business and probably I shouldn't ask you this, but did you talk to Lan about what happened?"

He asked so concerned that it hurt me. I always knew he loved me, never knew how much, until this moment. He is the closest to a father that I had and I always was honest with him.

"Yes, I talked to him. He promised to be patient!"

I say, leaving out the fact we already evolved with patience so far that even neighbours started to complain.

"Damn, I cannot kill this boy. He is just too good!"

He's serious and I look at him like he lost his mind. Soon he burst into laughter, and I joined him.

"That was mean and not funny at all."

"But your face was priceless. You love him don't you?"

"Yes I do! How incredible and unexpected it sounds, I did fall for him hard."

"God because he is a good boy, even if he is a little stupid for thinking I will let you marry him, without you loving him. Don't care if he does it for his mom or not!"

My face falls to the floor, if that is possible. As I stare at Vitaly, not carrying he can see the shock in my eyes.

"What did you just say?"

"Oh, don't play stupid now. I know you know. It wasn't until I had confirmation from Nikolai. You just didn't believe for a second, I believed you "just happened" to fall in love with a guy like Lan, in a matter of weeks. When you need years to say "hello" to anyone who wasn't me or Misha. Like I told you, I was always in the shadows! And be sure, I made sure to know what is good for you. And I know Lan is good for you, he loves you very much!"

By now, he was resting his big arms on my shoulders. What the hell should I say to that? Lan loves me very much? In what world would that happen? But, I will not disagree with the only man who is determined to protect me, no matter what. In return I just nod. A girl knocks on my door letting me know that it's time to make an appearance, I nod and proceed to wipe a few tears that manage to fall while talking to Vitally. He takes my bouquet and hands it to me.

"Well I see you have something blue in your bouquet… being made by a combination of white, red and blue roses my favourite flower… I will be something old and borrowed."

He says as we leave the room. We made our entrance in the same room I was admiring an hour ago.

"Don't let me fall!"

"I will never let you fall, trust me!"

I do as I'm told, without a second thought. Lifting up my gaze, I see Lan standing there waiting for me. I become so nervous that I'm shaking. Vitally is patting my hand, but I cannot take my eyes from Lan. He is wearing a black tuxedo, with black pointed toe dress shoes, a white shirt underneath his tux jacket, with his hair in that messy style of his and tears in his eyes.

I will cry!

I don't need to cry.

Once we are at the bottom of the only two stairs from this place, Vitaly lifts my veil, kissing me on the cheek and whispering.

"I will always be here for you, married or not!"

Taking my hand and placing it in Lan's.

"Take good care of her, otherwise I will chase you till the end of earth, without a time limit. And once I found you, you will wish I never did!"

He's so serious that I am afraid for Lan, but he smiles his most charming smile and I just whispers "Vitally!" as he winks at both of us.

Wedding starts with "the dude", how Lan's refers to him, saying his part and then proceeds to ask us if we agree to marry each other. When Lan turns to answer, he is so loud everyone starts to giggle. I follow his lead so no one will laugh anymore. When he says his vow I can see his seriousness and that means every word, even if we did not write the vow ourselves. My turn comes and I mean every word I say, only to add and "I love you", before I could refrain myself. I did it so low that only Lan heard me, except he didn't even move for a few seconds. Shit, I ruin the moment, now it was not the time. Why did I believe Vitaly? Before I could overthink this further and way before we could sign the marriage certificate, Lan lifts my veil and bends to kiss me saying "I love you more!" and closes the gap between our mouths.

He does love me. Vitaly was right. The officer informs us that my husband was too quick and we still need to sign. Of course, everyone laughs and claps for us. We go with the drill of pictures, religious part and so on. A soft hand touches me, when I turn around is Elena.

"Hello, I am so happy you could be here with us!"

I say, she smiles and asks me if we could talk somewhere a bit more private. I excuse myself as I guide her in the only room I know, the room that was designed for me.

"Is everything alright?"

I ask her once I make sure she is sited and the door is closed, so no one can hear us.

"Yes dear! Everything is alright. I just wanted a moment of privacy with you."

She said smiling lovingly, but nothing could have prepared me for what was to come next.

"I will tell you something and I want you to listen carefully without interrupting me…I nod and she carries on… Lan knows I have another five month to live, but actually my time is so close to the end. Please be honest with me and tell me if you really love my son. I don't want to know about the agreement between you, I want to know about your real feelings!"

She says calm but demanding, making my eyes widen and my face is pure shock I be,t as she smiles.

"Dear I have cancer, I am not an idiot. And even if Ruslan believes that he can hide things from me, he can't. I know my son better than he believes. He would never marry someone just to please me, so he must be in love with you to make such a huge step in his life. Please speak."

I swear this woman is something else.

"Well at the beginning, I couldn't stand him, but somehow I found myself in love with him. I have no idea how. I'm terrified that once our agreement comes to an end, I will be unable to live… without him."

She wanted honesty and for some reason I could not keep my mouth shut. She only nods and stands, but as she heads for the door she turns, like changing her mind.

"I am sorry for what happened with you nine years ago. I could not save you then, but I made sure your father will never touch you again. Not as long as your name will be Ivanovich, at least. I can assure you, unless you change your mind, my son will not change his. Like I said, I have cancer. I am not an idiot. For sure your father will want to speak with you tonight. You should listen, as it will probably be his last chance to do that. Just a piece of advice! …*she hugs me as she says*… Welcome to the Ivanovich family! I am so happy that you and my son love each other, because you will lead our legacy.

The most powerful way to do that, is through love."

She cups half of my face with one hand as she kisses my other chick and leaves the room. I stand there full of questions that maybe will never be answered. In what the hell I entered? Vitally's words come to my mind. I know he will be here for me.

Taking a deep breath I am heading downstairs. I find Elena talking with Lan. I would love to know what she said to him, but I cannot ask him that. I see Lan excuse himself and come to me. He says it's time for our first dance as husband and wife. A song I never heard before starts and we dance. Paying attention to the lyrics, I try not to think about the conversation I had with Elena. Our song comes to an end, only to hear my father question.

"Can I have the next dance?"

In the next second I feel Lan ready to action. I wrap my hands around him, remembering Elena's words. Maybe I should listen for what appears to be his last chance. I see now both Vitaly and Nikolai are with us and I smile brightly.

"Of course, a bride should dance with her father. I promise to save a dance for each of you gentlemen."

Holding my hand for my father to take it in. He does just that and the connection makes me vomit, but I need to play nice. It's hard to explain to a few hundred guests, why the hell the bride could not stand her father, without disclosing the whole truth and relieving the past. Now is time for neither one of the options.

As we head to the dance floor a slow song starts and my father asks silently for permission to touch me, which I give nodding slightly.

"I am sorry!"

He says. Sorry for what? I don't ask. I don't trust myself enough to speak, without causing a scene. Silence he takes as an invitation to speak further.

"I am sorry for everything I did to you. I have no excuse for the way I treated you, but if it makes it better, me and your mother had a very big disagreement and she wanted to leave me. I just took it out on the wrong person, without thinking about what I do. I tormented myself to this day for what I did to you. I was terrified that you will never be happy because of me, ever again. I am thanking you for not telling anyone, except Lan about what I did back then!"

"How do you know I told Lan? Did he tell you something?"

I ask afraid that maybe Lan went behind my back.

"He doesn't have to use words. I can see the way he protects you. I would do the same even worse for your mother. But now is pointless anyway. At the end she got the life she waited for. She's finally with the love of her life. The only difference is, she's at the bottom of the ocean. Hence the reason she's not here to cause a scene!"

I am fully crying now, but he holds me so tight, I can't even look him in the eyes. For everyone is a simple dance, for me it's yet another nightmare.

"What did you do?"

I asked full of hate, and he started to laugh.

"I have done nothing. She did it herself. She could not take no for an answer, so she killed Sergei and killed herself. All this happened a while after telling me to go to hell, because she's finally moved in with Sergei. I never believed it would be at the bottom of an ocean, but your mother is full of surprises. I have to admit. Consider this your wedding gift, for your new life. I will have one gift for you soon. Take care of Misha please. Not for me, but for him! And again, I am really sorry for what I did back then. Unfortunately, I cannot go back in time to make it right!"

He squeezed me in a tight hug for a few seconds. Letting me go, he's heading to the door and out of my life, as I will find out later.

Elena's words were true. Before I can react and go after him, none other than Nikolai takes my hand in his.

"May I have the pleasure to finish this dance?"

I nod because words are not forming anymore.

"I am sorry for everything that you have been through. I would like to know if I can do anything for you."

I stare at him with wide eyes and shake my head no, but he continues.

"I know what Elena said to you. It's a lot to take in. One of these days please make sure you find your way to her house. She will explain everything to you. I promise! Once you know everything and you are able to make a final decision, I will support you. No matter what. You were too young back then, but you are strong enough now and you are part of the family. Ruslan is like my son. I will always have yours and his back, even if I need to pay with my life."

The song finished, Nikolai bends down and kisses my forehead, like thanking me for the dance. I have so many questions in my head. I feel everything spinning. Things are happening too fast, the last half an hour or maybe half the day is a blur. I know Lan is next to me saying something, then Vitaly wraps his hand around my waist and guides me outside in the now cold air, heading to the forest. My mother is dead, resting at the bottom of the fucking ocean. Which ocean? My father left, telling me he will have a wedding gift for me. What would that possibly be? I am brought back to the present moment by Vitally's hands shaking my shoulders. Staring him in the eyes I speak.

"Is it true? Is she dead? Did she kill herself after she killed her lover?"

I am screaming, not carrying who is hearing me anymore. What kind of fucked twisted game is this?

"Yes it's true."

Vitaly says the truth, I know he never lied to me, never. No matter how ugly the truth was, he told me the truth always and forever. I know he will never lie to me. I start to cry and he hugs me, enveloping me in his huge bear-like arms. He provides the comfort I need in these moments. No matter what happened and how much disgust I had for that woman, she was my mother. It hurts like hell to know she didn't even look back to us. To Misha, her star, her beauty. She took her life so selfishly. I cry because I am angry and cannot control myself anymore. I knew no matter where they went disaster followed, it happened again. This wedding was amazing, until he showed up, only to ruin it. Only to destroy my happiness once again.

My father always did that to me, always took away the happy moment from me. This was supposed to be about me and Lan, not about him and his fucking selfish wife.

"I hate them, I really do hate them. They ruin everything once again."

I tell Vitaly as he caresses my bare back providing the comfort.

"I really don't want to be here anymore. I cannot go back there and pretend like nothing happened. Pretend that I don't know. I can't, this is too much. I fucking hate them!"

I am screaming and punching Vitally's big chest. He lets me take all my anger and frustration out on him.

"I will take you to Lan's car and make sure he will take you out of here. Fuck the wedding. They had enough for today. I promise you will be the most guarded woman in this fucking family. I will make sure of that, even if I need to pay with my life for that!"

The second person to tell me that in a matter of minutes. What the hell it's happening? Why is everyone so willing to die protecting me? As we make our way to Lan's Bugatti, I see Nikolai heading towards us.

"Are you alright? Can I do anything for you?"

He asks so calm and low. If I wouldn't be in this state, I would say that he is almost obeying me. Because I cannot speak, Vitaly says.

"Just bring Lan to take her home. She is in shock now, they had enough of a show." Exchanging a serious look, Vitaly adds.

"She is fine, just tired. A lot to process and more to come. She will make her way to Elena these days. I will make sure of that."

I start to scream

"Stop fucking talking like I am not here. I am able to hear you and what the fuck is going on? Where is Lan? Does he know about all this?" Power drains from me again. Everything moves in slow motion, people are talking but I don't understand anymore. I know I'm screaming, I don't know what. I see Lan arms come towards me, they are so far away. Before he could catch me, I fell at the bottom of the ocean.

My mother is there, her lifeless body lies down on the ocean floor, and somehow she is smiling at me. For the first time, she is proud of me. She is proud of who I am and who I became. Who did I become, that she is so proud of? I ask, but before she can answer me, everything goes dark. Like someone suddenly hid the sun and I can see nothing. Peace is nice, peace is good and I welcome her as I close my eyes, even if it is already dark.

When I open my eyes, I am in a room I have never been before. I need a minute to realise it's a hotel room. Lan is next to me in bed with his hands wrapped around my waist. I try to move without waking him but no such luck.

"Good morning!"

"Good morning!"

I can see it's light outside, but the drapes are closed so the light is not so bright, which is good because it's not hurting my eyes.

"Where are we now?"

I ask, more out of curiosity than the need to know.

"At the hotel, not far from where we got married yesterday. You fainted and I wanted you to rest.

Instead of driving to London I came to the hotel. How do you feel now?"

How do I feel? I have no idea, but I don't say anything. Instead I try to lift myself up. In a sitting position, I can see the room has magnolia colour for the walls, a cream carpet. The bed is double and in front of the bed glued to the wall a night stand, with an old version of plasma TV on top of it.

Clearly it's not 5 starts, but it's better than driving an hour and half to London. Lan sits as well gazing at me with concern.

"Seriously are you ok? They told me what happened and I don't know what to say or what to do. I am not good with this stuff, never been. However, I will do anything you want or need, even give you space if that's what you want or need. Not that I would like that very much, but I understand."

"I need your mother's address."

I tell him surprising the hell out of him and myself at the same time.

"Are you sure?"

He asked with curiosity this time in his voice.

"She has important things to discuss with you, but I am not sure you are ready."

"So you know? How much do you know and what the hell is going on"

Asking so fast and spinning at the same time, without intention I fly off the bed with a thud so hard that it knocks the breath out of me

"Hhhmm!"

I manage as Lan is next to me in a second, grabbing me by armpit and lifting me up.

"You need to move slower and faster. I don't know much. Mom told me she needs to speak with you first, after they will let me know as well. She did say to me, that if you ask me to drive you there, to do so. No question asked. I never could say no to her, you know that by now. I have to admit, this is very strange. She never acted so mysteriously, it's not her style!"

He explains to me.

"I really need to talk to her. I am not sure what is going on, but she knows everything about me including that night."

As I finish Lan eyes are nearly popping out of her sockets.

"What? I never said a word to her, you need to believe me!"

"I do! But, I still want to go!"

I did believe him, but I needed answers to all my questions. I needed to know why all these people are so willing to die for me, all of a sudden. Why if they did know about what happened that night, nobody bothered to do something about it? Why did my mother kill herself? What happens with my father? And so many other questions. I knew Lan was not the person to answer this. And no matter how much I will wait, I will end up in front of the same person. Why wait then? With that we went to shower and get dressed. We grabbed coffee and some sandwiches for the road from the hotel restaurant. It wasn't a long ride, about an hour or an hour and half depending on the traffic, except today traffic wasn't helping.

Two hours later I was standing in Elena's room waiting for her to start her story. Never expecting what this woman was about to tell me and the way that changed my life, from that moment on. I will always and forever be grateful to Elena for everything she did for me, even after she left this world forever.

Once we arrived at Ivanovich residence, which to be honest I did not pay enough attention to how it looked like, I was heading up the stairs. On the right, I was told, it's Elena and her husband's room.

I knocked softly and was greeted with. "Come in dear!"

I take in the surroundings, it's a beautiful room the colour of walnut wood with cream drapes, I was expecting to see Elena in the massive bed. Instead, I found her next to the window. Sited at a small coffee table in her chair.

"Welcome! Please join me!"

She says and I made my way to her, sitting on the opposite chair, facing her. She smiles warmly and lets me know the coffee in front of me is indeed for me and if I would like, she can tell her chef to prepare something for us. Or, if I am not very hungry she will have lunch, with the rest of the family, in an hour anyway. We agree to join everyone for lunch in an hour. Elena starts to speak.

"I believe you have so many questions that your head is spinning. I was like you once, maybe worse. Unlike me back then, you have me here to explain everything for you. I made sure of that long time ago…I look at her like she lost her mind and she laughs… dear I expect this day since you were born. With the only exception I never believe I will have so little time to see you here, I'm glad for the time I have anyway… A long time ago…she started to say looking out the window like looking in the crystal bowl, back in time…my father and your grandfather were very best friends. They grew up on the Altai Mountains, they were very brave men. Because back then times were hard for Russians, especially after the battle that took place between Russian Secret Air Service and U.S Marine MARSOC Forces. U.S Forces infiltrate a missile control silo taken over by Russian Ultranationalists in order to reach the control room and upload the abort codes, so they could stop the nuclear ICBMs from reaching the Eastern Seaboard of the United States. The plan went awry when a sergeant activated his emergency transponder, when landed by parachute. The SAS troops had to quit their silence and fight their way in. They took out an enemy convoy and pushed through several Russian troops to get to the silo and rescue their captain. They were able to rescue him, but they continued the attack. They destroyed the Russian power station, to disable the electricity of the base. Allied troops proceeded to launch an attack on the base. They fought a gunfight with the Russian troops in the centre, and later rappelled into the silos in order to stop the launch, using abort codes obtained through the Russian government. They fought their way to the war room, and deactivated the missiles blowing up over the Atlantic Ocean. Not before wounding a few Virginians. With the ICBM threat averted, the Allied troops fought their way out of the facility destroying not only the silo and everything around it, but half of our village as well. We needed nearly a decade to come back from the damage they created then. In order to make sure the story is not repeating itself later in time, my father and your grandfather founded an organisation, called Vory, that would guide themselves by a code, called Vory V Zakone. This organisation had as a president one man but it was actually led by a woman. A woman everyone would die for in order to protect. This woman was your grandmother…my mouth was literally hanging by now, what she was telling me? It could not be true…and many years after… myself. The rules of the code were simple and only eighteen in number. Later, I will show you what they are and how they look. Explain them to you…to me? Why to me? But I did not ask, I was just listening…because my father's family and your grandfather's family came from money and connections, they decided to help everyone rebuild our village. They made a treaty with all the countries surrounding us. Countries like Kazakhstan, Mongolia and China to help them sell their supplies, like guns, drugs and many other things, just let them use the passage they build through the mountain. In this way they will pass the border, without being checked. We had two conditions.

First to pay us a protection tax. Money we used to develop the Vory family and all people depending on us.

Second, to make sure any information they have on Americans, will be passed to us as well. To be able to take precaution for what was to come.

They weren't very happy to agree to this, but they needed the passage and the safety of their merchandise. So, they gave in. Things were going well, the village would slowly, but surely rebuild. People would turn to their new normality and us children would start to play outside, without the fear of people falling from the sky. In this way I met your father and became best of friends, until your mother. Well maybe even after, but it was more difficult. Your father was there for me and for that I want to be here for you. He was not a bad man, he just made the mistake to fall in love with the wrong person and fight everyone else away…her voice held equal parts hate and pain as she was talking about my parents. I could not picture a happy and good man in the body of my father…until it was too late.

We were close, so close we would say to whoever asked that we are brothers. For us it was comic back then, it still is as I recall. But, time passed and we grew. We were still friends, but like I mentioned your father fell in love with your mother, who was in love with Sergei. No one could change his mind, not even when they closed their eyes. He loved her until the last breath…her last breath or his last breath? No he was alive last night. Why is she talking like he died? …She was determined to be the next to rule the Vory. She had nothing that was needed in her to do so. When she realizes that Sergei is not in love with her and he will never love and support her to achieve her goals. She sleeps with your father in order to make Sergei jealous. Only to learn she was pregnant with you. That nailed all her chances with Sergei and she was forced to marry your father. Needless to say he was the happiest man I ever saw and the blindest, by far. His love for her ruined all of you. No matter how many times everyone, including your grandfather, told him your mother doesn't love him, he fought harder, fiercer to prove everyone wrong. Only to be broth to his knees, time and time again, by the same woman he fought so much for,.

She pushed him to play, made him go every night in that casino.   Nikolai, who was my father's right hand, had strict orders to not let him get close enough of the Vory table. Back then my father was the president and your grandmother the leader. In this way, both families would be in charge. It pained your grandfather to see his only son ruining his life, but family was above everything, the whole village and the surroundings were depending on Vory. We needed to be careful and diplomatic. We need to be able to smile when we want to cry. To control when we want to kill. Show no emotion in the deepest moments of sorrow. Your grandfather did everything he could to make amends with your father, the problem was that your mother was more demanding every time. Always being so unhappy with everything. Until, the day your grandmother passed away and your father lost every bit of power and support he had, up to that moment. I was next in line to lead Vory and Nikolai took your father's place as president, that's how I met my husband and became family to Nikolai. It was the most beneficial alliance we could do at that time. Dimitri was studying politics and wanted to be a politician.

Nikolai with me would rule the Vory and have more information coming our way, which helped to make the best decisions we could, in order to develop this family more and more, to the point where it is today. We made sure our people would be educated. Our children would benefit the chances to find better jobs and leading positions. We develop a spying system, as many refer to it. To us was a good intelligence service. We would support brilliant minds to go in the world and have a chance to learn more and more. When they came home, they would help us to put together the most performing system they could find in real time. We had children that we grew and helped working for travel companies all over the world. Mechanical engineers working in Aerospatiale factories. IT engineers, slowly we made our way up to politics and like that our family would grow stronger with each year. For those who could not or did not have the will or patience to study, we helped them to develop in other aspects. There were beautiful girls who would like the taste of money, they would sleep with the surrounding countries soldiers and bring new information. Or help us distribute and sell their merchandise. Of course, not everything was legal, but it was quicker to find the raw information and compared with official ones. It was a better way of staying on top of everyone in times of need. Being one step ahead would help a lot. Our only mistake in all this was that night, when no one was able to realise what your father planned. Would take years to clean his mess without creating a commotion and raise a lot of questions. Both me and Nikolai were still young and new to all of this at the time. Very in love with his partner, in my case I was lucky, I got to live my love story and still manage to lead Vory. This is what I want for you as well. Unfortunately, Nikolai was a different story. I knew about Ana, a perk of being a shadow in a family you lead, is that everyone talks to you and they have no idea who they talk to. I wanted what was best for Nikolai. Your mother on the other hand decided that is the moment to show her cruel side. She made friends with Ana and convinced her not to tell a soul, not even Nikolai, and that was her demise.

One night your mother asked Ana to come and babysit you, because your father was drinking too much again and he took Misha with him to the casino. When Ana got to your house your mother killed her to get back on Nikolai. She poured sulphuric acid on Ana and buried her in your room, under your bed. No one ever knew she was there, except your father, who came home too early and discovered all the scenes unfolding as your mother would dig Ana's grave. Nikolai found out she was missing a week after her being dead. He swore not to love again, until recently… *she winks at me and brings a finger to her mouth in a sign of secret. This woman is something else and I was to take aback of everything. It was like I was listening to a movie story or something…* Your father decided to fix her mistakes and found out who Ana was. She had a brother, your father made sure to frame as a drug leader that wanted to run away with you. Blaming him of rapping you and killing Ana. Nikolai was too raged to read between the lines and beat the man to death. From that day on, your father had leverage against your mother, they tried to turn their life in a way to be suitable for everyone in that family. He got a place in the Vory family pretending to find a mole we were looking for a long time. Your mother shut her mouth being able to see Sergei more often. But by now, Sergei would have Felicia and a family of his own. Life carried on like you most likely know. The day Vitaly told Nikolai you decided to leave your parents house, we all knew that was the day you decided to wake up from whatever happened with you. Vitally gently teach you to get where you are now. He was there to replace what your father did, even if he always kept your secret. Until recently, we did not know what your father did to you. We always assumed it was Ana's brother, we knew as a drug leader...that I was shocked it's understandable. I never expected this, any of this. She was telling me a different side of life that I knew, it was both terrifying and clarifying. Most of the questions I had about my past were answered by this beautiful, yet fragile, woman standing in front of me. The woman I was staring at looked like she was a ghost talking from a different era... Once you come to London, Vitaly makes sure you will know Arthur, who will be your right hand and the person who will inform you. Be there for you when you need the most. He was raised for that. And you made the first step towards him alone. You always had a brilliant mind, once Vitaly realised you are good with computers, we knew you will be a match for Lan, you are so alike that it was impossible not to… how do you say these days "hit it off?" … *And we started to laugh at her facial expression when she said those words, she wrinkled her nose and made a disgusted face, so sweet* …Of course you are both stubborn and you could not be introduced like normal people, or you would kill each other. We made it possible, on a level ground for you two. Hence the bug in Arthur's computer…now, *I was exactly like in cartoons… open mouth with tongue out, wide eyes, pretty much like Tom the cat when he sees that dog every time. Which makes Elena laugh so hard, she bends from her seat, after a while she continues* ….I need to admit, I never hoped to see you two get along well and for sure I did not understand at the beginning what drove him to marry you. As soon as I was able to connect the dots, I couldn't be more proud of my son and even more disappointed in your mother. But, that's a different conversation for another day. With all this being said, I think you can realise that you are the next Vory leader. And your father made sure I will tell you myself. That was the deal between me and him last night before he wanted to speak with you. I told him, I will speak with you if he would find the courage to ask for that forgiveness he prays so much for so long. I can be very convincing when your mother is not involved."

She said and smiled sadly at the end. I could see she loved my father and despised my mother for so long, but she was too kind to even admit that to me.

"I have so many questions, like why me? How would I be even able to do this, when I tried so hard to stay hidden from the world itself? What makes you think I even want to do all of this or even be part of this family?"

I have spoken so fast, I am left without breath. For some foreign reason, by the time I finished my questions, I was whispering and looking around the room to see if people would not come out of the walls. I was losing it. She just stayed there patiently for me to finish and said to me softly.

"Everything you need to know, will be dealt with. You will have time to prepare and take your place when the time comes, but I must tell you. Time may be here sooner than later, because I don't have long to live anymore."

"You still have at least five or six month don't you?"

I asked so afraid, for me, for her but mostly for Lan.

"I have less than a month. That much time you have to prepare and be ready."

Shock. Clear as day on my face, tears came down from my eyes as I asked.

"Does Lan know about this?"

She shakes her head no.

"It's better if he doesn't know. It is hard for him the way it is. He will find out soon about your position in the Vory. Please, let me be the one to tell him that. It will make it easier for all of us."

"Okay. I have a question: who will replace Nikolai at the time he decides to leave?"

"It will be Vladimir. So the two families will always be in charge but they will not be ruled by a married couple. Things could be hard when that kind of feeling will be added to the mix. Lan will take over the family business and take care of his IT company. While I made sure Julia will behave and not cause problems for you. I have a piece of advice too, make sure Felicia is respected, but at the same time don't let history repeat itself. Especially now, when your mother killed her father. She is a good girl, very hot headed and impulsive. Use her right because she could be a value to you, if you know how to handle her."

I wanted to say so many things and ask so many questions, but a knock on the door stopped my words as Elena said so kindly "Come in dear!" Julia opened the door and told us everyone is waiting for us in the living where the table is set. We exchanged a glance and for the first time I saw Julia really smiling at me. That made me smile back. Probably she was a kind girl with too many things to handle. Hell, I was a kind girl, with a rapist father and a suicidal mother. If I could master to find happiness she could too. We would work together in this even if we need to break heads first.

We made our way downstairs, finding all the men in the house sited around a square table, beautifully arranged and with a delicious roast dinner. As I took my seat next to Lan, across from Julia and Vladimir across from Lan. Elena and her husband sitting each at each of the tables ends. I looked in my plate and saw a nice piece of roast chicken, with roast potatoes, carrots, peas, cabbage and green beans covered in gravy sauce, sitting on my plate in a nice arrangement. As soon as the smell of cabbage hits my nose, I bolt for the garden door, not able to remember where the bathroom is in this house. Seeing a shocked Julia, smiling Elena and Dimitri, a confused Vladimir and a very worried Lan, following me to the garden, where I was able to clear my stomach content from the morning.

It's the 14th day in a row when I am sick, my period is late like 3 days now. It became harder to explain Lan why I am sick almost all the time. I am not stupid, I know this may be clear signs of pregnancy, but I was so terrified to do a test, I don't know what to do in case

I'm indeed pregnant. So I chose the easy way, I lied to me and to him that is the stress from the wedding and because probably I was too stressed with everything last night. I can see it is hard for him to believe, but doesn't push it either, which I am grateful for.

Returning to the table I apologize, and try to eat as much as I can. For some reason, it looks like this chicken is alive all of a sudden. After lunch I return to Elena's room and she carries on with showing me a lot of papers, explaining the rules code and many other things. When we finish she tells me to send Lan to her room and make sure I take a nap. I look very tired. She smiles at me knowingly.

I don't or maybe I don't want to know the exact same thing she thinks.

CHAPTER TWENTY

RUSLAN

As I was still glued to the floor, not being able to make my body respond or react, from what was displaying in front of my eyes. I could see Nikolai making his way and save Lana from the embarrassment of being left alone in the middle of the song that was supposed to be for her and her father's dance. People looking from outside will think that was a dance meant to be for two men, but I knew better. I would love to make my body react, run after Petrov and break his bones. The song comes to an end Vitaly makes his way to Lana and guides her outside as I am approached by my mother.

"We need to talk, dear. No worry Lana will be fine."

She is so calm. I stare at her as she grabs my hand so gently, making me move in what felt like an eternity. She takes me to a room I don't recognise, but I can see a lot of makeup and dresses, so I assume it is the room designed for Lana. What are we doing here?

"Listen very carefully at what I have to say to you. I raised you to know everything about Vory and the family, to be able to make decisions under pressure and be there for your wife when she needs you. Be her strength in time of need. This is one of these times, even if the moment it's not appropriate. Ivanka Petrov killed Sergei and then committed suicide..."

"What? How is that even possible? I saw Sergei yesterday morning."

I said shocked as hell. This must be a misunderstanding.

"It is possible and it happened. They wanted to fly to America, but unfortunately for Sergei he was too honest with Petrov's wife and never expected the outcome. You need to be there for your wife. I wanted to let you know earlier, but you didn't listen, telling me you need to dance with your wife. Now, you better listen because great things are about to happen. Petrov confessed where Nikolai's first love, Ana's body is hidden…"

"How do you even know about that? Actually don't worry, now is not the time."

I say bringing a hand in the air to stop her and scratching my forehead after and putting my other in one of my pockets, as I continue "Go on!"

"Petrov committed suicide and Nikolai was adamant to let it happen, or he will kill him. But, before any of these insane things went down, Petrov wanted to come clean with Nikolai and made sure to have a deal with me first. He handed me two envelopes each containing a letter, one is for Lana, I will make sure she will receive it tomorrow. When you will bring her to us no questions asked. The other one was for Nikolai, we read it earlier, before his dance with Lana."

She said to me, trying to appear unaffected, I could see it was painful enough for her. Why would she care about Petrov?

"Out of the whole day in this world he decided today to ruin her life more?"

I was screaming now. My mom was so surprised by my outburst that actually stepped back. Shit!

"I am sorry! I did not intend to scare you. I am just so angry at Petrov. What happened? Where is him?"

Mom being mom, she recovered so fast like nothing even happened in the first place.

"Petrov explained in his letter to Nikolai what happened many years ago. How Ana was killed and how he loved his wife too much to turn her in to Vory. You need to be there for your wife. Is nothing we can do about the past, but it's something we can do about the present. All this will only fuel Felicia more. Lana is outside with Vitaly losing herself in the pain, if someone could reach her is …you. If you do love her, then be there for her. This is your chance to show me… to prove to me, that you have feelings for this woman.

Your chance to stand true to your words from a month ago."

The same words that lead me to meet my wife, a couple of hours later.

"Of course I love her and of course I will be there for her, but please allow me to take a moment. This is a lot for me to take in. Where was Ana's body found? How Lana's mother even manage to kill Sergei and what the fuck is going on today of all the days?"

"Well apparently Ana's body was in Lana's room, under her bed for so many years. Her mother buried Ana there, nobody didn't even considered them as suspects. Petrov's wife ran with Sergei, but we don't know details since both of them are dead. I don't know why it happened today, but you need to be there for your wife!"

"Mother, you told me to be there for my wife so many times, it feels like you don't believe I'm able to do that. It's just a lot to take in, that is all. Do we know what is going to happen? What Vory will do and even better what Nikolai is planning?"

I am almost afraid of her answer, but never expecting what she said next.

"Petrov is at the bottom of the lake nearby, with his brain blown by now." She said so calmly, like she is telling me we are going to eat our meal now.

"What? He was very alive 5 minutes ago, you must be joking!"

Shock taking over. And just now I realise, she told me like two minutes ago, he committed suicide.

"I am not joking with serious things, you should know by now. He wanted to do that in front of his daughter, I managed to talk him out of that madness thinking. Lana had enough of his stupidest actions. I made a deal with him, I told him to go and speak with Lana and apologies for what he did, so he can find peace in his last moment. I promised him I will make sure she will receive his letter tomorrow, after everything is done. But of course Petrov being Petrov he told Lana about her mother. Vitaly is with her but she will need you now more than ever."

She explains. Well, if I am taken aback of all this, she will be in full shock at the end of the day. No matter what, they are her parents. Shitty parents for that matter, but still her parents.

"I am sorry to leave you here, but I need to find her because she is most likely destroyed about all this. I will make sure someone will be here with you shortly, I need to find my wife!"

I say as I head out the door and back in the reception room. She's my wife now, and the words sound so wonderful to say them aloud. Never believing I will enjoy them so much. I'm not able to give this too much thinking, because Nikolai comes looking for me.

"Hurry, Lana is in shock and she is screaming in the parking lot. Vitally tried to calm her, but it's not working."

He tells me as I follow him to the parking lot. I can hear a screaming Lana. Telling Vitaly to fuck himself and demand to talk to her mother, because she had enough of this game. Man she is worse than I believed. As I am getting closer, I reach for her just in time with her body going down. She faint. I guess the emotion of everything was too much to process. Hell I took it hard, not talking about her. As I put her in Bugatti, I hear Vitaly telling me.

"She needs to talk to your mother soon. She still doesn't know her father is gone and I think she is too tired after everything. However make sure she talks to your mother before anything else."

Okay why the hell everyone decided to be weird at once? And what exactly is going on here? But, I am more concerned about Lana than I'm about all the questions in my head. I get in my car and speed out of here to the nearest hotel I can find on GPS. As soon as I paid for the room I took Lana in my arms and headed there. Settling her down on the bed, I take a look at my sleeping beauty here. She is gorgeous and this dress is incredible on her. I am happy that I managed to pull out the wedding the way I did. She deserved to be happy and have a nice memory of our wedding. Except her father decided to end his life today of all days.

I am so angry, I would murder him all over again. Instead to calm myself, I started to gently take her dress off, thinking this was not the way I envisioned this going on. Then again, nothing is as I envisioned anymore. Once I finish, I cover her with a duvet and head down to my car and bring some change of clothes for her and for me. Thanking her that she did not take that bag out of the car. Returning to the room, I take a shower and slide in bed next to her, wrapping my hand around her waist. I pull her closer and sleep follows soon.

I wake up as she tries to squeeze herself out of bed, saying morning and talking for a few minutes. Lana tells me she wants to go and speak with my mother, I agree to take her. Partly, because she is still broken-hearted and partly because everyone at the party last night, told me the same damn thing. We shower change clothes, take something to eat and drive to my parents house. The drive is not long like an hour and half. We drove in silence, me not knowing what to say and her I think still trying to process all the information received last night. Once, at my parents place, I guided her to my mother's room and I headed to living where I found dad.

"Good morning, because it is still morning!"

He says with a smile and I greet him back, but no matter how much I want to, I can't bring myself to smile.

"How are you?"

"Good, I guess. I really don't know anymore. You know I am not good at this shit and seeing her so broken, I just don't know what to do."

I am being honest.

"Just be yourself and it's enough for her, and for everyone. You will see everything will come together. All of this will be water under the bridge."

How can he be so sure? I wanted to believe him, but I didn't have enough confidence in me.

"Your mother is explaining Lana how things are going to be and what she needs to do. When she is done, it will be your turn."

He says looking at me sympathetically and I furrow at him.

"What are you talking about?"

I am confused now. He goes to the kitchen and comes back with two glasses of whisky, in his hands. I refuse mine as he enjoys his.

"Look, we have been preparing for this day since you and Lana were born. It's not my place to speak, so I will let you mother explain. She is better than me. So, while women enjoy their conversation, call your brother and let's watch some football or shitty program on TV, until lunch will be served. What do you say?"

I agree with him as I head to Vladimir's room and bring him with me in the living. We watch some football and we talk about different teams from different countries. I am not into this football thing. I prefer watching MMA fights, but I have no chance between these two. Before we could debate more about what countries are or not good at football Olga, my parents' chef, informed us that lunch is ready.

Well better said dinner was served, because mother was not eating after three in the afternoon. Something with indigestion and whatever she said. We sat at a table when we heard the girls coming down the stairs.

I was across Vladimir hitting our legs under the table. It was something we did as children and carry on to this day, and probably till one of us will die. Lana across from Julia, who by now for some strange reason was looking at Lana with a genuine smile on her face. Mom and dad at each end of the table.

Our roast chicken was served and smelled delicious, I couldn't wait to taste it. But then, I see a bolting Lana heading towards the garden vomiting as soon as she was outside. I was so worried about her, I did not even bother to look at anyone around me.

"Are you okay? It's like a week since you are sick now. You sure is only the stress?"

"Yes I am sure. Don't worry I am fine."

She said and I didn't push it further, even though I wasn't so convinced it was just the stress anymore. Something was up with her and she was avoiding the answer.

I was terrified to think about it, if I let my mind wonder I will remember how mom was at the beginning. Vomiting, eating very less, sleeping a tone. No this could not happen again, Lana wan not having cancer as well. I am just too paranoid.

Coming back to the table I dived in my meal and finished in no time. When I looked at her plate was missing just a few carrots and a few green beans, untouched everything else.

This could be a serious problem, something is really up with her and I will make sure to find out what exactly is. I cannot think too much about this because mom takes Lana upstairs again. I'm back with dad and Vladimir, Julia heading out with some friends. Half the time I did not pay attention to what they talked about, but I am plugged out of my thoughts by a soft hand on my shoulder.

"Your mother wants to talk to you."

Lana says to me. I can see she is tired.

I let her take my place on the couch as I am heading up the stairs hearing Vladimir talk to Lana.

"Lay down and sleep, you look very tired. I will make sure no one steals you from here!"

They both laugh. These two have a connection of their own since the day they met. I am jealous and thrilled at the same time. Knocking on my mother's door she says "Come on dear!"

I walk in her room and find her at the coffee table sitting in one of the chairs, I take the empty one positioned in front of her.

"How are you? You look tired, are you sure you want to talk today? I can wait until you rest a bit, if you like!"

I offer but she refuses, waving at me.

"Nonsense. I am fine and what I wanted to tell you is important and cannot be pushed further."

She is very serious and this happens only when she has important news to share. Coming to think, she is even more serious than she was when she told me she has cancer. Does Lana have cancer too? So before I stop I ask.

"Does Lana have cancer too?"

Here, I asked. But the waiting is terrifying. What if she has? What would I do then? God cannot be so cruel. Except my mother's reaction is nothing of what I expected and I am confused now. She started to laugh at my question. Like a happy full laughter, which makes me laugh as well, not sure why I laugh, because I am a ball of nerves.

"No silly boy, she doesn't have cancer. She is fine, but that's up to her to tell you."

So she has something to tell. I knew something was going on with her, but for the life of me I can't think what it is.

"You know I am always honest with you and always educate you to be prepared for everything and anything. You will be fine with what is next, don't worry."

I'm in deep darkness by now. What is this woman trying to tell me here? Some would say, for a brilliant man I am pretty stupid right now, because I have no dam cluc what is going on.

"What I wanted to tell you is this. Lana is next in line to be the Vory leader and you need to be there for her, like your father was there for me!"

Do you know that cartoons where the character's mouth feels to the floor when receiving news like that? Well I was the guy with the jaw on the floor. Lana, Vory leader? This is some kind of twisted joke of my mother. She developed a great sense of humour since cancer. Before she says something else, I start to laugh so hard that my belly muscles hurt.

As I was laughing my mother was observing me. Waiting for me to finish my laughing moment, which only made it even worse. I could not stop, until she poured a glass of cold water on the back of my neck, making me snap at her.

"What the fuck?"

Without even flinching, she asked seriously.

"Have you finished?"

Coming back to my senses, I nod and stare at her.

"Well now that I have your attention. Yes Lana is going to be the leader of Vory and you will be there for her. Vladimir will take Nikolai place as you will run the family business and your company of course. There are so many things for her to learn and so little time. Especially, that my health doesn't allow me to prepare her as I would like to. I know you wanted to go and enjoy your honeymoon, and all that. Please allow me two months to prepare Lana before throwing her to wolves… literally."

I was looking at my mother like she was speaking from another dimension, and for the first time in my life, I was sure I would pass out.

"I expect you to be there for her, for your child and for your family. I have raised you for this. I educate you for it! I knew what was coming and I spent all the days of my life preparing you for this matter. I will do the same for Lana as well. As much time I have left. I will do that for the love I shared with Petrov and for the fact that Lana is your wife now."

She said to me, as I processed what she said. She shared love with Petrov? What the fuck she was talking about? What love with Petrov? I knew for sure my parents never fought or at least not in front of us.

"What are you talking about? What love with Petrov? Dad knows that you slept behind his back?"

As I was questioning her, I was getting angrier and angrier. By now, I was in her face and by the end of my last question, her hand connected with my face.

Making me realise that it was my mother I was talking to. I put my head down as she said.

"How dare you talk like that about me? When was the time I made you feel I would sleep with someone other than your father? let alone behind his back."

She asked me, calm and demanding. This woman was more patient than me and Lana together.

"I am sorry… I didn't mean it like that! I just can't control myself when it comes to that...man!"

I chose the word man carefully, because she was looking at me like a bomb about to explode and frankly one slap was enough for the rest of my life. I did not intend to get another one!

"Exactly, that's why you need to be next to her, and this is another reason why she will be the Vory leader. Your brother and Arthur will be her right hand. You will help her with everything she needs and be there for her. You have a brilliant mind, and I know your intentions are pure, but at times, instead of using that brilliant brain of yours. You decide that for unknown reasons it is better to toast whoever is in front of you! So now take a breath, calm down and take your seat. We need to carry on. Me and Peteov were best friends, before he decided it's better to ruin his life next to a whore thirsty for power...I made a shocked face as my eyes went wide like onions, at my mother's choice of words, she never spoke like that. I knew she couldn't stand the woman, but never knew how much...I wanted what is best for him, but for some reason he would not stop this crazy and insane downfall he took for that woman. Not even when she decided to kill herself so she could be with a lover who did not give a worthless penny on her. No, he went on leaving me to mourn a brother that I always loved, a friend that was there no matter what even when she was beginning him not to...by now she was crying, it was the first time in my whole life that I saw my mother crying. I didn't know what to do. She was mourning the loss of a friend who everyone saw as a monster, maybe she saw something we never had the chance to see...he was like a brother to me, we were unstoppable together. We swore no matter what, to be there for one another and we were, as much as we could. AND before you assume stupid things again, your father always knew about it... I knew he did something terrible that night, but I never knew what. Until Nikolai was reading that letter to me. I had a very deep desire to break his neck with my bare hands, it was too late. Because the cards were shared by now and he played his in the worst way possible. Even then, I would have gone against Nikolai to help him. Only problem with that was that Petrov knew me too well. By the time Nikolai showed me the content of the letter, Petrov was at the bottom of the lake with his brain out of his head."

"But you said he wanted to do it in front of Lana and you convinced him not to. I don't understand."

I didn't because her words would not match.

"I knew he wanted to do a stupid thing, but I did not knew what. I convinced him to talk to me first. The only thing he told me was to make a deal with him. I asked him what the deal was and he handed me two envelopes one for Lana, one for Nikolai. He apologised for what was about to happen and asked me what I wanted in exchange. I told him, I wanted him to apologise to Lana, because soon she will be the leader of Vory. He could not be more proud of her and told me to make sure she doesn't fail. I'm the closest family she will have left. And with that he turned on his hills and went. I have had time to make sure Lana will speak to him. I never actually believed he would commit suicide. I saw him leave the place, I signal Nikolai who tried to play it cool, as I went to look for Petrov and try to stop him from his path. As soon as me and your father were close to the edge of the lake, he looked at me and told me "I am sorry. I love you, but I love her more. I can't live without her even after everything." And with that blew his brain. I was grateful that your father followed me there."

I went to hug her. She looked even more fragile than she was. And my heart was breaking for her, but like she always said we cannot change the past, we only can change the future. After a while she calmed herself down, took a few deep breaths and cared on.

"Now you understand why?"

Frankly I did not. But that was not what she wanted to hear, so I just said "Yes!" caressed her cheek with my hand and took my place in the empty chair, as we talked further.

"So, what happens now? Okay, we are not leaving for honeymoon because you need two months to train, or explain or whatever you two will do, in order to make sure Lana is the best she can get to lead Vory. But what happens after? Do we need to move to Russia? Can we stay here? I don't know, I have so many questions. What is my role next to her? We never discussed these things."

I said stating a truth, we never discussed these things, but then again we never need it to.

"Like I said so many times, you need to be there for her. Will be times when she will have to make very difficult decisions. Maybe she needs to scream at someone, just let her be. Other times she will need information, make sure she can trust you with the situation at hand and provide her information. No matter how. She needs to know! So she can plan in advance. Between legal and illegal is just a thin line, used properly in your advantage, always. She is a good hacker, but you are better. She is self-thought, you went to the most expensive school for that. Make sure you keep and entertain our family connections and make sure you always have at least an ace up your sleeve. Blackmail is still the most powerful weapon a man can find. Used with your head, not with your trousers. I thought you to be better than that. Your bed is shared only with your wife, not because you are stupid or unattractive. But because in this way you will never get caught in any situation that can compromise you, or force her hand. You know that even the most illegal businesses are made at the most legal and expensive tables. Always have your eyes and ears open and talk to your wife. You don't build a marriage just with sex or primal desire. You build a marriage with conversation, even if sometimes that means to scream your lungs out. With respect, with loyalty and more important with support and unity. Let nobody come between the two of you and you will be unstoppable. Believe everyone and they will divide and conquer.

From the day she becomes a leader is not about you two anymore. Is about all the Vory family. You are not responsible for only your family. You are responsible for all those families and their children's future. Building an empire means providing for people in a way that they would want to come back and support you. Even if you lead them to the most certain death, they will not abandon you. That is what you need to make sure. That is what you need to know. And I promise, I will make sure that in these two months I will prepare Lana in a way that she will be able to deliver all this. She has the strength. It's in her, she only needs someone to push her so she can come out from that cocoon of hers. And yes, a trip to Russia will be necessary, but not in the next two months. She needs to be able to stand her ground in front of Vory. She needs to learn how to demand respect with only her presence. Most of all, she needs to control her feelings toward Felicia, and Felicia itself. This will be her test especially, now that Lana's mother killed Felicia's father."

I was speechless. In the end what more could I say, except "I will do all that for her, but mostly for you!"

After all this discussion we chatted nonsense for a little time and let her to sleep. I could see she was very tired after a day like today. I know for sure it took a lot from her to cry in front of me.

As I went downstairs I saw Lana still sleeping on the sofa with Vladimir next to her.

"She is very tired. I think the whole event started to take a toll on her. She told me that tomorrow at eight a.m. needs to be here and talk to mom. Will you stay or go back to the hotel?"

"It's better for us if we go to a hotel, it was a hard day for her and for me, and I just want to be with her, only. How do you know all that?"

I ask him to see what he knows and how much.

"I know everything. I know what is happening. I'm still young, but mom and Nikolai told me everything since you and Lana started dating. I think the better word is since you saw Lana at the café."

He says and winks at me.

"How do you know that?"

I asked him surprised, but we both answered in unison "Arthur!" of course it was Arthur.

"Once everything settles, I will tell you how easy it was to plant the bug in Arthur's computer and make you guide Lana on the server."

He says as he starts to laugh a little too loud, waking Lana.

"Hey, what time is it?"

She asks me with sleepy eyes. She is so beautiful that it pains. Lately she has like a special spark that shines on her face, the more I look at her the more I am falling for her, if this is even possible.

"It's nearly eight in the evening. We are going back to the hotel for the night and after tomorrow, we will organise in a way so you can be able to be here as much as it takes. Mom told me you two need to spend a lot of time together in the next two months."

"Yes we do!"

She says looking at me and then she turns to Vladimir and asks.

"Hey do you know if there is more chicken left? I am starving."

"Oh, I will have a look. Don't move!"

He looks at her furrowing, but when he says the last part he laughs and she smiles replying that she wasn't planning on running away. Vladimir informs us that is enough for all of us and we all join my wife, and have a late dinner. Looking at her how she eats makes me relax a bit. Maybe mom was right, she doesn't have cancer after all. Once we are through to our meal we head back to the hotel, I can't wait to have Lana in my arms again. I know the next two months will be hard on her. She will be forced to change her habits, learn how to keep that fire inside her, instead of letting go. So tonight, I will enjoy her with all her burning fire. I will make her scream my name, until sunrise. As soon as I closed the hotel room behind me, I pulled her to my chest and slammed my mouth to her.

Normally, I would go slow but by now she is used to me and for sure is more than comfortable with me touching her in this way. I deliver a very needy kiss, starting to undress her from this track suit she has on. She does the same with my clothes, and our clothes fill the hotel room floor. Once I have her completely naked, I push her softly on the bed, kissing her neck making my way to her breasts. Kissing each one of them, pausing just enough to play with her nipples building the need for me in her, slowly going down on her belly. Licking around her belly button and down towards her tights. When I'm face between her legs and my tongue hits her clit she starts to moan. I bring my left hand up to one of her nipples as I continue massaging her clit with my tongue. I penetrate her with two of my fingers, she moans and I feel her juice sliding down my fingers. This woman will be the death of me. Vory leader or not, she is mine and mine alone. No one will give her the pleasure I am able to give her.

"Lan…I…am…Coming!"

She says between breaths, I lift my head just enough to see her arching her back and I say "Come for me baby girl!" and she does.

She comes so hard that she is shaking and squeezing my head between her legs. I allow her a few minutes to come down from her orgasm rush and I start to kiss her again. She surprises me when she says.

"I want to return the favour!"

And wiggles her eyebrows. Damn, I did not expect that from her, but I'm not to stop her or complain, hello no.

"Please be my guest!"

Smiling she positioned herself on her knees in front of the bed, looking at me with a devilish grin on her face. She bends and starts to suck my dick. As soon as her mouth touches me, I am in heaven. All my blood head toward where her mouth is positioned, on my body. This is so good. Man I could die from this alone and I make sure to let her know saying "This is amazing, please don't stop!"

I support myself on my elbows, I need to see her. I need to engrave this in my memory. She is so good at what she is doing just now. She sucks and licks the tip of my cock head, I get harder and harder. Looking at me through her eyelashes, as she bobs her head up and down, I feel the pleasure forming in the lower back. I know I will not last long and I tell her "I am coming…you…Lana" but once I start to speak she increases the speed and I could not hold back.

I came in her mouth so hard that I saw stars. Looking at her she smiles at me, being so proud of her, like she just won the most wanted price of hacking competition. Taking her hand. I pull her next to me in bed telling her.

"I need a few minutes to get myself together and I will bury myself in you after."

She starts to laugh telling me she will help me to recover and she starts to kiss me and caress me. Scratching me softly with her nail on the sides of my abs and around my pelvis bone, man she was good, because there are my soft spots. In a matter of seconds, I am hard for her again. Bringing my hand up, I cup her breast and start to play with her nipple. I notice she loves that. Kissing her neck, this time she comes on top of me.

"You want to ride me? You naughty girl!"

I say as we start to laugh and I get an "Aham" at the same time she slides down my cock. Pulling one of her lips in between her teeth and rolling her eyes in pleasure. She starts to move and soon I move in sync with her. Keeping one hand on one of her hips and one in the middle of her chest between her breasts so it makes it easier to travel between her bouncing boobs. Her hair is open and slides down her shoulder. The way she is displayed in front of me, she is the most beautiful woman I've ever been with. She is my wife. I am a lucky man.

What I don't know yet, is that this exact memory will be all I have left when she leaves.

As she is panting and moaning I get harder… and harder. If she carries on like that I will come faster than she will. I do what I know she will get her there too. I support myself on the headboard and take one of her nipples in my mouth, swirling my tongue around it, I feel her tightening and she says "Lan… I …I…am coming…harder please!"

Who am I not to comply? Especially when she said please in that needy begging tone of her. I speed up my pace and tell her "Come with me baby girl!" We both come together. It is such a blissful sensation that I will not be able to describe it in words. I hug her, squeezing her to my chest telling her "I love you so much that it hurts!" this time making sure she hears me.

Lifting her head and looking into my eyes she says "I love you more!" using the same words I used when we married and she told me for the first time she loves me.

We fell asleep until the next morning when we headed to my parents house. Not before witnessing another round of vomiting coming from Lana. She tried to hide it, but the hotel room walls are too damn thin for that. I heard everything. This becomes more and more of a problem, she needs to go to hospital and check what is going on, for sure I will not be able to sleep at night not knowing if indeed it's not cancer. No matter what everyone is telling me, I know mom started exactly in the same way. Sickness and a few treatment and now she is fucking dying. I will not stand arms crossed and expect for them to inform me Lana will die soon as well.

CHAPTER TWENTY ONE

SVETLANA

As soon as I take Lan's place on the sofa Vladimir tells me.

"Lay down and sleep, you look very tired, I will make sure no one steal you from here!"

And we start to laugh. It feels good that for once I have someone to have my back. I drift to sleep feeling very exhausted after today and everything in general. I don't know how much I have slept, but I wake up when I hear a muffled laugh coming from Vladimir. Opening my eyes I see Lan talking to Vladimir. I ask what time it is and Lan tells me it is eight in the evening.

Man, I have slept a bit, but my thoughts are interrupted by a grumbling stomach. Now you are hungry hmm? I ask if there is more chicken from early today and we proceed to eat after the dinner when we head back to the hotel. As soon as the door closes behind Lan he pulls me close and starts to kiss me, not softly like always, but needy soon our clothes jump revealing our naked bodies. He pushes me on the bed and makes his way between my legs. Oh man that feels so good he is so skilled when it comes to sex and everything involved with a bed. Is hard to keep up with him. So like any good hacker when you don't know something you learn. I started to look at porns, so I get the most needed experience with this man. Hopefully he will never catch me. As he massages me and licks me, he introduces two fingers inside me and I am so close, trying to tell him but the words would not make their way out and he says "Come for me baby girl!" and I do. Every time he says this to me, it makes something in my brain that just to obey him so bad. As I try to find my next breath a thought comes to my mind, how about if I return the favour? I could try to see why the hell all that women love to give blowjobs and say it's lovely at the end? What could it be so lovely sucking a dick? So before I lose my courage I say "I want to return the favour!" he looks at me shocked, probably because he thinks I am joking. Never expressing my intentions to do that before, but after a few seconds he says "Please be my guest!" And of course, I proceed to begin my experiment. Now I understand what the heck they mean. It is something so powerful to feel the man you love becoming hard and so hard for you that it feels the need to explode. As I do my best to give him the best experience he had until now, I am so focused on what I am doing that I just hear my name coming out from Lan mouth and then feel something warm and salty feeling my mouth and of course I swallow. This is what they do in porns, so I do the same. Once, I finish Lan catches my hand pulling me next to him telling me he needs a minute to recover and I offer my help.

Morning comes too quickly, but by the time I open my eyes Lan has already showered and is half dressed.

Damn that abs and chest of his brings me back to life. My hormones start to dance, except my stomach has different plans and I bolt to the bathroom and vomit…again. For sure, I will not be able to brush this off longer. I could see he is looking at me like I will vanish soon or something. I inform him that I will take a shower and get out after, needing time to actually calm my stomach and find a new explanation for what is happening with me. I really need to take a test and do it. I know my period normally doesn't come regularly, the doctor said to me there is nothing wrong with that. It's just because my uterus had a trauma. I never vomit for more than one day and that happens when I eat eggs. Most likely this will be a pregnancy. Pregnancy? I don't know what to do with it.

Finishing my shower I head back in the room and get a new change of close. I find Lan facing the window looking lost in his thoughts.

"Is there something wrong?"

I say as he turns to face me only to see his eyes are red.

"What's wrong?"

I ask, scared it's his mother.

"I want you to go to the hospital and have some check-ups. You know my mother's illness started with the same symptoms. I don't want to go through that again, only this time with you. It was hell then and it will be even worse now."

Pour guy thinks I have cancer. I know it's not appropriate, but I start to laugh so bad I cannot stop. When a confused Lan is looking at me like I lost my head I say.

"I have egg intolerance, probably it was something in the food I ate in the last few days. I did not share this information with anyone, being too stressed with everything around, it slipped my mind. I don't have cancer, maybe too many eggs in my system."

And one that will grow during the next nine months, but I don't say that part out loud. My explanation must be good and believable because he relaxes visibly.

"You crazy woman, how bad is your intolerance? Because one, you scared the shit out of me and second, you know they could actually poison you?"

He screams at me by the last part, but is better than telling him the actual truth. First I need to be sure myself. We head to his parents house where I am being waited, by a very excited Julia and an amused Elena. Sometimes I don't know how to handle Julia's moods, but I bet it will get better or so I hope.

"Welcome dear!"

She says to me and Lan as we exchange hugs.

"Good morning Elena!"

"Good morning mom!"

We exchange the same greeting and hugs with the rest of the family and Elena says to me and Julia.

"Today will be a fun day. Today is the day my designer comes and visits, so we can change our wardrobe."

Amazing. Why do women like to shop and have ten thousand clothes, when they use a handful the most? I will never understand. But hey, now I will be the Vory leader and I need a lot of clothes. Double amazing. We had to go to Elena's room where we chatted nonsense for a good half an hour. With Julia explaining to us how she and her friends met some new guys in a club, how they had a nice time on the beach this summer and how much she loves the fact that she is so close to the water. This is something I can relate to. I remember the river in London and how much I like to walk next to it. From time to time I tell all my sorrows, my joy, and my concerns and the river keeps them all secret. I am brought back by Julia asking me something...

"Sorry, I drift out at the mention of water. I was thinking how much I love to walk next to the river!"

I say honestly and she lights up like fireworks.

"Really? Then you need to come and see the sea! Maybe we can take a walk later."

Officially confused and taken aback by her statement, I am thinking if she is planning to drown me in the sea. I mean from the first time I saw her, I could tell she doesn't stand me. Why the sudden change? Unless it is an understanding between her and Felicia to get rid of me.

"Don't worry I will not drown you there!"

She says as she laughs like reading my mind. "Julia!" Elena says.

"It's okay, I was thinking about that possibility too."

I admit as we both me and Julia laugh.

"Look it's not that I don't like you. Okay, maybe a bit I still don't. I did not know you back then and I know how painful was for Lan what Felicia did to him. I was trying to be protective of him. Let's say, I changed my mind once I realise Felicia is not who she says. Her intentions weren't as pure as she wanted to let me believe. I may be good and at times naïve, but I am always thinking of what people tell me and how they react.

Once the two don't match, I let them believe they fooled me, but I pay attention to what is happening. That is what pretty much happened with Felicia, as well. She told me she loved Lan and wanted him back, because she was a fool. But in the end she could not stop hurting Lan again and again. What she did with you at the restaurant, was in no way what I expected her to do. So with that, I am sorry because I told her where to find us."

Was she seriously apologising to me? I was looking at Elena, I did not know how to take this. Elena was smiling at Julia, so I was proud of her. I could see it was a lot for Julia to say this to me, and she really tried to make amends with me.

"I don't know what Felicia and Lan's story is, because we didn't actually discuss the subject, but I appreciate you looking out for your brother. You have no reason to apologize. I would however like you to know, I would never hurt Lan on purpose. No matter how strange it seems, I do love your brother with everything within me."

By the time I finished my response to Julia, she had her mouth covered with one hand and her eyebrow raised so high on her face they nearly met the line of her hair. When I turned around to Elena she had tears in her eyes, only making my eyes water as well. It was a nice moment we shared here, but we have been interrupted by Vladimir announcing the designer's presence, only to make Julia jump up and down in the room. The day went by trying cloth and changing from one style to another. I remember why I hate shopping so much. By the time we finished, I was more tired than after a day at the café. We had lunch at some point and now we are having a late dinner. I could see Elena is very tired and I announce that we will head to our hotel room but come back tomorrow to talk some more. After we take two days break, because I need to go back to London and announce the café owners to look for my replacement as I will be here most of the time for the next two months. We agree with Vladimir to help us look for a temporary place for these two months not wanting to stay at their house. Especially, because we had no room we could borrow, but mostly because I would really like to be with Lan only, at night. Soon after we got to our room I fell asleep.

Next morning was better, I actually managed to ask for a lemon from the reception desk before Lan woke up. Instead of vomiting my stomach out, I just sucked the lemon. I really need to get that test done and maybe talk to Elena about this, since she made some subtle remarks about how good pregnancy will look on me. I swear the woman is psychic. As soon as I caught a moment alone with her today, I knew I had to say something otherwise I will go crazy. Before losing all my courage I said to her.

"Elena I need to ask you something. Well it's more like, I need your advice and maybe your help too."

I say becoming more nervous. I mean she was friendly enough for me to trust her. She was the closest to a mother, well how a normal mother should be with her daughter, but at the end of the day she was still Lan's mother and no matter how many rules Vory had. You never cross a mother when it comes to her children, or that's how it should have been. That's how I imagine me being as a mother in the last few days. I know I would protect my children with everything inside me.

"Tell me dear!"
Elena said in a soft demanding voice, or maybe encouraging voice I really have no idea because I was terrified and the words wouldn't come out from my mouth. Like they decided to glue themselves on my tongue now. Seeing my struggle she asked me.
"You are pregnant?"
I think my reaction told her everything she needed to know, because as soon as she spoke the word my eyes tripled in size and my jaw was on the floor. Like I literally had my mouth open.
She laughed softly and she told me.
"Dear you don't have to say, everyone with two eyes can see. You are shining, you run to the toilet every now and then in the morning, you barely eat anything before noon only to eat the whole meal with the plate itself, if possible at night. You gain some wait, not much but enough for me to see. You cannot keep your hand off Lan, if your life depends on it. And I am not referring to inappropriate behaviour. I literally see you need to touch him in any form, sometimes to brush your fingers on his arm, other times to hold his hand, and so on. It's okay to tell me. If he doesn't know yet, I will keep your secret until you decide to share with him!"
As she was talking to me she cupped my check with her hand. It felt so good, but so strange at the same

time. Why could my own mother not be like her? And without a second thought I just told her.

"I am not sure about it, but I think I am. It's nearly three weeks now since I have morning sickness. At the beginning, I did not give too much of a thought, I put everything on tiredness and stress and all that, but now I know it's not that. I didn't do a test, too terrified to find out the truth, but Lan asked me in the morning what was wrong with me and demanded to go and have some check-up. He's afraid I have cancer. I laugh at him because of nerves, but I am not able to keep him at the bay with this. I'm not sure if he will be happy about it. If not what will I do? I ruined everything before it even started!"

I was talking so fast by now and started to cry somewhere in the middle of the story. If before I could not talk, now I could not stop talking. It was like my stop button for words would not work anymore.

She listened carefully and once I managed to stop she held my chin with both her hands and spoke with conviction, gazing straight into my eyes. It was both releasing and terrifying.

"Listen to me carefully, because I will say this once! You did not ruin anything! You are fine, and I am next to you, no matter what! I will always be even, if not physically. You mean more to me than you will ever know. I will send Olga to buy a test for you. Don't worry she knows to be very discreet. Once the test results come we go further. I will talk to my doctor and make an appointment for you! My advice is to tell Lan once you know for sure you are pregnant, but it's up to you!

And for Lan not to worry he will be the happiest you will see once he realizes what is actually going on. Poor child is blind with his eyes open when it comes to you!"
She says and we start to laugh as the door opens and Lan enters the room, only to panic when he sees me crying.
"What happened to you? Are you okay?"
In two long strides, his next to me holding my shoulders so hard that I will have bruises tomorrow.
"Easy tiger, you will bruise her by tomorrow. She is fine! She just hit her toe at the end of the bed and the pain made her eyes water. Relax would you?"
Elena beat me in speaking and I looked at her with grateful eyes, because I could not have come up with a better excuse than this. But I start to laugh as soon as she speaks the last question. The choice of words and the tone she used, more like a rapper voice and her hand gesture. Exactly like an American film with gangsters, she was so comic. I was laughing, and Lan turned his head to look at her, never leaving my shoulder as he asked.
"What happened with you and where is my mother?"
Turning to me.
"What did you do to her? She never speaks any other way than very posh queen's language, until this very moment. Did you ruin her?"
And we all laugh.
"Why did you come here?"
"Julia told me that she said to you about going to the beach together, is she planning on drowning you

there? Because you don't step out of the house, I am telling you!"
Both I and Elena said in unison "Lan she is your sister!" He was looking between us now.
"Wow you start to speak exactly the same and at the same time! Had my mother brainwashed you?"
And we laugh some more. He soon brings me in a hug and tells me that Julia asked if I want to go with her. She will wait for me downstairs in the living room. I use this opening as a distraction for Elena to do her thing and send Olga to shopping. Looking at Elena from where I am in Lan's arms I wink at her and tell Lan
"I would like to take a walk with your sister, do you want to join us? So you make sure she doesn't drown me, you know."
We laugh again, making our way downstairs and leaving Elena to rest. Once in the living room, we gather together. Me, Lan, Vladimir and Julia and we head to the seaside which is ten minutes driving.
It's a beautiful view, so serene. The way the water came to shore it was so peaceful. Lan was behind me, he wrapped his arms around me with one of his palms resting flat on the lower of my belly just above my pubic area. It was like he could feel I was pregnant and he wanted a connection with our child. I was brought to the moment by Lan whispering in my ear.
"You know after Felicia's betrayal. I never thought I would love again let alone get married...until the day I found myself promising mom that I will marry and expect a child before she passes away...*his words*

made my knees weak but I never interrupted him. This was his first time talking about his feelings and I was not ruining the moment! I just patiently listen as he carries on with the story... I know this sounds insane and mathematically impossible, but for some strange reason I would be thrilled to make my promise true to her. You know? I never lied to my mother, not even in my darkest moments, not until I told her I got married and have a child, which turned out to be true in the end. I mean the marriage part. I know at the beginning we agreed to divorce after she passed away, but I fell in love with you, like I really love you and if you give me the chance I will prove it to you, every day until the end of times. The way I love you, not even death can take away. So it needs to be the end of times. I know I was a dick to you at the beginning, but will you make me the greatest honour to walk next to me in life till the end of time?"

And as he was spinning me around he sat on one knee, with a ring box in his hand that was holding a ring with a blue rock the same colour with his eyes. I was in tears.

"Yes! I will walk next to you in life till the end of times!" And I mean every word. Now I know no matter what, he will be there. Once again, Elena proved she knew her son better than anyone in this world, me included. After sliding the gorgeous ring on my finger next to the wedding band, he stood wrapped his hands around my waist, lifted me in the air and spun me a few times, screaming like lunatic how happy he is that I agree to

spend the rest of my life with him, even if we were already married. I was laughing so hard. When he settled me down I was dizzy, but I could see Vladimir and Julia next to us.
"Finally you did something right, even if the order was wrong!"
Julia said to him only to get a middle finger in her face. Vladimir was laughing at them saying to me.
"Congratulations! But you don't know what you signed up, next to this man! Don't say I didn't warn you!"
He said to me, wiggling his eyebrows and laughing. After another ten or so minutes we turned back to their parents house and I went straight to Elena's room. She was waiting for me.
"How was the walk dear?"
She asked as I sat down on the empty chair at the coffee table.
"He proposed to me!"
I said as I lifted my hand in the air and she laughed at my expense.
"Well I know we are married, but he proposed to me and I am so happy. Elena I really want to find out for sure if I am pregnant and make him a surprise. He even told me about the promise he made to you and without him even knowing, he did stay true to his words. But please don't tell him yet. I want to surprise him!"
And I knew how to do that, but I needed all the help I could get. First, I needed confirmation that my suspicions are true. Second, I needed to talk to Vitaly and with Arthur.

Three days passed since I took the pregnancy test and I was starting at those two lines, meaning positive for pregnancy. Three days since Elena promised to accompany at the doctor's office. Three days since I was so happy, but the only person to really know my happiness was Elena. In this short time I spent with her, this super slim and super sick woman showed me more love, appreciation and respect than all people in my life, Lan included, since I know all of them. She became my best friend, my confident, my most trusted person, the best advisor and critic for everything, but most of all she became the mother I never had and I told her that every day. We made it a habit by now to meet every day and every night I will go to our apartment, but not before telling her how much she means to me. Now she is here with me in the doctor office waiting on pins and needles to let me know the blood tests results. When the door opens and the doctor announces.
"I have good news to share!"
I know what she is about to tell me, but Elena's excitement is more than mine as she asks.
"She is indeed pregnant?"
Me and the doctor laugh at her excitement. It's nice to see her showing feelings. She is a fireball like me, but never expresses her feelings. Probably a habit now, after so many years of controlling herself. We realise that we have a lot of things in common.
"Yes she is indeed pregnant!"

Seconds after Elena lifts from her chair and hugs me so tight, I am afraid for her more than for me. A tear slid down her cheek as she said.
"Now I am ready to depart from this world knowing I have lived this moment. Lan will be very happy!"
Oh my God I will cry now.
"Thank you! I am happy that you were here with me today! I am very happy for this moment."
And I was. Now, I could continue my plan to surprise Lan. As we head to Elena's house I say to her.
"I know time is not in our favour, but I would like to have a week with Lan in London, because I prepare a surprise for him and I have a few things to put together. I will come back after that. That's one thing and the second, I would like you to think of a name for your grandchild. Like a name for a boy and a name for a girl. I would really like you to be the one to choose the name. You would save a massive fight between me and your son. No matter how good or awful the name is, he cannot argue with you! I say and we both laugh.
"You made me the happiest person in the world, yes you can take a week off. It's not ideal, but I understand and I would be honoured to choose the name of my future grandchild. Thank you for this moment!"

CHAPTER TWENTY-TWO

RUSLAN

Since we agreed to stay in Southend-on-Sea, Lana and my mother were inseparable. At some point, I believed Julia would start to feel an outsider or become jealous but neither happened. My sister surprised the hell out of me when she told me she spoke with Lana, and made amends for her behaviour. This is strange even for Julia. I asked her what is going on and what she is planning. She laughed at me and told me I am too paranoid. Apparently mom explained to her Lana's role in our family and in Vory and told Julia that Lana is not a treat for her. Neither in the family nor in mom's heart. Julia used her brain for the first time in her life and instead of going to war with Lana, she tried to get to know her and was surprised… they actually like each other. So much that I find Julia slapping the back of my head one day.

"What the hell was this one for? And why is everyone slapping the back of my neck??"

"First you were a dick. Second, you have such a wide neck that my hand fits perfectly when I hit you!"

"What have I done to you to qualify me as a dick?"

"To me, nothing. To Lana!"

I furrow my eyebrows.

"What did I do to her?"

Man, that woman can be a mystery at times I swear.

"When I asked her how you proposed to her, she tried to change the subject and because I pushed so hard, of course because I know what you are capable of. She had no other choice than to admit you never proposed. May I know the reason for your stupidity toward this very important moment in a woman's life?"

Great job man! Play this one, with none other than your annoying sister that for some unknown reason decided to take sides with my wife and crucify me for not proposing. But, she started to tap her fingernails on the table we were sitting in the living room. That annoyed the hell out of my ears.

"Well I don't have one reason. I just didn't do it. I believed it's not necessary to propose, once I made my intention clear."

I said the truth.

"Well, I need to inform mom that for once you are more stupid and blind than she ever realised. You moron! For a woman, any woman for that matter, this moment is the most important. That woman needs to be able to tell the world how romantic her future husband was. How they made love after. How he sits on one knee telling her all these beautiful words...she says so dreaming, and I try to imagine Lana next to a bunch of girls talking about that. Not even in my imagination, the moment my sister describes, is right....sharing that exact experience with her daughter later on in life. Have you thought of that? You selfish man!"

At the mentions of a child of ours, I felt a punch to my stomach. Did I want children with Lana? A family of our own? The answer to all those questions was easy. Yes! I wanted that and more. I decided then and there that I will keep my promise of proposing her true. I wanted to do that before the wedding, but I couldn't find a moment. I have that now. Staring at my sister, I smiled that charming smile of mine and said.

"I will propose to her. But, I need your help and you are going to do it!"

"Aha, good morning sleeping beauty! What do you need?"

"First you tell me two things. One, where is the number of mom's jewellery? And second, what did make you change your mind about Lana, because it wasn't only mom. I know you and I know Felicia was your favourite. So speak!"

"You are not going to let this one go, are you?"

And I shake my head no.

"It was Felicia! Don't look at me like your eyes will pop, because it is creepy...and I start to laugh at her disgusting face...Yes, it was Felicia! I mean the way she spoke to Lana at the restaurant. What she did in here, the fact that she planned to ruin your wedding by telling Petrov where to find you. Only because, I mentioned by mistake the wedding location...she looked so sad and her eyes were shining. She was genuinely sorry. This crazy selfish person liked Lana and saw the true face of Felicia. Well she was growing, finally...I regret that even today. I don't know if I could forget myself if Petrov would have blown his brains in front of Lana… Man, stop looking at me like I am an alien! I talk to mom and she was always honest with me, like she was with you. Just because I act stupid sometimes it doesn't mean I can't see or judge the things. Look, I am sorry for the way I treat her then, but I am trying to make amends here, right!"

She did try and I could see she was sorry, so I did the only thing that I knew she would understand. I stood and took her in my arms giving her a tight hug and a "Thank you!"

"You, bear! You are going to smash me, and I will be no use to you dead!"

She said and we both laughed but I let go of her.

"I will bring you the number of the jeweller, but I need to see the ring before everyone. Actually, I will help you choose it, because you have terrible taste. We just need the ring size, but I know how to get it."

"Oh! My little detective!"

I said trying to sound like the guy that plays Lucifer, her favourite series. Rubbing my fingers from my right hand to one another, like I would pour salt on the table as I said the words.

Three days since I plotted with my sister to buy Lana an engagement ring. She kept her word and found out the ring size. After our discussion she took Lana to her room, pretending that she doesn't know what ring to choose for her new outfit. Putting Lana to try all her rings, it was so obvious for me what she was trying to do. I was surprised that Lana did not say a thing about this whole situation or she didn't even get the hint of it.

Today mom and Lana are gone to finalise some papers and arrange something else with the bank and I have no idea what else. I took the opening to meet the jeweller and still be back in Southend-on-Sea by the time mom and Lana will be home for lunch.

As soon as I came back, Julia was next to me making me show her the ring she chose. Adamant I have no taste when it comes to this, it is a beautiful 24 karat gold ring with a blue sapphire in the middle and smaller diamonds descending down either side of the sapphire to the middle of the finger. I ordered a special box covered in blue velvet to put the ring in it.

What I liked the most is that the blue sapphire had the same shade as my eyes. Another one of Julia's requests. I was so nervous about what was about to happen. I could not hold my hand from not being shaken. I don't know why? She was married to me already and she was not about to run anyway. Julia told me she talked to Lana before they went out today and asked her if she wanted to come to the seaside as Lana was joking if she was planning to drown her. I went upstairs to try and make Lana actually come with us for the walk. Once I got upstairs all the wind was knocked out of me as I saw Lana crying. On autopilot, I just went to her and grabbed her by the shoulders and asked her what was wrong. Mom explained to me that nothing is wrong. Lana just hit her toe in the corner of the bed. Thank God for that. A bit of drama and shock as my mom suddenly started to act weirdly mimicking some gangsters from an American movie, them talking the same words at the same time. Man that was weird, but soon we were on our way to the sea side and I was a ball of nerves. Once we were closer to water I placed myself behind her back wrapping my hands around her. I put one of my hands flat on her lower belly and for a second I was thinking how she would look pregnant. A big swollen belly filled with our child. After a few seconds I opened up and told her about Felicia and how I believed, I will never love again after her. I told her how I felt in love with her and now was the moment to say the magic words. My heart beat so hard in my chest it was like she could hear it. I had to continue with what I had planned "...I know I was a dick to you at the beginning but will you make me the greatest honour to walk next to me in life till the end of time?"

I was waiting for her response on pins and needles. I don't even know why I was so nervous. But she said.

"Yes! I will walk next to you in life till the end of times!"

At this moment I was the happiest man alive. As I stood, I wrapped my arms around her waist. I lifted her in the air and started to spin her as I was screaming.

"I am so happy, I can't believe you said yes! I fucking love you so much!"

My sister was laughing and Vladimir was congratulating us. Looking at Lana I was thinking that the next thing I will make sure is to put a baby in that belly of hers. I will keep my word true to my mother. We will expect a baby, until her time to leave this world comes. But maybe, just maybe I am lucky enough and she gets to meet her grandchild.

After this, days were passing by so fast. Lana was busy with mom and by the time we were back to our temporary apartment here, she fell asleep as soon as she hit the pillow.

Three days later mom and Lana are in town, I am trying to catch some work I neglect these days, when Nikolai calls me.

"Hey man how are you?"

Even if he is my uncle and I do respect him, he made sure that I will not call him uncle or talk to him in third person. He wanted to be my best friend and he did a good job for that matter. Don't get me wrong there were times when I would make him so angry he made me call him "sir" like he was some kind of monarchy or something.

"Hey!"

I say, but like always with Nikolai, he doesn't waste the time. Especially in matters so important like this one.

"Listen, you need to do your thing and go on the dark web. Somebody put a target on Lana's head and a 3 mil reward for who brings her, dead or alive. At an address that comes up empty land in Russia, on GPS. We tried to do our best in finding the track from my office here in London, but we came up with dead ends. You are the best in this. And don't mention anything to either one of the Vory women, until we know for sure if it is legit info or not."

He says as my blood runs cold. Lana a target?

"What the hell are you talking about? I can have a quick look on the dark web, but it will not be something to dig into because I'm at mom house. For deeper digging I need to be back in my London office."

"Well, I know Lana is busy with Elena, but you need to be here and try to sort this out. We know that it's a Russian source. It uses VPN and a lot of different servers to lose track, I have a guy I like you to meet. He is good, almost as good as you are and he helped me a lot. My only problem with him is, half the time I don't know what the hell is he talking about. And he speaks both Russian and English, except when it goes in full IT mode no matter the language, it's still freaking Chinese. Anyway the guy is good, so good that first he found out that Lana is a target and the price is 3 mil for her and second, the top most skilled assassins are on her track. Apparently, until now she is fine, because she did not use her real name in many transactions other than her wages from the café, which is shitty pay. Why does she work there anyway? And a pizza delivery at her old address. Except, we are talking about ex Special Forces here, they are paid top money to dig her out from the grave if need be, and you know that."

"Nikolai how the fuck this happened? I will be in London until 4 o'clock this afternoon, mom and Lana are out arranging some shit with a bank and papers. I will drag Lana to London, if I have to. I need to talk to your guy and know anything he knows. But, before that, are you sure you can trust this guy?"

I say as my blood boils with angriness, worry and fear. I cannot lose Lana, not after everything we went through. I will find whoever is behind this and I will blow his or her brain myself if need be.

Nikolai proceeds to tell me that the guy is trustable and he guarantees for him. Nikolai never guarantees for anyone. So this must be something. He goes on telling me he will speak with Vitaly and announce Vory. So they can put a tail on Lana and mother in this way she will be kept under surveillance. At all times.

I know Vory has some skilled ex forces as well. With some of them I would not want to mess up myself and I am not a small guy, and did a lot of training in Vitally's gym. I tell Nikolai that I strongly believe we need to inform both mom and Lana, before anyone does it for us. He is not happy, but agrees in the end.

As soon as Lana and mom come back from where they were, which at this point in time I don't even care. They are here and they are safe and sound.

"We need to talk in mom's room. It's important and I expect full cooperation."

I say very serious, but the last part I said was more to Lana than mom. I start to head to mom's room, because we have no time to waste here. I told Nikolai

I will be back in London at four in the afternoon. I would like to teleport there now, if possible. Once in mom's room both women look at me with worry. Mom is in her full mode Vory leader as she speaks.

"Dear you can tell me what happened, I saw worse in all these years. So before you lose it, speak!"

She still has her soft mother tone, but is demanding.

"Lana became a target with 3 million dollar reward for her, no matter if death or alive."

I said looking into mother's eyes, but soon I heard Lana gasp as she covered her mouth with one hand and her belly with another in a very protective gesture. She will be sick for sure. Turning to her I say.

"I promise, I will do anything I can, to find whoever it is behind this and put a bullet between his eyes. Until now, we know the source of the announcement on the deep dark web comes from Russia. Apparently Nikolai vouch for a guy that is very skilled and trustworthy in what he claims to find .."

I look to my mother who looks calmer that I know she is, probably for me and Lana who by now found her way to one of mother's chairs, at the coffee table next to the window.

"…we both know, Nikolai never vouch for anyone never. But, he said this guy is worth it. Except, he cannot understand what he's talking about when he talks about his findings. This made me laugh at his expense, on a serious note, we need to go for London now. You will have a tail soon, me and Lana as well, Nikolai orders."

Mom and Lana exchanged a look that I had no idea what it meant. These two started to talk on a different level, by now. A level that no matter how much I tried, couldn't reach it. It was both frustrating and comforting, first because at times, I would really like to know what they have in mind and second, because they both are the most important women in my life and I am happy they have such a strong connection, even if this means at times I am an outsider.

In about an hour we got in a Bugatti and made our way for London. I was way above legal speed on the highway and I am sure, I took all the speed cameras they had planted there. No worry, I will hack the system and eras the footage, this would not be the first time. Once in the security of my apartment I told Lana.

"This will be a very stressful period of time for you. Please do not argue with me and deny the guards, they will be here in less than twenty minutes. One, you will never win this fight. Second, if we start like that it will be a very long period of time and we will want to kill each other before everything is done. I know you are the soon-to-be Vory leader. But, I am your husband… and I don't want to go above you, to Nikolai with this. I know Vory better than you do and I have enough on them to make them obey me, before you."

Dick moved to threaten her like that but I just wanted her to be safe and honestly I need my head clear for what is about to go down. Twenty minutes later our intercom rings and a thick voice informs me

"Mr. Ivanovich, I am Yuri, Nikolai sent me to you!"

I let him in the building, five minutes later I opened the door for him and two other guys. Even, I'm shocked at their looks. Where the hell Nikolai finds them? And how does he select them, after his stature?

Yuri the guy with a thick voice was the first to step in. A tall guy, like 6' 1' broad shoulder, nearly as broad as my door was wide. For a moment, I was afraid he would not fit through the door. Thick arms, I mean his arm was like one of my wife's thighs. Why did I make that comparison? His hand was larger than mine, and his first looked like a rugby ball. He had hair only on the middle of his head, similar to a Mohawk, only difference was his hair wasn't straight up it was braided ending with a ponytail. His face a long oval with thin lips inward to his mouth. Surrounded by a not to think beard. His eyes are light green. It was like he was looking into your soul, when he was looking at you. On his left cheek he had a scar a bit too thick. It started on the top of his cheekbone heading towards his jaw, hiding in beard, not sure how long it was, but I could see it was thick. Like splitting his cheek in two, only adding horror to his rough look.

Next to come inside was a man looking like Jason Momoa, same height like Yuri, same thick arms, oval face, long dark hair and a longer dark bear. Dark brown eyes hidden in his head. Thin lips and a rough look. His voice was a bit lighter than Yuri's when he said.

"Hello boss, I am Boris."

The third guy was similar to the previous two, only he had bold, thick lips, and blue eyes and a blond short beard. A star constellation tattoo on his right temple.

"Hello, I am Sasha!"

Looking at them, I felt small in my own house and I was not a small guy myself.

"Good afternoon to all of you. I understand you were already briefed by Nikolai. Your main task is to keep this fireball of my wife under your surveillance, at all times. Make sure you don't let her go to the toilet, without telling you where she goes. And that is an order!"

They all look at me so serious only nodding in understanding not saying a word. I welcome them in the living room, letting my wife know her details were here and she should come and meet them. I was wondering how she would react seeing them. She specifically told Nikolai she needed someone to blend in. Well Lana's definition of "blend in" with Nikolai's one, was for sure totally different. I would love to watch this unfold.

As we entered the living room, I made sure to be the first, so I had time to turn and see her reaction. As I expected, she was more than surprised, but she mastered to save herself in time for the embarrassment.

As soon as she walked in the living, her eyes were wide like saucers. Her mouth fell open and her cheeks all red in a split of a second, but she was aware of her reaction and she collected herself and put a smile on her face.

"Hello gentlemen, my name is Svetlana Ivanovich! It's nice to meet you!"

She said in that mother posh language. I told you they started to speak the same, since they are nearly attached to the hip. Extending a hand to shake each of theirs. She smiled and said calmly.

"Give me five minutes, I will be right back!"

As she spoke, I crossed my arms from where I was next to the sofa in living, bend my head to a side and look at her, biting my lower lip not to laugh. By now, she was a ball of anger and these three next to me looked like the guys from Vikings. All deadly serious, just shaking their head as she speaks. If they did not mention their names a little while ago, I swear they could not speak. Turning on her hills she bolts out from the room so fast that she slammed the door behind her, looking at them I said.

"I give you 5 seconds until she starts to scream in her phone to Nikolai, like she would want to be heard from here to wherever he is."

I said lifting a hand with all my fingers displayed in front of them and I grinned. They looked at me like I lost my head, but soon we turned our head to the side of the living facing the bedroom, where my wife's voice was booming.

"Are you freaking joking with me? I said blend in. Not make me feel like Mahomet, with the only difference that instead of one mountain, I have three. Nikolai this will not blend in, so fix it!"

We all giggled as I stated proud of myself.

"I told you. God Luck and God have mercy of you, because believe me she had the best teacher in annoying the hell out of you. Many many years ago, I saw this exact same story going down with the exact same Nikolai. Different women thought."

As I told them, I recalled when my mother needed detail for a few months, it was a mess. It took my father, my grandfather and Nikolai to deal with her. In the end they agreed to have one guy tailing her everywhere. I don't see why now would be different. But, my thoughts are shortened by Lana coming in.

"Thank you very much for your time and all the inconvenience. I am sure Nikolai will pay good enough for that. Have a great day gentl... "

I was muffling a laugh, as she was talking to them and Yuri's phone rang. A couple of seconds later, I saw Yuri putting his phone on speaker as Nikolai's voice boomed through and Lana's eyes went huge. So huge that I was afraid they would pop.

"Yuri, you and the boys don't move from that apartment. Except if Lana decides to go somewhere. I don't care if she swears to kill you, for that matter. She is not to be left unprotected, Мы ладили? (Do you understand?)"

The last part he said was in Russian. Two options, first because he was too angry to realise that or because one of this two was not speaking English very well.

"ARE YOU JOKING ME?"

Lana went on full scream forgetting all about the lady like Vory leader…here she is.

I guess by now they are used to this kind of reaction, because Yuri just said "Understood!" in Russian. With that Lana turning on her hills and out the room again.

Well this was nice, but the show is over and I really need to talk to her.

Out of everyone, I know she will listen to me.

"Five minutes that's all I need."

I felt good to inform them of that. Laughing to myself, I went into the bedroom where I found an angry Lana pacing around the room taking a deep breath to calm herself.

"Hey!"

I said as I entered the room. She snapped her head up and fired.

"Did you know about this? It was your hand in the middle? I mean, I have three Everest in my living room and they don't plan to move from there."

Okay! I am alive! Even if she just wanted to chop my head off.

"Listen maybe they are big, hell they are big, because I am partly afraid of them and I am bigger than you."

I said laughing only to make her relax.

"I understand your frustration, but you need to understand this is how it will be from now on. This position comes with responsibilities and risk, a lot of risks for that matter. You are one of the most important people Vory and this family has. That is what you get, three mountains to be with you wherever you are. So if you need a minute to scream go ahead take it. But once you step foot out from this room, I expect you to behave like the Vory leader you are. Not a stubborn child. You spend too much time and work too much to be where you are. Don't put everything in the bin now. Life is not hearts and flowers. Life is like a rose! A very beautiful flower that many would like to have, but very few are able to hold it without stinging. You are one of those very few people. So think wise your next move and do not sting yourself in a little thorn. I will stand next to you, no matter what. I am going to tell you one thing that my mother said to me when I was a little boy. No matter if you are on the highest mountain or in the deepest valley I will be next to you as long as you don't lie to me. Vory is a big deal for both of us, but we can make it happen, if we are united. I will work as hard as I can to make sure that target goes off your back and give you the freedom you want. Until then, you take the three mountains from the other room. Deal?"

She was quiet for a couple of minutes, as tears slid down her face, but at the end she agreed with me. Well this will give everyone an easiest time to deal with this fire ball of my wife. I was so proud of her. She always got the right decision, even if the way there was not the most orthodox. Or in this case she threatened to leave all of us deaf including Nikolai.

Two months since I was working with Vory and all the people I knew in IT, to find the motherfucker who paid a big price for my wife's body, dead or alive. Two months of dead ends, of frustration and lately of threatening letters at her old address. How the fuck they found her old address? I tried to erase everything that had to do with Svetlana Petrov, which it was very little to begin with. She was always so careful about everything. This was the tenth time when I ran a scan to the same server and I came empty handed. I feel like I will explode, but before I can take out my frustration on anything, my phone rings. Vitally, it may be very important.

"Make it fast, I don't have time!"

I say, no pleasantries.

"It's your fucker, want the rematch, are you up for it or should I cancel like last month?"

Great, not that fucker again. But, I cancelled last month. I actually believed I have a lead that will help me find the other fucker name. I have a number one fucker with a nice car and number two fucker with what I think is a nice gun and a bullet for my wife. I think it's best, if I get rid of the fucker number one, so I can totally focus on the number two fucker, which at this point is the most important one. For some reason this time I cannot stay away from the race. Maybe, I need it because I need to loosen up, or maybe because it's a distraction from all of this.   I don't know. I know that I just agreed to a rematch to that fucker.

"I have one condition to be in the race tonight. He can keep all the money if he wants, but at the end of the race, when he loses, I want to see his face!"

I say to Vitaly because there's no way in hell I will lose tonight.

"Deal! I will tell him to make it your Christmas present for next week. Be at the usual spot at midnight."

He says as he laughs.

"Fuck you! I will be there."

I go into our bedroom and find Lana with a book in her hands, not paying attention to the book, I just ask her if she wants to do something funny tonight? She looks at me suspiciously and I start to tell her.

"A year or so back, I started to race. I was full of energy, all the time angry and I needed a way to let go. So I talked to Vitaly to get me in one of his races. I was the best, until a few nights after I met you. It's a fucker there that makes my life a living hell when it comes to this. A bit earlier Vitaly called me the fucker actually wanted a rematch. I don't know why, but I took the bet. Do you want to see me race? You know, like Renesme said to you, to go watch it with her. Would you like to come with me? You can call her or I can call Arthur to bring her if you want."

I offered. I wanted so much for her to come with me, because then I would not need to have my head split in two. I could focus on the race, I knew she was there guarded by everyone I know.

"Okay! It would be nice, but make sure Arthur will bring Renesmee because I will have no one to stay with."

"Deal. You need to be ready by twenty past ten, it's not far, but I would like to be there sooner than the fucker gets there."

And she only nodded. I make my way to the office and call Arthur telling him about the race and to make sure he brings that fury blonde with him. Twenty by midnight we were there. I wanted to make sure I get to see when he comes. Lana takes Renesmee in Vitaly's car, as I need to make sure my car is ready and equipped for the race.

We spent time around, until we were 5 minutes before midnight. Looking around I see Lana is nowhere to be found. I start to question Vitaly when I hear a very familiar roar by now. The fucker is here, and just like that I turn and head to my car. Heading to the start line. Forgetting all about my worries. I know Vitaly will find Lana and make sure she is safe til I finish this race. I will have a chat with her about disappearing like that again later. All too familiar ninja style clothes. Not to worry, tonight I will get to see who the fuck you are. We agreed the same route I lost twice, north side entrance of St James Park round the Queen Victoria

Memorial and back to the entrance. This time you are mine!

We take our places at the start line, me in my Bugatti Veyron and him in his Camaro. Nearly naked chick in front of us goes with her part and at "GO" we speed. Only this time the fucker is faster. Man, this guy never learned from anything? He is so fast that he makes the same mistake I did the first time, taking the round too large, making enough space for me to take him by the interior of the spin. Wow, how are the tables rounded now? I beat him with the same mistake he beat me, the first time. I won the race! I won the race! For the first time when I raced this fucker, I won. Dam! This feels good. At least, I will have a chance to see his face. That was the deal of the race tonight, if I win he would reveal his face, and now I will have a face to the car driver.

I was obsessed with this guy lately. I fully stop my car and get out of the car, only to be hugged and kissed by a brunette, who was behind Arthur. At first I thought it was Lana, so I hugged and kissed her back, but as soon as I wrap my arms around her I know this is not my wife.

What the fuck? Opening my eyes, I'm greeted with a brunette Felicia.

 "Hello Lan, I am so happy you won the race! Congratulations!"

She screams, full happiness, what makes my anger grow. Look at a terrified Arthur, joined by an equally terrified or angry Vitaly. What the hell? I didn't do anything, she jumped in my arms before I even finished getting out of the car. But, at the same time I hear fucker's engine roaring. He spins his car in a circle, two times before facing the north park exit. NO! He will not run away. Not now, after I kicked his ass in this race. Pushing Felicia, I try to jump back in the car only to be yanked back out by two strong hands. When I look at who touched me and try to push him away, I am coming face to face with a murderous Vitaly that says.

"If you know what is good for you, in the next couple of seconds… you will let her go!"

As the fucker speeds out from here and from my life as I will find an hour later. Coming back to Vitaly's words I make sense of what he said…he said …her. Let her go?

"Her? Who's her? Do you know this "her" who drives that Camaro?"

I see Vitaly trying to choose the next words he will use, but before any one of us had the chance to speak, Felicia states too happy for her own good tonight.

"Of course we know! And you know her as well! In fact you know her very well! She should be Nikolai's wife, but instead married you and took what was mine, to begin with."

She says as bending her head to right and smiles at me and Vitaly who tightens his grip on my shoulders, to hold me in place not to murder Felicia. If I wouldn't be so angry at all of them right now. I would actually thank him for that. But being so pissed I try to fight him off, as I hear Arthur say to Felicia.

"Keep your damn mouth shut, if you still want to be alive by sunrise! Even better, fuck off! You caused enough problems!"

He said angry and I have no desire to take Felicia's side, but I find myself screaming

"NO! Stay and if you know what's best for you, speak everything you know!"

I am so angry and demanding, I can see fear on everyone's face by the time I finish my sentence. Except, my head spins with so many questions. This is a cruel joke, made by a bitch who doesn't give a fuck what implication her word brings. I look at Vitaly, death in the eyes and speak with conviction.

"I will not touch her as long as she speaks. Now get your fucking hands of me!"

He starts to lose his grip and Felicia screams terrified.

"No, don't let go! I promise to talk, but don't let him go!"

This is fucking great. Vitally speaks for the first time since all this nightmare started.

"I will tell him everything he needs to know. Arthur, take Felicia out of here and make sure she will never come back again!"

Even though he speaks to Arthur he is staring straight in the eyes, and panic sets in. If they take Felicia for here he will tell me shit. Giving me the thing I have to cool down first. I start to fight him again.

"I will murder you all if she makes a step. I WILL FIND YOU!"

I scream at her as she goes shaking as hell, being held upwards by Arthur's arms. But Vitaly is stronger than I expected. Hell, I am not a small man and all the training at his gym is supposed to pay off. Except, he is still holding me in place only to add up fuel to my anger.

"Calm the fuck down and stop moving!"

He roars in my ears. Making my brain get out of that angry trance and made me still for a second. Taking a deep breath I put my hands in the air and say "Okay." I was contemplating to punch him square in the jaw, but that will serve nobody.

Because even if I knew where this "my wife" went, it will be too late to actually catch up. I look at Vitaly and wait for him to speak as he does after a few seconds.

"I tried to tell you earlier. If you remember I asked you once what makes you think it's a man and not a woman driving, but you were adamant it's a man. Anything of this, he gestures at the now empty parking, shouldn't be happening. She had a plan to tell you…he scratch the back of his head, and he does that only when he is nervous. I know no matter what is next I will not like at all...she wanted you to win this race. That's why there is no money for the race tonight. She said she has a surprise for every one of us, you in particular! She let you win! But she did it so subtle no one saw, even I wouldn't notice if she wouldn't say that to me before! Unfortunately, for you and for us, we don't know what the surprise was. But, I know for sure she wanted to get out of the car and reveal her face to you, he smiles, I even told her she is too dramatic!"

He's not talking about Lana, is he? But then again Felicia said she is married to me, the only marriage I had was with Lana.

"Just to be clear, you are talking about Lana now, don't you?"

"Man you're blinder than I believed you are, when it comes to her. For someone who sees through everyone's shits, you did not see what was right under your nose!!"

I look at him like he lost his mind and speaks Chinese.

"Of course I talk about her! She was the driver to that Camaro all along. That car makes her cope with everything she's been through. She even calls that car "FREEDOM" if you can believe that."

I am so stupid. I was so stupid. Realisation hits me hard and painful, she left because she saw fucking Felicia kissing me. Worst she saw me kissing her back, because for a second I believed it was Lana who kissed me. I am so sick that I start to vomit on the pavement. Once I can get a hold of myself, I look at Vitaly who now looks at me with concern and sympathy.

"I'm going to go home and hope that she will be there, so I can explain to her what she saw, it's not what it is. I had no fucking idea that Felicia is here. Let alone she will fucking jump on me like that. When I kissed her, I was hoping that Lana was kissing me. As soon as I realised it's not her I pulled back, but it was too late for that as you could see. I love her man! I love her more than the world itself. I really hope I will have the chance to tell her that. In a way that she will understand!"

I tell Vitaly, feeling the need to explain myself out loud, not sure if for him or for me. He nods in understanding.

"Let me know if I can help with anything I know she can be hard headed!"

We share a smile at that, I climb back in my Bugatti and drive home. I enter my apartment and I start to call her name, but nothing… just a deafening silence. I check the bedroom, living, kitchen, and bathroom. Nothing… I enter in my office where a song is playing on repeat, on my laptop "Kyo Happy now" and on top of my keyboard two envelopes, one larger straight on top of the keyboards of my laptop, and the other is more like a piece of paper folded in two and place it on top of the large envelope, on one side I can see my name on it.

Ruslan

To Lan,

I understand now why you did everything and why you were so adamant to get married for your mother. She's indeed a very nice and kind lady. I promise not to spoil everything you did for her until now, however please do not look for me. I will stay in touch with Nikolai, but he will have strict orders to not disclose my location, especially to you! I will take good care of me and of everything you gave me. I will cherish our moments together, all the good and the bad ones because you are part of me now. As you already know I was "the fucker" with a cool car. No matter how much you like this car I will still keep it for me, because he is my FREEDOM and the most precious memory of you and me driving. Every time I raced with you it was pure bliss, because I knew no matter how much we fought, we could find a way back to each other. But... tonight I understood you cannot find a way to the other soul, if it's not there to begin with. You always loved Felicia, even if the pain numbed you, while you were with me. She was right that the first time at the restaurant, you too are meant to be together. Because, no matter how much you fight you will always find a way back to each other. I wanted to believe that's me and you, but... I lied to myself so much, until now. You don't love me and you proved today. You always missed her, because you still love her.

You stubborn boy! Don't let your ego come between the two of you. She loves you so much that she will take you with all your flaws. So take my advice and be happy. Be happy for you, be happy for me but most important be happy for your mother, she deserves to see you happy. If you really care for her, give her this and be happy. Be really and truly happy. I will be fine and silent. I will do my duties toward my people and my family. But you must do the same!

In the envelope you can find the divorce papers, already signed. I have prepared them a long time ago and signed them, probably in the back of my mind I knew this moment would come.

Live your life to the best of it.

Goodbye Lan

As I read this letter, I had all the feelings mixed up. She didn't know a damn thing about me, or maybe she knew me all too well. I am sure I did not love Felicia, but she had a point no matter how many times I fought with Felicia in the past, we always navigated each other. Except, I never loved Felicia as much as I love Lana.

I never felt such a deep connection with Felicia how I feel with Lana. It was like something we don't know yet, connected us. A connection stronger than either of us. What she saw was a pure miss-fucking-understanding. I did not love Felicia! I loved HER and for sure, I did not want a divorce. Not a chance in hell! You will not get a divorce so easily. With that I stand

and swipe my hand across my work table making the things on top of the table fly everywhere. And for the first time it was silence, the music stopped.

That happy song telling me to be happy, because she will carry on with her life… shut! Tears run down my face, no she cannot be gone. I need to find her. Arthur! Grabbing my phone from my jacket, I dial Arthur. The second ring he picks up "She is not with me!" he says, but I know he is lying. "Arthur please, I need to talk to her! Please!"

"Man if you don't believe me, come to Hippodrome. I am here. I brought Felicia, so she can rest. She was so shaken, after seeing you like this. Whatever you have or had, talk to her. She needs a closure man. Maybe in this way you can carry on with Lana, once you two settle."

"I will be at the Hippodrome in half an hour and don't move from there!"

And with that I got out the door. I went to see Arthur at my uncle's biggest casino in London.

CHAPTER TWENTY-THREE

SVETLANA

Me and Elena took a moment before getting out of the car, this conversation was too emotional for both of us. Once we stepped into the house we found a very angry and concerned Lan.

"Lana became a target with three million dollar reward for her, no matter if death or alive."

Lan informed us and in time with his words, I brought one hand to my mouth, so I will not vomit on the carpet. And the other on my belly in a protective gesture. He does not know about our baby. They will not touch our baby, even if it's the last thing I need to do. I must have made a noise or something, because Lan soon turned to me promising that he will do anything to keep me safe. Me and Elena exchanged a worried look. We both thought the same thing, mine and Lan child. I will need to tell him sooner than later. Problem was that now was not the time, so I was thankful when Elena understood this and kept her mouth shut.

In about an hour we were on our way to London with Lan speeding so fast, I had no doubt that he had a picture of his car in all the speed cameras across the highway. This adrenaline feels good, it feels refreshing.

I have missed this sensation, this pure power that only speed will give you.

I was enjoying this moment thinking about my freedom in the garage. I didn't see that car in a while now, my fingers itched to touch the wheel and feel the car speed under me. Taking me with her at the same time. Pure bliss, but who knows how much time I will need to wait, until I will be able to have that sensation again. Especially, now that Lan went in full protective mode. Before we left for London, I spoke with Nikolai and told him, I understand I need to have a detail at all times. But I want someone to blend in. I don't need a person to tower over me. I know I am not too short, but compared with them I am a smurf. Except, I am not blue.

Once we were in our apartment Lan started to talk about how I should not deny the guards sent by Nikolai and not fight with him over this because I will not win.

He is so sweet when tells me that I am the Vory leader, but I will always be his wife and that does something to my insides. This man can bring me to agree with anything he says and obey him in so nasty ways just by smiling at me.

Few minutes later I hear the bell as Lan goes to answer the intercom. I head to the bedroom to change and fix my hair that is in a messy way after I was playing with my hands in it, all the way to London. I believe I lost the track of time, because Lan came to the bedroom and let me know my guards are here. Guards, as in plural. I seriously need to talk to Nikolai about this. This was not something that we agreed on, but as soon as I stepped foot in our living room, my face took a voice of her own betraying me in the worst way possible when my eyes met three mountain Gorillas. Recovering as fast as I could, I introduce myself and they introduce themselves. Then I just told them to wait for a few seconds, turning on my hills. I stormed out of the room straight into my bedroom and called Nikolal. "Hello. Are you OK? Did the boys arrive?" I was boiling by now, but I tried my best to sound calm as I said "Nikolai, I specifically said that I need someone to blend in, not three gorilla walking around with me."

"So I take it, they are there and you are not happy with them. I can arrange someone even bigger, if that will give you a piece of mind." Bigger? He lost his mind? I could not even phantom a thought where there will be someone bigger than these three from the next room that looks like they just came out from Viking movie. And in that second I lost it.

All the control and all those things Elena told me, went out the window as I started to scream at Nikolai over the phone.

As I finished my part, I pushed the end button before he had a chance to say something. Heading to living I start to tell this…men, that I appreciate their inconvenience, but Nikolai will pay them accordingly.

Except my conversation was cut short by Nikolai calling Yuri and making him put the damn phone on speaker. So I will hear him barking orders to them, I knew Nikolai for a short time. But I know enough people to understand that if their brain turns automatically in their mother language, they must be really angry. I did not care, I was about to be his leader, so I just screamed louder "ARE YOU JOKING ME?" only to have Yuri say "Understood!" in Russian. So matter of fact, I really wished to be able to smack his face right about now. Line went dead and I turned on my hills and stormed from that room for the second time in a matter of five minutes. Few seconds later I hear "Hey!" Lan says as he enters the room at the same time with my head snapping up and me firing at him. I needed him to tell me it was not him in the middle, otherwise I would lose my mind and really have a blast prepared for him. But, he surprises me when he starts to talk so calmly and makes me a deal, I cannot refuse even if I want to. He is so calm and understanding and has that charming smile that makes me do whatever he wants. I missed him and I missed being alone with him. So, after agreeing with the Gorilla guys from the next room we went to procedures, schedule, routine, new alarm for the entire building and our apartment. When I went to bed, I was so exhausted but so horny as well, man this pregnancy was slowly taking possession of my body. I used Lan to lose stress and he never complained. Making love until next morning and every night after that.

Two month went by like this. I was surrounded and followed everywhere by three Gorillas. Some would say I got used to by now, nope. I did not. It was becoming worse, even if they were good guys and I got to know them a little. Still maintaining a professional relationship at least I made them talk more than "Yes ma'am" "Understood" and "Thank you ma'am" like they did in the first two weeks. I told them, if they want me to behave they need to lose this monosyllabic conversation of theirs. Sasha and Boris laughed at my remark, while Yuri made some big eyes that looked like King Kong gorillas on his face.

I mean they had nice features and they were kind men despite their size and that grotesque look on their faces.

Today around two in the afternoon I talked to Vitaly and told him to arrange a race between "the fucker" and Lan. I still did not tell him about the pregnancy.

It was easier by now to go around with morning sickness and all that, because Lan was closed in that office for nearly 24 hours a day, with the exception of our time spent in the bedroom.

This guy needs some time off and needs to clear his mind. I tried the same trick last month, with no result. I tried today as well anyway. I am on pins and needles if he agrees or not. I spoke with Arthur and Renesmee to play along, if he does actually agree this time. As soon as I got the text from Vitaly that he agreed I was so happy. Lan even came to ask me to join him to race. Shit, I did not consider that, but I agreed so I will not raise suspicions. Once he went back to his office, I called Vitaly back and told him to use the spare car key he has and bring my car in the Square. Keeping it hidden, until I can make my way there. I packed a small backpack with my outfit and headed to Lan's Bugatti. This will be the night I will tell him about the baby and the competitions. This will be the night where there will be no secrets between the two of us.

As soon as we arrived in the Square we headed to Vitaly and his car. We found Arthur and Renesme there, Lan said he goes and checks his car before the race and I got the opportunity to change and tell the guys.

"I have a big surprise for all of you, but most important for Lan, stay close by, because tonight he will win this race."

All three of them looked at me surprised. Renesme even pushed me to tell her sooner, I knew once she knew everyone knew and I wanted Lan to be the first to know, well except Elena.

Taking our place at the start line, I smiled even if he did not see me. For the first time since I raced with him, I looked in his direction, he was so handsome. I loved this guy with everything I had and I will love him till the end of times. More now that he gave me a part of him to carry and have for the rest of my life.

This will make him even happier that it already is. I am sure of that. As the girls said "GO" we raced on the same route as the last two times. The only difference is that I turned the tables and sped up before he could. Going so fast that I knew I would take the turn to large and make space for him to overtake me. It was the same scenario as our first race. The only difference is that he will win and I will surprise him. I wanted to do everything so subtle that no one will argue he didn't win fairly. At the finish line, I turn my car towards him and open my door to get out. Only to be stopped by the seat belt that I forgot to unbuckle, but something made me look up before going for the seat belt button. What I saw was not what I was prepared to see, ever in a million years. After everything we have been through he was with a brunette in his arms. None other than… Felicia, who was congratulating him for his race. That was all the midnight phone calls? All the secret meetings he had with IT guys? How stupid I could have been? He was with her this whole time. The words I said to Felicia at the restaurant were cutting me deep in the heart. He was sleeping with me, but desired her. He was touching me, wanting to touch her. He did find a way back to her, after everything that happened. He was doing his duties toward his mother and Vory. He was raised like that. I know that, because Elena told me many times. It will be my duty to raise our child…well my child now, as the new Vory leader. It was there in front of me, but I didn't want to see it. I was the fool in this game. Closing the door of my car, I roared my engine and turned my car twice before speeding up from this park and his life.

I saw Vitaly stop him before being able to jump in his car and chase me. I will thank Vitaly later for this. I knew Yuri was home and the other guys were off today. Lan told them there's no need for all of them and we will be out just an hour. Where we go is safe enough for us. So they will not need it.

If I make it home in the next fifteen minutes I have enough time to do what I have in mind and pack a small bag of changes.

As I park in front of the building, not carrying if I will get a ticket or not, because I will not be long up there, anyway. I take the lift and enter my apartment, as soon as I open the door Yuri is in my face.

"Calm down King Kong, it's just me. Look, I need to do something in Lan's office and after I will pack a bag and head out. You are coming with me no questions asked and no phone calls to anyone."

As I was talking I was very angry and demanding. I could see I made him freeze for a few seconds.

That means something. Well, I think it is true when they say never measure your forces with an angry pregnant woman. I headed to Lan's office to download a song, just to piss him off further. It was a break up song on a happy melodic line. I put the dam song on repeat. I took the envelope with our divorce paper in it from between his books from the shelf. I made a copy of the papers anyway after we got married but I hoped to not use them, ever. Well, I was so wrong. He never planned to stay married with me anyway.

Taking a piece of paper, I wrote down some words, with each and every word my heart was breaking a little more. I did love this man to the last fibre of my cells, but I think that wasn't enough. I packed a bag with some changes for a few days. I will buy new clothes. Informed Yuri I am ready and headed down at my car, no ticket yet. Amazing, one last worry. Before I got in the car I said to Yuri.

"Switch off your phone, I don't need anyone to trace us."

He nodded and proceeded with what I asked. Once in the car Yuri said.

"You drive? This is a nice car, all Nitro modified and stuff, a really nice car. I seriously did not picture you as an adrenaline junkie. Shit, sorry boss!" I take the compliment and laugh as he realizes what he said and apologies.

 "No worry I will not take your head off. I have seen worse and been told worse. I may be a Vory leader, but at core I am still a girl who craves to be loved and appreciated. I don't know why I am even telling you this. But, I just need to tell someone, otherwise I will explode. Until not long ago, I was nobody. I had my car, this car, and I was happy with that. Once I met Lan, everyone expected me to behave in one or other way. I need to be this Vory leader and hold my anger. Just to fucking realise that the man I fell in love with. The man whose child I carry is in love with a whore who wants to kill me."

I don't know what actually made me snap the brakes in the parking of Hippodrome casino, but as soon as I did, I turned to Yuri only to see a stoned face.

"You know, this could be actually true, because no one actually took in consideration her implication in this mess."

Seeing him furrowing his eyebrows I clarified.

"I talk about Felicia! She has the most important reasons to hate me."

Parking my car in a far hidden corner of this parking lot, we jumped out of the car and headed to the offices of the casino. This was one of Nikolai's private casinos. This will be the last place Lan will look for me in. PAnd it had a hotel on top. I could use a room to sleep in and in the morning see how it goes, from here. First I need to make sure Nikolai doesn't inform Lan of my presence here, or that will be a major problem.

Once in the back office of a casino, which was Nikolai office. It was a big office with massive wood furniture, all in dark mahogany colour. A big bookshelves on the wall behind the office that instead of books would have all kinds of folders and files. An elegant wood office chair in burgundy colour behind the desk and another two matching chairs in front of the office. The massive wooden table desk that was quite wide and long. It supported three laptops, a penholder and a pile of files on one side of the table. A dark grey carpet on the floor and light brown walls.

The perk of this room was that it doesn't have windows. On the right wall as you were sitting at the desk you would have a screen TV that would show all the cameras from the hotel and casino. On the left wall I could see another door, Nikolai explained to me it's a panic room. I found Nikolai sitting at his office, looking at me questioning. So I went straight for the explanation.

"Before you ask me anything I kidnap Gorilla number one here!"

I said as I pointed to Yuri behind me and Nikolai raised his eyebrows so high it made him look funny.

"I doubt you could kidnap him, if he didn't want to be kidnapped. So what are you doing here and where is Lan?"

"Yeah about that. I would really much appreciate, if you wouldn't mention to Lan that I am here. Let's say we had a fight and I need time to process Felicia in Lan's arms and the kiss they shared!"

Nikolai went from shock to more shock.

"What the hell did you say it happened? Since when Lan's met Felicia and when did you see them together and where? Did you know about this?"

He says as he looks at Yuri, but I am faster.

"Before chopping the wrong person's head off, listen to me. I had something to tell Lan. I called him to talk privately and well let's say he decided to share a moment with Felicia before anything else. They were very close, as their tongues touched close…**both men muffled a laugh at my jealous comment**…and well I came here and I don't want you to tell him that. Please!"

Normally, I would go full mode commander, but I think in this situation is easier to go with being nice and pleading. And I was right because he says.

"Alright I give you tonight to calm down and you can talk to him tomorrow."

That's enough time to steal for tonight.

"Listen on the way here, I just had an epiphany. I was telling Yuri I don't understand how Lan would like to spend time with someone who has the greatest desire to kill me...I deliberately left out the part where I said to Yuri that I am carrying Lan's child. Yuri made no comment on that either. I made a mental note to thank this Gorilla later... I mean she has the best motives here. I did separate her from Lan, my parents fucked up to the point where my mother killed her father, I am the next Vory leader. A position she dedicate her life to, plus she really doesn't like me, if she decided to dye her hair blue black just to resemble with me in that."

As I was talking the two of them listened to me attentively. Taking in consideration and scaling every word that comes out of my mouth.

"I have to admit. I did not think of this and yes it could be a possibility. But who could help her put this insane plan of hers in action? These kinds of things take time to plan and a lot of funds. Money that needs to be covered to mask this type of action. Connections to get to these types of assassins. It's not like two chicks don't like each other and try to blow their head off in the parking lot, with a 9 mm. Here we are talking about heavy arsenal weapons, ex-military skills that only highly trained assassins possess, why would she go that far for a man?"

Dam he has a good point and I have no answer to that. I just knew somehow she was behind this masquerade.

"I don't have answers to all your questions, but I know this. She has enough motives and she has a background that comes from back home. I wasn't around at that time to actually know any of them, but you were, and you should think of that. The main source is Russian. Now this means two things. Or this thing started way back and it was not finished. Or she had help from back home. We both know that Vory did a lot of under the table business with a lot of people. People that for the right price they will sell their own mother. So think back Nikolai, because the answer is there. I know, you know!"

"Everything you say makes sense, but no one comes to my mind, even if my life would depend on it now. Let's take a moment. Go up! Settle in one of the rooms, try to take some rest and I will be here in the morning. I'm not going anywhere I promise. I will not tell Lan anything if he asks. Keeping this between me, you and Yuri is the best at the moment. Don't get me wrong, I don't for a second doubt Lan, and whatever the two of you had, I'm sure will come to a solution. But knowing this at this point will make his blood boil more and we need him to have a clear head for what he needs to look into."

He says as I turn my head to look at the monitors and I see Lan with Arthur in one of the game rooms and a brunette, Felicia joining. Out of every place they could go, they need to be in this one? Me and Yuri change a look.

His full of sympathy, mine full of concern that he will say something and when I turn my head to Nikolai, he is fuming red as he barks.

"What the hell are they doing here? But most importantly why is he with her, instead of looking for you?"

He turned to me waiting for an answer, like I was the one to piss him off in the first place.

"Maybe it has something to do with the divorce papers I left in his office? But in all honesty, I didn't expect him to let me go without a fight. Instead, here he is celebrating his new status. I know you are a man of your word and you need to understand we have a family to run here. Business to deal and precautions to take, it's not only about you, me and Lan it's about… it's about all of us. About how much our fathers worked to be here. Please Nikolai don't think with your emotions now. Think like you always do. Prove me that what they say about you is right. Prove me that you are my right hand and together we will rule Vory right. That you will help me conquer every fear and have you as my best advisor, until Vladimir is ready. And in return, I promise you I will stay away from Lan, until everything is dealt with and even after, if I need to. No matter how much I love him. But, please promise me you will let this go!"

I said to him, as I was crying now. It took everything in me to promise that to Nikolai. But it was what we needed. I know he will do right by me and by Vory and I know he loves Lan. However, I could see right now he would prefer to break his neck, instead of watching him being hugged by Felicia. Grabbing his arm partly to make him look me in the eyes, partly because I need it as a distraction to not look at the monitors I say.

"Do you promise?"

Never expecting what would happen next. He brought me in a tight hug and said to me,

"You were a child then and I could not save you. I am sorry for that, but I am here for you now and I will not let you down, again. Even if that means to go head to head with Lan for that. You are safe here!"

A few moments later when he let me go, we looked at the monitors again and saw Lan making his way towards the back of the room where offices are.

"I have to go before he gets here."

"Yuri, show her the back stairs to the hotel. I will call reception to give you the master suite on the fifth floor."

And with that we walked out the office and took the back stairs up to the next floor, so we could take the lift to the master suite. Once inside I said too Yuri.

"Thank you for not saying a word about me being pregnant. It did mean a lot for me and I know it took a lot from you to keep it from Nikolai. I don't know what is between the two of you, but I can see you have loyalty going on! So, thank you!"

"Nikolai is one of the few persons that helped me back in Russia, when things hit the fan with the military department. I will always be grateful and loyal to him. But, here is none of his business, if you are pregnant or not. If you decide to tell him it is fine by me, if not that is good as well. But, it's important for me to know this so I can plan things ahead. Is good to know this for the next time we go somewhere, to grab an extra bottle of water or more food. I will keep your secret safe, I had a fiancée and a child once. They are gone now, but I will love them forever, no matter what. I think Lan should know as well and your assumption of Lan and Felicia. I think this is wrong, because of the way Lan behaves with Felicia. It's not how I saw Lan around you. But, that's just my observation and it has nothing to do with your decisions."

Well, out of all people, Yuri was not the one I pictured to be on Lan side and less to talk so much. I mean this was the most he said to me in the last two months.

"You know, for a Gorilla, you make a good friend. Lan and Felicia have a history together. I cannot compete and don't want to compete with it. And maybe, one day you will want to open up enough to tell me what happened with your fiancée and child.

You know, I can be loyal and can keep secrets, not only you! But like Elena always says people open themselves at their own peace, it's not good to push the universe!"

"Go take a shower and lay down in bed. I will check the perimeter and take a seat on the sofa in front of the TV, if you need anything I am here. Good night smurf!"

He says and I laugh. I looked like a smurf compared with him. But, I was honest. I did want to know what happened with his child and fiancée.

The only problem with sleeping was it did not come, every time I tried to close my eyes, I would see the two of them kissing. I went out of the room and told Yuri I have some things to discuss with Nikolai and he should rest, because I would be fine to find my way to his office and back.

Except. I mixed up the floors, and instead of Nikolai office I got to the same floor Lan was standing in someone's doorway. What the hell? I did not make a sound, stunned by what I saw. My Lan in a girl's hotel room doorway, pleading with her to tell him something. As soon as she came closer to him, I saw it was…Felicia. You must be kidding me! She said to him she will tell him everything he needs to know, she bent and kissed him as the two of them disappeared behind a now closed door. This cannot be happening! Lan cannot do that to me. I did not want to stay here and hear the confirmation of what I saw. I made my way to Nikolai office.

When he saw me walking on the door he said to me.

"My nephew is the most official stupid man I ever met, but I just hope he has a very good explanation in the morning."

I shook my head no and started to cry. Nikolai holded me in his arms telling me over and over again that Lan loves me and he will have a good explanation for this in the morning. I did hope so! The only problem with morning was that I met Felicia on her way back to the room.

I saw her leaving on the cameras in Nikolai office and went to talk to Lan. Only, she beat me to the door and she informed me that they spent a wonderful night together… or, I think that was the word she used. Before, I had a chance to say something when a naked Lan was in her door. At that moment I knew, I did not have anything to look for there. He screamed after me that it's not what it looked like, but it was just like that. At the first fight he had with me, he jumped in bed with her. This was so unlike Lan, but then again they were lovers way before I met him and made the stupid mistake to fell in love with him. I knew this would come, but never knew how much it would hurt.

Days went by and now is Christmas. I hate Christmas! It brings bad memories around. The empty house that we always had because we would not have enough wood to make fire in the stove during the day. No Christmas tree, because dad would drink the money or play them in the hope for the big jackpot. It was too big and cold snow that was always around in winter. I always hated this season. A knock at my bedroom door brings me back to now.

"Come in Yuri!"

Yuri is the only one who comes to my room, in the master suite I live in, now close to two weeks. Since that night at race.

"Are you ready to go?"

No I wasn't, but I had to be. "Yes!" I say, but he knew me better than that.

"You are lying. You don't have to lie to me and most importantly you don't have to lie to yourself. It's OK to not be ready."

In this short time we spent together, we became best friends. This Gorilla in front of me did actually have a heart inside, it was not all rough looks and mountain strength. He opened enough to let me understand that he suffered a big loss when he was younger. Apparently his fiancée was 7 months pregnant when she was shot in a terrorist attack in Spain taking with her their son. We cried together the other night. But it felt good at least I knew he has feelings and he cares about the world.

He told me that he will protect me with his life if it means that I get to hold my child in my arms.

He could not be there for his fiancée, but he is here for me. I don't know if it was a curse or a blessing, to have him guard me like that, but I was grateful for a new friend.

We are going to Elena, she organised a Christmas dinner with everyone. Renesmee, Arthur and Misha included. I tried to politely refuse chickening out from our plan to make Felicia to talk.

I start complaining that I am not feeling well. When she appeared at my suit door, explaining to me that she knows what happens and she doesn't force me to play nice with Lan in front of her. But, she need me to be there like the strong woman that I am. And she said Felicia with Lan will be there as well. Bloody hell, how I should face that? Apparently in her belief, I could do everything. That woman was adamant to ruin me, I guess. What was this old fox plan here? I had no idea, but I will find out.

"Let's go!"

I said to Yuri and with that we left the building and went to Elena.

CHAPTER TWENTY-FOUR

RUSLAN

As soon as I set foot in my uncle's casino, Felicia's arms were around my neck. God, this woman could not take the hint to fuck off? I guess I will have to let her know, but before I could do that she said.

"Lan I am sorry, I really am sorry! I shouldn't have told you like that, but I guessed you knew who the driver was. I was so happy for you that I couldn't hold myself, not to share my joy with you! It was wrong and stupid from my side!"

Well that was something I did not expect from her, an apology? I am even surprised that this woman even knows the meaning of the word.

"What is done is done. You know, you can't unring a bell! But, do me a favour and stop claiming me like a monkey. I am not your tree."

I said as I took her hand off around my neck.

"How are you? How is everything? Have you spoken with Lana?"

I ask Arthur who approached me and Felicia. I will thank him later for not giving me another moment alone with this woman, for taking her away from me in the parking lot.

"I'm as good as I can be in the giving situation."

He said, making a gesture with his head to guide my gaze to Felicia.

"I tried to call Lana, but it goes straight to voicemail. It's like the earth swallowed her all of a sudden. I will try around, I will call anyone I know and see where she went. Problem is that Yuri's phone is off as well and his phone is never off!"

I was contemplating what he was saying and tried my best to think where she could go. But then again, it was a part of her I never get the chance to know. So, I had no fucking idea where she could vanish like that.

Suddenly the hair on my neck was up when I realised what song is singing. I knew I had to go out of here before, I would be too sick to even move. Out of all places and out of all songs, this song plays here in the same place with me. My wedding song! The song brings happy memories of me and Lana, memories when she was in my arms and we were happy.

I had to go out of here. But, instead heading to the door, like I planned, something pulled me to the other end where the offices were. I had to talk to Nikolai.

Once in his office, I am greeted with a boiling hot Nikolai. He is so red that I am afraid steam will get out of his ears, which makes me laugh only to have that anger guided to me.

"Do you think it is funny, to see me like that? Hmm? Tell me? What the fuck you was thinking, parading in front of everyone with Felicia dangling your neck, like a fucking medallion? Where is Lana?"

He was firing the questions at me, like it was hot charcoal on his tongue. What was his problem and how did he know about me and Lana??

"Well, Lana decided to vanish tonight leaving me with no other explanation than the divorce papers and before you chop my head off know that mistake is not entirely my fault. She decided to play hide-and-race with me. Unfortunately, Felicia was there and everything went to hell, before I even knew who was driving that car! So why don't you look for your precious leader. And ask her, what the fuck is in her mind?"

I scream at my uncle taking out the rage I had inside.

"I came here to ask you for help to find her, not to be greeted with a fucking ticking bomb. But of course my luck is amazing tonight and out of all places Felicia is fucking here! Here! Out of all damn London, she decided this casino will suit her needs the best tonight of all nights. So, my dear uncle you are not the only one angry in this fucking room!"

Seeing me like this he calmed down and tried again.

"What happened tonight at the race? Because, you know she had a target on her head and she cannot wander around like she please, in a market full of people!"

"Apparently a while back we raced and I made an obsession for her, not knowing who she was in real life. Tonight was supposed to be the revealing night, for multiple reasons. The only one I have at this moment in time is that she was the driver and she has a fucking great car. Can you believe, I did not even knew she possess a driving licence, let alone a fucking car. She told Vitaly she has a surprise for all of us, but specially for me. The only surprise I received was, her vanishing and the divorce paper waiting for me to sign them home. I doubt that was her intention, but two things are for sure. One, I'm not going to divorce and this will not go down without a fight. And two, I will find her no matter what. I just need that damn VIN (vehicle identification number) of her car because of course she turned off her phone."

"Let's say you found her. What do you plan to tell her? That every time you have the chance you let Felicia jump in your arms? What is wrong with you and that woman? Lana really loves you and you open your arms to your ex, every time you see her?"

He was looking at me with so much disappointment. It wasn't even my fault for Felicia's action. I never encouraged her to behave like a whore, but no matter the amount of explanation I will provide, they will not believe me. I am sick of all of them. With that I said

"You know something? Fuck you!"

Turned around and walked straight into the big room. Hippodrome was one of the biggest casinos in London. It has a huge theatre room like, that it was two floors tall and open space. In front of the entrance door, but across the room was a big stage, where different concerts or shows could take place. With a set of stairs on each side of the stage. The ground floor was now full of poker tables, roulette tables, and other gambling tables. All table green with different imprints on them, depending on the game that table served for, and a dark wooden leg that supported each table. Red carpet on the floor.

If you look up, from the ceiling, would come down multiple chandeliers in a globe shape, lit with a lot of strong light bulbs, so they will provide the light needed for two floors.

On the ground you could see from place to place the same globe chandeliers lit with the same strong light bulbs arranged in some kind of flower shape, they looked like unborn flower buds, grouped in a number of three.

First floor was more of a restaurant area that looked like an interior balcony with a lot of tables and chairs, the second floor was another interior area, but it was used only when a big event required extra space for chairs or tables otherwise it was left empty.

Being so angry, as soon as I walk out of Nikolai office, I head to the poker table. I was always good at poker. I was the best in my group of players. Many could not read me and even more hated me because I always knew how to play my card. Except, since I met a certain brunette I could not remember my fucking name correctly, let alone remember any card I hold in my hands. After about two hours of play and a lot of whiskey. I was drunk enough to remember I had unfinished business with Felicia, and she briefly mentioned that she would stay at the hotel on the fourth floor. That's where my next stop would be. Her room. She has some explanation to do. As soon as I knocked at her door she opened, dressed in nothing but a set of black lingerie and a black matching robe, which hung open. I had everything on display. Damn, she looked good and my mind was clouded by too much booze, but she was not Lana.

No, she was too skinny and her boobs were too small to be Lana. Why do I even compare the two? This woman will never be equal, to my wife. Because she was my fucking wife, mine no others man's wife. Mine!

"Hello Lan!"

Felicia's sweet voice brings me back from the memories. Why did I come in here? Oh yeah

"You need to give me some explanations!"

I say holding me upward by the door frame. If someone would look at us they would say, I tried to get in her bed tonight and that was way too far from the truth. I needed an explanation and I was gone. Except, Felicia knew me a little too well, for me to stay on track with my plan. She brushed her hand up and down my chest, looking at me through her lashes, and smiling sweetly when she said.

"Of course. I will tell you anything you need to know."

Looking past me, for a moment too long. She wrapped her arms around my neck, not this again. Pulling me inside her room as she kissed my neck. As soon as the door closed behind us I said.

"What the fuck are you doing? I told you I came here to ask for an explanation. First will be, why the fuck you act like a horny whore? You never were like that before?"

But, before she could answer, I felt all the booze coming up my throat and out my mouth. Fuck, I was sick. Well, I supposed that's what happens, when you drink your frustration out, on an empty stomach. Felicia helped me to find my way to the bathroom and after emptying my stomach for what felt forever, she helped me to bed telling me.

"This is exactly why I decided to leave you in the first place."

I was too tired to say something. I closed my eyes and saw her smile. I saw Lana happy and laughing, telling me how much she loves me. I saw her as a bride again. And we were so happy together, just like we always are.

When I opened my eyes again, a bright light forced me to close them back and a hammer headache pulsating in my head.

"Don't worry you will live! Here some Advil and water. Some bagels and orange juice and in five minutes you will be fine."

Felicia's disgusted voice boomed in my head. Doing as I was instructed, I took the pills and ate the bagel. When the headache was bearable I went to shower. On my way to the bathroom Felicia said.

"I gave your clothes to the laundry with an emergency tag on them. You should have them back in less than half an hour. I am going out, but I am back in an hour. Be ready till then, so we can eat lunch."

Amazingly, that means by the time I finish the shower I will have my clothes. I am not planning to get out of the shower before that. Lunch where the fuck is breakfast? Without a word I took my phone with me and entered the shower.

I look for a specific recording in my list and press play, only for Lana's voice to fill the shower. Her voice is so soft but so happy. Listening to her telling me about her day at the cafe or explaining things made me realise I love her voice, and one day I started to record her. It was at the beginning, when I barely touched her. I wanted to be able to listen to her anytime I pleased, because she was always in that café, I recorded her. For example one day I challenged her to talk about IT and why she loves being a hacker? What her dreams are? And found myself recording her story.

I did it so subtle she did not even realise I was recording her, took my phone and pretended to read a text when I opened the recording application and pressed the record button. Put my phone on the table face down, so she will not see the blinking light led on my phone. I used to listen to that recording every time she was not around, like now. She left and I'm in the shower of this hotel. Hot water caresses my skin and her voice brings a calm in me, that I will never understand. Even if I could tell what she says word by word, it's always a pleasure to listen to her voice. Before I knew what I was doing, I leaned toward the tile wall, bringing my left hand up to support my head on it and with my right hand I started to stock my cock.

Closing my eyes and listening to Lana's voice, I imagine she is here with me, she is talking in my year telling me all those words. But, of course in my head they have a different order and a different meaning.

She tells me what she says in the recording. She is talking to me and her hand strokes my cock, not mine. It feels damn good, so good I want to hold this feeling forever. As she says ...I love this part of hacking...in my head she is telling me that she loves me and loves this part with me, and with that I come so hard that I see stars and her smile between them.

I sit myself on the shower floor, my leg unable to support me anymore. I miss my wife, so fucking much that her voice and memory makes me come so hard.

After a few minutes I stand, shower and get out of the bathroom when I hear Felicia saying.

"Well me and Lan had the most spectacular night!"

What the fuck is she talking, but most important with who. I open the hotel room door and see a very red Lana, as soon as she sees me her eyes widen and she bolts to the stairs. Knowing it will take time for the lift to come. I tried to follow her only to realise that I have only a towel wrapped around my waist.

"Fuck! It's not what you believe!"

 Too late for any excuses. Felicia's comment and my naked wet body, tell an entirely other story. She will never believe me again. I know that. In her eyes, I cheated her with the first opportunity I got. Turning on my hills with an angry face I storm to Felicia, grabbing her arm I ask.

"What the fuck did you say to her? We did not sleep together!"

But she only smiles at me. Don't kill her! Don't kill her!

Taking a deep breath, I take my clothes from her hands, get dressed and storm into Nikolai office

"Did you see Lana?"

"Good morning. Yes I did! She left the building, so don't bother looking. Care to explain what I saw on my security cameras? Because, I sure as hell am in no mood to keep screaming at you. It's useless anyway, but I would like to know what your intentions are here. So, I know how far away from you to keep Lana. From what you are saying to what you are doing, are two different things."

He tells me to be calm at the same time, as he sits with one leg on the front of his desk, putting his hands in his pockets and raising his eyebrows, questioning and demanding an answer.

"I swear it was a misunderstanding. I went up to ask Felicia why she is doing what she does, but I got sick and I fell asleep in her room. When I woke up, I took a shower and I heard her speaking with Lana, I tried to explain but she ran away."

"Run away? Do you want to see what Lana saw? I in her place have blown your brain off."

And without any other comment, he plays a recording from last night when I was standing in Felicia's doorway and Lana a few feet behind my back. As I see the video running I feel sick again. From where Lana was standing, I looked like I was there for Felicia, and the way she grabbed me, well it left very little to anyone's imagination what was going to happen once that door closed behind us. I closed my eyes and I could not watch this again. I would blow my brains in that moment myself, if I could. How can I be so stupid?

"That's so far from what was actually happening last night."

But, even I realise how absurd this sounded.

"I need a chance to be able to explain to her, this is not what is happening. Nikolai you, out of all people, know me and you know I would never do that to her. I did not do that to Felicia, even after what she did to me. I would not destroy Lana like that, after everything we went through. Tell me you believe me?"

I was desperate here, all the evidence is proving I am guilty of something, I did not do. I do love Lana and I would never hurt her like that, the bigger problem was that I did not know how to prove her that.

"What I think or what I know, is not important. You ruined your marriage and you ruined a girl who loves you more than she loves herself. She was here last night trying to find a way to solve all this mess, only to be greeted with…well, everything that happened. I don't know if I can help you, this time. That's how bad you screw everything."

And like that, nearly two weeks have passed since last time I saw Lana. I have no idea where she is. It's like she vanished. That's the perk of being a hacker, you know how to disappear in plain sight.

It's Christmas, my favourite holiday since I was a child. I always loved the white snow from outside, our warm house with fire in the chimney. My mother was good when they baked in the oven. Her sweet bread, and the jacket potatoes that she baked in the stove oven. We would stay close by to be the first to get them out and we would burn the tip of our fingers. The big Christmas tree dad always broth home, smelling so nice of fresh pine from forest, up the mountain. It was amazing. I miss this in London. But today, it will be equal parts a blessing and a nightmare, this is the last Christmas I will have with my mother and I plan to enjoy it. But it's the first day I will see Lana in almost two weeks. I try to find her but… Nothing.

Dead end!

No cell phone.

No GPS.

No nothing.

I didn't have her car VIN, since I did not bloody know it was her, who was driving that car to begin with. I could not wait to see that car and maybe, I could plant a transmitter device under the hood. So I can track her for the next time she decides to run. I have everything prepared. I just need the opportunity. I will try to find one today at mom's. I am heading there with Felicia next to me. It makes me want to vomit. Last time I was driving this same route, I had Lana in this same car sitting where Felicia stays now. Not even her fake black hair did something to help her look like Lana. I mean, I don't know why she was so adamant to be with me, since I did nothing, but push her away from me any time she believed I needed a hug. I could not wait to be at my mom's, so I could put as much distance as possible between me and this woman that doesn't understand the meaning of the word "No".

I don't even know why she would drive with me in the first place. It was the horrendous ride I was forced to take with someone, in my entire life. And thinking once I cried after this girl, only be proven now how stupid I was to begin with.

Once I got to mom I looked around to see if Lana's car was here, but no. Maybe she is late or maybe she doesn't come at all. Getting in the house I can see the house is decorated in a Christmas spirit, a tree with a lot of ornaments in it, each one more colourful than the other, is placed in a side of the living room. A huge table covered with a cloth having a Christmas theme and ornaments on it, mom always had a thing with season table cloths and drapes. I always hate the winter ones but never could bring myself to tell her. Each plate across her matching chair, glasses and candle support in the middle of the table. Yeah, all mom and her old way. I knew what she was trying to do. She was trying to give us the Christmas atmosphere we always had back home. Knowing she will not be around for another Christmas to share.

The stairs rail was decorated with lights and elves and other Christmas specifics. Everyone was here from my brothers to mom, dad, Misha, Arthur, Renesmee and of course Felicia, who at this moment was everyone's motive of hate, giving the separation between me and Lana. Don't get me wrong I don't get her side, but Felicia here is not the only guilty.

Lana should at least try to listen to my part as well. After the greetings and all, I can sense a cold breeze coming from the front door, when I turn around Lana gets in with Yuri on her tail. I don't know if I should be grateful or jealous, she's with him. She is more beautiful than I remember, her blue black freshly dyed hair is longer than it was a week ago, she got a bit chubbier too, but she still look gorgeous as fuck. Her blue dress a bit loose around her waist is making my dick to stir with life, like only she can do to me. She has high heel boots making her appear taller than she is. Lana has this elegance in her, and I can see my mother's print in her behaviour. The way she keeps her hands next to her when she talks. The way she talks to people around, so mother posh. A real leader now, she goes around greeting everyone until she gets to me and Felicia and suddenly a deafening silence.

"Lan and Felicia, nice to finally meet you!"

Yuri says as Lana smiles, a fake smile.

"Me and Lana are very happy to see you!"

What the fuck?

"Me and Lana? Since when are you something to Lana?"

I snap as Yuri smirks.

"OK, easy you two. See Yuri and I got closer this week and decided to be…friends."

She says as everyone's jaws are on the floor including mine. I stare in her eyes so hard, that I might set her on fire. God please, if you are there and if you hear me, please give me patience to not murder him. And put her on my shoulder, walk out of here and imprison her in my apartment, until her senses are coming back to life. God please, give me patience! Please!

"Well, we are happy to see you too!"

Felicia says as she wraps a hand around my hand, moment that Yuri wraps a hand around Lana's shoulders, but in a more protective gesture than a lover's gesture. Something is seriously wrong here, I will find out what the fuck is going on.

"Alright since everyone is here let's sit down and eat."

Mom says so calm like we was just been introduced new people, not my fucking wife with her bodyguard. What the hell is this? Some kind of Witney Huston movie?

We take a sit, like usual mom and dad sit at the each end of the table, me and Misha face to face, followed by Felicia next to me and Julia in front of her, Yuri next to Felicia and Arthur in front of him, Vladimir next to Yuri and Renesmee in front of him and Lana next to mom too far for my reach. As drinks were served dad tried to do small talk with everyone and mom helped him to entertain the atmosphere. Half of what they were saying I did not hear as I was plotting how to kill "Everest " how Lana referred to him. Because he touched my wife. They became … friends. What was that even supposed to mean? But I was brought back to the conversation as soon as my mother said it to everyone.

"One year Dimitri was so clumsy with the presents that Lan caught him in fact and he had to say Santa dropped them in his hand and ran away. So now he had to put them next to the tree."

We all started to laugh, until Felicia decided to open her mouth and I was close to murder her.

"Lana, what is your favourite memory of Christmas?"

"I hate Christmas!"

She said as Misha bends down his head and closes his eyes. Renesmee and Arthur changed looks and Felicia couldn't take the hint and pushed.

"Oh come on! You sure have something dear to you about Christmas, or maybe about your parents, or your father?"

I did not give Lana a chance to answer or anyone for that matter to react, until I had my hand wrapped around her neck as I state.

"I will kill you if you open your mouth again!"

I could see she became blue, but I could not stop. I had to snap or I would kill her, but I could not. She was the reason I am not with Lana anymore. She was the reason Lana would not look my way. She was the reason Yuri was touching Lana, in a way he shouldn't even think of doing. I was brought to reality by Yuri's large hand squeezing mine

"Let her go before it is too late. Let. Her. Go!"

I did and he yanked me over my chair and out in the garden. Man he was big and strong.

Everyone was saying something Julia was screaming, mom was disappointed in me and Lana was next to Felicia. Out of all people, she was asking that bitch if she's OK. I tried to fight Yuri and get back to Lana. Scream at her what the hell is wrong with her? This woman would eat her alive without a second look back and she asked her if she is OK. My wife officially lost her damn mind.

But Yuri shaking the hell out of me, made me look at him "WHAT?"

"Are you finished? So I can talk to you?"

Mountain speaks and he wants to talk to me? Tell me what? How he fucked my wife last night? Wait what?

"Did you fucked her?"

I ask as he furrows his eyebrows, as soon as he realizes who I was talking about, his face falls at the same time with his fist.

"You son of a bitch! It's your wife! How dare you disrespect her like that?"

One punch and I was on my ass, trying to stand as fast as I could he warned.

"I have more where that came from!"

Putting my hands in a defensive gesture I said.

"One is enough! And I don't blame you, I was a dick!"

"Great! Something we agree on. Now! Between me and Lana is nothing. She just came with this crazy idea to lead you and that snake to believe that we would be close, because, and this you don't know it from me, Lana and Nikolai believe that your precious here tries to kill Lana. Man, I know you have some shit going on. But she loves you very much. This woman would die for you, if someone would ask her to."

This was the last thing I expected him to say.

"I would die for her as well, but she is too stubborn to even listen to what I have to say. I never cheat on her. At the race it was a fucking miss understanding. I believe it's her in my arms, not her competing against me. And at the hotel, I was too sick from the whiskey I drunk to even talk, let alone fuck someone for that matter."

"Well you have a skilled driver and a smart woman. She has a plan but you need to play along. Don't ruin it. She worked hard to be here today specially in her condition."

Her condition?

"Is she sick? I know she is sick, but they treat me like a bloody fool and no one tells me what she has. How bad is it?"

He looks at me with amusement in his eyes and says.

"It's nothing serious, she just swallowed too much ice and got a bit cold, nothing a good bath cannot fix."

And walk back in the house laughing to himself. After a few minutes, I walk inside just to see him hugging Lana in a protector gesture and whispering something in her ear that made her laugh. I go to Felicia and say.

"I am sorry for my reaction. I should not do that!"

I kiss her cheek as she smiles. It's not your victory is your burial… soon. That was a goodbye kiss! But if Lana wants me to go along with this shit I will. Looking at mom I say.

"I am sorry for my reaction, you raised me better than that."

I was sincere with my apology.

"Well what is a Christmas without a bit of drama?"

Mother asked and we all started to laugh. We went on with unpacking gifts and all that, at some point we were watching a movie, something with Santa Nicolas, they are all the same for me. Lana and mom went upstairs in mom's room and I wanted to be able to talk to her alone. I knew she would listen to me there. As I got closer to the door, I could hear Lana talking, but when I got close enough to the door I understood what she said.

"Next week I have one of the most important appointments and I want you to come with me, but don't tell him yet, please!"

I pushed the door and asked.

"Don't tell me what?"

They looked at me like I was a ghost from the shadows. Mother turned to her and said calmly.

"I will not, but you should. It's Christmas, make me this one last gift!"

And she smiled as tears ran down Lana's cheeks, she nodded and mother went out the room, but not before kissing my cheeks and whispering to me "Congratulations!" for what? I will not divorce that's for sure.

"Please have a seat, you will need it more than me!"

Lana said as she directed me to my mother's coffee table next to the window. I took a seat as she started to speak.

"What I have to tell you does not force or commit you to anything. If you would not want a part of it, I will understand and I will never ask anything from you. Ever again. I am sorry it took me so long to tell you, but

I could not find the right moment and when I did… well we both know how that finished."

What is she talking about here?

"Can you speak? I don't read minds and this is already driving me crazy!"

I said, as she took a seat. A deep breath and she looks me straight in the eyes saying.

"It's no other way to tell you than… I am pregnant!"

I was so shocked that my brain did not work anymore.

"You cannot be pregnant with Yuri. It's not possible!"

I say so fast. She looks at me, like I grew another head. She stands as she says.

"It's not Yuri's. It's yours! I never sleep with another man in the same room, let alone in the same bed. This child is yours but like…"

Before she can say something else, I slam my mouth to hers. She did not need to finish that sentence. Of course, I wanted to be in my child life and of course I wanted her. I loved this woman more than she could imagine. This is the second chance that I have with her and she needs to see this. I take her in my arms and lift her up and set her down.

"This is all true? You are pregnant?"

I say so loud that I was positive they heard me from down stairs. But Lana put a hand over my mouth stopping me from screaming further.

"Yes it's true but aside from Elena, Yuri and now you no one knows. I would like to stay that way, especially with the whole target deal that is going on."

"Why Yuri knows, you are pregnant before me?"

I ask, jealousy speaking.

"Because, that night at the race I wanted to tell you. I wanted to get out of the car but my seatbelt kept me in place. Only, to have the best show of you kissing Felicia. I sped to the apartment to write you a letter and left the papers. Once I walked out, I had a Gorilla follow me around. I was so angry at you, that I forgot he was in my car, when I was fighting with you and an imaginary you and it slipped my mouth. But he never said a word to anyone, not even to Nikolai. He was loyal to me. And he is a good friend to keep around. He is actually one of my best friends now."

She said as I wrapped my arms around her again, bringing her in a thigh hug.

"I knew something was different to you, but I could not know what that was. You have a spark in you that was not there before, pregnancy makes you beautiful. And I love you more than you could believe. That night at the race it was a misunderstanding, when she jumped in my arms, I believed it was you that's why I kissed her back. But, as soon as I wrapped my hands around her I knew it's not you and I pushed her away. Only she just doesn't want to leave. What you saw at the hotel was an even bigger misunderstanding, because I was so drunk, I could not even speak.

I went in there thinking to ask her why the hell she doesn't let me be. But I could not speak properly and she saw you before, I could have a chance to see you. She dragged me in her room leading you to believe we had an affair. When all she got was a drunk ass Lan vomiting all over her bathroom floor. Lana… I love you and you need to believe me! I loved you a lot before, but I love you more than my life now that you carry our child!"

I spoke with sincerity as I broth my hand to her belly that it started to round, and I understood her choice of outfit now. That's why she was sick all the time. And I start to laugh at the memory.

"I guess you have a tumour with eyes and ears and healthier than all of us, after all!"

We both laugh at that. God, how blind I was? After a few more minutes of kissing giggling and more kisses she said on a serious note

"We need to go down stairs angrier than ever. The night is almost finished, I will explain Elena what happens, later. You need to treat Felicia warmer than you would like to. Me and Nikolai are working on a theory and before we can dismiss it I need you to be my eyes and ears when it comes to Felicia. Can you do that? Please"

She said it was so nice and sweet, I would jump off the bridge if she would ask right now.

"I have one condition to do that!"

I say as I left the index finger of my right hand and she nods.

"Tell me, what appointment do you have next week?"

"How about I send you an address, you make sure you get there alone and I will show you?"

She says smiling again.

"It sounds good to me. So now what we start to scream like lunatics to one another?"

"I storm out from here in my Lana stormy style, you try to catch me. We fight some more, so everyone will believe. While you make sure Felicia buys all the show. I will stay where I was until now, which is a secret. I will contact you, to give you the address for next week and Nikolai will call you to look into something, as soon as I am sure of one thing before that."

"Don't put yourself in danger!"

I say and she replies loud enough.

"That is not your business anymore!"

As she turns and walks out the door. I smile at her and remember I have a game to keep and storm after her screaming.

"Don't you dare walk away again! I am talking to you and you need to answer."

But damn, she is fast and everyone from the living is looking at us curious as why we are boiling to one another.

"I told you the divorce papers are home already signed, so suit yourself and sleep around with whoever you want. I have the right to be happy as well. So what if I am chubby? I don't need to be a model to be loved and appreciated by a man. Well, what's wrong that Yuri here loves me, like you couldn't?"

In a split second all the eyes were on her and after on Yuri, who did not understand why the hell he was suddenly thrown under the bus like that. I felt sorry for him right now, but I am sure he will understand later. Plus, it was a nice payback for the "she swallowed some ice" thing that I will have to tell him.

"So what you came into my mother's place to show off to your new boyfriend? At the same time with the ink drying on your divorce papers? Or did you know him from the beginning?"

Three different voices called my name as I stepped in her face and her new best friend, a mountain of muscles blocking my way.

"I think you are close enough!"

He said so seriously, I was sure the marrow in my bones was frozen by now. I have to thank him one day, for this exact moment. Turning to Lana he said.

"I think we need to go!"

Looking to mom he continued.

"I am sorry for all the inconvenience our presence created, I wish you a Merry Christmas and happy holidays. It's better, if we leave before things go too far out of hand."

He puts a hand on Lana's shoulder in a protective gesture again, walking out the door. Everyone silent for a couple of seconds, and Vladimir starts.

"You really cannot hold yourself, can you?"

"What? You don't know anything. She started, but anyways she is out of here, so let's continue."

I said calmly, like I asked them if they wanted more cookies. Mom said.

"You are coming with me now!"

She started to claim the stairs to her room. Everyone was in a daze of what it was actually going on. They will be fine. I said to myself. Once in mom's room she said just a single word "Speak!" in her demanding tone. Gesturing for her to sit down, I made sure the door was closed before I started to tell her.

"I am sorry for everything. All was just a show for everyone to look at. Lana and Nikolai believe that Felicia is behind everything. I don't know the details myself. But, I can tell you that I will not sleep, if I have to find that connection. Meantime, I have the duty to entertain Felicia and try to make her tell me anything I possibly can, in order for us to find any connection possible. I am sorry I ruined your Christmas!"

"Dear when I hand in the invitations to everyone, war was the first I prepared myself for. I just believed it will go a bit different and Felicia will jump at Lana's throat, which would have been the case, if you would not have lost your temper. Lana knew. I knew. Even Yuri knew, that's why the table strategy. So, I make sure you don't kill the poor woman. I guess I am getting old, because I did not take into consideration your reaction towards Felicia. I should know better, when it comes to you and Lana."

We carried on talking for a little while longer, until I could see she was tired. I let her go to sleep and headed downstairs where I said goodbye to my dad and Julia, Vladimir being to piss with me to actually talk to me. Arthur and Renesme were already gone by now. It was just me and Felicia. I had to drive her back to London.

Two hours later, I was in my apartment trying to squeeze my brain why would Felicia want to hurt Lana, apart from jealousy. I repeat the conversation I had with Felicia in my head over and over again, aside from a few misunderstandings that we had as a couple, we did not discuss much. She did want to get back with me. But it was too late now, and it will always be too late for me and her.

Following week, I received a text from a new number with an address I partially knew, and a time. When I called the number it sent me straight to voicemail. This should be Lana, I typed the address in my Spyder GPS. When I got to my destination, it was a private medical centre in the middle of London. I went to reception and asked for Svetlana Ivanovich, the receptionist guided me on a hallway that made the connection between the reception area and the waiting room area of the gynecology department, where I could find Lana and my mother. She brought my mother here. "Hey!" I said as I took a seat next to Lana. "Hey!" she said

"Hi mom, how do you feel?!"

"Hello dear I am good. A bit tired, but good!"

I could see, lately she was more tired than usual. I think all this took a toll on her.

I did not have time to put to many questions, because Lana's name was called by a nurse and we all headed to that door.

Nurse looked at us surprised and Lana explained to her we are family. She smiled and welcomed us in a room, where a bed was next to an ultrasound machine that had a screen connected to it. A chair in front of the ultrasound, next to bed. An extra chair was broth in the room for mom as Lana proceeded to sit on the bed. I could see she was as nervous as I was. And for the first time, mom was nervous to. As I was standing next to mom, I saw the doctor starting the check-up procedure. She went on with everything, informing us that everything looks fine and everything is normal. She asked Lana if she would like to hear the foetus heart. Unable to form words Lana nodded. Seconds after, the room was flooded with the most amazing sound of a heartbeat. Well many heart beats, I was looking at mom. She had tears in her eyes. I squeezed her hand as I was looking at Lana. Mom pushed me gently toward my wife. I was a ball of nerves at the sound of my child's heartbeat. I step carefully towards my wife. She was crying too, as we listened to the beat of our child's heart. I hold her hand and I promise her, I will never let her go, not now, not ever. I looked up at the screen and I saw a line, very long. Damn, that kid will be very well equipped. "Is that his...?" I couldn't say the words, not because I was shy, but because I was shocked. As soon as the doctor realised what I was looking at she said.

"No, that is the umbilical cordon."

And everyone in the room started to laugh.

"For a second I was afraid here."

And the woman laughed harder at my expense. Doctor went on telling us, she could not tell us exactly if it's a boy or a girl, today. Most probably, next time she will be able to see it better.

Once we finished with the doctor mom told me.

"You can be sure, now I can rest in peace. You stayed true to your words."

"Don't you ever say that to me, again! You will see your grandchild. I know you will. You are the most strong and stubborn person I know."

She smiled at me, but did not say a word.

New Year and January went fast, and now was the end of February. Felicia was gone in Russia for a couple of months. Something to do with modelling was the official version, but buy now we knew that something big was coming down to our heads. After the day at the clinic with mom and Lana, I decided to up my game and I did my best to have some friends time at my house with Felicia, Arthur and another couple of people I knew.

The official news was I was still single, after the fight with Lana on Christmas. Arthur helped me to get Felicia drunk and plant as many listening devices as I could on her phone purse and all over her car. Not to mention about the tracking device I planted in her car. That happens when you mess with IT guys. They fuck you silent. After nearly two months of surveillance we could match a few names to a few crimes and cooperate with police to take them down.

Every hunt and every name crossed from our list was a bonus to Lana's life. Especially now that her belly was so big she was nearly seven months pregnant with our boy. The only problem was that as time was passing my mother became weaker and weaker.

As I found out, she passed the limit of time doctors gave her, a long time ago. Every day with her was a blessing we received from the sky. I really hoped that she would live to see her grandson born. I decided with Lana to come and stay here for a few weeks. This time, we rented a bigger house, Yuri, Boris and Sasha were with us, as well. Lately, Nikolai was visiting as often as he could. Dad took a break from his politics, Vladimir and Julia were around more. This house was so small, but so big at the same time. Even Arthur and Renesme came to visit from time to time.
Unfortunately, she grew only weaker with the time. I

could see that cancer was slowly taking ownership of her body, faster that she could keep up anymore. Some days she did try to stay awake more but others were harder for her to do that.

Today it was a beautiful day of April. In a few days would be Lana's birthday, I really hoped mom lived to see that day. But today, she called us one by one starting with Julia and Vladimir, Lana, Nikolai, dad and now me. She said to dad that she wanted me to be the last, because it's harder on me.

Despite my anger, I am the most sensitive from the family, always have been. As I was walking in her room, she was up righted in between pillows. Just a shadow from the woman I once knew. I sat next to the door, for a few seconds, she opened her eyes and said so softly.

"Come on in dear!"

This will be the last time I would hear her saying that. I approached her bed so quietly, I was afraid that if I made a noise she would disappear. As I was close to her bed, I sat in the chair that was already there and took her hand in mine. I try my best to keep my tears at bay. It will be my second time breaking up like that and I did not want her last memory of me to be with me crying like a pussy in front of her. She opened her eyes, smiled at me and said,

"You were always my first. My first child, my first time becoming mother, my first time bandaging wounds, my first unconditioned love. I love every one of my children equally. But, I do so because of you. You showed me how to. You guided me in the hardest times. You were my angry, sensitive and kind hearted one. You were fire and ice both at once. I am so proud of you! I am proud that you never gave up. That you worked so much and achieved everything you put your mind to. When you tell me you will get married and expect a child, I laugh so hard with your father. I even said to him, don't be surprised if he appears tomorrow with God knows what top model and presents her as your future daughter–in-law, pays a doctor and gets her a pregnancy certificate, just to make sure he makes me happy.

But instead, you came up with Lana and I knew even before the two of you, that you love each other more than you could realise. When she told me she was pregnant, I believed her. Poor girl was nearly having a heart attack that I will tell you. As soon as I heard that child heartbeat, I knew my time came. I just got to live a little longer. I want you to know, no matter what or where… I will always be next to you. High on the mountain or down in the valley, I will be there! Now you have a family, a responsibility. You need to be there for your wife and child. No matter what… be there! Come fire or high water you need to be strong for them, because you are the rock of your house. You are the anchor of your family and you will be the example your son has. You will set the standard for your son as how to treat people around him.

How brave to be in facing his fears. How strong to stand in times of trial. Always love and respect your wife, because like I said before she must trust you, no matter what! Be there for her, like she will be there for you. Because she will be there for you. Every marriage has downfalls, but it's important to be able to communicate, in order to find a solution, for any problem you have. It will be a day when you will see a woman, more beautiful and younger than her. Make sure on that day you don't forget who your wife is. What she did for you, and where you are, because of her. To share a bed with someone is easy. To build a family is completely different. I raise you to know the difference between the two. Use that brain of yours wisely, everything you need is there."

She spoke slowly, taking her time with every word she said. She was tired and I knew it would not be longer, until she left this world. I texted dad. I wanted him to be here with me. He was the man she shared her life with and I wanted him to be able to hold her hand in her last moment. I could not be selfish and take that from them. Door opened and dad got closer. He went to kiss her forehead as I said.

"I will always be next to you. I promise! I will make you proud every time."

She opened her eyes, looked at me and dad one more time and said.

"You need to let me go!"

She closed her eyes, and left forever. All this made me think of the Passenger "Let Her Go" song. But, it was so hard to let her go. Both I and dad cried out loud.

She was the woman that taught us how to live, how to enjoy life and how to be happy. She was the soul and warmth of our house. And now she is gone. As I held her hand I kissed and whispered to her "I will always miss you, more than you can imagine!"

I knew she did not hear me anymore, but I had to say it. She needs it to know. I will miss her so much, nothing will be the same for me, after her. I promised myself, I will make sure to tell my son about his amazing grandmother, who loved him even before she had a chance to meet him.

Today was the darkest day of my life. Today all my fears came to life. She. Was. Gone! And it was nothing I could do about it.

As soon as me and dad left the room and came down in the living room, Julia started to cry, Vladimir hugged her and tried to be brave for her. Dad hugged both of them. I went to hug Lana and buried my head in the crook of her neck. Nikolai was in between all of us, even Arthur and Renesme were here. We all lost something. We all lost someone. Today we lost a wife, mother, sister, best friend and a confidant. No one will ever replace her and she will always be in our hearts. We cried what felt like hours.

Once we had no tears left to cry, we started to put together the funeral arrangement. Someone came and proceeded with everything. Two days later we lowered her into the tomb that from now on was her new home, forever. The day was a beautiful sunny day. It felt like she was smiling from above to us. It was still hurting like hell that we could not see her and we could not talk to her, but they say time heals.

I say, time makes you get used to the absence. Human brain is made to accommodate. So that is what we do. We accommodate pain, to absence and to a new environment.

This was our new environment.

One without mom in it.

We now learned how to navigate life without her.

But like anything in life, everything has a reward.

No matter if it's the greatest pain or the biggest joy.

You will always pay a price and always will be rewarded for it.

CHAPTER TWENTY-FIVE

SVETLANA

As I see a coffin lowered to the ground, I am thinking that life is not fair. I lost more in this life than others in three lives. Today, I say goodbye to the most wonderful person, who even if it was not related to me by blood, she did love me like her own. Cherished me like the most important prize she had. She taught me everything I know, from how to speak and how to dress to how to lead the most powerful organisation Russia has to this day. And she taught me how to lead it from afar. She introduced me to people that will obey me and taught me how to hold my head high in front of them. She was patient with me and gave me the time I needed. She was there for me, when no one other was. Believed in me, when nobody did. She made sure I was guarded in more ways than I could think of. She was the mother I never had, the source of unconditional love. She was my support in times of weakness. And now she's... gone!

She said to me "Lana, when I first saw you. You were a little scared girl, but as soon as I heard how you handled Felicia. I admired you more than you could think of. You showed me that you have what it needs for a Vory leader. I could shape any woman and teach her how to dress, speak and behave. They don't have what it takes and that's the fire inside you. Use that fire in a positive way and you will always come out victorious. Let that fire consume you and you will burn yourself inside out. You have the power to do anything you like in this entire world, and yet, you are here next to me and next to my son. Preparing yourself to become the most important woman in Russia. Because, you will be more important than the first lady itself. Make sure you always keep your back straight and your head high. Don't let them take you down, you are stronger than all of them, in one place. It's in you! You just need to trust yourself. Listen carefully! When you will be in a situation without escape, make sure you will have the coat I gave to you. Never, but never change the tailor I recommended to you and tell Nikolai.

"In poker, I always love the black-hearted ace, he has a shadow of its own, but in the end it is all about love" he will understand what to do. Believe me, these words will save your life more times than you could think of. They did save mine a couple of times. Red is my favourite colour, wear it as many times as you can. Oh, please don't let anyone of them wear black. None of them need to wear dark clothes to grief me. They do it enough in their souls and that is just for them to know. Make sure they will be happy. You are the new "Madam of the house" and they need to obey you. I made the necessary arrangement, so you will not have too much of a headache. One last thing, before I let you go. Artem! Make sure one of the boy's names will be Artem. Don't forget! I will love you for what you are, even from beyond the grave. I am so proud of you and all the progress you made, in such a short time. Be well my special!"

That was the last memory with her alive. I will hold it in my heart, until the end of time. Looking around, I realise me and Lan are the only one who left by the grave. Even the guards took a few steps back, to give us a moment alone. This was my moment to break down. Now, I could let go, no one was here to see. As I fell to my knees, I started to cry. I cried until no tears came out. Lan was there next to me, not saying a word, just allowing me to mourn one of the most important people in my life. To mourn my parents that never cared for me, but they were gone. To mourn all the love that I did not have and the one that I had, but was taken away.

I don't know how much time we were there, after everyone was gone. Now it was getting dark, my knees started to hurt and the baby was moving inside of me, like he was about to race for the Olympics. Maybe because I was hungry as well. At some point Yuri came closer and helped Lan to lift me from the ground. I left a part of me as well. I buried my past next to this woman.

As I stood, I straightened my back, lifted my head high and spoke with conviction.

"From today, I am officially the new Vory leader. I will lead to the best of my knowledge. I will make sure to take care of everyone, help and support our new generation to come. Lead them with justice towards times of victory. I will be wise in times of trial and strong in times of war!" I don't know who I said this to, but I had to say it. Walking further from the grave I felt a cold breeze hugging me and I smiled. Maybe in her way Elena was next to me, even from beyond the grave.

Six month passed since we buried Elena. The emptiness is still in my heart, but it became easier to navigate this situation.

In June we welcomed our son, Artem Ruslan Ivanovich, into the world. He was our greatest gift, our pride and joy, our reason to live. He was a strong boy, blond with blue eyes. Chubby hands and legs and fluffy cheeks. It was looking so much like Elena, and probably Lan when was a baby. I am still to find what Elena prepared for me in Russia. Both me and Lan were very happy, the day I gave birth to Artem. I know, I will do everything that is in my power to protect this little bundle of joy, from everything and anything bad in the world

If before I could not understand why my parents did not love me, now I was beyond confusion, for the same reason.

How can someone not love a part of themselves?

I will never have an answer for that.

We arranged to fly to Russia next week, which will be a week before our first wedding anniversary. I wanted to be able to see what Elena prepared for me there. She gave a key and an envelope to open once I am back in our village. I had to go head to head with Lan for this trip, and made sure Vitally and Nikolai would be there as well. Lately, Nikolai and I decided to start involving Vladimir more and more, so the transition between the two of them will be smoother than mine with Elena was. Plus the sooner he knows more the better. He can start to shape after the way we are and think.

Felicia was still in the dark with what happened in London, partially because in the last nearly ten months she was in Russia, preparing the big plot of my beheading.

We worked tirelessly to find every piece of information we could put our hand on, to find out what she's trying to do and who helped her.

We could find out that she made some deals with a few members of Yakuza, and another few organised crime groups. She did want me... badly. I talked to our most trusted man and we agreed that before it is too late, I will be the bait. Of course we did not mention anything of this to Lan, even if Vladimir was adamant we should tell him. I knew, his reaction would be the one to give us Felicia, in the end. I made sure everyone stayed quiet. We were busy making sure everything goes as smooth as it can go.

We would travel private, with our baby for the first time to see his mother land. I left Russia nearly three years ago, thinking I would never come back again. And here I was, descending the stairs of our private plane in the Altai Mountains. The same mountains that were my home, my grave and now my happiness. I went away a broken scared girl and returned a strong, highly educated leader, for a family that has yet to know me.

We had our safe house somewhere close to the village I grew up in, and at a close distance from the town Vory had the "office" in.

When we arrived at our residence here in Altai, I saw it was a mountain wooden cabin, with small windows and a huge fence. Even if the house was entirely from wood, the surrounding fence was made from mountain rocks. It has a gate that was made from stainless steel, impossible to see inside the yard from outside. The fence colour was the natural colour of the mountain's rocks and the gate was silver.

The yard was big enough to park three SUVs in. I could see in the left corner of the garden, as you face the cabin, it was a swing. It must look nice in the summertime. We were at the end of October and it was freezing cold outside, especially because we were high up in the mountain.

As we got inside, we entered a large room that served as a living area. On the left wall of the room it has a floor to ceiling chimney that was decorated with mountain rocks as well.

In the left side of the chimney, a tall not too wide bookcase shelves, in the right side of the chimney, the same bookshelf only a bit wider with a cropped medium size TV.

A small coffee table in front of the same chimney, with a sofa and sofa chairs made from reddish leather, a red carpet under the table. From the ceiling hangs a chandelier made from deer antlers crown.

All the room colours were natural wood colour, it was so warm and welcoming. Not only because of the design, but because of the burning fire from inside the chimney. The smell of fresh burnt wood gave this place a peace that I was longing for a long time, now.

On the left side of the room was a door that led to a small kitchen, very rustic, with a small cabinet, an electric stove and a kitchen table. I wasn't planning to use the kitchen, apart from the coffee in the morning and maybe to heat some milk for Artem, at night. In the far end of the room was a big enough wooden staircase that led to the first floor, where there were four bedrooms, all designed to look the same. A big bed in the middle, with two night stands on each side of the bed and a big wardrobe on one of the room walls. In each bedroom a small bathroom with a shower, sink and toilet, all in white. It was the only place that would be white from the entire house, everything else being in natural wooden colour.

It was a nice warm and cosy house, big enough for me, Lan, Artem and the three Gorillas, I became accustomed to. We could say that we became close. I demanded that I wanted to know about them. I guess beyond this shield I put on after we buried Elena, I was still the same kind hearted girl that cared about everyone. I would still call them Gorilla boys, just to mess with them. Vladimir finally agreed to stay with us, because one, he would be close and easy to protect and second, he did not want to go and stay in their childhood house alone. I was even happier, I could use all hands with Artem, he was such a live boy for nearly four months now.

Once in our bedroom I realise we have a crib for Artem. A crib I did not order. I knew Lan must have. I went to him and planted a kiss on his lips, just to surprise him.

"What was that one for? Not that I complain, but I want to know!"

"For the crib. I guess tonight the bed is all ours!"

I said as I wiggle my eyebrows. Only to see a hungry Lan, smiling.

"I could make it now, why wait for tonight?"

"Lan, you will wake Artem and I wish you good luck with that, because I have to go to the first Vory meeting from here, in about an hour. I have enough time to take a shower and change my clothes."

I was wearing a pair of jeans with white tank top and plaid red and black flannel. I had a pair of winter black boots, I took off as soon as we were inside the house, and a thick winter jacket. It was so cold this time around in Russian mountains, especially because we were so close to Siberia. We expected snow tonight.

Later that night, I went to the casino in town. I made sure to dress as business as possible. I had a navy blue suit made from two pieces. Trousers and a suit jacket matched with a white shirt and a pair of heeled and very elegant boots. Like Elena always told me, I used the same tailor. She introduced us last year, when he made me a special, elegant, black winter coat with matching big buttons and of course my piece of resistance, my typical Russian furry hat, which was sitting elegantly on my head, leaving the lower part of my blue black hair on display, on my shoulders.

As soon as I was inside the casino, Yuri took my coat and my hat as we headed for the offices, where I was expected. What I liked the most at Yuri, was that when we were in the family company, he was friendly and open, but as soon as we were outside, he was all business and professional. Never once calling me anything other than "Ma'am" or "Boss". I knew I could count on him and he knew he could count on me. The day he met Artem, his eyes were watering and he cried more than Lan did. Who could imagine this mountain Vikings crying, I swear if I could tell anyone, they would laugh at me, but I knew better.

Inside the office, I realise it's a copy of Nikolai's London office. Or should I say this is the original office, after the London office was made. From furniture to colour, everything was an exact match. I think that was his way to be close to home and cope with homesickness.

The only difference here was that the room was bigger, it held more chairs and had a bigger table.

"Good evening gentlemen!"

I said as I took my place at the head of the table with Nikolai on my right and Vladimir on my left, both followed by men's whose names I did not know yet.

After introductions were made and they understood who I was, what my role was in this organisation they opened up. We start to talk business, informing them with what we know, then telling us what they could find. Who was our best connection with the surrounding countries and Yakuza. We made the necessary arrangement and we plan another meeting in the next two days, so we could put the final detail in order, before we go into action.

By the time we finished this meeting it was nearly midnight, I was exhausted. Couldn't wait to go home, take my son in my arms, kiss him good night and spend some much needed quality time with my husband. Damn, it felt good to be in Lan's arms as he was buried in me and both trying not to wake Artem.

We made love for the first time on Russian soil. Morning came too quick for me. When I opened my eyes, I saw Artem missing from the crib, before I could go ballistic and in full panic attack mode, I heard the shower and Lan talking with Artem in a childlike voice. I smiled at the sound of my husband's voice and the baby laughter that came from Artem. When they finished showering, I took their place. Once dressed I came downstairs, only to smell freshly cooked bacon, eggs, fresh bread and milk. And of course a lot of coffee. The three Gorillas, Vladimir and Lan, with Artem in one hand, all sat at the kitchen table that looked too small for such big guys.

The picture made me laugh. It looks like they were in the house of the seven dwarfs. To small objects, to large bodies. Vladimir made space for me at the table as I asked.

"Why didn't we go to town to eat? It's no need for any of you to cook!"

"I like to cook, it's not a problem. At least, I find something to spend time with, while in the house. Plus, I have Boris here to wash the dishes."

Yuri said and we all laughed. It was like we were a family, not like they were my employees.

"I talked to the guys and they will watch Artem for an hour or so, because I want to show you something. Make sure you dress accordingly, we are going up the mountain."

Lan said to me and I nod, letting him know I listen as I eat. In about an hour we were in one of the SUVs going up the mountain, towards the pine forest.

"Are you planning to kill me and take the three million dollars reward?"

I asked him as we laughed and an idea hit me, but I kept my mouth shut, I actually needed to speak with Nikolai first.

The car came to a stop and Lan told me we needed to claim on foot the remaining distance, until the top of the mountain. Once we were there the view was magnificent. From where we were standing, we could see all the villages and the town at our feet.

The slope of the mountain was covered with snow, fir trees seemed to rise from it. From the middle of the mountain downwards, began the villages, with their scattered houses.

Near the base of the mountain was the city. Everywhere you looked, you could see only mountains, fir, coloured houses like matchboxes and lots of snow.

Although I hate winter, the landscape seemed detached from the Christmas cards. It was beautiful and quiet. Lan bent to kiss me and we took in the view as he said.

"In the night time it looks even more wonderful! You should see all the lights there. I always loved around Christmas, when all the houses were covered in different colourful lights."

This we're the moments I crave the most. These moments were my favourite. Not money, not designer clothes, not who I was in their eyes, but these simple moments I got to share with this amazing person.

The way his arms were wrapped around me. The way he holds me close to him, so tender, but protective at the same time. The way my heart skips a beat every time he tells me I am beautiful and special. These were my favourite moments, because at the end of the day, this is what we have. These are the memories we hold on to when the storm hits the fan. And I knew for me and him, this was the quiet before the storm. I wanted to take all in and hold on to it, as long as I possibly could. We stayed there for what felt like forever, enjoying the peace and quiet. Lan would kiss me from time to time, just to make sure I did not freeze.

When we returned, I said to him that we needed to stop at his house, because Elena gave me a key and an envelope to open once I was in their home. We parked outside and I could see Lan taking a deep breath. His eyes were glossy and he barely kept his tears. It was the first time in many years, he came back home and his mother was not here. It took a toll on him. I could see. To ease his pain, I wrapped my hand around his and said.

"You don't need to come, if you think you can't. I will go alone, but if you want, I will be here for you. I will always be here."

He nodded letting me know he listened, wipe his eyes with the back of his hands and took a deep breath.

"It's fine! One day, I will have to come and make sure everything is okay, before going back to London. It would be better to be today that day, especially because you are with me."

With that, we got out of the car and got inside the house. It was an amazing house with floor to ceiling windows, chimney much like in the house we stayed in. Everywhere you could see a picture of them. Pictures showing they were happy and they love each other. Pictures with a happy and beautiful Elena. I never saw her so beautiful, she wasn't ugly when I met her either, but cancer would have had a print on her body. In these pictures she was stunning. This house was once warm, it was a home and you could see that just from looking around.

"This room was my favourite room, from the whole house. We would sit on the sofa, mom telling us different stories about bears. Dad would read his paper or do other things. Sometimes, we would just crawl on the floor in front of the burning fire in the chimney, with mom and dad on their hand and knees, playing with us. It was the most wonderful childhood I could have wished for, and life for that matter. Until, mom got sick and I never understood what I have done so wrong, that God wished to punish me like that. But, here I am today with you, and I cannot be happier for what I got from life, even if that meant to lose my mother. You have no idea how much I love you Svetlana!"

He told me and when he finished, he kissed me.

"If we carry on like that, we will never be able to make it back on time for Vladimir to go and meet Nikolai, and it's important for them to meet. I need you to show me your parents bedroom. Elena said that on her side of the bed, in the same spot she rested her head toward the wall, it has to be a star on that point of the wall."

"Fuck me, the North pole star, it always felt suspicious that is there and not on the ceiling. Let's take a hammer first. Don't move, I am coming back!"

He disappeared through the kitchen door and came back two minutes later with a big hummer, on his shoulder. With a smile on his face he said.

"Let's bring some wall down."

Wiggling his eyebrows. I laughed and told him.

"Crazy we are not going to destroy the house."

As we went up the stairs and into their massive bedroom, aside from the amazement that their room broth to me, it was a feeling of disappointment that I will ruin this amazing room. It was a massive bed in the middle of the room with a night stand on each part of the bed, with a small cute lamp in the form of a ballerina on it. A massive walk in closet on the right side of the room. It was a beautiful contrast in purple and red and orange.

We pulled the massive bed that was heavier than I expected, to a side and found the star. The thing was, that it was done in such a way. It would look like it was a piece of wallpaper miss placed on the wall, when in fact it was the door of a safe. Then, I understood why the envelope. "It's a shame I wouldn't use the hammer, after all."

Lan said, I started to laugh as I grabbed the envelope from the backpack I had with me. Once I opened, I had a piece of paper with a code that was the safe password. We opened the safe and found a few different items there.

On the first shelf of the safe, were three pairs of knitted baby shoes. Two blue and one pink. I could know that the pink one is Julia's one, and the other two are Lan's and Vladimir's. A few family pictures. So that was the family shelf. Next shelf, was holding a quite thick orange envelope and the last, which was the bottom of the safe, contained moulds for one, five, and twenty US dollar banknotes. I was looking at Lan, Lan was looking at me and we both held a shocked expression on our faces. Now, that was something that for sure I did not expect to find in here.

"Well, if my mother is not full of surprises."

He says and we both started to laugh.

"I think I should look in this envelope."

I took the envelope and opened, inside it was a very well organized folder with information, pictures, and detailed names of all the Yakuza leaders.

"Blackmail is still a powerful tool. Used wisely in your advantage! That is something she said to me before we got married. She was giving me information and guidance, all the time. Oh, mom!"

Lan said to me.

"Well this changed the game 100%. We now have leverage over the Yakuza. Let's leave the moulds in here for the moment. I will meet with Nikolai and Vladimir, try to get to a decision about this and how to use all this information we have… and if it's not working, we will involve the moulds."

We arrange everything the way it was before. And we left the house. Even if someone would have seen us, it would be more like we were here to go down the memory lane.

Two hours later, I was in our casino office with Nikolai and Vladimir. Staring at each other in confusion, shock and amazement of what I discovered.

"I knew she was onto something, but I did not know what she was onto. I know as well, she had a private meeting with Chenguang Noshimuri in London. But, I don't know the content of that meeting. However, I think you should contact Noshimuri and invite him here for a visit. See how soon he can come, and how long we have to prepare and put everything in place."

"Before I go on with that, I want to speak with the two of you something. I had this idea today, when I was up the mountain with Lan. I might know how to make Felicia speak, but you will not like it one bit."

I said it so sure of my words, staring straight in his eyes that it took him a moment to process what I said to him.

"Before I am certain that you lost your damn mind, can you please elaborate what you are talking about?"

He said, exhaustively. He raises a hand to one of his eyebrows and he furrows. Vladimir was only ears, curious of what I could say. I start to explain my idea and what I have in mind, but both of them start.

"And this is your greatest plan in making Felicia speak?"

Nikolai asked, still not believing what I just told him as Vladimir said.

"I think this is the most stupid and reckless plan you can come up with."

"It's not. However I need to make sure Noshimuri plays his part in this!"

I went on and explained to them further what I was thinking and my plan of actions. At some point, Nikolai was convinced I had lost my mind. Vladimir was totally against this and threatened he would tell Lan, but in the end, I managed somehow to make them agree and go on with my plan. I contacted Chenguang Noshimuri and agreed to meet the next day, in a safe house at the border with China. Once I was left alone in the office, I looked up to the ceiling and thanked Elena for everything she did for me. She stayed true to her words. She did love me from beyond the grave. I will always cherish her and keep her in my memory as the mother, friend, tutor and confident, she was for me until her last breath. I will make sure to look after all her children and grandson the way she looked after me, to protect them the way she protected me.

Next day at dawn we were at the border with China, in a safe house meeting with Noshimuri. It was an old wooden house with the windows covered with nailed planks. The house is so weak, that in case of an attack, the first thing I should avoid would not be the bullets, would be the walls of the house to not fall on me.

The only reason we met here is, because we are in neutral territory. I have to admit, the place is so well hidden on top of the mountain, It was a challenge to get here, and we had well equipped off-road vehicles. To get where we are now, you either have to come here intentionally, or know the place so well, that you know about this ramshackle house. Either way I would say we are pretty safe, for the time being. Of course neither one of us came here alone, I had my three most loyal Gorillas. He had a few men himself. Everyone was loaded to the teeth with guns and ammo, we didn't even bother to hide it anymore. This was the number one rule in the underworld, wear designer clothes and have the biggest and fastest gun.

"Mrs. Ivanovich, it's a pleasure to finally meet you! I do hope we can do business together, that will benefit the both of us."

He said in a strong Chinese accent.

"Mr Noshimuri, pleasure is all mine! I am sure we would come to an understanding to have prosper business together. In this world it is always better to have an ally, than an enemy!"

I said at the same time I was shaking his hand and displaying the most fake charming smile, I could master on this cold.

"What can I do for you and what is so urgent?"

He asked and I took out a green folder from my backpack and handed it to him.

"See, I have this information that certain people will pay top dollars, to put their hands on. As a gesture of kindness, I wanted to talk to you and let you know that, I am in possession of these precious papers. As you can see, there is clear evidence of the uranium you bought last year. I bet your wife will highly appreciate the new styles and positions you tried, with that beautiful brunette called Felicia, and not to mention that your son is so handsome. It would be to bed to mourn him one day, over a stupid accident."

I tell him all this with confidence, accentuating on the word beautiful, and trying to sympathise with him over his son. One thing that I am grateful for, is that not many people know about Artem. I will do my best to stay that way, he can be a powerful weapon in the wrong hands.

"I understand what you are saying. What do you want in exchange for this information?"

He was mine. Sincerely, I was expecting more of a fight, but I will not complain. Smiling, I said.

"I am happy that we can understand each other. As a show of kindness you can keep that file. Of course, you would understand that I was forced to have a copy of it. As a guarantee, that you will not have a change of heart. You know us women, can be very persuasive when it comes to what we want. So for the start, I would like to know what my little friend in there has in mind. After, I would like you to help and organise a meeting between me, you, my friend in question of course, a few other people. And of course, you would tell them how I helped you to extract the uranium from Russia to China."

In the last part of the conversation, he was confused and could not help himself and ask.

"Why would you like to take credit over a crime that you did not commit?"

And with that he was mine.

"Do not worry about that. I would like to know if I could count on your help. Of course, at the end of the meeting my man will go with the beautiful brunette, and you will go with that information you hold and a safe and happy family. Because, I know how to keep secrets."

I say as I wrinkle my nose. I gave him no other choice, than to practically agree with me.

"It's always a pleasure to do business with you Mrs. Ivanovich. Of course you can count on me, just let me know the place and the time that will suit you, for tomorrow's meeting. I will make sure everyone will be there. Have a great day yourself. Oh! And be aware that the roads here are very dangerous, if you mix the marking."

He smiled letting me know he had eyes on us, it was something that I expected. The perk of having Elena as my tutor all this time, was that she gave me details about everything and anything. We shake hands and part our ways. I had his help and that was all that mattered. Tomorrow, all this nightmare will be over, one way or another. Once I was back in the casino's office, I told Nikolai everything that happened and what I discussed with Noshimuri. I told him how proud of me I was, because I hold my ground like that in front of Noshimuri. The way I manage to keep my emotions in check and appear calm and collected, when actually, I was shaking from inside out. One wrong word, would give him the escape he needed, to get out of this messy situation. How happy I was, that after such a long time and so much work, we can finally put an end to this. I will be able to spend some time with my husband and child. This meeting needs to go according to plan. One small mistake and everything goes to hell. And they have a chance to flee. Then, all our work and sacrifice were in vain. Nikolai tells me he is proud of me as well and he was sure if someone could convince Noshimuri to do something, it was me. Sometimes, I think he gives me more credit than I deserve, but I will not complain.

I headed home that night and took a good look at Artem, he was sleeping in his crib. So peaceful and relaxed like the world was all hearts and flowers. Like no bad was around, and angels were watching over us. Well probably they were, but at this point in time I was not sure anymore. I went to bed and lay down next to Lan. I turned on one side so I could face him, gazing at him I whispered.

"I love you so much! Thank you for being patient and caring. Thank you for all your support and devotion. You and Artem are the best thing that ever happened to me. I want you to know that, no matter what. I will love you till the end of time!"

I start to kiss him softly at the beginning, but soon our kiss would go passionate, like always. He pushed me gently on my back and lay on top of me, positioning himself between my legs. He started to kiss my neck and caress my breasts over my pyjama top, slowly he slid his hand under the top of my PJ. Caressing my skin up to my breast, pinching my nipples between his fingers. It felt so good. Like every time he touched me. I came to life, lighting up like fireworks. At some point he lifted the top over my head, I made sure his shirt was gone as well and now we were skin on skin. It was a sensation I cannot put into words. I always love to feel him naked, on me. It was like we could mould into each other, as soon as he was inside me, we became one.

Two bodies into one, two hearts into one, and a huge love between us. He was mine and I was his. He moved, I moved. We were in perfect sync and that felt so good. When I came he followed. I try to be as quiet as possible, because we would not want to wake Artem and the whole house. I would always remember this night. It was the night, I gave him all of me. Until this moment, I always kept a part just for me. Today I surrender completely and no matter what was after tomorrow, he will always hold my heart and soul, he will always have me body and... soul. Him and no one else.

Next morning I was up before sunrise. I am not sure if it was, because I was stressed for today, or because of the time difference between London and Russia. But, I was up. I got dressed, made sure my boys are still sleeping and headed downstairs to the kitchen, to make myself a coffee. Vladimir was there, sleepy eyes and messy hair.

"Hey, what's with you up so early?"

"I can't sleep. You know, I was thinking and overthinking this plan of yours, I cannot come up with something better, but I am afraid of what will happen. What if Noshimuri decides to take the risk and doesn't show up? Or what happens if Lan doesn't want to leave Artem with the sitter? There are so many questions, I will lose my mind."

I took a few steps closer to him, put a hand on one of his shoulders, staring into his eyes, I said to him.

"I appreciate your concern, but the plan is good and we have been over it a few times now. I need you with a clear head, not overwhelmed by thoughts and situations. I know it's hard. It's hard for me as well, but…   I am here for you and I need you to have my back, more than ever. I am going to walk in between the wolves. I need to know you have a strong rope, to pull me out. Because no matter what, you are my family and I am yours. And... we both have Nikolai here."

I said and we both smiled. Man, I did not know I am so good at pep talk. Day went by with our morning routine from here. After, we went to the casino and made our final recap, over our insane plan. The meeting was scheduled to take place at eight in the evening, when it was dark enough to hide, but early enough so no one would get suspicious about what was going to happen. We chose a place, up the mountain next to the pine forest, close to a ravine, so it will be more credible. Before the meeting, I went to pick up my new winter coat, from the tailor that Elena insisted so much to use.

"Mrs Ivanovich, make sure you keep it close at all times. As you can see its cold outside."

And he smiled. It was a short old man too skinny for his own good, green eyes and white hair. His gaze is always kind and his smile warm. Every time I see him it reminds me of my grandfather, he was my happiness, then he passed away and I had no one, until Elena.

As we agreed at eight I was up the mountain meeting with Noshimuri.

"Did you make sure Felicia will bring Mr Ivanovich?"

I asked Noshimuri and he said.

"I can be very convincing, when I want to. She will be here with your husband soon."

As on queue Lan's SUV parked, next to mine. Here it goes! All I can wish for right now, is that everything will work according to plan. As he gets out of the car he says.

"Lana what are you doing here? You said you are with Nikolai on the other side of the town. What is going on?"

Noshimuri looks surprised by Lan's statement as he asks.

"He doesn't know?"

I look between the two of them, I can see Noshimuri realise what is going on as Las asks.

"I don't know what?"

But another car approaches, and we are stopped from our conversation. An angry Nikolai got off from his SUV, followed by my three Gorillas. Except, that instead of coming to offer me protection, they surrounded Lan in protective pose.

What the hell is going on?

This was not part of the plan, but I don't say anything. I am waiting for Nikolai to open his mouth. I will know exactly where to go from here.

"You betrayed me! You betrayed the family and the Vory. You betrayed everything we stand for! How could you? We trusted you. Elena trusted you!"

Okay this was definitely not part of the plan. What the fuck is going on?

"Care to elaborate?"

I ask Nikolai not too sure what to say.

"You said you have an important meeting. I didn't know that it was with him!"

Nikolai pointed towards Noshimuri, but from the way he accused me, it looked like I was having a romantic "meeting" with the guy. Something doesn't add up, but I follow what I have to do. If Nikolai chose this path, he knows something he cannot share, yet. I know exactly what my next word would be

"You know Nikolai, in poker I always love the black-hearted ace. He has a shadow of its own, but in the end, it is all about love. And I've learned, in love and death. We don't decide!"

"That is right, we don't decide!"

I see Nikolai taking out his gun... BANG!

A single bullet to the heart. The only problem was, it was... my heart.

For I don't even know how many times in my life, darkness wrapped me in her silence. It took a single bullet to the heart, to have all my life displayed in front of my eyes.

Memories that were long gone, surfaced from the back of my mind. Everything happened so fast, before I saw Lan with Artem in my mind.

I hit the ground.

I was numb.

Darkness became thicker... and thicker.

I was... gone.

CHAPTER TWENTY-SIX

RUSLAN

I knew today was an important day for Lana and Nikolai. But, I was so surprised when Felicia texted me, that she has information about my wife's infidelity. I nearly dropped the phone out of my hands.

What the hell was she talking about? What infidelity?

Lana was working at her case. We all were working to finally find that stupid snitch, inside Vory. Felicia was adamant that she has the evidence and I should not tell a soul, because she would show me what is going on. She was doing a favour for our Vory family. And bring the Yakuza leader's head, on a silver plate, to us. She promised me, tonight at eight she will prove me right and I will understand what is going on behind my back.

I knew this woman could be crazy, but not that crazy. I would like to see what she has on my wife, or more importantly how she plans to get my wife, in a trap with Yakuza members. I am not an idiot and I will not go anywhere, until I speak with someone. And that someone was Nikolai. I had big trusting issues when it comes to people, but I will always trust Nikolai with my life. I made sure Artem was with the sitter and Vladimir on his way home. I went to the casino's office. Once there, I told Nikolai everything that Felicia told me.

"Are you sure Felicia said, she will behead Noshimuri? Lan this is no joke and I don't need Yakuza, out of any clan out there, in my head. Especially, not in Lana's head, at this moment in time. How does she plan to do that? Behead Noshimuri, I mean. He is not a person you can easily get close to. Not to mention she wants to part his head from his body. So she must have a plan for that!"

He asked me, like I knew all the answers.

"Nikolai you saw the same messages, I saw. I don't know more than you do. I want to know where Lana is now, and why Felicia says she has proof that Lana is involved with Yakuza?"

"That, I have no idea. Lana, did not come here today. I'm in the dark, as much as you are."

He said to me. What the hell was going on? This was out of the order, even for Lana. She would not go out without Yuri, they were practically attached to the hip, lately. And now he was here with us and Lana was nowhere to be found. Nikolai went on telling me, I should accept Felicia's proposition to go with her, he will come with Yuri, Boris and Sasha, behind me at a safe distance. So Felicia will not know we are followed. Needless to say, the day went by excruciating. Lana's phone was off and she was nowhere to be found.

Felicia text came around seven in the evening, she was telling me to meet her outside the casino and we will go together, up the mountain. Up the mountain? What the fuck we would do up the mountain?

Once we were there, I was shocked to see Lana with none other than Noshimuri, according to Felicia. I never met the guy. It was a medium high Chinese guy. Around his forties, skinny but clothes made him look fatter. He was dressed in a grey suit and on top of it had a grey coat. He looked so surprised when he heard me ask my wife what is going on, like I should know something, but I have been left out of it. I tried my luck again as I heard Nikolai's car approaching. He got out of the car and he started to bark angry at Lana. She starts to talk about poker and hearts, and love… but she doesn't make sense. Lana doesn't know the rules of poker, let alone to play it. This must be a code between her and Nikolai and I am left outside.

What the fuck is going on? Something big is about to happen, but I never expect what is next

"That is right, we don't decide!" Nikolai says to Lana, and I see him taking out his gun… BANG!

Straight to Lana's heart

"NOOOOOO!"

I shout and start towards her, only to be halted back by Yuri and Boris.

"Let go of me, you fuckers! Get your hands off me!"

I was screaming. I can't believe he killed her. Did he lose his mind? This cannot be happening. No she cannot be dead, but I could see the pool of blood gathering around her and nobody was moving a finger to help her.

Why?

"What did you do? You idiot?"

I was screaming at Nikolai who as soon as he heard my voice, turned around and told me.

"What did I do? I eliminate the snitch from Vory. She was here to sell uranium to Yakuza. Meet Mr Noshimuri, who your wife was fucking."

Nikolai said to me pointing to the Chinese guy, who by now was very confused about what was going on. Everything was going on so fast, I had no time to process, or catch up with the events. My wife was now in a pool of blood, with seconds on her life. Yuri and Boris were holding me in place, while Nikolai was boiling. Noshimuri was so confused that he kept his mouth shut, waiting to see what was happening next. Sasha was behind me, somewhere. But, out of all Felicia was bursting in laughter. She was so happy for the course of these events.

"I seriously cannot believe that Nikolai believed Lana is the snitch."

She said laughing and looking between me and Nikolai.

"You are more stupid, than I gave you credit for. See the thing is. That your precious Lana, was here tonight, to actually make a deal with Noshimuri. Because she knew, I was sleeping with him....*she said so proud of her, like she won some Olympic competition on the continent*...She was trying to find out how she could trade him the information, for me. But, Noshimuri came and told me, because he knew once we make sure Lana is gone, you are gone… She pointed to Nikolai... I actually expected more of a fight from Nikolai, than from you. What can I say, you really love her in a way you never loved me, but it's okay. Now, she is gone and you will come back to me.

Because, I will be the next Vory leader. See, Nikolai shoots Lana. As we can see... she is innocent, and according to Vory he needs to pay. It was an injustice to her innocence. Vladimir is not ready to take Nikolai place, he is too young and he doesn't have the required experience. It's only me that is left to be next in line. What can I say other than "Thank you Nikolai!" You just avenged everyone with a bullet, including yourself. My only problem was Noshimuri. But, like every war has collateral damages, Noshimuri here is our collateral damage. Sorry Noshimuri, nothing personal, only business."

She says as Noshimuri starts to laugh.

"How stupid do you think I am? Do you think I don't know you were trying to use my nephew? He wanted my place in tirades. tKilling me and let him be the Yakuza leader? That would have been suitable for both of you. Doll, you are not that smart to come close to me, enough to take my head. I made a deal with Mrs. Ivanovich and you are their problem now. Even if I would take great pleasure, in showing you what it feels to have your head departed from your body. I have a word to keep. She is your problem from now on."

Noshimuri said the last words to Nikolai as Sasha went to grab Felicia and Nikolai thanked Noshimuri for the help.

As soon as Noshimuri was in his car and Felicia restrained in Sasha's hands, Yuri nodded to Boris and they let go of me. I bolted to my wife. She was alive, she was strong and she was going to live. Yuri said to me.

"Boss, let me take her up and settle her in the car. Tomorrow she will have an enormous headache, from that rock she hit.

"Headache? She has a bullet in herself!"

You idiot. I wanted to say the last part out loud, but I kept quiet.

"No, she hasn't. It's bulletproof. Because of the close range, she was pushed harder than she expected and hit her head. That is a bag of red paint, or fake blood made with some honey. Look!"

He sticks his finger in what is supposed to be my wife's whole in the heart and brings the finger to his mouth, licking the red liquid. If I wouldn't be so worried, I would consider it funny, but it felt horrendous and I was looking in between all of them.

"What the hell is going on here?"

I ask the question that was in my mind for the last thirty minutes or so.

"Son, I will tell you everything as soon as we are back in the casino and deal with problem number two, which is Felicia's punishment. Let Yuri take Lana up and in the car."

"No one touches her! I will take her home and come to the casino after." I scoop my wife in my arms and take her to the car she came with here. Giving my car keys to Boris, to bring my car. I got in the car with my wife and drove home.

They better have a good explanation for what was going on.

"How stupid of you to act like this. What the hell was in your mind? What now you are playing dead, every time when shit hits the fan?"

I was screaming at her, but she was knocked out. I was screaming my fear, pain, frustration and anger.

As soon as I got the car in park, I got off and rounded the car so I could take her inside. Vladimir was opening the door.

"Oh my God, they kill her in the end?"

"You knew about this as well? No, they did not kill her. She just hit a rock when she fell, she just knocked out."

I said to my brother, angry as hell. Once I had her on the bed out of that clothes and all secure under the sheets, I came downstairs and grabbed Vladimir's shirt collar.

"You knew about this idiotic plan of theirs?"

Before I could do anything stupid, Boris grab my hand.

"Boss, we couldn't tell you. If anything helps, Vladimir was against this from the beginning."

I felt like I was exploding.

"Let's go to the casino. And you are coming with us!"

I said to Boris. But, the last part was addressed to Vladimir.

"I will drive. You don't have a clear head for that!"

Boris said in a no argue tone, with his hand extended for the car keys.

We get inside the casino's office and I see Felicia, Sasha, Yuri and Nikolai. Staring at them as they stare back at me, a deafening silence for a few minutes. Nikolai would look everywhere except me, not because he was afraid of me. But, because he knew how pissed I was about all this, and the fact that everyone knew apart from me. I felt like an idiot that everyone played after their own liking. The guys knew their place in all this and even if I wanted to, they would not speak about this. They were too loyal to Lana, to open their own mouth. No matter how much I normally respect this, in normal circumstances, it sting when I was at the receiving end of the silence, but of course Felicia being Felicia she said.

"Well, it's nice to see that in the end, I accomplish something. I ruined your little family. Oh, how awful of me!"

She was sarcastic.

"Listen! Stop stepping on my nerves, because I had enough of you this year. If you wouldn't be tied to the Goddamn chairs, I would tie you myself to it."

I said to her, through my gritted teeth. Turning to Nikolai I said.

"I am waiting for someone to clarify all of this, because apparently I'm the only idiot that did not know what was going to happen. So?"

For the first time since I came in this office, Nikolai turned and looked me in the eyes.

"I will tell you everything, but boys please take this…lady, to the other room. And give us some privacy. Vladimir you can stay!"

He said and we waited, until everyone was out of the room except the three of us.

"As I told you before. Back in the day we had a mould between us. We could not figure out who the mould was, until Lana put everything head to head. It was like a piece of puzzle that was in front of us, but we need the right person to see where each piece will fall. That person for us was Lana, maybe because the rest of us were too involved and to blind to see in front of their eyes. I and Elena included. With all your help, but especially with the information Elena left for Lana, we were able to realise we have been played by Lana's mother and Felicia's father. They wanted to lead Vory for their own benefit. When they saw this would not happen, they just started to make justice after their own laws. They killed Ana and her brother, to cover the murder. Sergei educates Felicia to make you fall for her. The only problem they did not take in account was that I will find out about her affair with Ivan, and actually tell you. After that, they had no other option than to wait for the right moment, to plan their next strike. Elena's sickness was a bonus for them and our short straw, from life. But, she played her cards well. Elena knew Lana would be the next Vory, and no matter how much I hated Petrov, he did something good in this life. At the end he confessed everything and we were able to find out about Yakuza's involvement in all this situation. Elena always kept an eye on Lana, through Vitaly. As soon she heard Lana was going to try a career in makeup, she knew she needed it to involve Arthur, and from there to work out a way for you to bump into each other. The only problem with that was that Lana would not want to have anything to do with this world. So we knew she hacked and she is good enough. From there the job was easy. Plant a bug in Arthur's computer, ask for Lana's help and make sure you will give her enough headache to get "accidentally" logged into our server. It was a test and a risk we need it to take, in order to make sure she is reliable and we can trust her. We know how that turned out. When you two finally met, our job was half done. We just needed time to train her and teach her how to use her abilities to lead Vory. For once, in this insane situation, we were lucky. Elena lived long enough, so she could accomplish all this.

I knew at some point she met Chenguang Noshimuri in London. I did not know the actual content of their conversation, Elena said it is better this way and I never doubt her judgment. All I knew at that time was that Noshimuri is willing to help, no matter what. Why?

I had no clue. Knowing your mother, Noshimuri did not stand a chance. After you and Lana found the folder in the safe, everything made sense and the pieces of the puzzle started to fall in place, as Lana recalled every conversation she and Elena had. She and I had everything Elena told, you, Vladimir and what Felicia said to her in their exchanges. Petrov told Lana he has a final gift for her and he did keep his promise. Next to Ana's body, which was buried under Lana's bed, we found evidence of Felicia sleeping with both Noshimuri and his nephew. And the coordinates of the place where they would pass the uranium, across the border in China, from Russia. Of course helped by none other than our precious Felicia and at times Sergei. As soon as we were in possession of this information. Lana came with the idea to fake her murder and ask for Noshimuri help, in exchange of his family safety and the uranium trade being kept a secret. We used the same tailor we always use. Ordered her a bullet proof coat. I was supposed to be the one to shoot her in front of you. That would give Felicia the pleasure of getting her venom out and laugh, in our faces, at how mistaken we were, to kill our innocent leader. The only problem with that plan was that you informed me Felicia was planning to kill Noshimuri, and frame us for it. I texted Noshimuri to make sure he is guarded, but the plan goes on. I knew if I shot Lana in the heart she would "bleed" and the force of the bullet would push her to the ground, I had no time to tell Lana about Felicia's plan to kill Noshimuri. So, I speed up the murder process before someone could say something wrong, and everything go to hell.

She never slept with Noshimuri or anyone else for that matter, but we need a good reason to take you out of the house.

We knew that if she makes you think she's cheating, you will not fail. I need to give credit to Noshimuri for this. The rest you know it yourself."

I was astonished about what he was telling me. First, I could not be more proud of my wife that she had the courage to go on with a plan like this. Second, I could not believe what I was hearing, it was like some kind of action movie scenario.

"If it makes you feel better, I was totally against this. That's why they let me home to watch Artem sitter. A great piece of ass!"

He said, wiggling his eyebrows and smiling like a fool. Both me and Nikolai said the same thing at the same time.

"Please tell me you didn't fuck the sitter?"

He started to laugh

"You cannot blame me! She has a great ass and I need it a distraction from thinking that my sister-in-law is plotting her own murder."

"Oh God, I need to tell Lana to find a new sitter, if we don't want drama around the house. You better find another source of pussy next time. I am sick of changing Artem's babysitters because of you."

I warn him. Turning to Nikolai I ask.

"What will happen to Felicia now? And what is the plan for the future? Are we going to stay here, or go back to London?"

"We are waiting for Lana to wake up and see whether she decides to move to London or not. As for Felicia, we are working with police to frame her for as many crimes as possible, but let Noshimuri out of this."

We discussed the matters a little longer and I headed home together with Vladimir. Once in our bedroom, I was looking at my sleeping wife, still unable to believe what her mind is hiding, at times. She was the most beautiful woman I saw and she made me fall in love with her, because of that burning fire inside her.

Never believing what her mind can produce and what will expect me in future. I guess, I need to wait and see, but most important is to pray to God that no matter what, to keep my mind as sane as possible next to this spitfire smurf.

I made my way to bed from the door frame, where I was standing a couple seconds ago and slid next to my wife, wrapping her in my arms pulling her as close to me as possible.

My crazy smurf.

Next day, all the men in the house including Artem were in the kitchen eating when Lana came downstairs with her hand to her head.

"Can someone give me a painkiller or something? My head will not stop throbbing."

She said as we all looked at her. She had a pair of too short shorts, my shirt on, which was covering her shorts, making her look like she was in underwear. No bra and her hair all messy on her head. She looked like she just wake up from the most hot round of sex, my mouth went dry at the sight of her, as three different man cleared their throat and Vladimir said.

"Hey Lana, I love you and all that. But seriously, you need to reconsider your outfit in a house full of testosterone."

I turned to look at him, murder in my stare. He starts to laugh at my reaction, at the same time Yuri and Boris, slap the back of his head, make him bend and take a step forward.

"Sorry guys, but I don't care about anything at this point. My head is killing, worse than last night's bullet."

She attempted a joke. I went to grab some painkillers from a cabinet and as I approached her I said.

"Woman with you is like walking on a tightrope, with my heart in my throat. Next time when you plan your own crime, can you at least let me know in advance? I nearly commit suicide there. And we don't want to be some kind of Romeo and Juliet modern version now, do we?"

"I am sorry and will apologize properly tonight for that, but I couldn't have told you. Your reaction needed to be real and you could not fake that!"

She says as all the men, except Artem, were coughing at her words.

"How about you stop talking and I put some food in you?"

We all laugh at that.

EPILOGUE

SVETLANA

Two years have passed since that night. We managed to put Felicia away for a long time. Of course, I got points with Noshimuri for keeping him out of this. Points I will cash at the best time.

We made our permanent residence in London. We bought a nice house, in the Hampstead area. It was a house with five rooms. A large yard and blue fence. I know every girl's fantasy is a white fence, mine is blue.

I made sure to have it paint in a shade of cosmic blue.

It was a Gregorian style house made of red bricks, with an arched lantern holder, over the front steps. It looked nice, especially on Halloween, when we put torches in there. Fence is made from wrought iron, with lots of curlicues tied together and moulded leaves and flower heads.

Although since ancient times, homes could be built perfectly square by master builders, I have always liked a bit of shabby-chic with artfully roughened or 'rusticated' stone.

Inside we had a huge living room, with a real chimney. Lan loved them and I wanted to make sure he has one here too. A big sofa with sofa matching chairs and coffee table on the opposite wall. Huge screen TV on the same wall with the chimney. A dining table in the far end of the living, next to the garden door.

Normal size kitchen, where our chef made the most delicious dishes, and pastries. On the right side of the living next to the kitchen, was a room that we made our joined office.

It was quite a big room, Lan made sure to make the most elegant home office with a huge bookshelves, expensive office furniture with matching chairs and a sofa bed. For some reason Lan was adamant to put a sofa bed in there. A service bathroom with a toilet sit and a sink.

The staircase was close to the house entrance, it led to the first and only floor of the house where you could find four bedrooms. One of them was mine and Lan's bedroom. I decorated in a shade of blue and yellow with some purple from place to place, only for Lan to complain that I ruined the designer work with my purple. But I loved it.

We had a king size bed on one side of the room. I did not want the bed in the middle of the room. One time I fell off the bed and I swear then and there that my bed will be glued to the wall, and that will be my side to sleep. So, I kept my word.

A big wardrobe glued to the wall next to our bed headboard. And, because I wanted something to remember me of Elena, I made sure to have a coffee table and two chairs next to my window, which was facing the garden. Sometimes I would sit there, look at the sky and imagine her sitting here with me. Or thinking back to our conversations and all the advice she gave to me. All our time spent together, laughter, tears, secrets and everything we shared in the time we've been together. That was my tribute to her!

Of course every room had her bathroom, all of them the same design shower, toiled sit and sink, all in white. I always believed a bathroom should be white.

One of the bedrooms was Arthem's room, decorated with "Lighting" McQueen prints and paintings on the walls. A bed in the shape of the same car and we had to make sure the wardrobe door would open like a car door, so he would stop crying that he wants a car as a wardrobe.

The third room was originally designed for guests, but after Vladimir slowly took residence in here, I let him decorate the room after his own liking. I wasn't shocked at all when the designer, who was a gorgeous young woman left. And left him with the room half-done, after they fucked their head off for three days. I told him that will happen, but the boy was adamant this was different.

The last and my favourite room is our soon-to-arrive daughter. It's a light yellow room, with a summer scenery painted on the walls.

Nursery furniture on one of the walls. A crib in the middle of the room and a rocking chair next to the window. I could not wait for her to arrive so I could meet her. See what kind of eyes she has, her little hand with small fingers that will wrap around my fingers.

As I descended the stair to living, I felt the contractions kicking in, but I forced myself to breathe. It was still a week early for this and I had a house full of guests for Lan birthday. It was an amazing August day, I could not spend it in the hospital.

So breathe, everything will be okay, just breathe. I managed to hit the bottom step, when I felt that my water just broke.

Natasha, Yuri's fiancée stared at me terrified and asked.

"Did your water break or did you need it to pee that bad? I will clean, but I need to know what I put my hands in."

I had no time to form words because another contraction hit again. Oh man, this girl is adamant to be her father's birthday gift.

"AHHHH!" I screamed in pain and Natasha was watching at me, like a ticking bomb about to go off as she screamed for Yuri to come in.

"Yuri, I give birth! I mean she will give birth. Lana gives birth. Yuuurrriii, where the hell are you?"

If someone was looking at us from outside, we looked like we were in a screaming competition with each other. The living was full of people now. Yuri was trying to calm his fiancée as Lan guided me to the car.

"She will be fine. She is just giving birth, not exploding."

Yuri said to Natasha as she replied.

"I will never get pregnant. That looks painful."

All this would be so comic, if I wasn't in so much pain.

Five hours later I was holding my daughter in my arms. A bundle of joy with green eyes and small black hair. She was so beautiful and so little. I fell in love with her instantly.

"She looks like her mommy!"

Lan said and I was smiling. Looking at him I said.

"Meet your daughter, Elena Svetlana Ivanovich!"

My life started in the worst way possible and I went to hell and back. Only to prove myself in the end, that all the nightmares and curses, turned out to be my biggest blessing.

I started as a fragile, broken woman that was afraid of the world, only to prove to myself and everyone else, that I can be the best leader Vory had to this day. The best friend, sister, daughter-in-law, wife and now a mother for the second time.

It's a saying I like the most.

"When life gives you lemons, take them. And make the best lemonade you possibly can."

THE END

Printed in Great Britain
by Amazon